Partial Function

An Infinity Bagua Technique

JCM Berne

The Gnose House

ISBN-13: 978-1-961805-04-0

Cover art by J Caleb Designs

Acknowledgments

I have more people to thank than I can easily count, starting with my wife, Moneeka, without whose support none of the rest of this would have happened.

My alpha and beta readers who contributed immeasurably: Andrew, Karl, Katie, Jasmine, Isabelle, Zombie, Bradley, and Kate.

My editor, Sarah Chorn, who came onboard on short notice and saved you all from reading a much worse book than this. If any lines in this book read well, it's more her fault than mine.

My proofreader, Isabelle at Emerald Scribe Editing, who helped so much on unbelievably short notice.

Mihir, for extensive advice, especially regarding the cover!

J Caleb Design, cover artist extraordinaire, who brought Akina to life!

Jordan, Andrew (The Wizard), Craig, Boe, A.R., Kayla, Usman, Chris, HC, Esmay, Lezlie, and Raina, who brought me the thing I couldn't bring myself: more readers.

My web and marketing guru, Marc Greenwald.

The rest of my Twitter and Discord communities, who brought me so much encouragement and support.

Contents

1

Dog? Witch Dog?

"If this is the best food you have, I'm going to need another jug of wine. To numb my palate." Akina tapped the empty clay pot with a calloused fingertip.

The inn's proprietor glared through squinted eyes, an expression that probably passed for a hard look in this small town.

In a contest of gray hairs, aching joints, or shirt stains, the man would have emerged victorious. In this particular battle, however, he was no match for his customer, and he quickly broke contact with a sigh and a shake of his head.

"Seeing as how my wife hasn't learned to cook these past twenty years, I doubt today is your lucky day. But I can bring you more wine."

She nodded. "A bowl of scraps for my dog while you're at it."

He glared at the animal sitting on the grass beside its master, tail wagging as it licked its lips and grinned at him.

"We don't usually serve animals here."

She glanced through the inn's front door, her hand tightening on her cup as she saw a big man casually slap the woman at his side. *Ignore it, Akina. You're just passing through. There's more important business at hand.*

She looked back to the proprietor. "I don't usually eat food suited for them, so I guess we're both having an adventure today, aren't we?"

The inn was of solid wooden construction, painted green with a thatched roof and a well-swept dirt floor. In the tradition of this land, it was in a field away from the town, far enough that crowds inside wouldn't bother the nearby townsfolk no matter how boisterous they grew. About a third of the interior was walled off, presumably containing the kitchen and owner's living space; the other two-thirds formed an open seating area with eight large tables.

Akina had chosen one of the four unsteady wooden tables set on the inn's front lawn. She was used to eating outside; few establishments agreed with the notion of pets coming through the doors.

The innkeeper paused, eyes flickering from her to the rowdy group led by the slaphappy big man. The dog stood and pushed his snout against her hip, trying to shove her off the bench. She looked down.

"What's your problem? You want me to do something about them? It's none of our business. And we're on a mission, or have you forgotten?"

The innkeeper shook his head. "Don't get involved, ma'am. The big guy is what passes for the law in this town. Not worth your trouble."

"I was talking to the dog. But thanks for the advice."

The older man nodded slowly and looked her over, taking in her clothes, which were dusted from travel. "That's an unusual shade of blue. Your jacket."

Akina's shoulders tightened as a second smack sounded from inside the tavern. "Thank you. It's faded now, but it used to be azure." She reached down and scratched between the dog's ears.

A thud as the big man slapped the table, knocking two porcelain cups and a bowl of noodles to the ground. A woman at a nearby table quickly bundled up her toddler and hurried out of the tavern. The child looked at the dog as they passed, its face solemn.

The dog stiffened and shoved Akina's hip again.

She sighed. "I know, you're right. Maybe it's for the best. Shouldn't take long and I could use the exercise."

The innkeeper opened his mouth as if to ask a question, then reconsidered. "I'll get your scraps." He went inside, moving with the careful deliberation of someone nursing a badly flaring hernia.

Akina pushed a hint of qi into her voice, enough that her words echoed off the back wall of the tavern. "Hurry up with those scraps. Bad enough we have to eat this slop, it's an insult to make us wait for it."

The conversation inside paused.

Come on, boys, pay attention to me. I may not be a pretty young thing anymore but surely you're not going to let a woman, alone and well into her cups, just sit out here unmolested. Are you?

Akina scratched between the dog's ears. "I know, I know. I'm rusty, though. If they don't come out soon, I'll figure out a new plan." The proprietor stopped at the inside table, bending to exchange words with the man at its head. She spoke again, louder still. "And the noise from those louts isn't enhancing the ambience any."

The dog yelped as if in affirmation and twisted its head to lick her hand. She drained the last of the wine from her jug as she watched the big man set the end of a long bone staff on the ground and leverage himself to his feet.

The slapped woman and her friend, both underfed and underwashed with matching traumatized eyes, winced as the big man stomped his foot on the floorboards. *They're not much older than my girls.*

"In the name of Ku-Lo the Undying, you're right, woman! This food *is* slop!" He hauled his girth around his table and trod toward her. The heavy staff thudded into the wood floor of the inn, then the grass of the front yard, with every step.

She bent to her bowl of gruel, eyeing his approach under the brim of her broad straw hat.

The man continued, "A pretty thing such as yourself deserves better than this, am I right? Perhaps I could accompany you to a finer establishment. We could have . . . a discussion." One of the women eyed the big man and began to stand.

"No, thanks. If I want intellectual stimulation, the dog will do." She watched one of the big man's companions, a skinny boy with a pock-marked face, roughly grab their captive and slam her down onto her stool.

Akina looked down. "Are you seeing this? Do they not teach men manners this far east?" The dog's tail stopped wagging, then immediately continued.

The big man set his staff on the ground. It was formed from a six-foot-long rib as thick as Akina's fist, steamed and straightened, with thumb-size bone fragments or back teeth from a lesser Wedge embedded in three long rows along the striking surface.

"What kind of dog is that? Are those red markings? Reminds me of an Azure Dragon Clan warhound. Never thought I'd see one again."

Her eyes tightened. "They're brown, not red. He's just dirty. And he's no warhound, just a lapdog."

The man leaned over the tip of his staff and leered. "He's a lucky dog then, isn't he? That's a lap I wouldn't mind spending some time in myself. I don't mind a more—how do you say—mature woman."

She tilted her head toward his table. "What about them, then? Wouldn't they get jealous?"

"What, those two? Nah. Those two are rescues, they are. Village was overrun by sea ogres. Built too close to shore. We saved their lives, me and my boys, just taking them to the capital to sell. Only fair we recoup some of our losses."

The woman who had tried to stand slammed her hands onto the table and tried again. "That's a lie! There were no sea—" Another man slapped the back of her head, knocking her into silence.

Akina let out a long, slow breath and cracked the knuckles of her left hand, then her right.

The big man smiled. "You can call me Ox. Everybody does."

"Is it due to the smell? Or the brains? I can't tell which is a more compelling explanation."

"Oh, you're a feisty one. I don't mind, though. I like it when they start out feisty. I'll show you the origin of the nickname as soon as these breeches are off."

Akina stood, rolling her shoulders and cracking her neck. *My joints didn't used to pop like that, did they?*

The man stepped back, hefting the staff with both hands. "Come on now, little lady. Just a bit of fun, right? A little wine, a bit of a snuggle. Then we can each go on our way. You're not going to make me get rough, are you? Not that I mind. Just asking." He smiled again, his teeth showing black, cracked edges between his lips.

She looked at her pet. "What do I want here, Dog? Do I stare into his eyes, turn his bowels to jelly so he backs off? Or do I let him come at me so I can deliver the ass-kicking he so thoroughly deserves?"

The man shook his head, his smile fading. "If you think that animal's going to save you, you're kidding yourself."

"Dog? He wouldn't hurt a fly. Or something a fly would feed on. I told you already, he's no warhound."

"You named him 'Dog'? What kind of name is that?"

"Well, my late husband named him 'Stay.' Confused the poor thing to tears. 'Come here, Stay.' 'Fetch, Stay.' So I just call him Dog." She hopped once, then twice. Then she reached into her sleeves and pulled out strands of white cloth, quickly wrapping her hands.

"If not the dog, what hope do you have, little lady? Not even a weapon on you. This club is crafted from the fourth rib of a leviathan I killed myself up in the Wilds. You have no chance."

Akina quickly tied her hair back with a simple loop. "You should be ashamed of yourself. Not for being an asshole, that's to be expected. I mean for being a living, breathing trope. Big man, big club, taking advantage of young girls? Making an aggressive attempt to sexually assault a woman you've never even met? You're a villain in the opening act of a puppet theatre performance, but it's badly written and we can all see the stick up your ass."

Ox opened his mouth, jaw and tongue working as words failed to exit. He finally settled on some phonemes. "Bitch!"

Akina laughed, then folded her fingers into tight fists. "I've been in a mood, you know? Don't judge me, I have reasons. So I feel I ought to thank you. Because this is exactly the thing I needed, without knowing I needed it."

One of Ox's companions put a hand on the outspoken woman's shoulder and told both captives to stay put. Then he, along with the other two rough-looking men, walked over to where Ox faced Akina.

Ox snarled. "I'm done asking, bitch. You're coming with us. And you're going to wish you'd been nicer about it."

She smiled back, and something in her eyes made his knees buckle.

"I am on a mission of secrecy, so under the laws of my clan I am not required to give you my name. But as you will die today, by my hand, I will keep to tradition and tell you of the forms that are killing you."

He raised the club overhead, his qi spilling up into the haft and enforcing the length of bone.

Akina's knees bent as her weight settled. Her left hand crossed her belly button as her right caressed her angular cheekbone.

"And by the way, that's no leviathan rib. It's the shin of a rhinophant. They're basically pack animals, herbivores, barely count as Wedge. Still, not a bad-looking weapon."

The club whistled as it swung with enough speed and power to fell a mature pine.

To smash a boulder.

Enough to split the skull of a rhinophant or a three-horn, possibly injure a white tyrant.

Certainly enough force to crush Akina into paste, rendering her bones to dust and her flesh to jelly.

"Infinity Bagua: Lower Limit."

The club descended and she stepped forward at an angle, lancing a short, left jab into Ox's larynx. The rebound echoed through her arm; she spun, left leg planted as her right reached behind, and was nowhere near the club when it cracked into the inn's lawn and murdered an innocent patch of lemongrass, digging a crater deep enough to swallow two sheep and a rabbit.

Ox's three associates slowed as they saw her pop out from beneath their boss's swing and face them.

"You boys aren't going to run now, are you? After I went to all this trouble to get your attention?"

Dog was up on all fours, short black tail wagging hard. He let out a soft bark and grinned.

The henchmen drew blades crafted from tyrant teeth, each as long as their forearms and carved into a scrimshaw with elaborate runes.

Akina checked the table inside the inn; the captive women huddled together, too afraid to run. *Guess we'll have to do this the hard way.*

The oldest of the men, his hair nearly as gray as the proprietor's, came first, closing from her left. She stepped close to him, weaving so the slashing bone blades missed her skin by inches, then whirled around.

"Infinity Bagua: Subtraction." She continued her centrifugal motion, sweeping her leg through his ankles and taking him hard to the ground.

The second man turned to face her new position, then charged, his lips pulled back in a snarl that didn't match his panicked eyes.

"Infinity Bagua: Division." He brought his blades down in parallel arcs. She stepped between them, angling her body sharply so only her side faced him. With casual brutality she raised her left elbow, catching the tip of his jaw with the sharp pointy bone at the end of the joint.

He crumpled and she stepped around his falling body, putting it between her and the last of the goons.

"I'll get you, b—"

"Cubic Function." She skipped forward, feet punishing the ground with powerful, stabbing steps, and was suddenly airborne.

He held his blades in front of his head, but her knee rose up under his guard and cracked into his face.

As she landed, she launched herself into a bound to her left, getting well clear of the charge Ox was mustering behind her.

With a face as red as an Imperial army medical tent, he stopped, turned, and charged again, small sparks dancing across the nodules of bone studding the heavy club.

"Fractions."

She ducked under the swing and lanced quick kicks under first his right, then his left kneecap. Ox howled in pain, the massive warclub slipping as he fought to support his lumbering mass on suddenly fragile legs.

Akina took careful steps, closing on Ox without giving him a chance to swing at her again.

"I didn't come here looking for trouble, you know. I was just passing through. On my way to something more important. Infinity Bagua: Wrong Answer."

Her open hand lashed out in a tight arc, smacking across Ox's jaw with enough force to fracture bone.

He staggered, hands coming up to block, too slow. He caught his weight with his staff, eyes glaring baleful hatred at her.

"But you had to come with these two women. Not much older than my daughters." Her voice broke; she swallowed before continuing, "And looking worse for wear, as they say." Her eyes tightened. "Wrong Answer."

She smacked his orbital, the bone crunching upon impact.

Ox slid down to one knee, drawing wet breaths through bloody lips.

"Any other time, maybe I could overlook that. But, you see, I have those two daughters."

Her foot rose in a wide arc, intercepting his head.

"Sorry. Forgot to tell you what that was. Asymptotic Reunion." She sniffled back unwelcome tears.

"You don't know what I'm talking about. Let's just say it was the wrong day for you to pull this crap. Geometric Progression."

She stepped forward, crouching as she planted her right foot against his leg, then drove a fist up into his throat with a full extension of her body.

Ox leaned backwards, then fell, thudding into the ground with a last expulsion of air and a thin cloud of dust.

Dog looked up at Akina, mouth open, waiting for her nod. She acquiesced, hands at her hips as she fought to catch her breath.

Dog waddled over to Ox's fallen form, lifted one leg high over the big man, and let out a stream of dark yellow urine.

Akina took in the henchmen. Two remained on the ground while the third, the oldest, rose to his hands and knees.

She held his gaze as she stomped on the upper back of the pockmarked boy. "Differentiate." The boy's neck snapped beneath her heel.

The older man pointed to her and choked out some words. "Stop!"

She stepped to the second henchman. "Angular Momentum."

With a twist she ended his life.

"I know you! I manned a station by the Dreadwall, in the back when! You're the hunter! The Spiral Witch!"

She froze, then turned to face him.

"I wish you hadn't said that. I was going to let you live because you spoke when you could have yelled and touched when you could have hit."

He shook his head, eyes wide, one breaking out in streaks of broken blood vessels. "You're supposed to be dead! Or gone! There's a reward for you!"

"Is that something you think you should have told me?"

He looked at her, then at Dog, then turned to face the inn and the two captives. With a grunt he stood and began to run up the north road.

Akina looked at the girls, then at the running man. "Damn it."

She stepped toward him, not running, but spinning with each bound, covering distance as she twirled, faster and faster.

He was twenty feet away when she leapt into the air, feet brought tight to her chest, then drilled down into the ground as she landed.

"Basic Wave."

Energy pulsed out from her feet into the soil, raising a wave of dirt like a silverback gorilla jumping into a lake.

The pulse of soil and grass traveled away from her and toward the man, rising under his feet and sending him toppling face-first.

His head hit the ground with a thud, and he lay still as she stalked to his body.

"Differentiate." The man's neck cracked in her hands.

Panting with the exertion she turned to the inn.

The proprietor was long gone, as were any other signs of life.

Except for the two captives.

Akina walked over to Dog and rubbed the back of his head. Then she turned into the inn and approached the women. They looked up at her as she took a hunk of meat cooked tight to the bone off the table. She tore off a mouthful and tossed the rest to Dog.

"You two heard what he said?"

The brazen one, clearly the older of the two, nodded. "We won't say a word, ma'am. We swear it on our lives. We'll never forget what you did for us today."

Akina picked up another fistful of meat. "You'll talk. If the wrong people get to you—and believe me, they will—you won't have a choice."

The younger one shook her head furiously, her lips pressed together, her body close to her friend's. "We won't, we promise. We'll be good."

They think I'm going to kill them. Twenty years ago, I might have.

"You misunderstand." She chewed and swallowed. "I didn't plan on them knowing I'd come this far, but it's okay. Let them know. When they ask you, I *want* you to tell them. Tell them who you saw. Tell them that it was Akina Azure, Heiress to the Azure Dragon Clan, the Spiral Witch, Master of Infinity Bagua. Tell them I'm back.

"And while you're at it, tell them you'll be praying for their souls."

2

There, Dog!

Three weeks later, Akina brushed dust out of her jacket, the smell of water faint on the air.

A guard, well-equipped in leather armor reinforced with white raptor bones, stood before her and shook his head. "No dogs allowed in town, miss. Magistrate's order." He blocked the arch over the road, his expression somewhere between boredom and diligence.

Akina glanced at Dog. A boy dressed in stiff, clean clothes, free of dirt or stains, knelt in the street and reached out to pet the animal. A wide-eyed servant stood behind him, her hands alternating between reaching for him and pulling back to her chin.

She looked up at the guard. "That can't be quite right, can it? There are plenty of horses in there. Oxen as well. I saw a man herding sheep ahead of me. He must have come through this gate."

The guard looked over her shoulder at the queue of entrants beginning to form. "Beasts of burden and food animals are the exceptions, ma'am. Now you have to move along; you're blocking the path." He shifted his hands on the haft of his bone-tipped spear, more a reminder of his authority than an outright threat.

"But he's not a dog, you know. Not really."

The guard looked at her sharply, and the boy looked up from Dog's side. "Come again, ma'am?"

She smiled and lifted her straw hat so he could see her face. Her mouth was dry with road dust and a light sheen of sweat was accumulating under her faded blue tunic.

"Well, of course he *looks* like a dog. At least he does now. But he's not really. He's as much a person as you or I."

"Ma'am, I'm sure you care deeply for your dog, but he's an animal. Can't come in."

"I meant he's a person. Human." The boy looked at her, then frowned at Dog. The servant made another half-hearted grab for him, as if to pull him away, but preempted herself.

"I can see that he's a dog, ma'am."

"He just looks like a dog. He does now, at least. The thing is, he's a shapeshifter. It's a special technique of the Bosun Clan. Controlled lycanthropy."

"Never heard of it. Or them." The guard's brows furrowed.

"Of course you haven't! It's a special technique. Transform into a dog. They can sneak around, listen in on conversations. Everyone thinks they're just dogs. If people like you had already heard of it, it wouldn't work. Pretty cool, though, am I right?"

He scratched his nose, one dirty finger perilously close to entering a nostril. "You're saying he's a weredog?"

"Yes! That's it exactly. A weredog. And surely the magistrate didn't mean for you to keep people out. Just, you know, regular dogs."

"I'm going to have to see some evidence of that claim, ma'am. Perhaps if your . . . friend could transform into a person? I'm sure it would be fine for him to pass in that form."

"Oh, right. Sure. That makes sense. Except, you see, you don't really want him to."

"And why is that, ma'am?"

"It's his temper, you see. As a dog, he's lovely, isn't he? Even with a small boy pestering him, he just sits there, tongue out, tail wagging, pleased as can be." The boy snatched his hand away from Dog and hopped back on his heels.

"What are you saying, ma'am?"

"Just that as a dog he's sweet and kind. But in human form, well, watch out. He's liable to go around biting people, tearing off limbs, generally wreaking havoc. You don't want that, do you? I mean, if you're interested in taking responsibility for it, we can just ask him to shapeshift here and now. Hold on, let me get him a robe. Don't want all the manly bits flashing about."

She shifted her pack to her hip and reached in through the top.

The guard stuck out a hand. "No need for that, ma'am. It's just, it's odd. I thought shapeshifters were dangerous in their animal forms, not as humans. Isn't that how the stories go?"

She looked up at him, her eyes opened wide enough to show whites all around. "You think the animal form is dangerous? Tell me, good sir, have you ever spent time around dogs?"

"Well, aye. My mum had one. Sweet little thing."

"So you know dogs. And you think, between a dog and a man, it's the *dog* that's the most savage and cruel?"

He opened his mouth to speak, then shut it. He lifted his leather conical helmet, scratched at his hairline, and nodded. "Go on in. Please don't make me any trouble."

"Of course not and thank you! Oh, wait, before we go, I have a quick question." Dog stood, as if to leave, and stepped over to the little boy.

The guard sighed and once again eyed the growing line of peasants behind Akina. "Go ahead."

"I'm looking for a bar." The man nodded, relief flashing across his face.

"That I can do. Name?"

"Don't have it. But it's going to be the roughest, toughest bar in town. The one you go to when you want a cheap, strong drink and don't care if you make it out at the end of the night or end up in the alley with your throat cut. The kind of place you won't let your sister even speak about at her worst moment. Where the floors have never been cleaned and neither have the mugs." Dog licked the boy's hands, broad tongue completely enveloping the clean, slender fingers while the servant looked on in horror.

"Ah, that bar. Head up this avenue until you find the sewage drain. Turn right and follow that to the river. At the river, there's a tax office on the left, and to the right is the place you want. Doesn't really have a proper name, but you can't miss it."

"Thank you, good sir. We'll be on our way." She turned, winked at the finely dressed boy, and led Dog into the town.

•••••••••••

"Don't give me that look, Dog. I know it smells bad. It's a town. That's what towns smell like. It's not my fault you've been spoiled by living out in the nature and mountains." Dog ambled along at her side, pausing every few steps to sniff the ground, paying her no mind.

They passed one and two-story buildings, packed close, made of wood with shingle roofs. As nightfall approached, mothers took to the streets to gather wayward children inside, pulling more than a few away from their attempts to pet Dog.

"This must be it." The crowd thinned to nothing as they carefully crossed the sewage channel one final time and faced a two-story building that had seen better centuries.

"This predates the last Wedge Pulse. Seems like the right place. I'm going to have to tip that guard on the way out." Dog shambled over to the sewage channel and bent toward an enticing morsel.

"Stay away from that! We're going in. Though I'm not certain the floor in there will be much better than what you're poking your nose at right now."

Dog faced her and woofed.

"Come on."

Akina paused at the entrance, half expecting an unconscious drunk to be tossed out the door just as she was entering, but the bar was relatively quiet.

Her stomach was tight. *I'm not ready for this. Not after all these years. But I don't have a choice, do I? This is the plan.*

She crossed the threshold, bracing for the smell of unwashed person and never-washed tables. Dog walked in front of her, then stopped and happily sniffed the boots of a man slumped over a chair.

Akina crossed to a bar. The surface was, to her surprise, well-polished and splinter-free.

"One of something that won't kill me."

The bartender shrugged. "This might not be the place for you, sister."

She nodded. "Something that will kill me slower, then. Is Remy around?" *Or am I wrong, and dear old Remy isn't working at the worst bar in town?*

He picked up a wooden mug, turned to a series of kegs, and nodded to himself as he poured from one of the dustier ones.

"Depends. You here to fight or talk?"

"I'm good either way."

The bartender paused, mug held in the air.

Akina held her hands up. "I'd prefer to talk, though."

"He owe you money?"

"We're old friends."

The bartender shrugged and slid the mug over to her. "It's early. He'll be here in an hour. Unless he's drunk again. Then it will be two hours."

"You serve food here? Same preference, wouldn't want to die of food poisoning before Remy gets here."

"We have pork buns. Baked off-premises. Probably safer than the drink."

"I'll take two. And another for my dog."

He nodded and passed her the food. She found an empty table in a dark corner and settled in to wait.

Dog finished his bun, licked his lips thoroughly, then walked off to explore the bar.

A sailor, dressed in the canvas and cloth typical of river barge crews, approached her with raised eyebrows, stumbling over his feet as he neared. She shook her head, and he veered off in another direction.

"Dog, get away from there." Dog had advanced from licking one unconscious man's boot to climbing up his leg.

The animal paused, lowered his head, and trotted back to Akina's side.

The bar's front door swung open, letting in a chilling evening breeze. A shape filled the doorway.

He was big in every way: tall, heavyset with equal parts muscle and fat, a beard covering face, neck, and upper chest, and thick hands hanging from his wrists like hams. Leather straps were buckled around his shins and up his arms, laced with bones harvested from the toughest creatures in the Wilds.

Akina gripped her mug as a sudden unpleasantness in her stomach made her question her desire to speak to him.

I don't want to talk to him. Am I afraid of causing him pain? Or of hurting myself?

Remy stepped with the exaggerated care of a man just a cup or two shy of passing out, leaning in as the bartender spoke softly.

They turned in unison to face Akina's corner.

She nodded to him, her mouth as dry as her eyes were moist. His face was stone as he crossed to her table.

"Akina."

She nodded. "Remy."

He sighed, shoulders slumping as if he were a kite that lost its wind. With a sudden jerk he turned to the door, watching as it swung shut, then back to her. "Is someone after you?"

"You mean, coming after me here? At this moment? No, nothing like that. You can relax."

He nodded and pulled a chair over to her table, then sat on it backwards. He looked down. "Is that . . .?"

"Petrik's dog? Yeah." She didn't explain, but her voice was choked.

His eyes filled with sorrow as he worked through what that meant. "I take it Petrik—"

"Blood plague. Two years ago. It was quick." She sipped her drink, hoping the alcohol would clear her throat.

"Ah. I didn't hear."

"How could you have? Nobody within five hundred miles knew where we were."

"Right, right. Until now. Now they'll know."

She nodded and sipped from the wooden mug. Dog stepped to Remy and began sniffing the man's boot.

Remy stared at her while she took another sip.

I should probably say something. Explain why I came. She finished the second pork bun.

He stretched his arms and gave her a half smile. "You've come an awfully long way to sit there and not tell me anything. You want to start talking now or should I step away and you can let me know why you're here when you're ready?"

I didn't know it would be this hard. Not with Remy.

"Can we go somewhere else? I can wait until your shift is done."

He stood. "No need to wait, they won't need me for hours. The violent drunks come in later. We'll go to the bathhouse. Your clothes have five hundred miles of grime caked into them and your face doesn't look much better." He smiled as he spoke, his eyes twinkling.

She smiled back, the tension in her belly bending and fraying. "You forgot already? My skin is always dark like this."

"I remember your skin tone. *You* have apparently forgotten the difference between brown and gray. Come on. Bring the dog. You can't leave him here."

"I would have anyway. Dog goes where I go."

Remy spoke a few words to the bartender, then led Akina out the door and into town, away from the river.

She walked in his shadow, reminded of old times when she would shelter from the cold winds of the Wilds behind Remy's broad back. They didn't speak as he paid for a private room with two baths, or when he added hot water for Dog. Within half an hour, they were soaking neck-deep in barrels of steaming water. Dog snored contentedly.

"There's the brown-skinned girl I remember."

She let her shoulders loosen by act of will, letting the heat sink into muscles that felt as though they hadn't relaxed in years. "Not a girl anymore, Remy. I wasn't one when you knew me."

He waved a hand in dismissal, water dripping off his heavy arm and onto the wooden floors. "Sorry. You know what I meant."

"I know. It's fine." She trailed her fingers over the surface of the water.

"You look good now that you're clean. Put on a few pounds, maybe."

She laughed. "See how trim you look after birthing twins."

He laughed back. "If I'm birthing twins, my trim physique will be the least of my concerns. But I'm serious, it looks like village life suits you."

"Living on the ass end of the continent, as far away as you can get from the Wilds without falling off the edge of the world is what suited me."

"Well, I'm glad you went, then. Even though I've missed you."

She sank deeper, leaning back so only the very front of her face touched air. A moment later, she sat up.

"I missed you too. Us going away was never about leaving you behind. You could have come with us."

"I know, Akina. But for a while there I wasn't very pleasant company. Having your heart broken will do that to a man."

She cracked her neck. "I know. You had a rough time. You needed space. Maybe we gave you too much."

"It's not as if you had anything to do with my broken heart. And I'm grown. I made my own choices."

"You deserved better."

"I did. I still do. At least it gave me an opportunity to test that old saying, 'wine heals all wounds.'"

Akina snorted, blowing tiny bubbles on the surface of the water. "I don't think that's how that goes, Remy."

"It's not? Well, good, it shouldn't be. The wine barely helped."

"I'll keep that in mind."

"Look, I'm not holding any anger at you for leaving. I understand that you two needed to get away from all this. But I am more than a little curious why you're here. I assume you didn't come back to catch up old friends on news? You're not carrying an invitation to Petrik's funeral, not with him dead so long."

"No. We had to burn him fast, what with the plague and all. There wasn't time."

"I'm sorry, Akina. That sounds hard."

She took a deep breath. "This isn't about Petrik. Not really."

He nodded and watched her, waiting for more. Giving her space.

He was always kinder than he let on.

She tightened her shoulders and nodded. "Right. I need your help."

He smiled. "Is it money, then? I have some squirreled away. Didn't think you'd be falling short, not with the fortune you left with."

"I don't need money. More like, I'm on a quest and I need you to watch my back."

"Ah. But you have the dog. What's his name?"

"His name is Dog. And he's not watching my back, he's useless. But he's Petrik's dog, so I can't just . . ."

"All right, I get it. Why me, though? I'm old and fat and out of shape."

"I need someone I can trust."

"No, no. You're supposed to argue with me. 'You're not fat Remy, you're solid. Manly. And you're not old either, Remy. You're youthful at heart. Still limber, thanks to the relaxing effects of alcohol.'"

"I need someone I can trust, *and* I need someone who can get me a face-to-face with the Tae Kun Clan."

He sighed. "That's a big ask."

"I have a big need."

"You want to share some details with your old friend Remy?"

She leaned back, rinsed her hair again, then sat up. "I'm taking on the Reaver."

Remy fell into a very deep silence.

Akina squeezed water out of her hair, then submerged it again and wrung it out.

"Remy?"

"I am pondering why you want me dead."

"I don't want you dead."

"Yet you want me on your side as you take on the Reaver. Why don't we drown ourselves right now in these tubs? It will be faster and infinitely more pleasant."

"That's why I need the Tae Kun. And to get an audience with them, I need your voucher."

He ran his fingers through red hair, slicking it back to his skull. "You're not talking about an adventure; you're talking about a war. A big one. There will be destruction like we haven't seen since the last Surge. And that killed thousands."

"I hope not. But if that's what it takes, then yes. I'll have a war." She studied him. Was he going to lose his nerve?

He leaned forward, water sloshing down the sides of the tub, and stared into her face. "You're not joking."

"When do I ever?"

"I thought you were after a bit of the old excitement. A quest for treasure. Steal the penis bone of Ku-Lo from the Emperor's castle. Loot the claws off the great rainbow tyrant from where it fell under the Spine of the World. Something fun. But this . . ."

"I wouldn't ask, but I need your help. And you used to say you'd do anything for me."

His voice rose in anger. "I would! I've proven I would! Time and again. Don't you dare question that."

"So do this. This falls under 'anything.'"

"But why?"

I don't want to say it.

I have to say it.

She slid under the water, rubbing her face clean with both hands. When she came up, Remy was still staring.

Another deep breath. "They took my girls, Remy." Energy dripped off her in pulses. Waves rippled and broke in both tubs; Dog stood up and barked; the door creaked against its hinges and the assortment of brushes and footstools littering the floor slid away from her.

His eyes widened and his shoulders shivered as if an ocean wind had gusted through the door. "Are you sure?"

She let out a long breath, calming herself. "Two of the men who came for them are dead, and I found the Reaver's tokens on their bodies. You think anybody else would leave a trail like that?"

"What if someone wanted you to go after the Reaver? Some common enemy?"

"I checked already. Multiple times. The Reaver sent me a message. Definitely from him. One of the girls' scarves."

"Ah."

"Silk from a giant spider. Nobody else has a scarf like that. Not that far from the Wilds."

"Ah. So he definitely has the girls and he wants you to know it."

"Right. Which means he really wants me, not them. Because otherwise . . ."

Remy rubbed his hands through his thick, unruly hair. "But why? This can't be revenge, can it? After all this time?"

She shrugged. "I don't think so. I don't even know who the Reaver is. Not for sure. Are there really that many people who hate me enough to go to this much trouble for revenge?"

"I'm not going to answer that."

She shook her head. "Seriously. But come on, you know why he'd want me."

"The Millennium Qi."

"My grandfather's legacy. With a weapon like that the Reaver could rule the martial world for a hundred years."

Remy nodded. "He could. But for him to get it, you would have to die. Which means this is a trap. Kidnap the girls, draw you in, capture you, steal the Qi. It's not even a clever trap."

"No."

"How are you going to beat the trap?"

"You've known me for twenty years, Remy. How do I beat traps?"

"I seem to remember something about walking through the front door and ramming your fist down the throat of everybody involved."

"I'm glad I left an impression."

He dipped under the water, then came back up, rivulets streaming down his wide body. "We're just going to bust down the front door and take them out, are we?"

"I wouldn't, Remy, honestly, I wouldn't. I tried to leave all this behind. But he took my girls."

"My brain says I should be worried for us, but my heart says I should be more worried about the people you're going after."

"Listen to your heart, Remy, and hand me that robe."

3

Dog on a Bone

Five days sailing up the river on the barge *Bone Rich* had Akina feeling antsy and impatient. She walked the foredeck, tracing figure eight patterns until the shape started to imprint on the planks, cycling qi and trying to let go of her worries.

She was taking a break belowdecks when shouting interrupted her rest.

In her eventful forty-plus years of life, Akina had learned how to sort all kinds of generalized shouting into distinct categories. There was the 'we can't believe you finished the last cask of wine' shouting, the 'we've been going the wrong way for half a day and have to turn around now' shouting, the 'there's something in the distance and we're not sure if it's a threat or not' shouting, and, finally, the 'monsters are attacking us and are already eating some of the crew' shouting.

This shouting was the last type.

Her assessment was confirmed when an arm fell through the hatch, bouncing along the floor of the hold. As it slid to a stop, all the crew members in sight grabbed weapons and scrambled to climb the stairs to defend the ship.

I should probably find out whose arm that is. But first things first.

She stretched and cracked her back, visited the privy, took care of a small errand, and walked to the hatch.

The shouting had intensified, combining with a chorus of sounds somewhere between growls and the squelch of wet boots plunged into mud. *And here I thought I'd heard everything.*

She leapt up the ladder, touching only one rung to help control her direction, and landed on the open deck.

The air was close to its midday hottest, the nightshades that would block out the sun come evening too far away to see. She smelled fish and decaying grass, which was typical of the wide, slow-moving South River.

She sought out Dog first; he was perched on the front railing, facing the deck, tongue hanging out as he watched the fighting. He spotted her and let out a bark.

The side rails of the ship were swarmed by creatures roughly the size of a human. They were covered in pale green scales with wide mouths full of sharp teeth.

Remy stood near the center of the foredeck, feet planted, a whirring sound coming from him that she hadn't heard in over a decade.

He cast her a quick glance, his attention on the attackers.

"Nice of you to join us. Have a good nap?" He held a pair of slender ropes with heavy bone darts attached. They spun so fast the darts were only a blur.

He twisted his wrist; the dart released and whistled out, lancing the face of one of the monsters.

With a sharp tug on the rope Remy pulled the dart out of the creature's head and set it to spinning again.

Akina shrugged. "We paid for passage, didn't we? It's not our job to defend the ship."

One of the creatures broke past the spotty line of defense the crew had formed. As they approached, she slid forward, leaned back, and kicked its chest with enough force to send it airborne and back over the railing.

"Infinity Bagua: Horizontal Axis."

Remy sent his second rope dart into another creature, splitting its forehead, then turned to survey the deck.

"We did not, in fact, pay for passage. We were hired to be guards on what should have been a very uneventful journey."

She stepped around him, avoiding the areas where she knew the darts would be spinning, and put her back to his. "Oh, right. Because the regular guards met with unfortunate accidents in a tavern brawl and needed medical care. If we're the guards, we really should be doing more to help fight off these . . . things. What are they?"

"Yes, we should." Remy stepped forward, angling his wide body, and flicked his ropes, sending darts out in two directions at once, resulting in a severed arm and a leg cut off at the knee. "These are sea ogres. How do you not know what sea ogres are? Didn't you live on the coast?"

Dog barked again as one of the sea ogres grabbed a crewman and prepared to drag him over the side. Akina ran, twirling with each step, then leapt and kicked the ogre's head hard enough to spin it completely around. "Infinity Bagua: Zero Point Tornado."

As she landed, she turned back to Remy. "I was on the west coast and so far south we could see the edge of the world. You have to be closer to the Spine to see monsters like these."

"I didn't realize you were that far out. Must be nice. What did you do for money?"

She ran along the barge's railing, killing ogres from behind and supporting the crew as they finished off the last of the attackers. She lost sight of Remy as she passed to the back of the ship, striking the surprised ogres from the back, rounding the back rail, and running toward the prow.

By the end of her circuit the battle had been reduced to a handful of injured ogres being finished off by the sailors.

Akina stomped on a final sea ogre neck and stepped over to her friend. "I was a farmer, Remy. That was the plan, remember? Petrik and I retired and went south to start a farm. Live in peace."

"Of course, I remember the plan. I just never thought you'd follow through. Figured you two had wound up as warlords down there or something."

She sighed and walked over to Dog. He panted and licked her left hand as she stroked his head with her right.

Remy knelt and wiped his darts off on a clean cloth, then spent a minute plucking nuggets of flesh out of his beard.

Akina looked at him. "Well, that's not what happened. The most I've used my martial arts in these ten years is clearing tree stumps and boulders out of new fields."

"Until the last few days."

"Yes, until the last few days." The barge's captain, a woman with weathered, leathery skin, stalked over to them.

"Nice to see you two finally decided to lend a hand, seeing as how that's what I'm paying you for."

Akina nodded. "You're welcome. Given how peaceful this river usually is I was sure your crew could use some practice repelling boarders. Looks like I was right since they didn't do so well. You'll have to send someone to clean up belowdecks."

The woman's face reddened, stark against the white streaks in her hair. "It's not your job to train my crew. It's your job to do what I pay you for, which is defend this ship."

"Exactly! Which it is, as you can see. Defended. You're welcome! Now, tell me, how often do sea ogres attack this far upriver? Because I remember someone saying something about sea ogres not coming up past Dragon's Mouth, and we are definitely upriver from there."

The captain looked at Remy, who shrugged, then back to Akina. "It is rare. Not unheard of."

"Really? Because I've never heard of it. Those things stink like old fish."

The captain shook her head. "I have work. You two stay out of trouble."

Akina saluted. "Yes, ma'am."

Remy touched her shoulder. "Maybe you could be less antagonistic? She's not your enemy."

"I'm not in a good mood. Don't ask me to repeat the reason."

"I know, and you have every right to be angry. But not at *her*."

Akina sighed. "You're annoying when you're right. Remind me why I let you speak to me that way?"

"Because nobody else is dumb enough to try. And you have a streak of masochism." He held one of his rope darts to the light to examine it. It was a single obsidian-colored tooth the size of two fists held together, its tip carved to a sharp point. A loop was cut into the top with a rope knotted through.

"I'm glad to see you kept those."

"Why wouldn't I?"

"You know. Not exactly necessary, a pair of black tyrant teeth, not when you're just a bouncer in some random tavern. You could have sold those and bought a nice house in the country."

He smiled. "I never needed money that bad. And I never wanted a nice house in the country. Besides, I have a lot of nostalgia for these." He sheathed the weapons and tilted his head to ask her to walk with him.

They strolled around the deck, checking the sides to make sure there were no lingering ogres.

The river was broad and peaceful in stunning contrast to the recent violence. The friends stood side by side at the back railing, watching as the water churned and bubbled around the bodies of the slain ogres.

Remy leaned over the rail, bending double and reaching down to the water just out of reach. He stood back up. "You think that was about you?"

"You mean the sea ogres? Did the Reaver do something to send them here?"

"That's the question. As you said, they don't usually come this far upriver."

She scratched her neck and lowered the brim of her straw hat for shade. "Could be. We'll see. If it's about me, he won't stop at a few sea ogres. There will be more trouble ahead."

Remy breathed deep as they listened to the splashes of bodies being dumped into the river. "Are you worried about calling out your style when you fight? It's not like there are hundreds of Infinity Bagua practitioners running around. Someone's bound to make a connection."

"I would be worried if I was sneaking my way north. But I'm not. I want them to know I'm coming."

"That's what I thought you'd say. You realize, and you know I have all the respect in the world for you, you can't take on the Reaver's army by yourself."

"I'm not by myself. I've got you, don't I?"

"Great. You realize we can't take on the Reaver's army together, don't you?"

"That's why I need an audience with Tae Kun."

"Tae Kun has no reason to fight the Reaver. And if they did, they're barely a match for him. Even if they were, they can't afford to march with the northern animal clans, the rainbow dragon clans, and the instrument clans waiting for a chance to gain favor with the Emperor. They know that. I know you don't think much of Arha Tae Kun, but he isn't as stupid as he looks."

She studied his face. "What are you saying?"

"I'm saying you'd better have an actual plan."

"Don't I always?"

"No, Akina, you don't. In fact, you almost never have a plan."

"That's not true."

"Really? What was the plan when we killed this black tyrant? The one whose teeth I'm using for darts?"

"The plan was to run up to it and beat it to death. Which is what we did."

"That's not a plan! That's barely a goal. And that worked with the black tyrant, but it won't work with the Reaver."

She nodded and looked at the river. "I do have an actual plan this time, Remy. It was a long walk from home to Dragon's Mouth. I had time to think."

"So there's an actual plan?"

"I said so, didn't I?"

"We're not just going on a suicide run? Go out with a flash and a parade? I really need to know. Well, I don't *need* to know, but I'd like to."

"I swear on the lives of my daughters, Remy. There's a plan. If it were just about me, maybe I'd be okay going out with that flash and parade, but they deserve more than that. So yes, there's a plan."

"Okay. We should check on Dog."

She laughed. "Dog is fine. He's the one thing you absolutely don't have to worry about."

••••••••••

Something poked at Akina's backside.

"Mmm, Petrik, not now, I'm—" Her eyes snapped open to a dim view of the wooden wall of the hold. "If you're not Remy, you have three seconds to live."

"Hush. It's Remy. Get up, we have an issue."

She sighed and rolled off the hard bunk. There was a minute's scramble while she pulled on her loose brown pants and faded blue tunic. She laced up her split-toed boots as Remy briefed her in a whisper.

"Pinch point up ahead. The river gets broad but shallow and there's only a narrow place where ships this big can pass. It's fortified and they run inspections."

She settled her straw hat on her head and looked up at him. "You woke me for a customs inspection?"

"It's not the Emperor's men manning the customs right now. It's the Reaver's."

"Then you should have woken me sooner. What are they demanding?"

"We got word from ships coming downriver. They're searching everybody. They won't let anyone pass without being boarded."

She stood and followed Remy up the ladder to the barge's deck. A third of the crew—eight men—milled about as the barge floated in place. She imagined there was an anchor of some sort holding it against the current. The captain was talking in hushed tones with the first mate, a tall, skinny man with a missing ear.

The mate spotted Akina and Remy, nudged the captain, and continued talking.

Akina surveyed the deck. "Where's Dog?"

Remy pointed. "Sleeping inside that coil of rope. The noise doesn't seem to bother him."

"That dog can sleep through a lot. What do you think? What are our options?"

He stroked his long beard. "We can grab a raft and head for shore. Hope the Reaver's men don't spot us in the dark and come after us."

"Or hope that they do."

"Nah, they'd sink the raft from a distance. You don't want to fight them on water."

"What else?"

"Convince the captain to turn around."

She shook her head. "Unacceptable. We need to get upriver at least as far as Divine Fork. Going around will take too long."

"Well, if we have to get across the checkpoint, we need the captain to ram the blockade with this barge."

Remy turned at the sound of a throat clearing behind him.

"You need me to do what exactly?"

"Oh, uh, excuse me, ma'am. We were just wondering what we should do about those customs boats."

The captain squinted at him in the dim lantern light. "Why do my guards feel the need to have an opinion about the customs boats?"

Akina knelt and ran her fingers over Dog's back. "Those aren't the usual customs people. I'm sure you've noticed."

"I might have. What difference does it make?"

"The Reaver's men are here to give me a hard time. Since I'm on your ship, they're more than likely going to give you a hard time as well."

The captain turned to her mate, who nodded and fingered the hilt of something nasty poking out at his waist. She turned back.

"Which sounds to me like a great reason to dump you over the side. Or hand you over to the Reaver's men myself."

Akina nodded. "Absolutely, that's right. That's exactly what you should do. Smart lady. Hand us over, invite the Reaver's men over for a chat. Maybe serve some tea. In fact, hey, you there, start a fire. We're going to need some hot water."

The captain shook her head at the first mate's questioning glance. "Why don't you sound more concerned?"

Akina looked at Remy, who shrugged, then pointed at herself and opened her eyes wide. "Me? Concerned? But why? Remy and I might be taken by the Reaver, but what are we really losing? It's not like we have a very fancy ship with three very powerful tyrant bones built into the keel that are about to be confiscated, leaving us with nothing."

The captain leaned in and lowered her voice. "What are you talking about?"

"You know, the tyrant bones. Three of them. Reinforcing the keel. I bet that's how you ride so low in the water, fill that cargo hold with juicy, profitable . . . stuff. Scrape the bottom, no problem, wooden beams might splinter but those bones just absorb the impact. Still, bones of that size? That's a fortune built into this ship. I'm sure the Reaver's men will be very sad to take the bones and leave you with nothing."

"Those bones are hidden. There's no way they'll be found, not by a search. Are you going to tell them about the bones? Why would you do that?"

"Me? I won't tell them anything. I'll die before I let them take me. I'll try to kill them, and if I fail, I'll die. Who knows? Life's a gamble."

"Then what are you saying?"

"I *might* be informing you that the seals hiding those bones have been broken. That they're not as hidden as you thought. Sure, a regular inspection won't spot them, but the Reaver's men know their bones. And their magic."

The captain half drew a cutlass from her belt, showing a foot of gray edge before resheathing it.

"Why?"

Akina bared her teeth in an expression nobody would confuse for a smile. "You have kids?"

"No."

"Then I don't think I can explain. I didn't mean for you to get in the middle of this, but you are. Now you can help us break through that blockade or lose your ship. Your choice."

The captain took a pinch of dried leaf from a small bag at her hip and stuffed it into her gums. "So I turn you over and lose the bones, keeping my ship together, or I let you lead us on a suicide mission and lose my life *and* my ship in one big massacre. That's not a great set of options."

"The only massacre you're going to see are the other guys. Get us in close and Remy and I will clear the Reaver's men and end the blockade. Then you take us to Divine Fork, we disembark, you never see us again."

The captain spat over the railing. "What makes you think you two have a chance against a shipful of the Reaver's men?"

Akina grinned and cracked her neck. "What makes *you* think they have a chance against us?"

Remy stepped forward and put a hand on her shoulder. "I'm not the kind of man to throw my life away. If we have a platform to fight from, I promise those men don't stand a chance."

The captain chewed some more, then spat again and looked to her first mate.

The tall, angular man stepped close and lowered his voice. "Were you really using Infinity Bagua on those sea ogres?"

Akina nodded.

The mate turned to his captain. "We have a blockade to run, ma'am."

4

Dog Eat Dog World

The captain stuffed another wad of leaf into her cheek and chewed furiously. "I shouldn't have given up the pipe."

Remy nodded. They stood side-by-side at the prow of the barge, eyes switching between the war barges blockading the river and the edge of the nightshade crossing the sky from the east, light streaming down behind it. The unimaginably large slab had been passing overhead for about eight hours, blocking most of the sun's light.

"Another quarter hour and we'll have enough daylight to attack, Captain. And I agree, you should have kept the pipe. Nothing would help now more than a good smoke."

She looked up at the big man. "Explain why we're waiting for dawn?"

Remy smoothed his beard over his chest. "Have you seen the way my beard glistens in the morning light?"

She grunted and shook her head.

He held up his hands as his face twisted in mock offense. "Dear captain, I sense doubt in your tone. We hunted the Wilds for a decade. We can handle a few of the Reaver's men. The light makes it easier for me to protect you from arrows."

She shook her head again, turned, and walked the perimeter of the deck, stopping to point out an occasional loosely knotted rope or empty water bucket.

Akina looked up from where she squatted, rubbing Dog's belly. "I think you were really reassuring, Remy. She seems very confident now."

"Well, you weren't helping. Try to look, I don't know, dangerous or something."

She stood and dusted off her hands. "*Looking* dangerous was always your job. I'm here to *be* dangerous."

He looked around to check for eavesdroppers. "Are you still? Dangerous? It's been a long time, Akina. You've been working a farm, having babies."

"Having babies is significantly harder than anything you've done in the past ten—no, in your entire life."

"I know, but it's not the same as combat. You have the Millennium Qi, which is awesome. But do you have your fighting edge?"

"Enough to take care of this batch of third-rate hunters. Now get ready, dawn is coming. And no more flirting with the captain."

"Was I? I don't think I was. Not my type. The first mate, maybe. If I was drunk enough."

Akina gave Dog a final rub and straightened. She took in the busy crew, then pointed up. "You know, in the south, they study the holes in the nightshade."

Remy looked. "The lights?"

"Yeah. There are patterns in the holes. Petrik studied them, too. He could tell the date just by looking up at night. Three hundred and sixty different nightshades just floating along."

"Then what? After they pass?"

"The first one comes around again. Or there are more than three hundred sixty, and they repeat the patterns. But if that's the case, it's an exact match."

Remy shrugged. "So they know the date. That's neat, but I know it too and I didn't have to memorize those patterns."

"They think certain combinations are auspicious. If you want to get married. Or conceive a child. You'll do it under certain nightshades, but not others."

"Does it make any difference? Are their marriages better? Their children kinder?"

"Not as far as I could tell."

They watched a curtain of light, extending as far as they could see to the north and south, advance on the river. As dawn touched the water, the captain called out for the crew to start moving the barge.

Oars splashed and the ponderous boat picked up speed.

Akina checked on Dog snoring inside the coil of rope he'd made his home, then looked at Remy. "Just like old times."

"I think we remember the old times differently. Starting with us having three other hunters at our flanks."

"Yes, well. We work with what we've got."

Remy unsheathed his rope darts and set them spinning overhead. Akina crouched by the railing. Sounds carried over the water; lookouts on the war barges were calling out that they'd spotted the cargo barge's advance.

Akina pointed. "Ram the one on the left? I'll hop over and take out the one on the right. You cover the barge."

Remy nodded. "You don't need to keep repeating it. I'm sober. Depressingly so."

The barge turned to the port, cutting a rough path across the river toward one of the warships. Dog snorted and woke up. He climbed over the rope, scanned the deck, then turned back to the coil and began to vigorously hump it.

Arrows flew from both of the Reaver's boats, splashing harmlessly into the river.

A voice shouted from behind Remy. "Arrows!"

The big man shook his head, beard shaking in the breeze. "Just keep going! I've got it!"

The first mate called out. "Stroke!" Oars splashed into the water, the barge lurching forward as the crew grunted and strained and pulled.

A flight of arrows came close enough to spray Akina's face with droplets of water.

"Stroke!"

Remy hissed as he sped up the rope darts. "Way of the Bear: Greater Den." A dome of energy spread from the rope darts, lifting over the top of the barge and enveloping it.

"Remy, how long can you keep this up for?"

He laughed. "No idea. But I wouldn't stop to take in the view if I were you."

Shouts from the warships escalated as the cargo barge closed on their position. Arrows arrived in a continuous stream, pouring in from both sides. As they struck the dome of Remy's den, they bounced off or were redirected into the water. Soon ballistae were brought to bear, heavier shafts joining the arrows. The port warship started to turn, its crew struggling to move away from a collision.

Remy grunted with the strain of deflecting the hail of projectiles.

Akina pointed. "Impact in ten seconds. Brace."

The big man planted one thick foot on the deck behind him, rooting so hard the wood warped and bent around his feet. His rope darts continued their hum, twin bundles of death.

The ship shuddered and shook as the prow hit the rear quarter of the warship.

Had the ships been simple wood frame construction they might have both sunk after impact or been torn into unusable fragments. But some monster had chosen, for reasons not fully understood, to come east along the Spine of the World. It had died, slaughtered by human hunters desperate to protect their lands and kin. The creature had been rendered into bone and skin; those parts had then been used to reinforce keel and hull until they were all but indestructible.

The rear of the river barge swung out and around, leaving the prow pointed directly at the warship they'd struck and the west bank of the river behind it.

Soldiers dressed in the purple and black livery of the Reaver swarmed to the edge of their ship, tossing ropes and ladders over the side to help them board the barge. The cargo boat's crew rushed forward, armed with cleavers and pikes to knock them back into the water.

Akina stood and exhaled. "My turn. Keep an eye on Dog. Infinity Bagua: Spiral Sprint."

She leapt toward the back of the barge and the warship beyond it. Her right foot struck the deck; as she rebounded into the air, she turned, landing facing backward.

With the next step she spun around, then completed a revolution and a half in the air. Every bound carried her further along the length of the barge and had her completing more, and faster, revolutions.

Her last step shattered the aft deck of the barge and launched her through Remy's shield and across a hundred yards of river.

Spinning in the air, she spotted dozens of soldiers milling about on the war barge's deck. More than a few were firing arrows at her, then drawing swords and axes and bracing for impact.

The crew yelled wordless notes of confusion.

The men on the warship watched Akina fly, clustering near the spot where she was going to impact their boat.

Bad move, guys.

She hit the deck like a meteor strike; like a boulder shot by a catapult; like the descending foot of a leviathan; like a very angry, very powerful woman landing on the deck of a ship full of men who were trying to stop her from getting her daughters back.

Energy pulsed from the impact, flinging all but a handful of soldiers off the sides of the barge and into the water, most screaming at the pain of shattered limbs and distressed joints. The deck rippled like ocean waves, splintering and warping in concentric circles around her. The masts of the barge bent and broke, leaving pale, jagged stumps behind.

Akina landed in the hero's pose: right knee on the deck, right hand palm-down next to it, and left arm extended to the side, eyes looking down.

She slowly raised her head, looking up through the rim of her straw hat, eyes stormy and violent.

"Intermediate Wave."

Splashes could be heard around the barge as more soldiers took the most direct path away from her.

The warship rocked, the front rising back out of the water after Akina had pushed it down almost far enough to swamp. With a lurch it straightened, bobbing back and forth in the disturbed river.

A slow clap sounded from the shattered superstructure.

"Bravo. Really, bravo. That was a wonderful entrance. Worthy of the Spiral Witch. I barely dared to hope that I would see the Millennium Qi in action."

The voice was so oily Akina wanted to rag out her ears. It was also familiar.

"Bao? Little Bao? Is that you?"

"Don't call me that. Nobody calls me that." A shape emerged from the wreckage. A man, an inch or two below average height, slenderly built, dressed in the black and purple of the Reaver.

Akina pulled lengths of cloth from inside her sleeves and wrapped her hands. "You *are* Bao! It's been years. You still wetting the bunk? Oh, they teased you for that."

"I know what you're trying to do, but I've grown beyond my childish temper. As you'll soon see." He strode forward into the light, chains crafted of linked vertebrae trailing from his hands to the necks of eight stumbling, broken men.

She panted, a bit light-headed from her exertions. *I thought I was in better shape than this. I should buy some time, but not too much time or Remy will get overwhelmed.*

"Why are you here, Bao? What do you want?"

"Why do you think? I'm here for you. More specifically, to bring the Reaver the treasure of the martial world that you hold inside you." He tugged the chains, forcing the eight battered individuals to stumble forward. They wore civil service colors, yellow and tan uniforms typical of customs inspectors at a distant outpost. The Emperor's people.

"You sure? You're not trying to grab the Millennium Qi for yourself?"

He smiled, blackened teeth showing between thin lips. "You can't divide me from the Reaver. What he's working for is too important. It's time to unite the martial world before the next Wedge Pulse comes and plunges us into another dark age."

Akina straightened and cracked her neck. "I won't stop you from uniting the martial clans or banding together to stop the next Pulse. But you can't have my daughters."

"Nobody wants *them*, not really. But we need the Millennium Qi. Your grandfather almost ruled the world with it, once upon a time. Now the Reaver will finish the job."

"He can't have that either." She clapped her hands, the sound sharp and clear in the morning air. "Time for your last words, Little Bao."

"I will have you chained at my side when I bring you to the Reaver, Spiral Witch. I do believe I'm going to enjoy the journey."

She skipped forward and launched a kick toward his chest. "Infinity Bagua: Horizontal Axis."

He turned his body, parrying the kick with both arms; her foot drove in with enough force to catch his shoulder. The impact sent him stumbling to the side.

She turned to follow him, stepping forward and across his body, lancing out a left jab. "Lower Limit."

He yanked on the chains, pulling himself just out of the path of her punch, throwing a kick up at her head that she deflected with her cloth-wrapped right arm.

She turned to face him again and he reset his stance, hands by his cheeks.

His eyes flashed. "My turn. Way of the Eel: Stun the Pond."

His eyes flashed again but with actual sparks; they danced from his pupils, circling through the whites, then out into his hands and across the deck of the warship.

Electricity sizzled through the bodies of nearby unconscious soldiers, their flesh smoking and bubbling. Lanterns along the deck exploded, oil flaming and shattering their glass covers. Two of the captured Imperial soldiers shied back, their skin blackened by the discharge.

The wave of lightning continued. Akina danced backward, leaping from foot to foot, each step digging fresh ruts in the wooden deck. As she reached the prow, nowhere to go but into the water, she leapt, flipping in the air as the wave of lightning passed.

She landed on both feet and stared at Bao with wide eyes. "I guess you've grown up some."

He bent over, panting, his qi exhausted by the costly maneuver. "Nice move. I'll. Get. You. Now."

"I don't think you have anything left to get me with. Surrender and I'll let you live. Out of respect for the kid you used to be. The one who brought me wine and washed my clothes after a hunt."

"I'm. Not done. Yet." He straightened, took a deep breath. "Reaver's Reap: Drain."

Black light dripped out of his hands and over the polished bones of his chains. The soldiers flinched from the light, eyes wide and jaws slack.

The light oozed onto two of the men, covering their wrists, their hands, then their forearms and climbing to their shoulders. The men fell to their knees, then sat back on their heels.

Akina watched as their bodies collapsed in on themselves, the black light roiling and sucking at their skin, pulsing aura traveling back up the chains and into Bao.

His posture straightened as the life force of the soldiers poured into him, replenishing his qi. His lips curled into a smile as his breathing eased. "I follow the Reaver for many reasons. This is one of them. This is the power that will let us stand up to the Wedge. This is the future!"

Akina shook her head. "Sorry, Little Bao, you've lost your way. I would give you a lecture about morality and becoming worse than the monsters you fear, but it would be a waste."

"Why? Do you think I'm stupid?"

"No, I think you're about to die."

Bao snarled and dropped all eight chains, letting the two corpses and six dazed soldiers fall to the ground. He crouched down. "Way of the Eel: Rush."

Akina knew the technique.

It used electricity to fire the muscles directly, causing muscle contractions far stronger and faster than those driven by neurological impulses.

He came at her in a blitz, the air cracking with his speed, lips parted in an ugly sneer.

Akina retreated as if underwater, shifting from side to side with the tight angular footwork characteristic of Infinity Bagua. With less skill, Bao was still pressuring her, his overwhelming speed and physical power too much to handle.

He landed one punch, then a second, on her centerline.

She coughed specks of blood onto the deck and wiped her mouth with the wrapping around her right hand.

He stood back and grinned. "I expected more of the Millennium Qi."

She twisted left, then right, then stomped the deck with her foot. "Infinity Bagua: Simple Wave." The wood pulsed and shifted, disrupting Bao's balance.

She stepped forward once more, eyeing his movement as his arms spread to catch his fall, leaving him airborne and defenseless for a single, precarious, precious moment.

"Lower Limit." Her fist snapped into his throat, crunching bone and cartilage.

Bao stumbled backward, hands at his throat, his eyes pulsing again with power as he poured qi into his neck, furiously working to open his airway. He turned to look over each shoulder, eyes searching for the chains that sagged limply over the floor.

"Speed doesn't matter if you can't root yourself, Bao. It's like you learned all the advanced techniques but never quite got the hang of the basics. Your teachers should have had you stand in place for another five years before showing you that stuff."

"Bitch!" The word was choked, barely audible.

She hopped forward and swept at his legs. "Subtraction." He leapt out of the way, turning a full somersault in the air.

Blood leaked through the fingers at his throat as he landed, but he crouched and grabbed a chain with his other hand. He smiled at her through bloody lips. "Not. Over."

She exhaled, fluid moving unpleasantly in her lungs. *Shit. I'm almost done. Can't let him absorb their qi.*

"Infinity Bagua: Horizontal Axis." She twitched her hips as if to kick Bao but saw that he was ready for it.

No choice.

She pivoted and speared her left foot into the forehead of the prisoner at the end of the chain.

The man died without a sound.

Bao's eyes widened as he reached for another chain.

"Infinity Bagua: Angular Momentum." She killed the second soldier, breaking his neck with a quick, efficient twist.

Bao looked at her.

"What? Did you think I was soft? Wrong Answer." She slapped the stunned expression off his face, channeling all the weight of her hips and legs through her torso and hand.

A spray of blood fountained out of his mouth and over the deck. Bao recoiled, facing her again, coughing as pieces of his larynx tore and gave way.

"Did you think I would be merciful? Hold back? Because I'm a woman, perhaps? You always did think less of me, didn't you, Little Bao? Wrong Answer."

Another slap left his eyes milky and dazed.

"You and the Reaver think because Petrik's gone I'm going to fall apart? Take to my knees and let you pull the Millennium Qi out through my throat? Because I have nothing left? Vertical Axis."

She lifted her hand high, then dropped her hips, bringing the tip of her elbow down into Bao's shoulder.

His collarbone broke with an audible snap; Bao cried out as his arm spasmed.

"You've taken everything from me. But that doesn't make me less dangerous. In fact, it makes me the most dangerous thing you've ever seen. You're worried about the Wedge Pulse? A tsunami of monsters riding east, trampling all of civilization before it, stretching north and south to the ends of the world?

"You should be a lot more worried about me.

"Angular Momentum."

5

Wish Upon a Star

Four days later, upriver from the battle with the Reaver's soldiers.

Remy twisted a peanut in his hand until the shell disintegrated. He tossed a nut into his mouth and slipped the other one to Dog. "What are their names again? Wait, can dogs eat peanuts?"

Akina nodded from her position: cross-legged on the foredeck of the *Bone Rich*. "I don't know about other dogs, but this one can eat anything. Whose names? You mean the twins?"

Remy nodded and picked another peanut from the rough canvas bag that sat between them. Dog chewed and settled back on the deck, resting his head on his paws. "Yeah, the girls. I never met them."

"The older one is Pooja. She's the serious, dependable one. Sneha's the troublemaker."

"Older? I thought they were twins?"

"Yes, they're twins. But they don't come out at the same time, side-by-side, you know? Pooja was first by a few minutes."

Remy looked up, then shuddered and returned to his peanuts. "I never thought about it."

"Men usually don't."

"How old are they?"

"Eleven. Almost twelve."

Remy tried to see her face through the shadow cast by her straw hat.

"Pooja. Sneha." His mouth worked wide around the unfamiliar words.

Akina nodded. "They're common names near the edge. Different people there. Darker, like me. Poor Petrik always stood out with his thin beard and light skin. We wanted the girls to have every chance to fit in."

Remy nodded and fed another nut to Dog, who moved just enough to lick it off his fingers.

"You said two of the Reaver's men died? Grabbing the girls? They had guards?"

"They didn't have guards. They weren't supposed to need any. They were grabbed out of a village school. Mud walls. They were learning to write, scratching in the dirt with sticks."

"Then . . . Was Dog there?"

"No. Remy, they're eleven-year-old girls. But they're *my* girls. You think they'd just scream helplessly when a bunch of soldiers tried to grab them?"

"Ah. Killed two grown men."

"He's got some very skilled men if they only lost two."

"How did the men get away?"

"You mean, why didn't I catch them?"

He wiped his broad hand across the polished wood of the deck, gathering shell fragments and tossing them through the railing. "That is what I mean, yes. No way were they faster than you, especially not with captives."

"I'm not sure. Dog caught their scent and we followed them northeast. Lost them halfway to the next village."

"So Dog's a tracker."

"Not a great one but not the worst. We're talking about a band of men. And my girls. There's no way Dog would just lose that scent."

"What do you think? Did they have griffins?"

She sighed. "I don't think so. The griffins would have had to be kept in the woods, right? We would have found signs. Griffin scat. Well, Dog would have. I have no idea what griffin scat looks or smells like. Besides, only the Emperor's men are supposed to have griffins."

"We stopped counting on 'supposed-to' a long time ago."

"Hey. I'm already taking on the strongest hunter clan west of the Great Sea. Let's not be in such a rush to add the Empire to that."

"Okay. Not griffins. What else?"

She ate a peanut and sighed. "I think the Reaver has Star Clan help."

"You think they came in through a gate all the way from the Wilds?"

Her voice sharpened. "Are you trying to irritate me? I don't know, okay? We lost the trail. They either flew away or they opened a gate. As far as I know, the only people with teleportation magic are the Star Clan. So either the Star Clan or some of its members are working with the Reaver. You think I like that? You think I'm overjoyed that another monstrously powerful clan is part of a plot to kidnap my girls? I'm not."

"Okay, okay, calm down. Please."

"Your strategy, when confronted by an angry woman, is to tell her to calm down? You don't have many female friends, do you?"

"No, not really. Not since you and Petrik left. And Rei."

She sighed. "Well, it's not an effective move."

"Noted. I'm just trying to understand what we're dealing with so I can help. You're not alone, you know."

"I know."

He stroked his beard, smoothing out the edges with calloused fingertips. "The crew isn't very happy with us. Does that worry you?"

She shrugged. "I'm not here to make anybody happy. You think they'll try to get rid of us? It's been days since we passed the blockade, what are they waiting for? Seeing if any of them grow a pair of ovaries and find the courage to make a move?"

"Is that how the saying goes? Grow ovaries? I thought it was testicles."

"I've given birth to two kids. I've also seen how fast you go down when hit in the testicles. You sure your parts are the ones I should associate with toughness and courage?"

He held up his hands. "I concede your point. Regardless, what are we going to do about the crew?"

"Tell me what you think they'll do."

He paused. "I doubt they'll attack. Seeing what you did to the Reaver's soldiers put the fear of the Emperor in them. So to speak."

"Exactly. A frontal assault will not be to their advantage."

"I did overhear an awful lot of muttering. More whining, really. Especially about the sailor who lost an arm to those sea ogres."

"Oh, please. They made enough money looting the bones off the Reaver's men to pay to grow that arm back three times. Turn that sailor into a complete freak."

"Still, they think we should have been quicker to defend them."

"Right. Back to what I asked. What do you think they'll do?"

"I don't know. We've stopped in two small towns since the blockade. Don't you think one of them is going to whisper in the wrong ear that we're on board? Send a message to the Reaver?"

"I do." She leaned back, hands on the deck, and tilted her head toward the sun, showing him her smile.

Remy swallowed another pair of peanuts. "That is not a face full of worry and thoughtful concern."

"No, it is not."

"Care to share why the thought of our location being leaked doesn't worry you? Because it worries me."

She locked her eyes on his. "What do you think the Reaver will do if he hears that we're on this boat?"

"I don't know. Send people here to kill us, maybe? No, he'd kill me and capture you. I don't like either option."

"I don't like them either but work with me. How will the soldiers he sends get here?"

"Um. I'm not sure. I suppose they won't be riding griffins."

"I don't think they will."

"You're hoping they come with someone from the Star Clan."

She reached out and scratched the back of Dog's head. "Let's just say I'm tired of the pace of this boat. Have some more nuts and I'll tell you the plan."

•••••••••••

Something rough and wide and wet slid across the back of Akina's neck.

"Mm, Petrik, I'm ti—" Her eyes snapped open. "If you're not Dog, you have two seconds to make peace with your divinities."

Dog woofed on the back of her neck. "What's wrong, boy? You hungry? Had a bad dream? What do you dream about, anyway? Humping new and exciting tree stumps in exotic locations?" As she spoke, she pulled her tunic down over her head and laced up her boots, eyes scanning the dark interior of the hull.

"Did you wake Remy, boy? We're going to need him. Actually, he should be up and on watch. Where's Remy, Dog? Take me to him."

She looked down at the animal, who looked up at her and huffed again, tongue dangling from the side of his mouth.

She pointed up the stairs. "Take me to Remy." Dog woofed and bent to smell her feet.

She stood and stepped over to the ladder. "I told Petrik, let's get a smart dog. One that's good for hunting. But no. He wanted you. Because you were sweet and useless, and he said we had room in our hearts for something sweet and useless. By the Emperor, I wish you wouldn't try so hard to prove how right he was. About being useless, I mean, not about our hearts. Feh."

She reached down and lifted Dog up under her arm, then crept up the ladder. "Good thing we're on a boat, right, Dog? Completely safe. No way anybody can attack us out here on the water. We are feeling very secure and unprepared. Not ready at all for any surprises. Certainly not another attack. It's nice to feel so safe, isn't it?"

Akina popped her head up through the hatch, pulling it back down immediately. She looked at Dog tucked under her arm, their noses almost touching. "You see anything? Why'd you wake me, boy?"

Dog licked her face. "Fine. I'll check it out."

With a hard tug on the ladder rung she pulled herself up through the hatch and across ten feet of deck, landing in a crouch to try to avoid being seen by anybody onboard.

Remy's bulky form was slumped against the prow, the handles of a pair of blades jutting out from his chest. Her shoulders tightened, then relaxed. *It's been so long, I forgot how good he is at playing dead.*

Akina pivoted slowly, staying close to the deck, and caught flashes of movement from the rear of the boat.

They're clearing the deck. Be back this way any sec—

Whistling from both sides interrupted her train of thought. Akina tossed Dog toward Remy's prone body and dropped flat to the deck.

Dog flipped in midair, lips split in a wide grin as he sailed across the deck before landing on the big man. Twin sickles cut the air that Akina had just vacated before the ropes attached to each caught them and pulled them back toward their throwers.

Black bone. Looks like they were cut from a three-horn skull. Not cheap.

Akina kicked out, launching herself away from the origins of the two sickles while staying low to the ground.

"Look, Dog, it's a surprise attack. We are sure to face defeat, since this attack is so completely unexpected. How ever did this happen?"

With deft movements practiced daily for a quarter century she wound strips of cloth around her fists. Dog stood on Remy's belly and woofed.

Two of the Reaver's men moved in parallel, trying to keep her between them. They were covered head to toe in purple and black cloth armor reinforced with ribs, skulls, and long limb bones taken from smaller tyrants, saurids, and leviathans. Twin-bladed sickles, a foot and a half long, twirled over their heads on silk ropes.

"Look, Dog, they have me surrounded. I have no choice but to retreat across this deck." Her tone was flat, showing no hint of fear or concern.

She charged the soldier on her left, twisting as she ran to avoid the sickle he hurled. It flew past her shoulder and she scraped along its rope as she closed on the man.

"Infinity Bagua: Constant Value." She landed a palm strike on his chest with enough force to splinter the saurid sternum protecting him and send him flying through the air.

Without looking she ducked, planted a hand on the deck, and shoved off, sending her body feet-first at the other sickle wielder.

"Infinity Bagua: Rotational Momentum." She struck the soldier with a crack and landed in the hero's pose. Dog barked once, looking past his mistress.

Akina stood slowly, uncoiling from her crouch joint by joint, one vertebra at a time, snapping around to face the back of the barge and the rest of the Reaver's men at the last possible second.

"Look, Dog, I'm outnumbered and surrounded. I seem to be thoroughly trapped."

Twelve uniformed hunters faced her in a wide arc spanning the width of the barge.

The six on the left and five on the right were the Reaver's, dressed in black and purple uniforms heavily reinforced with bones worth a small fortune. They carried swords and sickles and staves carved out of the corpses of various Wedge with casual competence. Their eyes were hard and unimpressed by the fact that she'd just taken out two of their associates.

In the middle was a shorter female, slender, dressed in the white-accented raincloud gray of the Star Clan. She squatted, hips to heels, leather gloves with ogre knucklebones sewn in covering her hands.

Akina nodded to the woman. Possibly girl. "Are you here for me or looking for directions? I'd point you to the nearest decent dim sum place but I'm afraid it's out of your range."

The Star Clan warrior hissed. "I am Zhu Hsa Star. You are returning to the Wilds with me as my captive. It's up to you whether you come with or without functioning limbs."

Akina nodded and dropped her hands. "Okay. With limbs, please."

Zhu looked at her with wide eyes, then turned to the men flanking her, who shrugged. "What did you say?"

"I said, okay. I'll come as your captive. Me, by myself, fighting you and all these guys? It's pretty hopeless. Might as well surrender, right?"

Zhu nodded, her eyebrows creeping closer together as she studied the last master of Infinity Bagua. "What are your terms?"

Akina shrugged. "I don't know. I'm not in a position to dictate terms, am I? But maybe you could leave my dog alone."

"Your . . . dog?" Zhu tried to force out a mocking chuckle, but her delivery was choked by uncertainty.

Akina pointed a thumb over her shoulder. "Dog. He's a good boy, won't hurt a flea. I promise." She held her hands out, palms up, and started walking toward the men to her left.

The warriors backed away, that side of their formation retreating while Zhu looked on. "Lash her hands. She's surrendering!"

The man on the end turned to her. "That's the Spiral Witch, though!"

Zhu grunted and rolled her eyes. "Why did you think we came here? Did you think we were bringing sweet buns or a formal invitation to a ball? We're here to capture her!"

The man shook his head, eyes on Akina. "It's a trick. I'll fight her but I won't let her walk up to me like that. Look at her, she's smiling."

Akina spread her arms wider. "Whatever are you talking about? Who would think innocent little me would trick anybody?" She advanced further and the line of hunters pivoted, the men on her right coming around behind her, the formation moving around the superstructure in the center of the deck.

Zhu moved with them, coming around behind Akina as the older woman continued to pursue the soldier. The Star Clan adept raised her voice.

"Enough of this nonsense! Akina, swear on your honor as a knight errant that you'll surrender peacefully, and we'll leave your animal in peace."

Akina turned, moving along the railing, having chased the Reaver's emissaries around to the port side of the barge. "My honor as a what now? I didn't hear you." Her hands were still up, her eyes gleaming in the dark.

Zhu's nose twisted. "A knight errant. You've been a member of the martial world since before I was born, both a huntress and a warrior. All of the Five, including you, are legends. I grew up on stories of the Spiral Witch. You inspired me. I know your word is impeccable."

Akina looked down, covering her face with the brim of her straw hat. The Reaver's men froze, waiting for her response.

Zhu continued, "Give me your word, Akina Azure. We can end this now. No bloodshed." She glanced at Remy's fallen form. "No *more* bloodshed."

Akina lifted her head, then lowered it again. The soldiers closest to her edged closer, weapons at the ready, eyes tense.

She looked up.

"I *was* a knight errant before you were born, Zhu Hsa of the Star Clan. Not just any knight errant; I was the pride of my clan. I mastered every move of Infinity Bagua by the time I was fifteen. By eighteen, I had cultivated my qi to such purity that my grandfather, the terror of the martial world, declared me the next recipient of the Millennium Qi, our clan's most powerful sacred treasure.

"With Petrik, Remy, Rei, and Mau-rhi I formed the Five and roamed the Wilds for years. We harvested enough bones to buy a kingdom of our own. We upheld the status of our clans in more duels than I can remember and faced down every challenge with laughter and scorn.

"Through those years my word was my bond. My honor was as important to me—no, more important—than my life or the lives of my friends.

"That is who I was. It's lovely, really, that you were raised on stories of the Spiral Witch. Lovely that you found them inspiring.

"The thing you're forgetting, though, is that I left the martial world. I took my share of those bones, dissolved the Five, and went to a new place to live a peaceful life."

She had made a half-circle around the barge. The soldiers stood in front of Akina, facing her; Remy was prone against the railing on the other side, at their back, Dog on the deck beside him facing the confrontation with bright eyes and a lolling tongue.

"Once I was there, I found something I valued far more than my honor, reputation, or pride. I found something—something*s*—for which I will happily lie and cheat and steal and kill.

"And then . . . then the Reaver took them away from me."

Dog barked.

"Infinity Bagua: Simultaneous Equations."

6

Uncertain Outcomes

When Akina had first come north to cross the Dreadwall and hunt the Wilds, seeking her fortune, local martial artists had mocked the southern martial arts styles.

Northern arts were quick and dirty. Warriors assigned to the border had just months to either learn to fight or become food for the Wedge. They mastered punishing kicks and brutal weapons, fighting in groups to kill the monsters that threatened the human settlements to the south.

How ridiculous were the southern clans, they had said. Training for years by standing in one place. A decade spent simply learning to breathe. How *soft*.

Akina knew there was truth to those claims. The southern adepts would hold positions, breathing carefully, cultivating their internal energy for years before practicing a punch or a kick. Her own ancestor's Bagua, brought by warriors from another world to fight a Wedge Pulse, adapted that training only slightly; they walked tight circles, circulating energy while they moved, constantly turning, constantly shifting, combining their spiritual cultivation with motion in a way they believed more applicable to combat.

The Azure Dragon Clan had climbed the ranks of southern clans only after a further innovation: They twisted the Bagua circle into infinity walks.

From the time she took her first steps, Akina had paced the figure eight traced into the floor of her clan training hall, waddling about, eyes locked on the far wall. Circle, pivot, circle again, pivot. Repeat. No less than five hundred times a day. On good days, thousands of times.

The pivot, the sudden change of direction at the center of that pattern, was the core of Infinity Bagua. Adepts moved their qi in a matching pattern, the center of the shape held in the body's core, just below and behind the belly button, energy pulsing out and back, then behind and down, tracing infinity.

Ten years and a million cycles spent on that pattern meant Akina could change direction with an effortless grace that, to the less trained eye, bent the laws of physics.

She shifted her weight to the left, then to the right, the sudden movements causing men on both sides to flinch and raise weapons into defensive positions.

Another shift, a drop, and her elbow drove into the unprotected belly of one man. Another shift, then back, then forth; she kicked into the lower leg of a confused man on the other side, snapping his shin and sending him howling to the ground.

Three more steps put Akina between two of the remaining soldiers. She blurred, a whirlwind of shifts and feints that had both men backing away and covering their vital points.

One went down when a palm heel strike sent a wave of qi into his heart.

The second dropped when she reached around his guard and slapped the side of his head hard enough to separate him from consciousness.

Zhu's voice rang out over the scuffs of shuffling feet and the thuds of falling bodies. "Path of the Star: Father's Gate."

A fist struck Akina's jaw. She spun, dissipating the impact with the motion, stumbling slightly.

"Grandfather's Gate." A foot appeared out of the air and stabbed Akina's abdomen. Her breath whistled out between tight lips as she slumped to the ground, catching herself on one knee and a hand.

Zhu continued, "You're as skilled as the legends indicate. But you're no match for an adept of the Star Clan."

Akina coughed. Two of the soldiers, Tae Kun trained adepts carrying four-foot shields cut from the frills of a three-horn skull, closed to her flanks.

Zhu, twenty feet away from Akina, threw another punch. A hole opened in the air in front of the Star Clan adept, paired with another hole just in front of Akina's face.

Her fist entered one hole and emerged from the other, cracking solidly into Akina's nose.

Akina fell back, rolling with the motion and coming to her feet. She leaned forward and let blood drip onto the deck. "You're quick. I don't know that I've ever seen that technique done with such speed."

Zhu sneered. "You're not the only genius in this generation. This is your last chance to submit before we start hurting you."

"I don't think you're part of my generation. And I'm not done yet."

Akina shifted again, left to right, landing palm strikes on the centers of both shields. The heavy implements rang with the impact as the two soldiers were forced to take heavy steps back. *Time to use Partial Function? It would go right through these shields. But it's too soon for that.*

A sudden whistling from behind Zhu made her duck and step to the side.

Two of the soldiers at the ends of the formation went down, ebony bone darts embedded in their necks.

Remy's voice carried to them from the front of the boat. "Way of the Bear: Twin Strikes."

Zhu spun to face him. "How?"

He shrugged as he pulled his darts back to his hands and set them spinning. "Hibernation technique. The knives your men stuck me with barely penetrated my armor."

"That's armor? I thought you were just that fat."

He grinned. “I am kind of fat. Just not all the way. That’s part of the technique.”

Zhu tsked at him, then turned and stepped through a hole she’d torn in space. She reappeared on the other side of Akina and immediately launched a flurry of kicks at the older woman.

Blood dripped down Akina’s chin and her breathing was ragged after the kick she’d taken to the abdomen. She blocked and sidestepped Zhu’s strikes, eyes darting from the Star Clan adept to the two men with shields who flanked her, edging closer with every step.

Dog barked and took in the scene, tongue rolling out of the side of his mouth.

Of the thirteen soldiers who had arrived on the barge with Zhu, seven were dead or incapacitated. The shield bearers were concentrating on Akina while four more faced Remy.

Zhu paused her attack, stepping back to catch her breath, and Akina stomped the deck. “Simple Wave.”

A ripple rode through the planks, disrupting both shield bearers and knocking Zhu two steps away.

The wave came up on the four soldiers facing Remy from behind, pushing them off balance. Remy tossed darts at two of them, the sharp tips catching each in the throat. The other two recovered their balance and charged him, short swords with red bone blades in gloved hands.

Remy pulled both darts back and held them in a reverse grip, pointed end down. He began to rain hammer strikes onto the two soldiers.

“Way of the Bear: Bite.”

The shield bearers crab-walked to stay on Akina’s flanks. She alternated strikes on their massive shields with frantic evasions of Zhu’s attacks from the front.

The Star adept kicked forward into a hole in space, her foot emerging from behind Akina, forcing the older woman into Zhu’s arms.

Zhu wrapped her arms around Akina, shouting at the shield bearers to close and lock her in place.

Dog barked and trotted toward the two women.

Akina saw the shields closing in, tucked her chin, and whipped her forehead into the bridge of Zhu's nose. Remy hooked his blades into the torso armor of the two soldiers he was facing and cracked their heads together, dropping the men to the ground.

Zhu fell backward, bringing Akina with her to the ground. Akina smiled at her with reddened teeth and watched a line of blood leak off her chin and onto the smaller woman.

"Now we're even."

Dog stopped about ten feet away and barked at Zhu.

The shield bearers closed on the fallen pair, lifting the sheets of bone to reveal sharpened spikes along the lower edge. Remy threw his two rope darts out to the sides toward the sea. As they neared the barge's railings, he yanked on the ropes, turning them on an inward arc that buried each in the back of a shield bearer.

Akina stood as the men fell. She stepped back from Zhu.

"You should have brought more men."

Zhu pushed up onto her elbows, then to her feet. "Maybe I underestimated the Millennium Qi." Blood leaked down her face, her own mixed with Akina's.

"You underestimated *me*. And Remy."

"You've both been away from the martial world for over a decade. Who would have thought you could still fight?"

Akina laughed. "You should have asked around. Maybe talk to someone who actually knows us. We're two of the Five Fangs. We're legends for a reason."

Remy set his darts to spinning again. Dog walked to Akina's side and nuzzled her leg.

Zhu shook out her black hair and surveyed the fallen men. "You two shouldn't have been a match for these thirteen. They're all high-grade hunters."

Akina nodded. "They were beaten because they're afraid of me."

"You mean of the Millennium Qi inside you."

Akina shrugged. "Either way. Their fear made them hesitate. If they'd come forward more aggressively, you'd be the one making demands of me. Instead . . ."

Zhu smiled, her teeth shining white in the night's darkness. "You're not exactly in a position to make demands of me yet, Akina Azura. I'll be embarrassed, yes, but I'll be going now. I'm sure the Reaver will be interested to hear that you two are working together."

"Is that what you think is going to happen? Sure. Go ahead. We'll wait." The older woman pulled a cloth out of her belt and wiped the blood from her face.

Zhu formed a circle in the air with her hands, brow furrowing as the hole she expected failed to materialize.

"What the—?"

Akina blew her nose in the cloth, eyeing the bloody mess inside it with disgust. "Oh sweetheart, did you think you were trapping us? I'm so sorry. You're confused."

Zhu looked up at her, then turned to Remy. The big man continued twirling his rope darts. He smiled. "Way of the Bear: Greater Den."

Zhu raised her arm as if to rush the big man, but Akina stepped forward and grabbed her shoulder from behind. The older woman reached around and held a small blade to the Star Clan adept's throat.

A head poked up through the hatch below deck. Dog trotted to it and barked; the sailor retreated.

"Zhu, this was always about trapping you. Well, not you specifically. I had no idea who you were. But I was pretty sure the Reaver would send some hunters here to take care of me and, given the distance involved, I was equally sure he'd send someone from the Star Clan. And I knew you wouldn't be able to form a gate from inside Remy's Greater Den. It's something we discovered quite accidentally about fifteen years ago."

"Fine. I'm trapped. What do you want? Killing me won't get you anything. We're one of the most powerful clans in the Empire. You'll be sleeping with one eye open for the rest of your short, miserable life."

"Oh, you cute darling. You might be backing the Reaver but there is no way the Star Clan as a whole is behind him. Even if they were, there is no way they'd declare a blood feud against me for taking out an assassin who was here on a personal vendetta. No, I think I'm safe from the Star Clan, thank you very much."

Zhu looked to Remy, then back to the fallen men, some of whom were stirring on the deck. "I still don't understand. What do you want? You're not trying to scare off the Reaver by killing me, are you? He doesn't care about me that much."

"I'm sure that's true. But you're misunderstanding. I don't want to kill you."

Zhu sagged a bit in her arms. "What, then?"

"I want your help."

Zhu snorted. "You want me to help you take on the Reaver? Just slit my throat, I'd prefer it."

Remy laughed. "That's what I told her! We were in a bath, though. You should ask for a bath."

Akina cleared her throat. "You don't have to fight the Reaver's men. I just need more mobility."

"You want me to gate you around. Take you to his fortress."

"We have a few stops along the way."

Zhu paused and swallowed as the blade creased the skin on her throat. "What exactly are you asking?"

Akina locked eyes with Remy, who nodded. Dog stepped over to Zhu and eyed her leg lasciviously. The older woman tightened her grip on the knife. "Swear on qi and clan. One hundred days of service. No fighting the Reaver's men directly."

Zhu spat. "One hundred days? There's no way you two are going to live that long."

"Then you'll be free of your oath, won't you?"

"I can't give you one hundred days. I have commitments to my clan that supersede your claim. Some things are more important than my life."

"You'd rather I spill your blood over this shiny deck? That won't help your clan any."

Zhu grunted. "If that's what has to happen, then that's what has to happen."

"Forty-nine days. Seven weeks. On the fiftieth day you're free to go . . . but you swear not to act against me, Remy, or my girls for the full hundred days."

"Forty-nine days of service and fifty-one days of parole? In exchange for my life?"

"That's what I'm offering."

Remy sighed. "Take the deal, lass. It's a good one. She won't ride you to death or trick you out of your honor. She's a mum, after all. But make up your mind fast, because I'm growing tired and if you haven't sworn the oath before I have to release the Greater Den, we'll gut you like a fish."

Zhu glared at them with cold eyes.

Akina tightened her lips and spoke into Zhu's ear. "This is how the martial world works. How knights errant work. If we all fought to the death over every disagreement, there'd be nobody left to face the Wedge. I guarantee if the Reaver himself were here, he'd take the deal."

Zhu spat again, glaring at Remy. "Fine. I'll swear the oath. On qi and clan, I'll give you seven weeks of service and one hundred total days of parole. And when it's done—"

Akina quickly jabbed her knee into the small of the woman's back. "Stop there. You can wish vengeance upon me all you want, but don't make it part of the oath. There's no gain in it and plenty of risk." She released the knife and pushed Zhu to the ground.

Remy relaxed the spinning of his darts and knelt next to Zhu. "Don't break the oath, sister. If you do, it will twist your spiritual channels into knots. Using your martial powers might become impossible. Or it might kill you."

He gripped her shoulder and hauled her to her feet. She shrugged him off. "I know how oaths work. I'm not a kid."

Remy laughed. "What are you, fifteen? I've taken shits that lasted longer than your entire life."

She sneered at him. "Sixteen. And young as I am, I was still the one the Reaver trusted to come here and take you two out."

Akina blew her nose clear of blood. "Didn't work out for you, did it? Why don't you open a Greater Gate and send these men back to the Reaver."

Zhu did as she was told, dropping the men one-by-one through rifts she opened.

Remy woke the guards that had been knocked out by Zhu's men and told the captain that the deck was clear of enemies. Sailors busied themselves by resetting the sails and checking their course.

Akina sat on the railing, resting her elbows on her knees and clearing more blood out of her nose. Dog nuzzled her leg, whining until she bent to scratch behind his ears. Remy sat next to her.

Zhu finished tossing the last of the Reaver's men back across the continent and walked to the pair, her spirit dim and drained of energy.

She faced them, waiting for one of them to speak. They didn't oblige. Finally, she huffed.

"How did you know?"

Remy tilted his head. "Know what?"

Zhu sighed. "How did you know you would beat me? How did you know the Reaver wouldn't send more men? Stronger men?"

Akina smiled. "Is that how you think it works? Remy, remind me, was I ever that young?"

Zhu shook her head. "What do you mean? How what works?"

The older woman wiped her nose again. "You think we always know how things will turn out? That we make plans and set traps because we know the outcome?"

"Well . . . You said you planned this."

"I did plan it. My plan was to either capture you and have a chance to take out the Reaver or to die on this barge if you come with forces we can't handle. Or get taken back to the Reaver in chains. I didn't 'know' anything, except that this was the only way to get my girls back."

"You went to sleep every night, knowing that it might be your last? That instead of me with these twelve, it might have been my brother with twenty-five and you'd be done for?"

"That's exactly right. You're surprised?"

Zhu shrugged. "I guess I am." Dog started to climb up her leg; Akina grabbed him by the back of the neck and pulled him back.

"Honey, that's how I go to bed every night. That's how I've gone to bed every night since I entered the martial world. It's just more acute since my daughters were taken. If you can't sleep soundly knowing that you have a decent chance of not living until dawn, knowing that terrifying creatures are gathering to make sure you don't, then you need to get out of this life."

Zhu looked at Akina, then at Remy. The big man nodded. "She's right. Listen to her."

Zhu sighed. "As long as I'm sworn to your service, I don't exactly have a choice."

7

Dog Days

Remy's every breath was agony.

Sweat trickled down his forehead, disappearing into his thick red beard only to re-emerge, triumphant, in a torrent that coated his neck and turned the dense mat of fur on his chest into a swampy, sticky mess.

Heavy muscles bunched and writhed as he reached down, grabbed a gray tyrant knucklebone by its crafted handle, and snatched it overhead with one powerful extension of his body.

Zhu stood facing him, staying several feet clear of the circle he had painted with swings of the weight and sprays of perspiration.

She wrinkled her nose in disdain. "What are those things? And what are you doing with them?"

Dog walked up to her leg and nuzzled the side of her knee, eyeing her calf with lazy lust. Akina was walking figure eights behind them, further from the prow, and the rest of the crew was busy elsewhere on the ship. The martial artists had taken over the front of the upper deck and everybody on board seemed happy to let them have it.

Remy put down the knucklebone, running his hand over the Imperial seal etched into the side. He exhaled hard but inhaled slowly, willing his heart and lungs to settle down before responding.

"You're not from a merchant family, are you?"

Zhu shrugged. "I was born into the Star Clan. I've known nothing but hunting."

Remy nodded. "These are used to weigh products for trade. Grain or whatever. We used them for exercise, so when I saw the full set onboard, I knew I'd have to give them a swing for old times' sake."

She nodded and stepped closer, nudging the head-size weight with her foot. "Does that make you a better fighter?"

The big man wrung out his beard, leaning forward so the stream of liquid would miss his legs. "Doesn't hurt. When I trained with these regularly, they said I had endless stamina."

Akina paused. "Wind. We said you had endless wind. We meant that you never stopped talking."

"You were just jealous because I could talk. Even high up in the Spine, where you were blue-lipped and panting for air, I continued to entertain and distract with soliloquies on the nature of the universe."

She grunted. "That's true. I almost started to believe you when you said you weren't fat, you just had huge lungs."

Remy laughed. "Both can be true! And it's a good thing I stayed fat, you know. My martial arts depend on it."

Zhu scoffed. "You should lose weight so you're faster and more mobile."

The big man wiped his shoulders with his hands, launching sprays of liquid. "You should hesitate before giving advice to people who have beaten you in combat."

She sneered but didn't say anything. Dog put his forepaws up on her thigh and started to climb her leg. Akina reached down and pulled him off. "Bad Dog."

He looked up at her with sad eyes. She sighed and crouched beside him. "Okay, fine. Not bad dog. Mildly annoying dog. Better?" He licked her hand.

Zhu turned to Akina. "Why are we wasting time on this boat? Don't you have things to do?"

Akina looked up at the teenager. "What's your rush?"

Zhu shrugged. "I don't really care. I'm just bored."

Remy laughed. "You've been on this barge for a day and a half. Why are you impatient?"

Akina turned to him as the big man picked up a bucket of water and poured it out over his shoulders. "Do you not remember being a teenager? They're all like this. Bored, looking for something to do, seeking risks."

Dog eyed Remy as the man shook himself dry. "We were like that, too? You're right, it's been so long I've forgotten."

Zhu stomped the ground. "I'm serious. Not that I care. It's fine with me if you waste the next forty-seven days on this stupid river. It's just weird."

Akina eyed Remy, who nodded to her quickly. "We have some questions." Remy stepped to a dry patch of deck and sat down. Zhu sat across from him.

"It's about time. Ask away."

The older woman scooted over and sat on the ground near the first two so they formed a triangle, Dog waddling up to lie down at her hip. "First, how many Star Clan adepts are with the Reaver?"

Zhu straightened. "There were three of us."

"So two now. Or will they replace you?"

Zhu shrugged. "How am I supposed to know?"

Akina's brow furrowed and her eyes darkened. Remy held up his hand. "Zhu, we don't know why you were there. Did the Reaver contract with the clan for three adepts? If he did, they would replace you. Or were you there for some other reason?"

Zhu rubbed her crown. "Oh. No, we were volunteers. The clan asked who wanted to go and we were the only ones who offered. So I don't think he'll find a replacement. At least not soon."

Remy nodded. "Okay. How many hunters does he have other than those two?"

Zhu shrugged again. "I don't know. A lot. Place was swarming with them. Every half-assed hunter in the north half of the Empire seems to wind up with the Reaver at some point or another."

Akina scratched Dog's head. "Why?"

"What?"

"I asked why. Why do so many people flock to the Reaver's banner?"

"I don't know. He's the best hunter, I guess. Goes after the tyrants, even the leviathans. The three-horns. Takes a big team with him when he does it. In fact, more often than not, the Wedge come right to his fortress. Like they're aiming for it. After the hunt, there're plenty of bones left for everybody. A year, two years with the Reaver and you can stick around and try for real status or cash out and head south, buy a farm somewhere."

Akina and Remy briefly made eye contact. Akina turned back to the teenager.

"The other two Star Clan members. Stronger than you? Weaker?"

Zhu snorted. "Ren is almost as strong as me, but only because he's four years older. My brother, though . . . he's strong. That's why I came, you know. My brother volunteered and I always try to do whatever he does. Tag along, copy him. It's not as if he or my mother ever make time to actually train me."

Remy tapped the deck with two fingers. "Do all these men learn the Reaver's Reap? The qi-stealing technique? Like Little Bao?"

Zhu's eyes narrowed in confusion. "Little who? Oh, Bao!" She snorted. "He is kind of small. But no, only the Reaver's inner circle learn that. The lifers. Most of these guys come with their own sects' techniques. They're really not that special. As you two figured out."

Remy leaned over and grabbed a bag of peanuts out of the small bundle containing his clothes, gear, and armor. He passed them around.

Remy twisted to either side, stretching his back as Akina fed peanuts to Dog.

Zhu ate two peanuts and looked up. "So, when do we go in? Tonight? My qi is restored, I'm ready."

Akina looked at her sharply. "Go in? You mean to the Reaver's place?"

Remy snorted. "Girl, we're not going to just storm the front gates of the Reaver's fortress. Are you crazy?"

Zhu crinkled her nose. "It doesn't have gates, really. More of a jawbone. Look, I can sketch it for you."

Akina shook her head. "Normally, I'm the one advocating for a frontal assault. But Remy's right, that's not going to work."

"I thought you wanted me to gate you over to the Reaver's fortress so you could sneak attack him. Or raid the place and take your girls back. If that's not it, what's your plan? Wait, do you even *have* a plan? You don't. I'm going to die on this quest. By the Emperor, my asshole brother was right. I'm going to die young and a virgin." She cast a quick glance at Remy, who blushed and held his hands up in defensive positions.

Akina sighed. "We can't sneak the girls out. He'll expect that and it's not a good idea to depend on your opponent doing something stupid. Besides, just getting away doesn't do us any good if it leads to us having to run from the Reaver for the rest of our lives."

"I was right. No plan."

"I do have a plan. That's just not it."

Zhu rubbed her head. "I used to want an older sister but now I have had you for one and a half days and you are just so, so aggravating."

Remy reached for Dog, who trotted over to his side for some petting. "She grows on you. A bit like a fungus."

Akina crushed a peanut shell. "The Reaver took my daughters. I think it's because he wants to get to me, but I can't let that happen. I can't let him have the Millennium Qi, and he can't have me, or my daughters. The only way we'll be safe is to take him out."

"You mean kill him."

Remy shook his head. "Or convince him that the price he'd pay to have them is too great."

Zhu ate a peanut and looked out over the railing. The river, broad and slow moving, stretched as far as she could see. The coming nightshade was still a thin black line, barely visible in the eastern sky.

"That guy's a little crazy, you know. All that stealing other people's life force. He's obsessed with you."

Akina froze. "Is he now?"

"Oh, yeah. Talked about you all the time. Said the Millennium Qi would help him stop the next Wedge Pulse. Said it was worth any price."

"Did he? That's interesting."

Zhu shelled and ate two more peanuts. "Yeah. He was always off in some corner with Faceless, talking about it." She popped another peanut in her mouth, her skin pale under the bright sunlight.

Remy held out a hand, waiting for Zhu to notice and give back the bag of nuts. "Zhu, do you know how the Reaver found Akina? Is it something to do with Faceless?"

Zhu shrugged. "I don't know. They had a big reward out for information about her. You guys know Faceless?"

Remy and Akina shared a look. The older woman shook her head. "We know of him. I didn't realize he was working with the Reaver."

"Oh, yeah. Faceless is basically his right-hand man. I bet he's going to come after us soon."

Remy smiled. "Perhaps this is something you should have mentioned earlier?"

"Maybe. I don't know. I'm sworn to your service, right? You ask questions, I answer them. You tell me to move bodies, I move them. None of that includes me taking any kind of initiative, does it?"

Akina nodded. "Smart girl. And fair point. Now let me ask you, what do you know about Faceless?"

"Not much. He's close to the Reaver. He has connections to the Hound Clan. I think he led the team that took your girls. Other than that, I know he's strong. Stronger than my brother. Maybe as strong as the Reaver."

Remy nodded. "Anything else?"

"Just the face thing. Not having one. It's not just a clever name."

Akina snorted back a laugh as Dog waddled back to her side. She fed him the last of her peanuts.

"Zhu, how far can you gate us? Can you open a King's Gate?"

Zhu nodded. "That's my limit. My brother can do an Imperial Gate, but I can't stabilize one yet."

"Can you make one big enough for the four of us to pass?"

"Four? Oh, you're counting Dog? Sure. But that's pretty much my limit. Drains all my qi."

"How long to cycle your qi up to full strength?"

Zhu tapped her cheek. "If I focus, a day. Maybe a few hours less. But only if I'm not doing anything else. Like fighting or opening smaller gates."

"Okay. What do you need to open a King's Gate? Can you do it based on a map? Say, to a place you've never been before?"

"Depends how precise you want me to be. If you want to be put in a specific room, it needs to be someplace I know. If you want me to drop us just somewhere around a particular town, I can do that from a map. If it's a good map."

Remy narrowed his eyes. "It's hard to find a good map. What if it's not such a good map? What happens then? Do we appear inside a mountain or something?"

"I mean, you could. But not really. Haven't you ever been through a gate?"

The big man shuddered. "I have, but I don't trust them."

"It's like a door. If I open one into a mountain, then when you look in, all you see is rock. You can't step through. You don't, like, die or anything."

He nodded, his beard flopping against his chest. "Good. Good. I'm all in favor of postponing my death as long as possible."

Akina gave Dog one last rub and stood. "That fits with what I was expecting. And it goes with our plans."

The young woman glared at her. "I don't think you've told me what those plans are. You just said we aren't going to attack the Reaver's fortress."

"Not yet, we aren't. We're old and out of shape. We need an army if we're going to take on the Reaver and Faceless. An army and maybe a few sacred treasures."

"Is that what we're doing next? Raising an army and gathering weapons?"

"Something like that. For that I need you rested. And I need a better map. In two days, this ship will reach Divine Fork. It's a big enough town that we can sell our share of the bones we looted and use the money to buy a map. Once we have that, you can gate us to the next place."

"Which is . . ."

"Which is the very interesting place called You Don't Need to Know Yet. I will tell you it's pretty far west, so take that resting seriously. You should do some qi cycling."

Zhu shrugged. "I'm not good at that. It's fine, I'm a genius. My qi recovers really fast on its own."

Remy shook his head and stood. "All the more reason to learn the exercises. You want to be as strong as your brother, don't you?"

Zhu opened her mouth to argue, then saw the expression on Akina's face.

The older woman touched her shoulder. "I can teach you Infinity Bagua cultivation. If you want."

"That's not an order? Because, if you forgot, I'm under oath regarding orders and following them."

"No. Just an offer."

"Are you allowed to teach me?"

"Why not? I'm the reigning master of the style. I get to make the rules. If the Reaver is going to teach Reaver's Reap to idiots like Little Bao, I can certainly show you how to cycle your energy."

"After that, will you tell me the plan?"

"No."

"But I'll be, like, your disciple and everything. Doesn't that mean you trust me?"

"I trust you to walk around in connected circles and cycle your energy. That doesn't mean I trust you to keep your mouth shut."

"Okay." Zhu stood and eyed the pattern Akina had worn into the wooden deck. "Why should I start learning this now when I'm only going to be with you for a little while? Seven weeks and I'm free. One hundred days and I'll be fighting against you."

"You can spend those seven weeks learning or not. Either way, at the end of it, you'll be seven weeks older. If you study, you'll have seven more weeks knowledge of Infinity Bagua than almost anybody you'll ever meet. Make a choice."

Zhu nodded. "Okay. It can't hurt, right?"

"You'll taste some bitter, holding some of the stances. But you're strong, aren't you? Little hunter that you are."

"My mother did always say I have more toughness than smarts."

Akina looked at Remy, who shrugged. "That's the spirit!"

The big man grunted as he stood. He snapped his fingers for Dog to follow. "I'm going to feed him. Be back soon."

Akina nodded and began to show Zhu how to walk the infinity pattern, using light touches at the young woman's hip and shoulder to correct her alignment.

After a few rounds, Zhu stopped suddenly. "Can I ask you a question?"

"I haven't stopped you yet."

"You asked me a bunch of things, but you didn't ask about your girls."

"No, I didn't."

"Why?"

Akina exhaled slowly, her face angular and tight as if chiseled out of hardwood.

"I know they're alive. If the Reaver kills them, he has no bargaining power over me.

"So the possibilities are that they're fine or that they're not fine. Either way, there's nothing I can do about it other than try my best to rescue them, which I'm already doing, right?"

Zhu nodded, her skin losing color as she felt the intensity of the older woman's aura.

Akina's eyes were focused upriver. "But if I ask you how they are in a moment of weakness and you tell me that they're not fine, then I'll know.

"I'll know that you were there, that you saw them harmed. Maybe even took part in harming them.

"And if I thought, even for a moment, that you harmed my girls, I'm not sure I could stop myself from tearing you into very, very small pieces and feeding you to Dog.

"So I won't ask, and you won't answer, and we'll all just try to get along."

8

Mapmaker, Mapmaker, Make Me a Map

Zhu Star's dark eyes were wide as she took in the noisy crowds of Divine Fork. The city center's narrow streets were packed with colorfully robed people walking, haggling with sidewalk vendors, engaging in thoughtful conversations over cups of steaming drinks, and looking out for people with prices on their heads. Like Akina.

Remy reached over and pulled Zhu's hand off her face. "Don't pinch your nose like that, it's rude. It doesn't smell that bad."

Zhu turned to him and opened her mouth. "It's so crowded!"

Akina chuckled. "At least they have real sewers here. You should have seen where I found Remy."

The big man shrugged. "You'd be surprised what you can get used to."

Zhu shook her head. "I'll never get used to this. How do you pay attention to it all?"

Akina pointed down a relatively sparse alley. "Down this way. I think."

Zhu turned to the older woman. "What do you mean, you think? You don't *know*?"

"We're visiting a cartographer. How are you supposed to know where to find him? If you already had a map, you wouldn't need a cartographer."

Zhu held up a hand, her eyes twisted in confusion as Akina marched down the alley. "Wait, what?"

Remy clapped her on the back. "Don't worry. It will make more sense when you're drunk. Which will hopefully happen soon after visiting the mapmaker."

Akina continued, "I'm just saying it's an inherently flawed business model. Dog, do not eat that! Do you have any idea how long it's been dead? Do these streets look clean to you?"

Dog looked at her plaintively, then left the bird carcass behind and trotted to her side.

Shop doors slammed shut as they passed. Remy sniffed. "We're not making a good impression, Akina."

"They know where they can shove their impressions. It's always like this. They sneer at us until they see the polish on our bones. Then it's all 'yes, sir,' and 'right away, ma'am.'"

"True enough. Speaking of bones, are we ever going to see our share of the profits when the captain of *Bone Rich* sells the weapons we took?"

Zhu looked up at him. "She's going to sell those?"

"Of course. Spoils of war. Or something. What did you think she would do? Send them back to the Reaver?"

"Won't he be angry?"

Remy laughed. "We killed his men. You think it's their weapons he'll be angry about?"

She nodded slowly. "I suppose. Seems odd, that's all. To take their stuff."

"You're a strange girl."

Akina stopped short. "I thought it was right around here. Remy, you remember?"

Remy pinched the bridge of his nose and closed his eyes. "Let me think. We're close. Maybe another block up?"

"All right. C'mon, Dog. This way. No, don't eat that either. We just fed you!"

Zhu followed as Remy walked. "Are we getting our share of the money or aren't we? I don't think I've ever had any money. All our hunting was done in a group and my brother took all of it."

Remy looked at her. "I don't think you understand how shares work. Your share of the profit we made from killing the men you led in an attack against us is exactly zero. To be honest, it should be less than zero. The Reaver should charge you for the cost of losing those men."

Zhu frowned. "Oh. That's not good. But are you two getting the money?"

Akina shook her head. "We're not. The Reaver will have people in town waiting for the ship to come to intercept us. I had you gate us while it was still a day away to avoid them. I thought I explained this to you already."

"I stop listening to you after you talk for a bit. Can you buy me some new clothes? These are starting to smell and I can't get all the bloodstains out."

Remy slapped her on the back. "You're starting to grow on me, little Star Clan child! You remind me of a young us. Now be patient. We'll get your things washed soon enough."

Akina snapped her fingers. "You were right, this block. Right there. I know that sign. And she's not like us, we were never that young." She led them to one of the brightly painted doors that lined the alley, each with a fragment of map hanging on it along with a printed sign. "Remy, guard our backs." He nodded.

Bells tinkled when Dog and the two women crossed the store's threshold. Dog sneezed as the unfamiliar scents of parchment and ink struck his nostrils.

"Hello, good sirs!" A high-pitched but masculine voice came from the back as someone shuffled toward the front counter.

Cylindrical cases of wood or leather crowded the shop alongside tables stacked high with rectangles of parchment, some as small as a handprint and others large enough to make a blanket on a cold night. A pair of oversized wooden desks dominated the rear, weighed down by wood-and-bone constructs that looked suited for a geometry class at Imperial University.

They lined up in front of a long counter of polished wood. Bone-tipped pens were strewn about near glass jars of ink.

The man who wafted forward was thin, dressed in a dark blue robe covered in blotchy patterns of darker blue and black that effectively disguised any ink stains. His jaw was clean shaven and visible below the delicate wooden mask that covered his nose and eyes.

The shopkeeper reached up and slid glass lenses from his eyes onto the upper part of the mask, flicking down a different set of discs and focusing on his patrons. He looked like a four-eyed owl.

"Please excuse me, madams. My vision isn't what it used to be. At least not when looking at faces. Maps, however . . . Well, rest assured Kai's Cartography has the highest reputation. Is that a dog?"

Akina bent to grab Dog by the neck. The animal strained valiantly to get around the counter and sniff Kai's robes. "He won't hurt you, Kai. It's been a while."

The cartographer reached to his face and flicked up the lenses over his eyes, flicking down a new set and leaning closer to Akina. "Is that you? The Spiral Witch, in my store?"

"It's me. In the flesh." Her tone was neutral, not the golden warmth typical of greeting an old friend.

Zhu leaned toward the man. "You know her?"

Kai smiled. "Aren't you the cutest? Akina, where did you find her? Is she yours? She doesn't look like you, with that fair skin and those oval eyes. In fact, she looks like one of the Reaver's, unless I'm mistaking the cut of that dreadful outfit for something else. Though the colors are wrong."

Akina showed her teeth in an almost-smile that didn't affect her eyes. "She was one of the Reaver's. She's mine now, on parole." She gave up restraining Dog and let the animal wander.

"I see." Kai swapped the lenses again and leaned back. "I am glad to see you again. It's been too long. How long exactly?"

Zhu stepped to the side and stared at a map of the city pinned to one wall, showing the confluence of the East and West rivers flowing from the north and forming the South River.

"About fifteen years. Give or take. Dog, get away from his leg."

Kai looked down without expression. "That sounds right. I don't want to sound ungracious, but you need to know that there is a bounty out for you. I can't guarantee your safety. Or privacy. My shop is secure, but you waltzed in here off a public street."

"Don't worry about the bounty. Worry about whoever comes to collect it."

He smiled and tapped the counter. "That's the Spiral Witch I remember. What brings you back here after all this time? And where's that lovely man whose heart you stole? It was the talk of the town when he broke his betrothal to run off with you. Not that I blame him, of course."

Akina scratched her head. "Petrik's dead."

Kai's eyes widened behind his spectacles. "I'm so sorry, honey. That's awful. You're here for revenge, I take it?" He shivered. "I almost pity whoever took Petrik from you. I always said, of the Five Fangs, you were the prettiest but also the most dangerous. People thought I was mocking, but . . ."

"No, Kai. Not revenge. It wasn't that sort of death. Anyway, we need maps."

"Then you've come to the right place. What kind of maps and for what?"

Akina elbowed Zhu, who returned her attention to the cartographer. "What? Oh, maps. We need gate maps."

Kai's eyes widened and he flipped lenses again. "You're Star Clan? That explains the colors you're wearing. And the reason you came to me."

Akina shook her head. "Not the only reason, Kai. I also knew I could trust your discretion. As a friend."

"Of course, of course. I have a selection of maps precise enough to allow you to focus a gate. But to where?"

Zhu looked to Akina, who nodded. *As we rehearsed.*

The younger woman cleared her throat. "The Imperial palace in the capital. For a start."

"I see. Akina, what does the Emperor have to do with this?"

"I have business with the Reaver."

"Good business or bad business? Never mind. Knowing you, of course it's bad. Is that wise?"

Akina flashed her teeth. "I'm famous for any number of things, Kai. Is wisdom one of them?"

"No, I suppose not. Still, what does that have to do with the Emperor?"

"You think I'm going to take on the Reaver by myself? I'm not stupid. I need the Emperor's help."

Kai nodded. "Should I ask what you have over the Emperor to have him help you?"

She smiled. "Come on, Kai. A girl has to keep some secrets, doesn't she? But between you and me, it's no secret the Emperor would love to get his hands on my bloodline. That's why he put a bounty on me. I'm the last of the Azure Dragon Clan."

"Sweetie, I don't think it's his hands that he wants on your, er, bloodline. You think he'll take your side in a fight against the Reaver for that?"

She smiled and leaned in. "I'm not in the habit of taking 'no' for an answer."

He sighed. "I'm aware. Poor Petrik never stood a chance."

"He did not."

Kai turned and opened a waist-high cabinet, then began poking around the map cases that stood vertically inside it. "Capital. Capital. Where are you? Akina, can I ask why you have it in for the Reaver? You know I love a little gossip."

Her voice was cold enough to draw the midday heat out of the air. "He stole my girls. He wants me to come after them, so that's what I'm going to do. It will be the last mistake he makes."

"Ah. Well, that's a good reason. I'm sorry. Never had children myself, always too busy with my maps, but I hear one grows quite attached to them. Here we go, this will get you to the capital. What else?"

Zhu cleared her throat. "Um, we'll need to make a few other stops. For, er, stuff. The ruins of the Seventh Dynasty capital, for one."

Kai nodded and rummaged further back in his cabinet. "You're going weapons shopping. Probably a good idea. You should reassemble the rest of the Five Fangs while you're at it. If you want to survive against the Reaver. With them, and the Millennium Qi, there's a chance I'll see you alive again."

Akina swallowed. "You know where they are? Can you tell me where Rei is?"

Kai grabbed a map and stood, handing it to Zhu, then turned to Akina. "Why would I know?"

"You said it yourself, you love gossip. Where can I find her?"

Kai tapped the desk in front of him. "You did give me news about Petrik, so I owe you. Last I heard, she was with the Order of the Pink Lotus. You know it? Near the Dreadwall, but at the far western edge."

"I know it. Can you give us a map?"

"Let me think, let me think. I don't have anything to get you there from here, but I can map you to the Dreadwall center and from there to the west. Does that work?"

Akina looked at Zhu, who nodded. "I can do that. It will take a few days, but sure."

"Okay, good. Give us that. Can you tell me where Mau-rhi is?"

Kai frowned. "No, I haven't heard a whimper about Mau-rhi in years. But I have news on the Bear. What was his name? Remy. He's in a town at the far end of the South River. Drinking himself to death."

"Actually, I can do you one better. He's sitting outside your shop watching the alley and wishing he was at the far end of the South River drinking himself to death."

Kai smiled. "So you've already started. What else can I get you?"

Akina and Zhu traded glances. Akina cracked her neck. "We need a couple of distractions."

Kai looked at each of the women. "What do you mean?"

"We need pieces to throw the Reaver's men off our tails. We'll leave something in a bag where someone can see it so they can run off and tell the Reaver. Or Faceless. Keep them guessing and chasing false leads."

Kai nodded slowly. "If Faceless is going after you, then that would help. Maps to dangerous places, I take it? Just to make it fun?"

"That would be perfect. Any suggestions?"

"The Leviathan's Graveyard, for one. A natural place for you to go."

Akina nodded. "It's in the Wilds, though. Do you have a map?"

"For you? Of course. Assuming you have the bones to buy it."

She touched her belt and shook a faded canvas pouch. "You know I have the bones, Kai. Always do."

He walked to the far corner of the shop and opened a different cabinet, then called back over his shoulder. "What else? Temple of Surge's End?" Dog waddled over to him and sniffed his backside.

"That'll do. Nobody gets out of there alive. I'm sure it will challenge even Faceless. How about the Cave of Ten Thousand Swords?"

"Done. You're looking at three hundred shards worth of maps already. Is that enough?"

"It's enough." Akina opened the pouch and shook thumbnail-size bones, black and polished, out onto the desk.

Kai turned and shooed Dog away. The animal walked a circuit around the shop. Kai returned to the counter and laid out the maps.

Akina tapped her parolee on the shoulder. "Check them."

Zhu nodded and unrolled the maps, squinting to verify the level of detail.

Kai smiled at them and eyed the pile of bones on the desk. "Is that for me?"

Akina nodded. "Assuming the maps are all you said they are."

"Oh, please! When have I ever steered you wrong?" He fingered the bones, rearranging them. "This is more than I asked for."

"I know. I threw in a little extra to buy your silence."

"What do you mean?"

"Faceless will be here asking what we wanted, what you sold us, where we're going. I want you to mislead him."

Kai put a hand to his lips. "You wound me! I would never betray a friend, despite not having seen them in over a decade."

"I know, Kai. You're a good friend. A good man. But it's Faceless. You're going to have to talk to him. I want you to lie. Consider the shards . . . extra motivation to do so."

"Of course. I'll forget all about the map to the capital. And to Rei." He put his hand over hers where it rested on the counter.

She smiled, she hoped warmly. "Thank you. I knew I could count on you."

"Absolutely. I hope you get your girls back, Akina Azure."

"Me too. And thanks."

"Give Remy my best."

"I will." She packed the maps away in her backpack and whistled. "Come on, Dog."

Dog ran up to Kai, who bent to pet him, and licked his hand.

"Come on, Dog. Time to go." One last lick and Dog followed Zhu and Akina out the door.

The pair found Remy facing the alley, eyes sharp.

Akina put her hand on his shoulder. "You doing okay?"

"Of course. What do you mean? Is something wrong? Do I look sick?" He patted his cheeks.

"No. But you haven't been drinking much. I just noticed."

He laughed. "Rumors of my alcoholism are somewhat exaggerated. I'll survive cutting back a bit. Wouldn't mind one or two this evening. Do we have time?"

She shrugged. "I think so. *Bone Rich* is due in port tomorrow. I don't think Faceless will be looking for us until then. I say we find an inn, get clean, have a nice meal, and gate out of here tomorrow. Zhu, you up for that?"

Zhu's face brightened. "I am! But where to?"

"You know the plan."

Zhu's nose crinkled. "I thought I knew the plan. But you told Kai something else."

"Let's walk." They put several blocks between themselves and Cartographer's Alley before she spoke again to Zhu.

"Kai will give us up to Faceless."

"Will he?"

Akina shrugged. "He's not a hunter. And he doesn't owe us anything. I knew he would. So I gave him the wrong information."

"You didn't even ask him for the map to the Temple of Surge's End. And I thought that's where we were going."

"I didn't ask for it, but I got him to offer it. When he gives us up to Faceless, what do you think he'll say? Assume you're Kai and you *want* Faceless to find us. So that you get a reward. Or at least get out of this with your skin intact."

Zhu screwed up her nose again and concentrated. "I'd probably say you were heading for the palace, or for that place on the Dreadwall. And that the other places were decoys."

"Exactly. Even if Faceless suspects what I did, he has a lot of choices to make. The chances of him heading for the Temple right away are very low."

"Won't that get Kai in trouble?"

Another shrug. "Not the time-to-pick-an-outfit-for-his-funeral-pyre kind of trouble. Beyond that, it's not my problem."

9

Not Far Now

Zhu sighed a dramatic, explosive exhalation that conveyed her complete displeasure with the state of the world in the way that only a teenager can ever adequately express.

"Are we there yet?"

Akina turned to Remy, who walked by her side as they passed between low-slung green hills. "Tell me again why I shouldn't kill her, Remy. And please try to be convincing this time. Your arguments are wearing as thin as the soles of my sandals."

Remy turned back to Zhu, who trailed them by thirty feet. "Child, don't be so annoying. How can you complain this much after a single day of walking? Aren't you a hunter in training? You're supposed to be in peak physical condition."

She grumbled something unintelligible, then spoke up. "I am in good condition. It's not that I *can't* walk all day, it's just *boring*. I'm Star Clan. When we need to go somewhere, we just . . . go."

Remy shook his head and turned to Akina. "And you. Why do you let her get to you? You know she's just looking for attention. Aren't you a parent? You should know this. Even I know this, and the closest I usually come to children is, well, never. Not close. Far away."

Akina snorted. "I'm a parent, yes, but I never said I was a *good* parent. I'm just trying to settle into a fun family dynamic. You know, she complains,

I threaten to kill her, you step into the middle and calm things with a joke or a snack. I'm waiting for the snacks."

His eyes widened. "Is this how you and Petrik were? Actually, don't answer. It must have been. Knowing Petrik."

She sighed. "Mostly, yes. Fine, I'll try to restrain myself."

Zhu pointed at the sky. "The nightshade is coming. Are we going to walk in the dark?"

Akina pointed ahead. "I think we're close. Let's crest that hill and check. If I'm right, we can set up camp in this depression, then enter the temple in the morning."

"Fine. But I need to rest if you're going to ask me to gate you to the far end of the continent tomorrow."

Akina turned to her, walking backwards. "You're not cycling qi while you walk? What kind of adept are you?"

Zhu opened her mouth to argue, then snapped it shut. Opened it again. "I am. I just want to rest or I'll be cranky."

Akina spun back to the front. "We certainly don't want that. Come on, up this hill."

Dog barked and led the way to the top of the grass-covered hill. The humans followed.

Remy breathed deep as they neared the crest. "Are we sure this is a good idea, Akina?"

"Quiet, there are guards on the next ridge. And no, this isn't a good idea. None of these ideas are good. This is just the best out of all the bad ideas. Now hush."

They dropped to hands and knees, then their bellies, Akina leading the way and Remy, then Zhu, following. They squirmed to the top of the hill, parting the grasses to peek over into the valley beyond.

Zhu, lying flat to Akina's right, turned to her. "That's just another hill."

Akina bared her teeth and shook her head. "That's not a hill."

"What?" Zhu squinted and looked again.

"Look closer."

"Are those . . . bones?"

A large field stretched before them, rocky and barren save for a handful of twisted, off-color weeds peeking out sporadically. The ground was stained, streaked with neon greens and putrid purples not usually found in nature, hazy and obscured by a gaseous emission that bent light like a candle flame.

Across the half-mile field, the ground rose sharply to a lump a full fifty yards high and two hundred yards long, stretching across their view.

Akina turned to her parolee and watched as she took in the white streaks that looked like stone but, on second examination, proved to be ribs. Then a pelvis. And a skull opposite.

Dirt had collected in the crevices and gaps, but the hill was formed out of the body of a creature large enough to swallow entire towns in a bite.

Zhu looked at her with wide eyes. "Those are Wedge corpses? This far from the Wilds? How did that happen?"

Remy laughed. "Haven't you heard of a Wedge Surge, lass? That's the Great Surge. Wiped out the Seventh Dynasty, nearly destroyed the Empire. Well, it wasn't an empire then, but it nearly wiped out human life on this continent. This is where the Great Surge ended."

Akina nodded. "Those are corpses of the Greater Wedge. Monsters over two hundred yards long and fifty yards high. Big cousins of the leviathans. Their bones are so powerful they can't be shaped or used, not by anybody living today. The ground is stained and corrupted by their remains."

"How in the Emperor's name did they stop that thing?"

Remy shrugged. "They say it took a death curse from every knight, from foot soldier to emperor, burning their qi to fuel a set of desperate techniques. Hence the end of that dynasty."

A breeze picked up. Dog sniffed, then sneezed.

Zhu wrinkled her nose. "Is that what I'm smelling?"

Akina nodded. "It's not going to hurt you. Not in the short term. But if you breathe it in day after day . . . let's just say, don't do that."

"What about those guys?" She pointed at figures moving in the distance. Dog barked.

The older woman grabbed the animal by the back of his neck and pulled him to her side. "Hush. Zhu, those are guards from the Boneshaper Clan. This is their temple."

"I know that much, but how are they walking around like that? Is it a martial technique?"

Remy shook his head. "They wear protection. Cloths over their faces filter out the gases so their lungs aren't damaged."

Zhu nodded. "We're fighting through them?"

Akina rubbed Dog's back as he lay flat, sighing heavily and relaxing into the grass. "We could, but that's not the plan. They're not here to keep us out of Surge's End. Those guys are patrolling to make sure nothing inside the mounds gets *out*."

"Nothing . . . as in what?"

"You'll see. Not today, though. It's late. Nobody wants to enter Surge's End at night. We'll camp at the foot of this hill and go over there in the morning."

"I want to know what they're keeping in there. Is it more Wedge? I thought they all died. If they didn't die when the Surge ended, is it really over? Should it be Surge Still Going On? That sounds terrible."

Remy put a finger to his lips. "Prattle on if you must, but do it quietly. Come and help me set up camp."

"Won't the guards find us?"

Akina wiggled down the hill, standing only after she'd descended far enough to not be visible from the other side. "They're not interested in stopping us. I told you. I think they like when other clans try, and fail, to get into the temple. Makes them feel extra tough."

Zhu grunted as she slid through a patch of wet earth, scrambling to scrape the mud off her pants before it could soak in. "Will you please explain to me what's in there?"

Akina stopped moving. "Seeing that you used the magic word, I will. There are no regular Wedge inside. Some smaller Wedge from the Surge remained inside the bodies of the Greater Wedge that fell here and were twisted into new, unique varieties by the poisons in those corpses."

Zhu swallowed. "Are they more or less dangerous than the Wedge out in the Wilds?"

Akina shrugged. "It's hard to say. Nobody who faces them lives to tell us."

"That's not very comforting."

Dog trotted behind as the three laid out sleeping rolls and unpacked food. Remy waited until they were settled and set up a perimeter of spells that would alarm if penetrated.

Akina bit into a sausage roll, greasy pork sausages baked into thick shells of bread, the fat soaking through and keeping the crust soft enough to chew even after days in a pack.

She tore off a hunk and swallowed it, quickly washing it down with a pull from her water skin. "By the Emperor, I missed travel rations."

Remy looked at her. "Your sarcasm is uncalled for. We've eaten worse. A lot worse. These aren't even that bad. Nicely seasoned."

Zhu coughed. "You've eaten worse?"

Akina swallowed another mouthful. "We were young. We did a lot of stupid things."

The teen looked at Remy, who didn't elaborate, then back to the older woman. Akina tore off a chunk with her hand and held it out for Dog to eat. Dog sniffed the roll, turned away, took in the lack of alternatives between the hills, and ate the roll.

Remy coughed. "What are we doing here, Akina? You're after the pearl?"

Zhu's head snapped up. "What pearl?"

Remy sighed. "Don't they teach you anything in the Star Clan?"

"Of course they do. Well, they try. They talk. I stop listening after a bit."

The big man looked at her with wide eyes while she ate her dinner. "You're honest, I will give you credit for that.

"The Ancestor Pearl is the sacred relic of the Boneshaper Clan. They keep it in this temple for its safety."

"Why would they keep their own sacred relic in a place that nobody can get out of alive? I mean, sure, it's safe, but they can't use it."

Akina shook her head. "They can. They make armor out of the skin of the Greater Wedge. The creatures inside won't attack anyone wearing it, so they can get in and out without a problem. In fact, they're due to visit the Relic in two days, so there will be a big procession from the clan coming this way."

Zhu nodded. "I see where you're going with this. We're going to steal the armor and use it to snatch the relic, right? We just have to beat up a few Boneshaper Clan members. No problem, they're a minor clan and I hear they haven't had a true inheritor of their art in a dozen generations." She cracked her knuckles, face lighting up in anticipation of a fight.

"Nope." Akina ate another mouthful.

"What do you mean? That's a great plan, isn't it?"

"It would be, except they'll have half the clan coming to see their representative visit the relic. We need to get the pearl without anybody knowing it was us. Which means we need to sneak in and get it before that procession gets here."

"Oh, okay. Don't want another clan coming after us, not when we're already dealing with the Reaver's people. So I guess I'll be gating us into the temple, right? We snatch the relic, gate back out before anybody notices we were there."

"Nope."

Zhu slumped. "I think you're doing this just to tease me."

"Not *just* to tease you, but I can't say I'm not enjoying that part of it."

"Why aren't we gating in?"

Remy pointed to the Temple. "The bones of the Greater Wedge do something to space around them. You can't gate in or out. I'd be surprised if you could even form a gate from this camp, given how close we are."

Zhu jumped to her feet. "Seriously?" She pursed her lips and put her hand up in front of her face. "Father's Gate!"

Nothing happened.

She looked between the others. "I can't gate? How am I supposed to fight?"

Akina shrugged. "You really should learn how to fight without your clan techniques, you know."

"Great, I'll add that to my training syllabus. But what am I supposed to do tomorrow?"

Remy pointed at the ground. "Sit down. You'll be fine. We won't let anything happen to you."

Akina muttered. "Much."

He agreed. "Anything much. It will be good practice."

Zhu flopped to the ground. Dog walked over to her and buried his nose in her belly. She scratched his head and continued her meal.

Akina twisted her head to her left, then right, shoulder, cracking her neck. "I'm kidding. We'll keep you safe. Remember, I need you for a few more things to help me rescue my daughters. I can't let you die right now."

"But later, after I'm done helping, then you can let me die, right?"

"Then it won't be my responsibility anymore. Your life will be in your own hands. Weren't you the one who said you'd come for me when your parole was up?"

"I—fine. Have it your way." She twisted around and faced away from them, continuing to eat. Dog whined and pushed his face further across her belly.

Remy looked at his old friend. "You do have a way past those Wedge, don't you? I don't think we could have fought our way in and out of the temple even in our primes. Maybe not even with all five of us together."

"If it were easy, the pearl would have been stolen ages ago, no?"

"That statement is both true and not an answer to my question."

"Petrik and I had an idea on how to get to the pearl. Came up with it years ago. What we didn't have was a way past the guardian."

Remy sighed. "But you do now?"

"Yeah. Getting the pearl away from the guardian is the one piece of this I'm sure of. It's the plan for getting into the temple past the Wedge that's kind of iffy."

"Iffy."

"You know, Remy, you repeat a lot of what I say back at me as if you're not sure I heard myself say it."

"I repeat stuff you say because I'm not sure I believe what I'm hearing."

"I never said this plan was based on certainty, did I? You and me taking on the Reaver? We never had much of a chance."

"There's a difference between betting your life on a bone toss and betting your life that the bone will land balanced on its edge."

"It's not that bad."

He drained the waterskin and nodded. "I guess that's good enough for me. What do we do tomorrow?"

"We need to enter the southern corpse."

"The temple is in the middle one."

"I know. We need something from the southern body first." She didn't continue.

"You know, a more sensitive person might have their feelings hurt by the fact that you aren't sharing more of your plans with me."

"I guess it's a good thing you're my partner, then, and not someone more sensitive."

"That wasn't my point."

"I know."

"You're not going to change, are you?"

She sighed. "What do you want from me?"

"I don't know. A little trust? For a start?"

"Trust you? To what, keep my plans secret? I do trust you, Remy. I trust you not to give away my plans. But you know what I trust even more? You not giving away my plans when you don't know them."

"I wouldn't."

"Are you sure? What if Faceless was torturing you? What if Faceless was torturing Zhu, and the only way to save her was to spill your guts? What if the Emperor himself asked you?"

"The Emperor? Is that how far we're going?"

She paused before answering. "I've thought this through from every angle I can imagine, and there are a few where it goes that way. Not likely, but possible."

He grunted. "What are you going to do with the pearl, Akina? We can't sell it. I don't think you can use it. Can you? Is this an ability of the Millennium Qi?"

"No. The Millennium Qi is a huge power source. It doesn't let the wielder do anything new, just *more*. And harder. And faster."

"Only the Boneshaper Clan can use the pearl. Are you going to ransom it back to them? If you need money, there are probably better ways to get it."

"It's not about money. Zhu, turn around. We know you're listening.

"I'll tell you both the plan when it's safe."

Zhu spun around but kept her lips pressed into a pout. "When will that be?"

"When it's over."

••••••••••

Akina woke to the gentle pressure of a hand on her shoulder. She kept her voice low.

"Remy? What is it?"

His response was just as soft. "You were dreaming. Go back to sleep now."

She half sat up, eyes straining against the darkness. This far north, very little light was visible from the southern edge of the nightshade, and the light that came through it from the sun overhead was dim and forlorn.

"Why'd you wake me?" She could make out Zhu curled into a ball in her bedding. Dog was rolled up against her side, legs up in the air, snoring softly. Remy was facing away from her, his big back blocking her view of the hill below which they camped.

"You were noisy."

"What do you mean noisy? I was sleeping!"

"Shh." Remy rolled over, shifting so he wouldn't crush her. "You were crying."

"I was not! Was I?"

He nodded. "It's okay. Zhu's still asleep. You get some rest now."

"Crying? Did I say anything?"

"Just names, Akina. It's okay. Go back to sleep."

She touched her face. Her cheeks were wet. "Names. Huh. Sorry."

"Don't be. We'll get them back."

"I know we will. Thanks, Remy."

"Anytime."

10

Thin Line Between Courage and Stupidity

They woke before the line of dawn's light struck their camp. Remy broke his perimeter spells; Zhu trotted back to a nearby stream to fill their waterskins; Akina rubbed Dog's belly and planned their day's work.

Remy turned to his old friend. "What happened to the bedrolls we used to use out in the Wilds? They were so much more comfortable than these. Or is it the ground? Is the ground extra hard near the temple?"

Akina bent over her backpack and tucked away her belongings. "The bedrolls are the same, Remy, and the ground is normal. You're just old."

"It's not fair. I'm very well padded, I should be more comfortable than this."

Zhu returned. "I filled the waterskins."

Akina held out her hand for her own skin. "Thanks. Are you ready?"

Zhu interlaced her fingers and stretched her arms forward, palms out. "I don't have a choice, do I?"

"You absolutely do have a choice. You can tell me you aren't ready. But that doesn't mean we won't be going into the temple."

"Then I guess I'm ready."

Remy grunted. "The girl is learning."

Zhu stuck her tongue out at him. "Don't call me a girl. I'm a woman, thank you very much."

He held up his hands in surrender. "Sorry, bad habit. The woman is learning."

"Enough of that. Time to get started." Akina pointed at the hill. "First we go back to where we were yesterday and watch the guards. If I have the timing down, they should be walking away from us now. Once we verify that, we head for the southern mound. Questions?"

Zhu held up her hand like it was a clan classroom. "What are we doing in the southern mound?"

"It's the least populated. We need to fight and kill about a dozen Wedge."

Zhu nodded. "Let me guess, you're not going to tell us why, but we'll find out when we need to know. Right?"

Remy smiled. "As I said, the woman's learning."

"Let's go."

They paused at the crest for long enough to verify a clear path down the barren side of the hill, across the desolate valley, to the side of the nearest mound.

Halfway across the valley Dog began to sneeze. Akina held a hand up to stop the party and applied an aromatic balm to his nose. "Anybody else?"

Remy smeared some over his mustache; Zhu sniffed the balm and shook her head. "Suit yourself."

They continued.

Zhu's head swung wildly as they walked. "I can't believe nobody's trying to stop us."

Akina watched as Dog nuzzled something on the ground, then peed on it and walked away. "We told you. They're not worried about people trying to get *in*. They're worried about not-people trying to get out."

"It still feels wrong."

Remy coughed. "Shouldn't we hurry?"

Akina shook her head. "Conserve your energy." The three stopped short as they neared the wall of bone emerging almost vertically from the broken ground and marking the border of the southern mound.

Zhu cleared her throat vigorously, leaned over, and spat on the ground. "The smell here is awful. No, it's not just the smell. My stomach isn't right."

Remy looked around. "Sausage rolls too much for you?"

Zhu took a knee. "Something else."

Akina stepped over and patted her shoulder while Dog rubbed his head against the younger woman's hip. "It's not your stomach, it's your core. Your bloodline martial ability is tied to control of space. This area is twisted by the Galaxy Clan techniques they used to kill these Wedge."

Zhu spat again, her face pasty white in the bright dawn sun. "What's a galaxy?"

Akina shrugged. "No idea. From what I can tell, that's the old name for the Star Clan. Maybe it's just a place. Exhale slowly, keep your lungs empty. Cycle your qi. If you can, stand and do ten infinity walks."

Zhu bent far enough to touch her nose to the ground, one hand pressed to her belly and the other clutching Dog to her side, then stood. "That was a mistake. Smell is even worse down there."

Akina watched as the Star Clan adept walked a figure eight and breathed slowly.

"Better?"

Zhu nodded as color began to return to her cheeks.

Dog walked over to an exposed pillar, thirty feet wide with a smooth gray surface, in the side of the mount. He lifted one hind leg and marked its base.

Remy pointed. "They seem bigger up close. Ribs."

Zhu whistled and leaned back to take in a fuller view.

There were other pillars, partially obscured by accumulated dirt and a tangle of thorny weeds, slick mosses, and off-color fungi. The plantlife joined one rib to the next, the totality knitting into a solid wall.

Akina touched the wall, shuddering as she did. "Not that I had any doubts, but this is definitely it. Help me find a way in."

Dog barked, then trotted east, pausing to sniff the base of the wall every few yards.

Remy watched him go. "Does he know what he's doing?"

Akina shrugged. "How should I know? He's just a dog. Maybe he smells something."

Zhu followed as Dog continued to the next rib. The others trailed behind.

Dog stopped in front of the wall, turned, and barked. Then he faced it, tail wagging in rhythm to the shaking of his tongue, and waited.

Zhu waved. "There's something here. More of a not-something. I don't feel sick when I stand in this spot."

Akina stepped over to the wall and put her hands on the plants. "This is it. Good job, Dog."

Remy stood by her side. "How do we get in?"

"There's an opening here."

"I see a solid wall of shrubbery. Where's the opening?"

Akina turned to him, smiled, then stepped into and through the wall.

"What do you know. Just like being born. Not that I remember that far back." She stumbled through a slit torn into the fabric of space, her eyes watering as she was struck by the heavy fumes contaminating the air inside the mound.

Dog popped through the rift and let out a small yip as he ran to her heels. Zhu came after, stumbling and coughing as she took in the air, followed by Remy.

The big man turned and faced the space behind him dubiously. "What was that?"

"Shh." Akina backed up to a spot closer to the wall. "Remember that entrance. No idea how long it would take to find another one."

The cavern was dimly lit by fluorescent fungi casting diffuse pools of pink and green light. The floor was lumpy and uneven, obstructed by growths and protrusions of no obvious provenance.

Things moved, always out of sight, shadows darting from one hiding place to another in the distance.

Zhu pointed up. "The ceiling looks higher than it did from outside."

Akina nodded. "That's spatial distortion. All of these mounds are a lot bigger inside. I tried to make a purse with this technique. Didn't work."

Remy walked a slow semi-circle around the two women, rope darts in his hands. Noticing him, Zhu pulled a pair of tyrant-tooth-tipped punch daggers over her hands. Akina wrapped her hands with quick loops of cloth.

Remy twitched as something moved off to the side. "Akina, my dear, I seem to have forgotten the plan."

"What do you mean?"

"I'm sure you coached us with a foolproof plan for this situation, but try as I might, I cannot remember any of it beyond 'get inside the mound and kill some Wedge.'"

Zhu cleared her throat. "Yeah, neither can I. What was the rest of it?"

Akina cracked her neck. "Hush, child. Remy gets to tease me, but you haven't earned it yet. And to answer both of you, that's the plan."

Dog barked as a trio of shapes came hurtling out of the darkness.

"Way of the Bear: Lesser Den!" Bear had his rope darts whirring in the air. The moment a shell of energy formed around the humans, three Wedge crashed into it, snarling and biting as the shield stopped their forward momentum.

Normal Wedge were lizards. Walking on two or four legs, scales coming in every color of the rainbow, they ranged in size from a little larger than Dog all the way up to trample-buildings-underfoot.

They all had the teeth of carnivores, and most had heads that tapered in the front like a snake. Hence their name.

These Wedge were a bit longer and skinnier than Dog: angry bundles of scale, teeth, and savage hunger. Their bodies were streaked in garish fluorescent colors Akina had never seen on a Wedge before, monstrous even by Wedge standards, mutated and twisted by the poisonous energies of the Greater Wedge corpse they stood inside. Tentacles and twisted limbs jutted out from their bodies at odd angles, spikes of bone and armor erupting from them in chaotic fractals.

Akina stepped forward to the edge of the shell. With timing borne of years fighting side-by-side, Remy stopped his technique and Akina spun through the three, lancing fists and feet into each of the creatures, stunning them further. "Infinity Bagua: Simultaneous Equations."

Remy reached out and gave Zhu a shove. The young woman nodded and stepped to the bodies, finishing each with an efficient thrust to the skull.

Remy started twirling his darts, spinning on the silk ropes that connected him to them. "Toss the bodies through! That's what we're here for."

She lifted each corpse on the end of her dagger and tossed them back toward the inside wall of the mound. Each body seemed to hit the wall, but instead of bouncing off, they hung in the air, suspended for a moment, then slipped through a crack in space and disappeared.

Zhu held up her hands and concentrated. "I can make gates in here, as long as they don't lead outside! I can fight too!"

Remy grunted. "Good. Because more are coming."

Growls and screams grew louder in the distance. The far walls of the cavern weren't visible, lost in shadows.

The growls grew louder and closer. A scratching sound started, claws scraping against bone and fungi and stone and petrified wood and the remains of long-dead monsters.

Zhu exhaled. "Wow. That's a lot."

The Wedge struck Remy's wall of qi like a tidal wave, breaking against it as twisting bodies flew off to either side.

Remy moved his right foot forward in a sweeping half-circle, then settled his weight and rooted through the ground, rope darts spinning above his head. "Greater Den."

The shield pushed out, knocking the swarm of Wedge away from the humans. Dog ran up to the edge and barked at the creatures.

Remy paused his shield, Akina leaping through to attack.

A moment later, the Greater Den was back up, catching two Wedge the size of oxen. Remy grunted with the strain of holding back the larger creatures.

Zhu pointed. "Can you open that side? I'll kill that one."

Remy nodded and relaxed his grip on one of the rope darts. "Way of the Bear: Spring Thaw."

Zhu darted through the opening and began stabbing the creature's neck.

Dog was behind Akina, barking at the Wedge that tried to attack her. She twirled, sidestepping and taking a new angle with each step, lashing out at rhythmic intervals with tight fists and callused feet.

"Infinity Bagua: Rotational Transformation. Get away from that, Dog. It's not for playing."

Dog stepped away from the fallen Wedge he'd been about to hump.

Zhu dragged the bigger Wedge back and into the mound entrance while Remy fought its sibling. One of his rope darts was caught in its mouth, but the other was held tightly in his fist as he crashed into the creature, tearing gashes along its side with the point of the dart.

Akina grunted as she saw a fresh wave of Wedge approaching. She tossed a small body into the air. "Zhu!"

The younger woman nodded and opened a gate in front of the body. The creature disappeared, reappearing in the same moment forty feet away at the mound's entrance. The carcass hung in the air, then squeezed through the portal, disappearing from the cavern.

"How many more?" Remy had two daggers embedded in the earholes of the big Wedge. With a snarl he twisted, breaking its neck with a snap audible even to Akina. He stepped back and threw the body at the entrance.

"Four more should do it."

Dog faced away from them and barked. Zhu pointed down the cavern toward a massive oval formation of bone that looked a lot like a giant pelvis hanging above the floor in the distance. "Incoming."

Remy snapped his darts down, throwing off arcs of blood and body fluids. "I can't hold off that many, Akina."

"Help me with these! Zhu, open gates!" She picked up another carcass and tossed it into the air. Zhu barely had time to process the crushed skull as it went through her gate and into the cavern entrance.

Remy picked up two more, muscling them through the air as Zhu opened a gate for Akina's last tossed body.

"Go! Get out!"

Zhu watched as a fresh swarm of ravenous creatures rose behind Akina.

"You're too close!"

Akina shook her head. "Get out! Take Dog!"

Dog barked and trotted over to Zhu's position as Akina turned.

Zhu looked at Remy, who shook his head. "Do what she said! Remember, she has the Millennium Qi!"

Zhu nodded, picked up Dog, and sprinted for the entrance.

Akina stretched her arms and twirled. Once, twice; on the third turn she leapt high in the air, easily clearing twenty feet.

As she landed, she stomped her left foot onto the ground. "Infinity Bagua: Greater Wave."

A ripple of force lifted the earth in waves that expanded away from her position in concentric circles. As they reached Remy, they threw the big man through the cavern entrance. The lead wave touched the first of the Wedge, tossing the creatures back and away from the Spiral Witch.

Akina panted, a stabbing pain in her knee telling her that she wasn't prepared for the strain of the technique or the uneven floor. She hopped toward the entrance, using bursts of spiritual energy to keep her balance when her leg refused to support her weight.

Zhu and Dog were clear, leaving Akina alone with the Wedge.

Not yet. Can't die yet. The girls need me.

A wall of creatures flooded to her position, jaws snapping at the air, growls and yelps softening as they saved their energy for running.

Faster and faster they came.

Akina stumbled on a lump of exposed bone the size of a kneecap, once again nearly hitting the floor.

Just a few more steps.

She hopped high in the air, watching as the leading Wedge sailed underneath her, and landed with a fresh technique. "Infinity Bagua: Lesser Wave."

She felt her energy nearly deplete as the wave knocked back the Wedge.

She stumbled, her left leg useless, and fell.

Reaching out to break her fall, her hands slipped into the tear in space that led through the wall of the mound and to the outside.

She blinked, eyes tearing up in the bright sun, as Remy caught her and pulled her away from the wall.

"Are you okay?" The mound rose behind Remy's back, his eyes focused on his friend's face.

Akina pointed behind him. "You have to den up the entrance! They're going to come through any second now!"

He dropped her to the ground and spun to see weeds part as a black snout, dripping green bile, broke through.

"Emperor's balls! I don't have enough left to create a den!" Rope darts jumped into his hand and he stabbed the nose, driving its owner back through the portal.

Akina landed heavily and scanned the area. Zhu was on the ground, panting with exertion while Dog licked her cheek.

"Good dog." She struggled to a sitting position.

Remy took a step back away from the mound and began spinning the rope darts in alternating circles. As tongues, noses, paws, and the occasional tentacle poked through the wall, a dart was in place to slice across its surface. The air hummed.

Akina shouted. "Hold them there!"

"I can't keep this up much longer!" A triangular face split down the middle, spewing blood and saliva over the grass before the body was pulled back into the mound.

"Zhu! Can you do something?"

The younger woman squinted. "Like what?"

"I don't know, but that portal is a technique from your clan! Can you close it? Seal the hole? Didn't they teach you *anything*?"

Zhu opened her mouth, blew away a strand of dark hair that had fallen across her face, and closed it. She turned to the wall.

"I might have something. Hold on."

She rolled her shoulders, then walked a quick figure eight, eyes on the portal in front of Remy. Walked it a second time. A third, her steps quickening with each repetition, head pivoting to keep her focus unerringly on the mound.

As she reached the center of the pattern for the fifth time, she paused and extended her hands. "Path of the Star: Rift!"

Remy stepped back as the stream of Wedge halted. He let his rope darts fall to the ground and wiped his forehead with the inside of his sleeve. He turned to Zhu.

"How long can you hold that?"

She maintained her concentration. "It's easier than it looks. It's a small block, so it's not usually very useful, but that portal is so thin that it's working."

He looked at Akina. "Can you stand?"

She shook her head. "Not yet. But they'll give up soon."

"How do you know?"

"I told you, Petrik and I researched this place years ago. We were going to steal the pearl. Figured out everything except the final guardian."

Remy sighed. "Fine. What do we do now?"

The thuds of creatures battering into Zhu's spell slowed and softened.

"Now you two help me skin these Wedge."

11

Fearless

Dog barked as Akina pressed a Wedge scalp over his head. She tugged it back, then forward again, making sure it left his eyes uncovered.

"You okay, Dog?" She was sitting on the ground, her face close to his.

He sneezed, then let out a low, pining wail.

"I know, it's disgusting. But that's the plan. You going to be okay?" He barked.

Remy loomed over her. "I should be asking you the same question. Can that knee even hold your weight? How are we supposed to continue?"

She leaned over and double wrapped a length of roughly scraped Wedge hide over the outstretched, injured leg. "It will hold. I'm already cycling qi through it."

Zhu stood next to Remy. "Why is this so tough, though? Don't you have the Millennium Qi? Shouldn't you be all, I don't know, bam, bam, kapow? Finishing these guys?"

Akina exhaled slowly. "It's not that simple. And it isn't your place to ask questions. You're sworn to follow orders, that's all."

Zhu huffed and turned away. Remy watched as Akina continued to pull pieces of skin over herself, his lips tight.

With a grunt and a hand for support Akina stood and faced the others.

Zhu was holding a Wedge skin at arm's length. "Do you really expect me to wear this?"

Remy looked into his own piece, formerly the torso of the largest Wedge, and wrinkled his nose. "Yes. But I'm not stupid; first I expect you to complain and moan about it until I get so annoyed I give Akina permission to kill you so we don't have to listen to you anymore." He lowered the skin and put his leg through one opening.

Zhu shook her head and looked at Akina. "You're serious?"

Akina nodded as she stuck another piece onto Dog, covering his hindquarters. The animal stared at Zhu plaintively.

Zhu shrugged and pinched her nose shut as she wrestled her fresh, dripping Wedge hide over her shoulders. "By the Emperor. I think I do wish you'd killed me back on the *Bone Rich*."

Remy squeezed another tube of skin over his leg, losing his balance as his grip tore a strip of flesh away from the piece. He caught himself and growled. "Where did you get this idea from, exactly?"

Akina grimaced as her neck covering caught in her hair. "We snuck in to watch them visit the temple, Petrik and I. It's like a test for the head of the clan. They all come to the central mound and hang out while she goes in and communes with the pearl."

Zhu shook her head. "The head of the clan isn't a she."

"They were at the time. Grandma Kwo put on a suit made from the skin of the Greater Wedge and danced into the central mound like she was invulnerable. We thought the skin was just really tough. Armor. But if it were, they'd have used it in battle with the Tae Kun. So we figured it must just deter the Wedge inside. Keep them from sensing her or keep them from attacking."

Zhu grunted as she pulled one skin over her thigh like a cavalry boot. "Like camouflage."

"Exactly. But that was the skin of a Greater Wedge. It's going to hold its qi, or at least some portion of it, for centuries. Maybe forever. With these guys, who knows? Hopefully a few hours, which is enough time for us to go in there and get the pearl."

The Star Clan adept stuck a finger down her side to scratch an itch she didn't want to think about too carefully. "If it's that easy, why is it such a test? The clan head, whoever they are, puts on the suit, walks inside, masturbates with the pearl or whatever, and walks out."

Remy stood and adjusted his pack under a cloak of skin taken from the largest Wedge body. "The real test is the guardian inside. I don't think that's even a Wedge."

Akina pulled Dog away from one of the bodies he was sniffing. "Don't eat that. And yes, it's the guardian. The fear demon. It's related to the Seventh Dynasty martial artists who ended the Surge. It's their ghosts, or spirits, or a manifestation of their most powerful techniques. It feeds on fear and it's basically unstoppable. At least by anybody currently alive.

"That's the real test. The elder is proving that she, or he, can control their emotions well enough to face the fear demon and walk away. It requires a spiritual presence very close to full enlightenment."

Zhu pointed at Akina, at Remy, then at herself. "That does not describe anyone here. How are we supposed to manage?"

"You'll see. For now we have to get to the central mound. Remy?"

"What?"

"Get us over the mound."

He leaned back and looked at the steep rise of the ancient ribcage. "We can't go around?"

"It's too far, and they'll spot us. Come on."

"Fine." He withdrew a rope dart, gave it a pair of twirls, and threw it, then pulled back on the rope so the point drove straight into the side of the mound, far overhead. The end sank into a knot of bark and bone, wedging in place. "Happy now?"

He handed the end of the rope to Akina, who wrapped Dog around her back like a baby and began to climb. A moment later Remy had a second rope ready for Zhu, who followed.

They climbed until Akina reached an area flat enough to stand on. She coughed. "Smell's even worse up here. Zhu, you want the ointment for your lip? It really cuts the stink."

Zhu pulled herself up onto the top of the mound and held out her hand. "Gimme."

Remy laughed and gave a final pull on his rope to join them, the mound thudding like a drum as his weight settled onto it. "Pride finally broke down, did it?"

Zhu shrugged and rubbed the ointment onto her upper lip. "I nearly passed out trying not to breathe on the way up here. I'm not sure you guys would go back for me if I fell off."

Remy slapped her back. "Of course, we would! Never leave a comrade behind."

Akina cleared her throat. Remy smiled and continued, "Fine, *rarely* leave a comrade behind. But we still need you, Zhu. And as they say, the foundation of every true friendship is mutual need."

Zhu looked at him. "Who says that? Nobody says that."

He shrugged. "Maybe not, but one day they will. For you shall tell tales of this grand adventure into your dying days, beguiling taverns full of eager listeners with stories of the majesty of my beard and the luscious—"

Akina growled. "Keep it down. Voices carry."

"Sorry." They reached the apex of the mound, Akina waddling to accommodate her stiff left leg, Dog sniffing the air from his position strapped to her back.

The central mound lay directly in front of them, across a half-mile stretch of wasteland. The east and west mounds were visible, rising out of the broken earth, the north mound obscured. Akina could see the retreating edge of the last nightshade as it headed west to grant darkness to the next continent.

The sun, as always, beat down from its lonely perch at the center of the sky.

Remy stood in place while Akina posted an arm on his chest for stability, leaning her weight away from the injured leg.

"Do you want me to carry you down?"

"I'll jump."

"Are you sure you should be using your energy like this? I know your qi cycling techniques are good but you're going to drain yourself."

She moved her hand up to his beefy shoulder and squeezed. "I'll be fine. We're not fighting our way through the next mound. Maybe you could carry Dog for me?" She unwrapped the animal and handed him over to Remy.

"Who's a good boy?" Dog yipped. "Come here, under my arm. Good boy." Remy scratched between Dog's ears.

Zhu looked down the slope as Akina leapt off the edge, the loose edges of her tunic flapping where they peeked out from the Wedge skin armor as she floated down to the flat ground below. The big man followed, skipping down the edge of the mound, tapping its surface every twenty or thirty feet to control his descent. He lowered Dog to the ground. Zhu brought up the rear.

Akina led the way across the field, pools of opaque gases lapping at their feet, slick mosses and sudden suctioning patches of mud slowing their progress.

Zhu let out a low squeal as she reached into her trousers, grabbed something, then flung it across the field. "There was a chunky bit sliding down my leg. I'm going to bathe in boiling water when we get to the next town."

Dog started to trot after the thrown bit; Akina called him back. The animal returned to heel, face low and dejected.

Zhu wiped tears away from her eyes. "When do you think Faceless is going to catch up to us?"

Akina looked back at her, then refocused on the central mound ahead of them. "What makes you think he will?"

"Come on, this is Faceless we're talking about. He's an outcast from the Hound Clan but he was supposedly their most gifted adept. He can find anything. He can find water in the desert. True love in a whorehouse. He can—"

Akina interrupted. "Can he find brains in a Star Clan adept? Hush, girl."

"I'm not a girl. And I need to distract myself from this . . . ick."

Remy patted her shoulder as they caught up to Akina. "Speak softly and she won't bother you."

Zhu reached a hand over her shoulder and down the neckhole of her tunic, stretching to reach a spot farther down her back. "How did you get together, anyway? When you formed the Five Fangs?"

Remy smiled. "You're asking how we met?"

"Yeah, I guess. I've heard stories about you guys but never that one."

They walked along the unsettling ground. Remy adjusted the Wedge skin that covered his face. "We met at a tavern on the edge of the Wilds. Leaking . . . no, Dripping Bucket. Terrible place. If you ever have a chance to eat there, don't."

"Noted."

"In a way that turned out to be all too typical, my good friend Akina managed to attract the attention of a group of Tae Kun adepts."

"What do you mean attention? Did she steal something?"

"Not that type. Their intentions were of a more amorous nature. At least, their leader felt that way, and the others were inclined to support him."

"Oh, I know about that sort of thing. Happens to me all the time."

He eyed her barely pubescent body skeptically but continued, "Regardless. Well, as you can imagine, Akina was undeterred by the fact that she was outnumbered five to one; she was ready to fight them all."

Akina grunted. "I would have beaten them, too. I was in the mood for a fight. I'd just lost my favorite hairpin in a bet."

"We never did find that hairpin, did we?"

"Never."

Remy stepped over to a spot between the women and patted her shoulder. "You'll have to forgive our interference. We didn't know that it was you picking on them, not them picking on you." He turned back to Zhu. "Petrik—I was already friends with Petrik, we were there resting up for another run into the Wilds—was furious at the Tae Kun for their lack of chivalry, for ganging up on a woman. He was about to leap to Akina's defense when Rei broke a bottle over one of their heads. Mau-rhi saw three of the Tae Kun go after Rei, so he jumped in—he and Rei are siblings—and Petrik pulled me in to make it even."

Akina paused to pull her injured leg free from a patch of mud. "We were never allowed back into that bar after that night. But Petrik gathered us to go to another place, and when he struck out for the Wilds the next day, we all tagged along."

Zhu nodded and pointed at the hill ahead. "Yeah, great story, thanks. But look there. Is that the entrance? I don't think big guy here is going to fit through that."

The four converged on a cave mouth, darker than it should have been and barely navel-high on Akina. Dog barked once and began to sniff around the opening.

Akina ducked into the cave. "Come on. Remy's more pliable than he looks."

The ecosystem inside the central mound matched the southern. It was vast: the ceiling too far away to see clearly and the far wall completely obscured by dangling columns of decaying flesh and billowing mist. Glowing patches along the walls cast a dim light over the space, shifting and moving with subtle air currents just enough to obscure the flickering shadows cast by moving creatures.

Things ran and jumped and shifted and, most of all, breathed; the darkness pulsed with scrapes of scale on bone and claw against stone.

Zhu coughed. "What is that? I feel bad here."

Akina glanced back, checking on the youngster. "It's just like the other place with the aura of the guardian added in. Exhale slowly. Walk the pattern if you need more stability."

Zhu nodded and turned a tight figure eight around Remy.

A saurid, standing eight feet high on two legs with a bird's posture and a mouth large enough to swallow an adolescent whole, stalked over to them, its slender forked tongue tasting the air as it approached.

Zhu had her punch daggers in her hands, but Akina put out a hand to restrain her.

"Wait."

The big Wedge walked closer, nictating membranes opening and closing over its vertically slit eyes. It turned and walked away.

Zhu let out a breath. "I just peed myself and it actually made the smell better."

A laugh from Akina. "I told you this would work. If these Wedge fought each other, they'd have died out centuries ago. To them, we're just funny looking Wedge."

Dog barked softly and trotted forward. The humans followed.

More Wedge approached. Walking on two legs, the Wedge species inside the mound were like miniature tyrants or big saurids: thick legs, long tails counterbalancing their heavy heads, short, almost vestigial arms clutched to their chests. They were scaled in green and red and purple and yellow, many crusted with heavy plates of bone and armor in odd locations. A few had glowing tentacles emerging from oozing sores along their sides or feathered wings too small to lift them from the ground.

The Wedge neared the group, sniffed them, and left.

Dog moved deeper into the mound.

With every step the spiritual pressure coming from further inside the mound grew in intensity. It pushed against the humans like a wave of hot breath or the proximity of a heavy weight, a wall of stone teetering on the edge of a fall, ready to crush all who came near.

Zhu coughed. "Is that the guardian?"

Akina nodded. "That's the test. The head of the clan has to walk up to that thing and touch the pearl."

"How powerful is it?"

"Nobody really knows. Nothing has survived a fight with it. It's a fear demon, though. It only fights you if you're scared."

Remy sighed. "I'm quite terrified. Judging by the liquid trickling down Zhu's legs, she is nearly as scared as me. Are you able to get the pearl?"

A shape manifested out of the shadows ahead, a smaller structure of bone and flesh the size of a farmer's hut. Dog stood in front of its darkened entrance and yipped.

Akina walked up behind the animal. "Come here, boy. Are you ready? Can you get the pearl for mama?"

Zhu and Remy traded glances. Remy cleared his throat. "Dog is going in?"

Akina nodded as she held her face close to her pet's. "Can you be a good boy? Go get the pearl?"

Dog barked and wiggled free of her hands.

She stood and turned to her friend. "He'll get it."

"How will he escape the demon?"

"I told you before, Dog isn't afraid of anything. The demon won't attack him. Two minutes tops, and we can leave. With the pearl."

They stood and watched as Dog trotted into the building, tail wagging as he ran. The pressure of the guardian's spirit was so strong that none of them could have taken even two steps toward it.

Zhu scratched at her waist. "How long is this going to take?"

"Not long."

The largest of the Wedge came close to them again, sniffed, and left. Remy cracked his neck as the creature walked away, tearing the ground with raptor-like claws at every step. "That's quite a dog. You should keep him."

Akina nodded. "He's family. I'd let one of my girls go before I'd let go of him."

Dog came running out of the guardian's chamber, tongue hanging out the side of his mouth, jaw opened in a grin.

"Did you get it? Did you get it?" Akina knelt to receive him.

Dog barked and nuzzled her chin. "Give me the pearl, boy. Open up."

Dog barked and opened his mouth. Aking bent lower and dug her fingers around inside it. "Oh, no. No, no, no."

Remy knelt next to her. "What? He didn't get it?"

"I'm pretty sure he got it. He wouldn't have just come out here otherwise."

"Then, what's the problem?"

"I think he swallowed it."

12

Waiting for Dog to Go

The next day; far away from the temple.

Remy sniffed, taking in the smell of the redwood and pine that dominated the forest. The forest sounds were drowned out by the stream that ran with cold, clear water thirty feet from their makeshift camp. He arched his back, grunting softly as vertebrae cracked and popped with the motion. As he straightened, he worked on the straps holding his armor together, tightening them again to account for the girth he was losing.

"I'm fading away, Akina. I need more food, more wine, and significantly less exercise if I'm to have any hope of maintaining my manly physique."

Akina looked up from where she squatted. "Are you so dense that you're actually choosing this particular moment to complain about not getting enough food? With me wrist deep in Dog's waste? Because I'd happily give you my share of our rations if you want to take on this little task."

Remy pointed at Zhu. "You have a parolee right there, oathsworn to take on any nasty job you assign her. Why are you even doing that?"

Zhu spluttered at the big man, her mouth working hard but not finding any words to spit out.

Akina finished working the pile while Dog watched with his head tilted quizzically. "He's my dog, it's my job to take care of it."

Zhu pouted. "You just don't trust me with the pearl."

The older woman chuckled. "As if you'd know what to do with it. You'd need months, maybe years, to get anything out of the pearl. You young ones don't understand the first thing about sacred treasures."

"Maybe I don't. Why don't you explain it to me?"

Remy stepped over and patted her back. "Sacred treasures have their own spiritual energy. It takes time to cycle your qi so it resonates with the treasure. One doesn't simply pick one up and transform into a great warrior."

"My teachers never showed me that. We do that by walking the infinity pattern?"

"That is the first step of Akina's technique, so yes, it can start with that. There are other methods. Probably as many as there are clans."

She exhaled loudly. "Why are we staying out here, in the middle of nowhere? There's not a town for fifty miles. It's been a whole day. I have enough energy to gate us somewhere useful."

Akina stood, holding her arms apart to avoid staining her clothes as she walked over to the stream and found a clear spot on the bank. She squatted again and worked her hands in the cold water. "We need the pearl for the next step in my plan. And I mean I need it in my hand, not inside Dog's gut."

Zhu kicked the ground. "I can't believe that with the amount that dog shits the pearl still hasn't passed through."

"If you were paying attention, you'd know he's been bound up since yesterday. He knows he did a bad thing and is upset about it. But he's calming down, things are starting to move again now. I think."

Remy stood over their makeshift kettle, a hollowed-out fire turtle shell suspended over the woodpile on a crude trestle he'd carved from damp branches. He tossed tea leaves into the simmering water. "I prefer wine, but tea beats water any day."

Zhu sniffed. "Is that Azure Dragon Clan tea? Is it part of your spiritual cultivation techniques?"

Akina stood and patted her hands dry on her trousers. "It's just tea, Zhu. We drink it because it tastes good. You should walk your pattern. Build up your energy. We'll need a gate out of here as soon as we have the pearl. We've wasted too much time already."

Zhu nodded and continued walking her pattern, carefully timing her inhalations and exhalations to the different steps, gaze focused on a mountaintop far to the west. As she walked, her internal energy cycled through a matching infinity pattern, her core at its center building and purifying itself.

Dog turned suddenly, eyes on a movement in the bushes, then took off at a sprint.

"Don't go far, Dog! Hey, Zhu, run after him! If he shits again, we have to know where it happened!"

"On it!"

Remy took a half step after Dog, then stopped. "What is he after?"

Akina shrugged. "That's his 'chasing squirrels' mode, not his 'watch out, I sense something dangerous' mode."

"Why do they do that? Chase squirrels, I mean. Do they ever catch them?"

"This one doesn't. I think he just likes it. He does a lot of things that make no sense. Why does he try to hump your leg all the time?"

Remy frowned. "I don't think that's the same thing."

She raised her hands, inspected them, then flicked them, shaking off excess water as she stood. "You want to understand the mind of a dog? You're becoming philosophical in your old age, Remy. I need you a little more focused on what's at hand."

"Fine, I get it." He faced the forest, watching the branches still trembling from Dog's passage. Akina walked up behind him and wrapped her arms around his waist in a hug. He patted her hands as she pressed her face into his broad, warm back. "What's this for?"

"I walked up to you after ten years and asked you to drop everything and risk your life to help me. You didn't even hesitate. I figure you deserve a hug for that."

"Did you think I wouldn't come through?"

She hesitated before answering. "No. I knew you'd come through. That doesn't mean you don't deserve the hug."

"I owe you my life. You and Petrik. More times than I can count."

She released him and stepped back. "I owe you mine, as well. More times than I care to count. I think our friendship is beyond ledgers."

He shrugged. "I didn't become a hunter because I planned to live forever. I honestly didn't think I'd get out of the business alive. These are all bonus years. If I can spend them getting your girls back, that's more than worth it."

"I get it. Still doesn't change the fact that you deserve a hug." A smile crept up her cheeks.

"Don't make a habit of it, please. You'll spoil me. Affection from the Spiral Witch. I'll forget what a cold-hearted bitch you are."

She slapped his arm. "Watch it! You can't go around calling a mother that."

"Sorry—" A shout from the forest interrupted him.

"Guys! He pooped! Over here!"

Remy turned and met Akina's eyes. She nodded and took heavy steps toward the source of Zhu's voice. "Let's go." Dog stood at the edge of the clearing, his tail wagging.

"Oh, shit."

Akina sighed. "We know, Zhu, we heard you."

The woman came running out of the forest behind the animal, her dark hair a sharp contrast to pale skin. "No, not that. I feel a King's Gate opening."

Remy hissed. "Faceless. Should we run?"

Akina shook her head and jogged toward Dog. "We can't. We need the pearl! Where did he go?"

Dog stood and barked, his tail rigid in the air. Zhu pointed. "Right here! He was coming back to you!"

Remy spun in place. "I can feel the gate. Over there."

Akina shouted over her shoulder as she sprinted for the pile Dog had left. "Hold them off!"

"I'll do what I can." He started spinning two rope darts at the ends of silk ropes held in his massive hands. "Way of the Bear: Lesser Den. Go, get the pearl!"

Energy flowed from his core, circling his body and solidifying into a spiritual shell just outside the reach of his darts.

Akina crouched by the steaming pile of excrement. Dog had, indeed, relaxed, and the results were spectacular, though less than charming. Zhu spun to face her. "What should I do?"

"Just stay out of the way."

"Can we run?"

"Not until I'm sure the pearl isn't in here. Just protect yourself! Stay ready to open a gate out of here! Remy can hold them off. Probably."

A pop of equalizing air pressure echoed through the clearing as three figures stepped out of a hole in the fabric of space.

Akina paused to look up.

"Faceless, is that you? I can't imagine anybody else would have bad enough taste to wear that mask in public, but I've been wrong before." She resumed working through Dog's waste.

The figure in front paused. He wore a cloak in an oak-tree brown that almost matched Akina's trousers, cut to fit close to a square-shouldered and lean-hipped physique that had been a good match to his rugged good looks in the years when he'd been considered the most handsome man in the Clan of the Hound. The hood was tucked into a mask carved from white tyrant bone, a smooth oval marred by two holes: one upper-left where an eye might be and one near the bottom right.

The eyehole focused on Akina as the man twisted his hands in the air.

The taller figure to his right stepped forward and began to speak. "Spiral Witch. Come peacefully and no harm will come to your girls. Or to your companion." He was the tallest human Akina had ever met, over seven feet, with limbs so long and lean she could hardly believe him capable of standing. He was dressed in the skin of a black tyrant, glossy and smooth, with a wide cape and a face-covering cowl built into a pair of leathery ornate ears flanking his temples.

Got to buy time.

"Bru Wei. It's ironic, isn't it? You being Clan of the Bat and acting like a lovesick puppy to Faceless. See? He's actually of a dog clan, and you're . . . not appreciating the irony, are you?"

The third figure emerged from behind the first pair as the gate squeezed shut. "Phew. That's a big one. I'm going to need a break before opening another gate!" Shorter, the light-haired man was dressed in storm-gray linen matching Zhu's. He spotted her a moment later. "Hey! Why are you working with them?"

Faceless signed some more; Bru Wei spoke. "You, hush." The Bat Clan acolyte's voice projected across the clearing with an unnatural, piercing clarity. "There's time to do this peacefully. You know we have no ill intentions toward your girls."

Akina snarled. "Then you never should have gone near them, Faceless. You should have known better."

More frantic hand twisting.

Bru Wei continued, "I agree. It was a mistake to take them. Regardless, you have to come with me. We'll let your friends live, let your girls go. Just surrender now."

Akina found a hard object, pulled it out of the muck. A pebble. She tossed it aside and dug furiously through the next lump.

"My grandfather ruled the martial world for half a century with the Millennium Qi. You think I'm going to trust that kind of power to the Reaver? Especially after he kidnapped two little girls to force my hand? I'll see the Wedge eat every human on this continent before I'll trust him with the Qi."

Hand motions.

"You leave us with no choice."

Remy released a dart, sending five pounds of razor-sharp bone on a straight trajectory to Faceless' single eyehole. "You've had plenty of choices. Starting with not working with that psychopath. I know you, Faceless. You're aware of the dangers of the magic he plays with. You should know better than to be part of this."

Dog barked.

Faceless sidestepped the rope dart without turning, standing as if unconcerned as the deadly weapon sliced the air next to him. His hands worked.

Bru Wei spread his long, thin arms, the folds of his cloak hanging off them, night-black wings of leather. "Another Surge is coming. Psychopath or not, the Reaver is our only chance to stop it. Now drop your weapons."

Akina found another hard bit. She rubbed it with moist, sticky fingers. "I'm not even carrying weapons. Having trouble seeing with only the one eye?"

Zhu turned her head between Faceless and Akina. She leaned in and whispered, "Can we go yet?"

"Do I look like I'm done?"

Dog barked again, tail stiff, eyes focused on Faceless.

Faceless' hands moved. Bru Wei nodded and opened his mouth.

The air shimmered in front of the tall man's face, carving a path toward Dog. The ground in front of the animal erupted in a blast, dirt and stones blowing a dozen feet into the air.

Dog hopped back, taking two steps from the small crater Bru Wei had created, and barked again.

Akina growled. "Leave him alone. You said to drop our weapons, right? He doesn't have any. For that matter, neither do I." She examined the lump, tossed it to the side. *Another pebble. Dog, why do you eat these things?*

Remy looked over his shoulder at his old friend. “He’s attacking with sound. My den techniques only partially deflect that. We’re going to have to try something else!”

“I know that, Remy! Just . . . think of something! I’m almost done.”

Bru Wei rose with a quick flap of his arms, his light frame and wide wings finding purchase in the air. Faceless reached to his waist and drew a sword, an arm’s length of juvenile red tyrant rib harvested before hardening fully, steamed straight and sharpened to an edge fine enough for shaving. If he had a face to shave.

Faceless closed on the edge of Remy’s den while Bru Wei floated over the top.

Zhu waved her hands in the air. “Mother’s Gate!”

A rift opened in front of the flying Bat Clan adept. He passed through it and was suddenly at the other end of the clearing, smashing face-first into a stout tree.

“Zhu! Don’t get involved.”

“I’m not letting Bru Wei get close to me. He never smiles. It’s creepy.”

“Remy’s taking care of it. Don’t fight them, that’s an order. Get a gate ready to the place I told you would be next.”

“Fine!” Zhu retreated behind Akina, putting the older woman between herself and Faceless.

The masked man slashed at the edge of Remy’s technique, his sword cutting away at the field of energy.

Remy sent another dart at the Hound Clan adept as sweat dampened his thick beard. “That thing is sharp. Akina, I know you don’t need me to tell you this, but hurry up.”

Bru Wei staggered to his feet and spun to face the clearing. “You’re not going anywhere!” His voice was deeper, the tone more guttural, changed to show he was speaking for himself.

Faceless deflected Remy’s dart.

The light-haired Star Clan adept pointed at Akina. “You want me to do something?”

"No! Let the adults handle things."

Bru Wei's seven-foot frame launched into the air. Remy retrieved his darts and set them to spinning.

"Way of the Bear: Den of Dawn!" A fresh sheet of qi fell in a wall between him and Faceless: invisible to the naked eye but to esoteric senses it shimmered like woven starlight.

The thinner man slashed at it again, relentlessly dissecting the shield.

Bru Wei flew in a straight path over Remy and onto Akina's position. Remy tossed a dart up, forcing the Bat Clan adept to twist out of the air or risk tearing his wings.

Dog trotted over to where he landed and stood several feet away, barking.

Akina bent over the last bit of undisturbed fecal matter. "Please, be in here." Zhu stood closer to her.

"There! Right there, by your left hand!"

Akina flattened and squelched the material through her fingers. She *felt* the energy of the sacred treasure as it touched her skin. She nodded, half to herself and half to Zhu, and stood.

"Faceless! I'll overlook your interference today, but that's all you're getting. If you get in between me and my girls again, your face will be the last of your worries. I'll take something else. Your arms maybe. Or legs."

Zhu shouted. "Yeah! How would you like to be called 'Assless,' huh? See how that feels! She can do it, too! You'd never be able to sit down! Sounds tiring, doesn't it?"

Akina turned to the young woman. "What? How would you do that? What are you talking about?"

"What, that wasn't good? I thought that's what you were going for. No?"

"Stop talking and open the gate. You're embarrassing."

Bru Wei got to his feet, swiping at Dog with stiffened fingers. The animal backed away, barking.

Remy panted as he dropped another Den of Dawn between them and Faceless. He backpedaled toward his friends, nimble for a man of his size.

amazon.com

Order of November 23, 2023

Qty.	Item
1	**Partial Function: A Wuxia-inspired Epic Fantasy** Berne, JCM --- Paperback **1961805049** 1961805049 9781961805040

Return or replace your item
Visit Amazon.com/returns

0/GvCnxBLkC/-1 of 1-//DUT2-CART-B/next-1dc/0/1127-20:30/1127-15:01

SmartP

Akina pointed at her pet. "Dog! Heel!" The animal stopped barking and trotted toward her. "Zhu! Gate."

Zhu nodded and traced a circle in the air with her hands, palms rotating with the motion.

Faceless was signing frantically while the light-haired man looked on, slack-jawed. Bru Wei faced Dog and the three humans, his lips curled into a sneer below the leather cowl that covered the upper half of his face.

Zhu exhaled loudly as a hole opened in space in front of her.

"Dog! Go."

The animal hopped through the gate, Akina close on his heels. She landed on a steep hillside a hundred miles from the clearing.

She fell, rolling to a stop at the base of the hill, and turned to see Remy, then Zhu, come through. The gate closed with a pop behind them.

Akina ran filthy hands through her pack, looking for the empty silk purse she'd sequestered there a week before.

"Dog, I cannot believe what you've driven me to. If you weren't so cute, I'd have Remy serve you for dinner."

Dog walked up to her and licked her elbow.

"Here!" She pulled out the purse, smaller than a palm and suited for carrying enough bones for a day of light shopping, and dropped the soiled pearl inside.

Remy rolled to a stop a few feet away, his big chest rising and falling with his panting.

Dog walked over and licked the big man's face.

Zhu stood over Akina. "Won't they follow us here? That Faceless guy seems to know where you are."

Akina nodded. "He can track."

Zhu turned. "So what are we doing? Trying to ambush them?"

Remy climbed to his feet. "I think we need something cleverer than that."

Akina shook her head. "Zhu, get ready to gate us again. East, anywhere. At least fifty miles." She closed the purse, shuddering as the filth on her hands corrupted the fine silk.

Zhu opened another gate; Akina ushered Dog, then her friends, through it.

The four stood in an orchard; trees twice Remy's height formed even rows all around them, branches heavy with cocovado fruits.

Zhu fell to a knee. "I can't keep doing that."

Akina nodded and let out a long, slow breath. "You don't have to; we're safe."

Remy looked at the purse in her hands, then at Dog, who barked once. "Are we?"

"Yeah. Remember the concealing spell on the river barge? I didn't break it; I stole it. It's on the purse. Faceless could sense the pearl if he were, say, already in this field, but he can't track it at any great distance."

Zhu looked at Remy, who was nodding and running fingers through his beard.

"Is that the real reason you took the spell? You knew you'd need it for this? Not to force the barge captain to run the blockade?"

"Why choose?"

The big man laughed. "Let's get you cleaned up."

13

Sick as a Dog

Dog snored softly from his spot in the corner of the underused barn they'd rented, paws twitching occasionally with his dreams.

Zhu sat on the ground with her back against the barn wall, a few feet from the animal, wincing as she adjusted her position. Remy sat across from her, tending to the small fire they'd built. Akina knelt by a tub of water, dressed in a thin shift, and scrubbed furiously at her clothes.

Zhu wiped the back of her hand over her forehead, then looked at the streak of sweat it left behind. "There's one thing I don't understand."

Remy looked up at her and chuckled. "Only one? Child, when I was your age—"

Zhu stuck her tongue out at him. "Not that again, okay? It's about Faceless. Look, I get that the pearl is hidden by that seal. But if Faceless found us by sensing the pearl from halfway across the continent, why doesn't he just track the Millennium Qi? Isn't that, like, even more powerful? Shouldn't it be easier for him to find? I mean, the guy is creepy, but he isn't stupid."

Remy turned to see if Akina was preparing an answer.

She wasn't.

He poked the fire again, then settled their teapot over it. "The Millennium Qi is special.

"Every person's qi is unique. It matches their personality, their thoughts, their temperament. That's why the Reaver's techniques are so dangerous. The qi he steals interferes with his own, corrupting his soul.

"Masters of Infinity Bagua can use their cultivation techniques to purify that qi. When they do so, it loses all its characteristics, all its . . . personality. That way, they can pass it on to an heir, who can add its power to their own.

"The Millennium Qi is the purified spiritual power of the first master of Infinity Bagua, added to the power of his disciple, and the disciple after him, and so on. It's been polished, purified, and cultivated for a thousand years."

She pointed a finger at him. "So that's why it's called that!" She coughed softly with the exclamation.

"Yes. But because it has no personality, no flavor of its own, there's nothing for Faceless to track. You might say it has no scent."

Zhu tapped the ground. "The combined power of every master of Infinity Bagua for a thousand years? That sounds amazing."

"It is a potent weapon. Which is why the Reaver is so desperate to have it. He wants to tear apart Akina's soul and harvest it from her."

Akina turned to them. "It's been more than a thousand years, actually. It was eight hundred years old when they first gave it that name. It's been twelve hundred years since then." She lifted her tunic out of the water and twisted it to wring out excess water.

Dog snorted and rolled over. Remy leaned forward to drop tea leaves into the pot.

Zhu coughed again, then eyed the back of her hand. "Guys, I think something's wrong with me."

Remy stood and stepped to her side, grabbing her hand. He looked at Akina. "Blood. She has internal injuries."

Akina nodded and started ringing out her pants. "Getting sloppy. Bru Wei must have gotten her. I didn't even see it."

Zhu looked between them. "What did he do?"

Remy pointed to her abdomen. "His clan uses sound, just like a bat. Stronger adepts can attack with it. Hard to see and harder to dodge. He must have blasted you during the fight. Eventually you'll learn to protect your internal organs against that, after some more years of cultivating your qi, but you're still vulnerable."

Her face paled. "What do I do? Can we fix it? Take some kind of medicine?"

Akina rubbed her forehead. "We need a doctor."

Remy shook his head. "It's not safe. They don't know where we are, but they probably have a general idea. The Reaver will have men out watching."

"Sure, Remy. Great. Remind me of the time you spent studying medicine? Because I remember a whole lot of you eating, fighting, and drinking, but somehow I've forgotten all the hours you spent with your nose in scrolls memorizing meridian lines and practicing your needle techniques."

"She can cycle her qi, heal herself. Can't she?" His eyes widened as he looked at the girl.

Zhu coughed again.

Akina pointed at her. "She's never been trained properly, Remy. Look at her. Yes, she's a genius with her clan techniques, but her foundations are terrible. How do you think Bru Wei got her with a half-hearted attack? It wouldn't have affected either of us. She needs a physician."

Dog woke with the noise, trotted to Zhu's lap, and licked her face. She rubbed his back. "Well, I'm no good to you dead. Just leave me here. I'll find a doctor in the village."

"He'll want money and most doctors won't be able to fix this sort of thing. We have to hope they have something more than the typical village bonesetter."

Remy rubbed his head. "They'll be looking for you, and Zhu probably shouldn't walk. I'll go find a doctor, bring them here."

Akina looked ready to argue but stifled it. "You're right. You go. Here, take some bones. Show them you'll make it worth their time."

He waved her off. "I have plenty. Just watch her. Make her drink. I'm not sure how much blood she's losing. I'll tell the farmer where I'm going. Maybe ask for directions."

"Yes, Dad. Thank you, Dad. I have no idea what I'd do without your sage wisdom, Dad."

He pointed at her with a rude gesture as he left the barn. "Yes, yes, I get the point. Just trying to be helpful!"

The doors shut behind him.

Akina knelt by Zhu's side and checked the younger woman's pulse, then gently kneaded her abdomen in several spots.

"I feel weak."

"That's appropriate. You *are* weak. You barely understand the basics of your own martial abilities."

"You're mean. And that's not what I meant. I feel weaker than normal."

Akina mumbled as she counted out heartbeats. After a minute, she pulled her hand back and nodded. "As I said, you have internal injuries. First time?"

"Yes. You don't seem very worried about it."

"I'm not the one with internal injuries."

"Oh."

Akina smiled. "Would you prefer me to wail and cry and tear at my hair and clothes? Don't say yes, because I'm really not the tearing-hair sort of person. I am worried, but you're not in grave danger at this moment. We'll get you fixed up."

"Am I going to die? Are you being cheerful so I don't suffer in my last moments in this world?"

"Yes, you're going to die, but probably not today. As for my demeanor, do you really think I'm that nice of a person? Expend all that energy just to make you feel better? Remember, I'm the Spiral Witch."

"That's true. I guess you wouldn't."

"That's the spirit. Let me finish drying these clothes. I'm sure Remy will be back in no time."

••••••••••

Incense mingled with old dust and heavy pollen in the air as the doctor tapped at various points on Zhu's body.

She was stretched flat on a bed of fresh straw, her eyes wide and nervous as she was probed and poked. Remy stood in the doorway, his back to them, affording some privacy to the exposed woman. Akina watched the doctor with suspicious eyes.

"You don't look old enough to be a licensed physician. Where did you say you studied?"

The doctor turned a very round face to her and smiled, showing her two more chins than was typical for a health professional.

"I studied at the Imperial Academy itself. Graduated with a gold sash. I am older than I look. I assure you I am more than qualified for this situation."

"Why would a man with a gold sash from the Imperial Academy be living in a remote village like this, where the most interesting cases are undoubtedly impotent old men and lame livestock?"

He nodded and smiled. "Quite so, quite so. Yet my dear mother lives in this village and I don't have the heart to leave her. I'm sure you understand. One only ever has one mother, isn't that right?"

"I guess. Mine was a real bitch, though. I did everything I could to get away from home as fast as I could. Still, it's in our favor that you're here. What's the verdict?"

He looked to Zhu, then back to Akina, and wiped sweat off the back of his neck. "Verdict?"

"Yes. Judgment. What do you say? Prognosis. Or diagnosis. What's wrong with her?"

"Ah, yes, verdict. I see. You confused me, as I am not, in fact, a judge, though when taking the Academy entrance exams, it was remarked that I had a natural aptitude—"

Akina's hand rose to her shoulder and the words 'Wrong Answer' formed on her lips.

Remy's voice lashed out from the doorway. "Akina, no."

She turned to him. "Fine! Doctor, get to the point, please."

His eyes widened as some primitive part of his brain recognized the level of danger he was in. "Yes, of course, so sorry. I don't usually see cases—"

Remy cleared his throat. "You should get to the point, Doctor."

"Right. The patient does, in fact, have internal damage. It is unusual, as I see no external evidence of a wound. Perhaps some sort of blunt trauma, though there isn't sufficient bruising to be consistent with that diagnosis."

"She was hit by a very loud sound."

The doctor nodded, his jowls wiggling with the motion. "Yes, that makes sense. Unfortunately, injuries of that sort are too diffuse to easily treat."

Akina rubbed her forehead. "What does that mean? In plain words, please?"

"If there was damage to an organ at a particular point, I could surgically repair it. Instead, the patient is presenting with slight damage spread over entire organs. There is nothing to cut or sow. No single point I can address."

Zhu struggled to sit. "What's going to happen to me?"

The doctor shrugged. "There is little I can do. This is, well, it's reminiscent of a chariot race. One chariot is the damage killing you. The other is your body healing itself. If I knew which chariot would win, perhaps I wouldn't have lost so much money gambling at university."

Akina looked at Remy, who shook his head. "Saved by the Bear. Are there any ways to help her along? I thought medicine was all about coaxing the body to heal itself."

"That is one school of thought, yes. Not my specialty, but certainly applicable. The exercises that circulate and strengthen qi would help her recover more quickly. Speeding up that chariot, as it were."

Akina put her hand on Zhu's chest, pressing the younger woman back into a prone position. "Let's assume that's not doing enough. Because it isn't. What else?"

The doctor wiped his neck again. "There are herbs I can administer. I don't think they'll suffice. I can use needles to encourage the circulation of her own qi, but I doubt the quantity she is manifesting in her current state will be adequate."

Remy spoke from the doorway. "Can she take from outside? A donation?"

The doctor shrugged. "Only if the qi provided is exceptionally purified."

Akina looked at Remy. "Your purification techniques are terrible. Your qi would kill her."

He nodded and looked at Dog. "He doesn't have enough. Not that he knows how to use it."

Akina sighed. "We both know I have to do it."

The doctor shook his head. "The process is very inefficient. Even if you can purify your energy, the amount she would require would be prohibitive. If we had a hospital with a team of donors arranged, we could help her. Or a monastery, perhaps."

Remy looked at Akina. "Do we have time? Is there any place close enough?" Then he said to the doctor, "You should know this area. How far to someplace that can help?"

"Er . . . I'm not entirely sure. I can't think of anything within several days' travel."

Akina looked at Remy. "Step outside with me. Doctor, keep an eye on her."

"Yes, of course." Zhu tried to sit up again, but he restrained her gently.

The old friends closed the barn door behind them and walked off through the cocovado trees.

Remy looked down at her. "You're thinking of doing it yourself. Can you?"

She laughed. "You're questioning how much qi I can use?"

He paused and looked up at the sun beaming down at them from its position directly overhead. "You're strong. But you've always been strong."

"What are you saying? Or asking? Are you asking something?"

"Your grandfather was an amazing talent. But you and I both know you were a greater one. If you had fully acclimated to the Millennium Qi, you'd be much, much stronger than you are now. But I've seen you fight, and heal, for the past few weeks, and that's not what's happening."

"Those are observations. Still no questions."

"I don't want to ask questions. If you wanted me to know more, you'd have told me more. I trust you have your reasons. But if you can't utilize the Millennium Qi, you don't have enough power to heal her."

"I have enough."

"Not without risking your life. Come on, Akina. She attacked us. Let her die. Or abandon her. Let the doctor take her to some hospital somewhere and fix her up. We'll move on. You need someone for transportation? We can set a trap, capture the blond Star Clan kid who's been gating Faceless and Bru Wei around. Or go catch a couple of griffins."

"If we don't save her, she'll die. They'll let her die, Remy."

"Maybe. But what's the cost of saving her? What if it kills you? I can't rescue your girls by myself. I would if I could. They're counting on you."

She plucked a cocovado fruit from the tree they were under and peeled the soft skin, exposing a creamy interior. She scooped the flesh out with a calloused finger and licked it.

"No."

"What do you mean, no? What part of what I said are you arguing with?"

"All of it. None of it. I'm not arguing. I'm not reasoning with you, not disagreeing. I'm not making any points. I'm just saying no. I'm going to save her, and my girls, and if the fates, the heavens, and the Emperor himself stand in my way, they're going to regret it sorely."

He plucked his own snack and peeled it.

"Then we might as well get to it."

••••••••••

"Hold her down." The doctor wiped his neck as he switched needles, pulling a thin shard of sea ogre bone from one spot and deftly inserting it into another. His eyes shifted quickly, gleaning information from Zhu's thrashing that completely escaped Akina.

Remy shook as waves of energy radiated outwards against him. He had two hands planted on Zhu's chest, his considerable weight pressing down on her.

"I'm doing my best!"

"Well, do a bit better. I need her stable."

Remy sneered but didn't answer. He exhaled, muttering, "Hold the Cub" under his breath, and formed a bubble of energy around his hands.

Tendons stood out on Zhu's neck as she struggled in vain against the renewed pressure.

The doctor looked into her eyes. "Try to relax! We're helping you!"

She nodded tightly, clenching her jaw and breathing in frantic gulps of air. "Hurts!"

Remy grunted. "It's supposed to hurt! It's like training. Everything that's good for you hurts a little!"

The doctor shook his head. "Actually, this shouldn't hurt. Not this much. Perhaps their qi isn't compatible."

Remy glanced at Akina. "You need to purify it better before you shove it through her channels. Focus."

Akina nodded and exhaled slowly.

Focus. Concentrate on the energy, not on how much you want this girl to live. Or how much you miss your own.

She redirected her attention, tracking the flow of energy as it circulated inside her body through a fixed center below her belly button. Through a loop extending behind her, then back in toward the center, through another loop in front.

Tracing the symbol of infinity.

The streams of energy rubbed and collided in the middle, scrubbing clean.

From that center she extended a tendril, then a line, then a full arc of energy that darted through the air and entered Zhu's body through the tip of one thin, conductive bone needle.

Focus on the center. Keep the lines mixing, colliding. Rub them clean.

Forget how much you want her to live. Let it go.

Remy panted. "She's relaxing. Is it working?"

The doctor nodded. "It's better now. The only question left is how much she'll need."

••••••••••••

A rough, wet band of flatness dragged along Akina's forehead. "Dog, how many times have I told you not to lick my face when I'm—"

Remy interrupted. "It's me, Akina. Relax, everything's fine."

Sunlight peeked in through spaces between the boards making up the barn's walls. The air smelled of hay and dust.

"Why were you licking me?"

Remy laughed and held up a cloth. "Just this, Akina. You have a fever. I was cooling you down."

"Huh. I suppose this means I survived."

"You did. As did Zhu. It was close. The doctor proved unexpectedly competent."

She grunted. "Help me sit." He eased her up and handed her a waterskin. "Thanks." Dog tucked his head into her lap; she scratched his chin.

Remy sat across from her, legs folded into a lotus position. He slapped his belly, smiling at the thumping sound it made. "I'm glad I haven't faded to nothing. At least not yet."

She smiled and glanced at the makeshift mat where Zhu was sleeping. "When can we go?"

"Doctor says you need a week to rest, so I assume we'll move on tomorrow. Faceless will find us here if we wait too long. Someone will have noticed that the doctor went somewhere, start asking the farmer questions, and . . . you know how it goes."

"I do. One night of rest. We'll leave with the dawn."

"Good. Where to?"

"You were saying something about griffins."

14

Much Ado About Griffins

By the next day, Zhu had recovered enough to gate them to their next stop. Barely.

She was on all fours in the back of a dark cave, shaking as she finished heaving the meagre contents of her stomach down a dangerous looking crack in the stone. Dog licked her foot, then climbed onto her calf.

Akina called out to him. "Get off her, Dog. She's feeling sick enough." He paused, then turned and trotted away.

Remy struck a pair of stones together, using the spark to light a torch that looked centuries old. "I can't believe the Wind Clan doesn't know about this place."

She walked the perimeter of the cave, squinting into the dark shadows to check for whatever surprises might lay in store for them. "This location has been passed down through the Azure Dragon Clan for generations. Since before they developed Infinity Bagua. I always thought it was stupid. Who cares about a hidden cave within shouting distance of the griffin breeding grounds? Now I look like the dumb one and my ancestral secret is going to save our plan."

Remy grunted as the torch caught and flared to bright life. "How did they find it, anyway? Or am I not allowed to know?"

"The cave? My ancestor was in the fight. The First Emperor came back from the East, changed into whatever you become when you go far enough East, and took on the entire martial world, uniting the continent. This whole area used to be a plain. The techniques they used in that battle carved out the valley they turned into the breeding grounds.

"The dragon clans already existed, though I don't think they looked much like what they are today. My ancestor was part of that battle. He barely escaped with his life, using the last of his energy to crack open this little cave. He rested in here for a thousand days, licking condensation off the walls and eating insects and moss while he recovered."

Zhu retched again, drawing an answering whine out of Dog.

Remy looked to the back of the cave. "Should I check on her?"

Akina shrugged. "Probably. But don't coddle her. She has to learn to whine less."

"She did nearly die just two days ago."

"Please. If nearly dying is going to stop her from doing her job, then we're all in trouble."

Remy nodded and headed to Zhu with a water skin.

Dog trotted to Akina. She squatted down and let him lick her hands. "How are you, boy? Had enough excitement? Sorry to tell you, we're just getting started. Have to find the girls. Okay?"

He leaned back on his haunches, barked softly, and continued licking her hands.

She chuckled and stood. "Zhu, you okay? Can you stand?"

Zhu lifted an arm. "One minute." After a few dry heaves, she stood. "I'm okay. Just pushed a bit too far. I'll be fine."

Remy looked at her. "Which is it? You're okay or you will be fine?"

"Just tell me what you need and I'll tell you if I can do it."

Remy looked at Akina, then nodded. "That's a good answer. I'll take it. What's next?"

Akina pointed to the narrow cave mouth. "We check out the grounds. Or airs. I supposed you'd call them airs." She led them to the mouth, a winding space between rocks barely large enough for Remy to walk through sideways. The path led to a ledge overgrown with thick bushes, with room for two of them to stand side by side.

Remy lowered his voice to a whisper. "Will they see us? The Wind Clan?"

Akina looked over her shoulder at him. "The grounds are more than a hundred miles around. They can't possibly guard every yard of it. They're counting on the dome to keep the griffins safe. Just don't make any big movements. Or loud sounds. And don't fart. Or think too hard."

"I hope that comment about farting was a poor attempt at humor, because it came far too late."

Zhu grunted from behind him. "He's not kidding. We're all in terrible trouble."

Akina shook her head and crept out between the bushes.

Below her the ground dropped sharply away into a nearly vertical cliff that lined a canyon a mile deep, several miles wide, and fifty miles long.

A shimmering dome of air rose up from each side of the canyon, joining in the center, pockmarked with floating ceramic vessels covered in magical seals. At its peak it rose half a mile above the lips of the canyon. Wicker huts floated at the dome's apex, spaced half a mile apart, barely visible from Akina's ledge.

Remy joined her on the ledge and whistled softly as he took in the size of the breeding grounds. "All this so the Emperor can have his griffins?"

Akina nodded. "Imagine the power it took to carve this gorge out of stone and earth. If he wanted griffins raised here, who was going to argue with him?"

As Zhu poked her head between them, a flock of griffins flew by a few dozen yards past the shimmering air that confined them. They had the heads of predatory birds: fierce eyes facing forward over a beak large enough to eat Remy in three bites. Their wings were thick and heavy with feathers, their front legs long and lean, ending in taloned feet. As they flew past, the humans could see muscular hindquarters, their animal legs trailing loosely in the air.

Zhu let out a breath. "Are those wild?"

Akina waved them back into the cave. "This is where they grow up. The Wind Clan maintains the dome. They can also open doorways in it. When they need to, they drop inside and find a griffin to tame. Once it's done, they bring it out."

Zhu nodded. "So we're here to steal some griffins?"

"No, we're here to let them go. As soon as you have your strength back. Go sit."

••••••••••••

Remy's voice was weak. "Akina, I'm not comfortable with this plan."

She sighed. "What's the problem, Remy? You're afraid of Faceless? Or of angering the Hound Clan? Or the Star Clan?"

"No, that's not it."

"Then what? You don't want to risk the wrath of the Wind Clan? Or is it the Emperor? You think you'll anger His Holiness?"

"No."

"Well?"

He cracked his neck and ran his hands through his beard. "I'm afraid of heights."

A different flock of griffins flew near, led by a large black specimen who skimmed close to them, his cold eyes meeting Akina's gaze square.

She swallowed. "You're going to have to deal with it, Remy. This is the way."

He nodded. "This is the way. Well, it's your way, and I guess for now it's my way too since I agreed to follow you on this mission."

Zhu shook her head. "You want us to walk out on that? It's not even a thing. It's air. I don't want to walk on air."

Akina pointed up the dome where Dog was trotting toward one of the ceramic spheres anchoring the dome's magic. "It's safe. Even Dog knows! Now come on!"

"But he's not afraid of anything, remember? That doesn't mean it's safe!"

"Wait, he's not supposed to go yet. Dog, get back here!"

Dog turned and looked at her, head cocked to one side, then trotted back to their ledge over the floor of hardened air.

Remy put two hands on the edge of the dome and leaned forward, slowly shifting his weight onto it. "It has give to it. Like a mattress. They should make beds out of this."

Akina pulled Dog off the dome. "I'll make sure to suggest it at the next meeting of the Clan leaders. Now, are we clear on the plan?"

Nods answered her. Dog barked once.

She exhaled and pulled the silk purse out of her belt, opened the top, and lifted the Ancestor Pearl out.

The size of the last joint on her pinky finger, the pearl's surface was lustrous to the point of luminescence.

Zhu stared at it. "What do we do now?"

Remy pointed at the pearl. "We wait for Faceless to sense it. Then he'll come and, well, you heard the rest."

"How long will that take?"

The big man shrugged his bulky shoulders. "No idea, really. Could be hours. Could be days. Get comfortable."

••••••••••••

Zhu bolted upright from the rock she'd been draped over. "They're here."

Akina uncoiled to her feet, cracked her knuckles, rolled her shoulders, then twisted her head to either side. "Where?"

Dog nuzzled Remy awake, interrupting the big man mid-snore. Zhu pointed out along the dome of solidified air.

"That way."

Akina squinted as she looked up over the curve of the shimmering dome. "You two know the plan. Keep Faceless off my back."

Remy rubbed sleep out of his eyes and nodded. "I would tell you to be careful, but you wouldn't listen. You'd probably just say something cool and tough, like, 'It's Faceless and Bru Wei who need to be careful.'"

"You know me too well, Remy."

Zhu held her hands over her eyes. "Path of the Star: Griffin Gate."

Remy looked over her shoulder. "What is that?"

"It's a tiny gate, just big enough to look through. I can put the other end as far away as I want, and when I look through this end, it's like my eyes are over there. Gives me sight like a griffin."

Remy grunted. "I don't like the way those griffins are looking at us with their actual griffin eyes."

She snorted and leaned further into her hands. "They're coming."

Akina straightened the brim of her hat, pulled strips of cloth out of her sleeves, and wrapped her hands tightly. "Good. I was tired of waiting."

She locked eyes with Remy, saw his acknowledgement, then hopped onto the dome.

A shadow skimmed over the dome in the distance: Bru Wei with leather wings outstretched flying toward her. His voice reached her easily, focused by the Way of the Bat techniques his clan had developed to manipulate sound.

"You are delaying the inevitable. The end result for you, Akina, will be the same. All you're doing is making things harder for everyone who survives you. Don't you care about any of it? All these people?"

"You're getting repetitive, Bru Wei. Try a different approach."

"Your adept can't keep gating you away from us. She's not strong enough to keep up this pace. You're going to have to stand and fight, and you can't win."

"You think you can take me, Bru Wei? When did you become delusional?" The shadow was growing as he closed the distance between them.

Another dot appeared behind him. *Probably Faceless trying to keep up on foot.*

"Maybe not alone, but I'm not alone, am I?"

She stepped to her right, then left, walking the arms-reach version of the infinity pattern, collecting energy below her navel. Her hands shifted with each twist, back hand protecting her jaw, front hand near her belly button, chin tucked in and back.

The shadow resolved into a set of features: pale jaw below a black leather cowl, gnarled ears built up above the skull, leather wings pulled tight between hand and foot to let the Bat Clan adept glide.

His mouth opened.

"Infinity Bagua: Circle." She spun her hands, palms flat and facing out. A wall of energy radiated from them; her face tightened with concentration, but she put only a fraction of her strength into the technique. *Remy is so much better at this. But I need him for a different task.*

Bru Wei opened his mouth; the air shimmered in a cone of violent disruption as a spear of intense sound emanated from him.

The sound struck Akina's shield, weakening significantly but passing through. She jerked back and away from the beam, but it vibrated through her abdomen.

Akina fell to one knee and coughed crimson flecks of blood. They stuck to the dome, hanging suspended on an invisible layer of air.

The leather-clad man landed softly in front of her. "You should have kept up your training."

She coughed again, bracing one hand on the dome to stabilize herself, and looked up at him through the brim of her straw hat. "You can criticize me after you give birth to a couple of kids."

"I don't remember the Spiral Witch tolerating any excuse for weakness."

"I never have." Her body extended, force spiraling through her frame from her planted right foot, up through her straightening knee, rotating pelvis, around her core and shoulders, then up into her extending right hand.

"Upper Limit!" Bru Wei took the brunt of her strike on forearms crossed in front of his face. Her palm knocked him back and he was sliding across the dome.

Have to keep making him think I'm weaker than I am. She coughed again, letting her gaze linger on the bright spots of blood she sprayed on the dome.

A pride of griffins passed beneath them in a dizzying rush, feathers scraping the dome, their eyes on the beads of blood.

She glanced toward the top of the dome and the wooden hut where Wind Clan sentries were supposed to be posted.

"They won't help you, Akina. They'll never reach in time."

I don't want them to reach.

She cast a quick glance toward Faceless' approach, then to Bru Wei's position, and finally at the hut above and behind her. With a huff she turned to her left and began to run.

"Don't drag this out, Akina!" The Bat Clan adept's voice was harsh and gravelly.

"Infinity Bagua: Sine Sprint." She took off, her motion cutting broad curves across the dome, first to the right, then the left, no two steps ever forming a straight line.

Faceless reached the edge of the dome near the cave mouth. Remy stepped out of concealment, planted his feet on the dome surface, bent his knees, and growled, "No further!"

Faceless drew his sword, red bone sharpened to an edge that cut the air instead of parting it.

The sword flashed.

Blood spurted in a slender geyser.

"Way of the Bear: Hug."

The big man lurched forward and wrapped massive arms around the slender swordsman. Dog ran up behind Faceless and let out a series of barks.

Bru Wei glanced back, but Faceless' arms were trapped; he couldn't give any commands. The Bat Clan adept turned back to Akina's retreating form.

She climbed toward the dome's peak, covering nearly as much distance side-to-side as progress, her movement too erratic for him to track.

"You're wasting time!"

She yelled over her shoulder. "I won't let you have me! Or the Millennium Qi!"

"You have nowhere to go! Emperor spare me." He leapt into the air, unfurling his wings to a full stretch, and pulsed energy through his body to gain altitude.

As the leather-clad man flew to intercept Akina, the smaller woman leapt and spun through the air, her motion jerky with fits and starts and pivots and sudden changes of direction. Every time he closed in, she spun away and sprinted off in another direction; every time he thought he knew where she was, she surprised him with a shift and a leap to safety. After four passes, he was growling his aggravation. He turned back to check on Faceless.

Blood soaked through Remy's trousers, but his arms were still affixed to Faceless, squeezing with such apparent effort that it seemed the smaller man's eye would squeeze out of the hole in his mask.

A soldier came running across the dome, dressed in the finer clothes of an officer. "Stop! By order of the Emperor and the Wind Clan! This is sacred ground!"

Remy shouted. "Akina, run! They don't want me, they want you! Get clear!" Dog hopped toward Faceless' back, stopping short, then stood and barked at the struggling man as Faceless worked the wrist of his sword arm free and slashed at Remy's back with shallow cuts.

Akina spat more blood onto the dome. More Wind Clan soldiers, dressed in the royal blue and brown colors of their clan, ran across its surface toward her. They jumped as a second pride of griffins flew too close, three of its members slamming heavy bodies into the dome's underside. The soldiers stumbled and nearly fell.

She poured panic into her voice. "Remy!" *Don't overdo it, Akina.*

He twisted from side to side, shaking Faceless the way Dog might shake a dead squirrel. "Run! I'm fine!" Blood pooled at his feet; he held steady and rooted as a pride of griffins thudded into the dome directly underneath him.

She muttered under her breath. "You're not fine." Bru Wei soared over her head. *Where's Zhu?*

The soldiers were focused on Bru Wei's broad wingspan, ignoring Akina. She saw two prides of griffins sweeping across the underside of the dome, their predator eyes focused on the activity. Faceless' sword, swinging almost loose from his wrist, cut a shallow slice into Remy's calf.

Akina sprinted out to her right as Bru Wei swooped through the space she'd been occupying. A pride of griffins, led by a large, red-feathered male, flew by. The Bat Clan adept climbed again.

Zhu ran out across the dome. *Good girl. Everything's in place.*

Akina spat a mouthful of blood onto the dome.

The second pride of griffins pummeled into it, angry beaks digging into the solidified air, questing for blood.

Akina dropped to a knee. *Just fake a stumble. Let him think you fell.*

Bru Wei halted in mid-glide, opened his mouth, and sent a blast of sound toward her, loud and focused enough to obliterate a fortress.

The Wind Clan soldiers shouted with hands up and palms out, "Stop!"

Akina continued her fall, rolling onto her hip and away from the tsunami of sound.

Under the position she'd maintained, Bru Wei's martial scream shattered the ceramic sphere inside the dome itself. Akina saw his eyes widen through the eyeholes of his leather mask as he recognized the damage he'd done. The soldiers reversed course, backpedaling from the impact, taking broad qi-assisted leaps toward the hut further up the canyon.

I wonder what happens when that sphere is destroyed?

Wind qi blew away from the dome in a rush. The air beneath Akina's feet lost its enchantment and sublimated into a cool breeze.

Akina plummeted through the dome, nothing between her and the ground but a mile of air and two griffin prides.

15

Old Dog, New Trick

Akina turned her face to the side as rushing air pulled the breath out of her lungs.

The *good* news was that the ground was very far away, so she would have plenty of time to find an escape before impact. The *bad* news was the same: The ground was very far away indeed.

Need something to bounce off of. What have I got?

One of the griffins, brown fur and white feathers, spied her falling body. It dove, beak outstretched as it sought to snatch its lunch out of the air.

Akina waited, sucking air in through barely parted lips, and flipped just as it struck. She tapped her feet against the top of its beak.

"Infinity Bagua: Reflection."

The technique reversed her momentum, sending her straight up with the same speed she'd accumulated by falling. *Grandpa could use that to bounce off a stiff breeze. No solid object required. Wish he'd taught me the trick.*

She rose near the level of the dome. Griffins were streaking back and forth in a flurry; two of them had dared the dome and passed through the missing section. They flew tight circles above it, gaining altitude quickly. Bru Wei rocketed backward, the gust of air released by the destroyed section of dome too much for his controlled glide to manage. Wind Clan soldiers were sprinting across, long staves in their hands as they batted at the escaping griffins in a vain attempt to corral them back into the canyon.

Remy was on an intact section of the dome, Faceless still in his arms, while Zhu knelt at the edge, her hand tapping at the missing section in front of her. Dog stood by her side, tail stiff, barking in Akina's direction.

Her eyes locked on Zhu's as she hit the apex of her trajectory and began to fall again.

A griffin flew by, buffeting her with wings as far across as a minor hall of the Emperor's palace, sending her into a twisting tumble.

Akina's arms and legs windmilled as she tried to stabilize her path. Another griffin crossed her line of sight, hungry eyes focused on her mid-section.

As she spun back to it, Akina dropped a hand to the tip of its beak. "Reflection." Her momentum shifted again, sending her back up into the air.

Wind Clan soldiers were closing on a dark lump of leather: Bru Wei collapsed on the hard dome. More griffins were spiraling into the sky, screeching calls summoning other prides from farther up and down the canyon. The soldiers who had been trying to force the griffins back were lying on the dome, slashed and bloody.

Almost forgot how draining Reflection is. If I'm lucky, I can do that twice more before depleting my qi. This might not have been the best plan.

Zhu climbed to her feet, standing at the edge of the solid portion of the dome, and held her hands up to frame Akina's position. The Spiral Witch hit her apex and fell again.

The snap of wings cutting into soft air; spots of color as stray feathers lazily twirled down into the canyon; a subtle smell of musk that lifted as soon as Akina noticed it. The griffins were gone, the immediate area empty.

She fell faster.

Another pride of griffins was closing on the opening from farther up the valley. Akina measured the distances with her eyes; by the time they arrived, she'd be far beneath them, plummeting to her death.

Crap.

Dog barked again, the sound growing fainter by the second.

I need something solid as a focus for the Reflection, and I need it soon. If I wait until I hit the ground, I'll be moving too fast for it to work.

She grabbed at the ties for her outer tunic, fingers pulling at the knots that held it to her for a moment before she simply tore the strings with a curse.

Akina turned to face the sky and pulled the tunic free, fingers gripping hard so she didn't lose the material to the fierce wind driving by her. She tucked her head and rolled facedown, the tunic in her hands. She took a breath.

One chance at this.

She pushed the tunic down with a double hand thrust so simple the technique didn't even have a name.

The tunic dropped, then snapped back toward her.

"Reflection."

She bounced off the tunic, flying back up into the air and toward Zhu.

Please, please, do your job.

As Akina reached the highest point of her flight, she watched Zhu, her eyebrows furrowed in concentration, shape her hands into the spell for a gate.

The world opened up beneath Akina's feet.

She fell through it and landed hard on the dome behind Dog. She lay still, breathing hard, and let the animal lick her cheek.

Zhu knelt at her side. "Are you all right? Did I get you? Did I snip off anything important? That happens sometimes, you know. It's not pretty."

Akina smiled and pushed herself up off her belly, then to her feet. "I have all the important bits still attached. We need to get out of here; the Wind Clan won't stay distracted forever."

Zhu nodded. "Remy is still wrestling Faceless."

Akina turned to see her old friend, blood streaming from a half dozen cuts, continue to squeeze the Hound Clan adept. If Faceless was affected by the pressure, it was hidden by his mask.

Zhu pointed. "If Remy lets go, he'll get cut open like a hog on Return Day."

Akina cracked her neck and let out a long breath. "I'll separate them." Dog nuzzled the side of her leg.

Bru Wei was upright and fighting the Wind Clan soldiers. The first two prides of griffins were almost out of sight, experiencing freedom for the first time. The blond Star Clan Adept was standing two hundred yards away, watching, his hands empty and held out at his sides.

Not enough time to try anything else. Akina ran to her right and lined up to a spot where Remy's body blocked Faceless' view of her. She bent forward at the waist, planted one leg behind her, and took off in a full sprint at her friend's spine.

"Infinity Bagua: Partial Function."

Her palm struck the big man directly in the center of his back.

Remy felt nothing.

The energy of the strike passed through him and into Faceless, who sailed out of the bigger man's grip like a frog dropped onto a hot pan.

Remy dropped to a knee. Akina circled him, examining his cuts with a practiced eye, identifying the most serious wounds. When she looked again, she saw Faceless drop into the surface of the dome as if a well had been dug into it.

Akina turned to Zhu. The young woman shrugged.

"I couldn't just let him walk away, could I?"

"Where did you send him?"

"Only about six feet down. Which happens to be the other side of the dome."

Akina watched the blond Star Clan adept drop to all fours and start tracing patterns into the dome surface. "You think he'll rescue Faceless?"

Zhu shrugged. "Probably. You want me to kill him so he can't?"

Akina pulled a cloth out of her waist and wrapped the spurting cut in Remy's thigh. "We don't have time. Get us out of here."

"Yes, ma'am."

••••••••••

Remy rolled from side to side on the thick cotton mat, shifting his heavy frame away from a position that put pressure on a wound only to find another cut newly aggravated.

Akina sat near him, back against the wall, enjoying the warmth of the sunlight. "You want some more tea, Remy?"

He exhaled. "Maybe in a bit. The more I drink, the more I have to pee, and getting up aggravates my leg."

She nodded. "I'll put more salve on those cuts in a bit." Dog's barks sounded from the courtyard beneath the window, followed by the sounds of children laughing.

"I didn't think you'd mastered Partial Function. Sending your energy right through an object to the other side."

"I hadn't when I was here. But peace and quiet left me with a lot of time to train."

He grunted and turned again to face the window. "The abbot was quick to give us shelter here. You want to tell me why that is?"

She stretched her arms overhead, tensing and relaxing the muscles along her shoulders. "Petrik and I made a sizable donation to this orphanage. It's not the kind of thing you forget."

Zhu swallowed the crunchy sesame sticks she was eating. "Is it okay, though? Aren't you putting all these kids in danger?"

"Not really. I know Faceless, he's no maniac. Even if he finds us here, he's not going to slaughter a bunch of children just because they happened to be hanging around the building where we were hiding. Now, help me switch out these bandages."

Zhu and Akina bent over Remy, ignoring his grumbling as they rewrapped his wounds, applying generous layers of salves that the abbot had provided.

Remy relaxed as they worked, and when they finished, he was snoring softly.

Akina caught Zhu's eye and pointed to the door.

They left together, winding down the main staircase and out into the courtyard. Dog was playing fetch with the children, who found his incomprehension of the game endlessly funny.

Zhu chuckled. "How does he not know how to play fetch?"

Akina sat on a broad stair and idly scratched at the ground with a stick. "I think he's teasing them. But it's entirely possible that he's just really stupid."

"At least he seems happy."

"That's more than most people get. Certainly more than most animals. You shouldn't just stand there, Zhu. Walk the pattern."

Zhu slumped her shoulders. "My clan never taught me this. We always cycled qi while in one place. And we would just spin our core. None of this making shapes or moving."

"And that's why you're not good at using your qi in a fight. Do you fight while standing still? Do you use your qi in a fight by spinning it in place? No. So don't practice that way."

Zhu began tracing infinity symbols in the dirt, her gaze focused on the main gate across from them.

Akina watched Dog playing with the children. *Reminds me of the way he played with the girls.* Images of her old life flashed through her mind.

Keep a cool face. If I start crying now, my reputation will be ruined.

After a hundred cycles, Zhu turned to her. "Are we leaving soon?"

"We have to wait for Remy to heal."

"That could take days. Weeks. Can you afford that kind of delay? I thought you were in a rush to get your girls back. Isn't that why you trapped me in the first place? Now Remy gets hurt and we just chill here and play with these kids?"

Akina drew the character for 'brat' in the dirt, then scrubbed it out. "It won't take days, or weeks. By tomorrow, maybe tomorrow night, he'll be healed."

"I'm not a doctor but I've seen wounds before."

"You haven't spent much time with masters of the Way of the Bear. Healing is one of their skills."

"But he isn't doing any techniques. He's just sleeping."

"You really don't know, do you? He cycles qi in his sleep."

"Are you serious? That's what he's doing, right now? Snoring away, cycling his qi, healing those cuts?"

"Yes."

"Why the hell am I walking these stupid circles, then? Why don't I learn to cycle qi in my sleep? That sounds awesome. Let me do that!"

Akina smiled. "You have to have the right temperament for it. And it takes a long time to learn."

Zhu slumped. "Fine. What does sleeping have to do with being a bear, anyway? What is a bear?"

"Didn't your mother teach you any of these stories?"

"No, my mother hates me. She taught me to stand on my own two feet and not one thing after that." Zhu traced something in the dirt with the tip of her boot, mimicking Akina, then wiped it out.

"Bears are mythical creatures. Walk on two legs, run on four. Big and furry. Bigger than Remy."

"What does that have to do with sleeping?"

"You've heard stories of a world where the weather changes, right? Where even in the lowlands it gets cold for months at a time, then warmer?"

"I guess. I don't know, sounds dumb. Like the world where the sun moves through the sky. Who makes these things up?"

"I don't get it either. But the stories keep popping up if you look at the notes written by the old masters."

"You mean like the Emperor? People who went east, then came back?"

"These aren't tales from the east. These are from the heroes who came to fight the Wedge. The round-ears." She touched the top of her ear to show which part on the strangers was round. "Generations of them came here from some far-off place, fought the Wedge, left us their teachings, and died or left again. Some stayed. That's where we got Bagua from. Nobody taught you all this?"

"Nope. I told you, my mother hated me. Father didn't think raising children was his responsibility. Especially not with my brother to keep him busy."

"I'm sure she didn't hate you. Motherhood is just complicated."

"People say that to me. But only people who have never met my mother. She definitely hated me, told me so herself. Many times."

Akina shook her head. "I'm sorry, Zhu. Some people are filled with anger. Did she explain?"

"Not really. Not that I heard, that's for sure. I mean, what valid reason can you give for hating your own daughter?"

Akina looked into Zhu's eyes. The younger woman's gaze was dry and bone hard.

"I suppose nothing."

"I'm sure you never said things like that to your girls."

Not out loud. "I don't think so. I did get angry with them, sometimes. We fought. That never meant I didn't love them."

Zhu wrote something else in the dirt, rubbed it out.

"Maybe if I get strong enough, she'll love me the way she's supposed to. If I'm as strong as my brother."

Akina put her stick down. "Maybe. Probably not, but maybe."

"I still don't understand what sleeping has to do with bears."

"In the stories, when it got cold, food would be scarce, so the bears would sleep. For months at a time."

"No! Get out! Months? That's crazy."

Akina smiled. "Isn't it? But maybe they'd think the same as you. I bet right now there's some girl around your age on one of these worlds, hearing about our world and thinking it sounds like a fantasy."

"Our world is normal."

"Of course, to us. Maybe they think the Wedge are crazy. An endless stream of scaled monsters marching along the Spine of the World, relentlessly heading east."

"What's crazy about that?"

"Why are they going east? Where do they come from? Why don't any come back?"

Zhu scratched her head. "East is where you go. That's just the way it is."

"Just the way the sun holds its place in the sky. Yet they say on other worlds it weaves back and forth." Akina poked at Zhu's ribs with a single finger, near the back as she said 'back,' then closer to the sternum as she said 'forth.'

Zhu giggled. "That tickles! Cut it out!"

"Maybe tickling is what you need!"

"I think it's what you need!" Zhu poked back at the older woman. Dog trotted over and got between them, barking. Three children gathered in a circle and chain-tickled each other.

Akina grinned and with a duck and a lightning-fast pivot she exited the pile and stepped away. *Laugh while you can, child. You'll lose the chance soon enough.*

••••••••••

As the shadow of the nightshade crossed the courtyard, Akina climbed up the stairs to wake Remy. The big man stank of anxious sweat and stale blood, but his eyes were clear and his bandages were free of any signs of infection.

He moved to sit up, grunted at the pain, and lay back down. "How long?"

"We spoke this morning. Night just fell. So, not long. How are you?"

He glanced at the window. "Mostly fine. I think. Not ready to move yet, if that's what you're asking. I'll just start bleeding out again."

"You need to heal fast. I can't handle the girl on my own."

"Taking her hostage was your idea. I thought she was growing on you?"

Akina smiled. "I'm teasing. She's fine. You thought I was serious? The day I can't handle a whiny teenager is the day I retire from the martial world."

"I thought you did that ten years ago?"

"Don't use facts against me, Remy. You know what I meant."

He smiled back. "I do. By the Emperor, from the smell in here you'd think I died from those wounds."

"You are definitely ripe. You up for a bath? Or should I have the monks pour rosewater over you?"

"Give me until morning."

She sniffed, wrinkling her nose, and nodded. "I'll make the sacrifice."

"Thanks. You mind telling me why we went to such elaborate lengths to release the Emperor's griffins? Do you have some plan that requires us to make an aerial escape from the palace?"

"What do you mean, release the griffins? We didn't do that."

Remy scratched under his thick, chest-length beard. "We didn't?"

"No. I was there, you were there. Did you see me attack the dome? Damage the spells?"

"No. But Bru Wei—"

"Exactly. Bru Wei did that. I was just in the vicinity. Maybe I was even trying to stop him. Did you think of that? I mean, we were fighting."

"I suppose you were. Why would Bru Wei—"

"How would I know *why* an adept of the Bat Clan would attack the Emperor's aviary and set the griffins free? I can only imagine it was an attempt to make the Wind Clan look bad. The Aviary is their charge, after all. Isn't it?"

"So you want the Wind and Bat clans set against one another."

"By itself, that's not useful. But what do you think will happen when a northern animal clan and an elemental clan are at odds? You think they'll fight alone?"

"No. They'll call in their allies."

She gave him a thumbs-up. "Exactly."

"You're starting a war."

"I told you this was going to get ugly, didn't I?"

"Where does the pearl fit in?"

"It doesn't. Not yet. That's the next step. I'll explain."

16

Dawning of the Age of Akina

White Dragon Fortress straddled the Turtletail River, which to Akina's mind would have been better named the Turtletail Stream or perhaps even Brook, based on its meager flow. *I think Dog has taken pisses heavier than this river.*

She faced the front gate, a structure clearly designed more to intimidate visitors than to offer any aesthetic or practical value. The gate, along with the exterior wall lining the square footprint of the fortress, was woven from Wedge bone. Long tyrant tibias, ribs from three-horns, and leviathan femurs provided the rough outlines on all sides while smaller bones, tied together with leather strips and twined tendons, filled the spaces in between. At a glance, Akina spotted parts from ogres, saurids, rhinophants, and every breed of tyrant; red, black, white, and ivory bones were all carefully placed and reinforced with enchantments to present an impenetrable barrier.

The wall was strong enough to withstand a Wedge Surge, at least temporarily, and represented five generations worth of bones harvested by members of the White Dragon Clan.

More than that, the precise placement of the bones, the angles and intersections, were a form of writing unique to the dragon clans. The walls spoke, at least to those who understood the script, of the history of the dragon clans.

Especially the White Dragons.

The front gate was five men high and ten men wide and watched by sentries standing on a platform behind the thick bones at the top edge.

Akina looked up, shielding her eyes from the sun. "I'm here to see the Dragon."

One of the guards swatted at a bug or piece of dust in the air. "She's not taking any visitors, ma'am."

Akina looked down and nodded. Dog lifted one hind leg and released a stream of urine on the base of the gate.

A second guard pointed and shouted, "Oy! He can't do that!"

Akina tilted her head. "It's so nice that the White Dragon is still providing jobs for the intellectually challenged."

The first guard scowled. "What?"

"Your friend there said my dog can't do what he clearly just did. And your mistress is kind enough to give him a feeling of purpose by letting him stand up there and pretend to be useful. What happened? Was he born this way? Was it head trauma? That happens, you know. Take a solid enough blow to the head, some people never recover their wits. A shame, really."

The second guard sputtered. "I'm not—tell her, Quinn! I'm just a regular guard, aren't I!" He looked at the first guard, sudden suspicion in his eyes.

Quinn sighed. "Of course, you are, Jet. She's mocking you, is all. Ignore her. Miss, I'm going to have to ask you to leave."

She nodded. "All right, then, go ahead."

"What?"

"You said you're 'going to have to ask' me to leave. I said, 'go ahead.' Ask."

Quinn looked at Jet, softly stroked the ivory spear at his side, its tip sharp enough to cut flecks of dust falling from the sky, and turned back to Akina. "Please leave this area, ma'am. No visitors today."

Akina knelt and stroked Dog's neck. "I'm going to have to insist. Besides, you haven't even asked who I am."

Quinn nodded. "No retinue, no retainers. I know who you aren't. Go beg for alms somewhere else."

"I'm no beggar, Quinn."

"Of course not, ma'am. Still."

Akina straightened. "Tell the Dragon that the Azure Dragon is here to speak with her."

Jet sputtered again. "She's mocking all of us now, Quinn. All the dragon clans. I don't like her. Let's go down there and deal with her."

Quinn, his hair long and dark, held up a slender hand. "Wait. You're the Azure Dragon?"

"I am. Akina Azure, the Spiral Witch, the Azure Dragon, Grandmaster of Infinity Bagua. Grandmistress? I don't know. I'm here to speak to your dragon and I am losing patience waiting out here without a hint of White Dragon hospitality to alleviate my temper."

Quinn cleared his throat. "Beg pardon, ma'am, but why should I take your word and notify the Dragon of your arrival? Do you have any proof of your identity? You're alone, no clan, no soldiers, no papers of introduction."

She looked down at Dog, who stared up at her, tongue hanging out of his mouth. "You hear that, Dog? They don't believe I am who I say I am. How should I convince them? Kill them both? That seems rude. I am, after all, here to ask a favor."

She lifted the collar of her jacket. "It's blue. Isn't that enough?"

"Sorry, ma'am, lots of people wear blue. They're not all the Azure Dragon."

She nodded and picked up Dog. Then, she squatted, placing her left foot behind and across her right, twisting so her shoulders faced left and her head was turned all the way back, her right hand over the top of Dog, the left turned up and below the animal.

"Infinity Bagua: Axis Climb."

She uncorked, twisting back to the right as she rose and leapt to the top of the wall.

Jet stood with his mouth open as her feet settled onto the gate header; Quinn took two steps back and held his spear at the ready, its savage tip directed at her.

"Come now, Quinn. I'm not attacking, I'm just here for a little visit. You don't want to disrespect the head of a dragon clan, do you?"

Quinn looked at Jet, who shrugged bony shoulders in response. He straightened, set his spear to the side, and bowed from the waist. "No ma'am, I do not. I apologize for not recognizing you. Please allow us to escort you inside."

"It would be my pleasure."

Quinn turned to Jet. "Watch the gate. Hopefully, I'll be back shortly."

Jet leaned in and spoke in loud whisper. "But how do you know she is who she says she is, Quinn?"

Quinn sighed. "I don't, Jet. But she just jumped to the top of the gate. She could snap both our necks before we noticed. No reason to try to stop her, is there now?"

Jet nodded. "I suppose not. Good day, ma'am. And your little dog, too."

Akina smiled. "Thank you, Jet. When I'm in charge, I'll keep you as a guard here. You're doing excellent work."

"Thank you, ma'am. Wait, what did you mean—"

Quinn silenced him with a sharp cut of his hand.

••••••••••

Behind its bonescript walls the White Dragon Fortress remained unchanged from Akina's previous visits. An array of barracks, kitchens, storage, and training areas were separated by small, artful gardens and neat hedges. In the center, a stone building perched over the river held a large open space for ceremonial visits.

Akina sat in a smaller room, at a table large enough for twelve, and sipped tea while she waited for the White Dragon. Servants came and went, offering treats and snacks, arguing in whispers about her identity, and occasionally questioning the appropriateness of Dog's presence.

Akina fed the animal one of the fine cookies that had been brought and sighed. "How long do I wait before raising a fuss, Dog? I'm not Akina, the Patient Witch. Or Akina, the Long-Suffering Witch. They wouldn't have dared leave me just sitting here ten years ago."

A rustle of robes and quick movement from the hall outside caught her attention.

"She said that? You're sure?"

A woman, hair as white as the snow on the Spine of the World, half a head taller than Akina, dressed entirely in robes of white trimmed and belted in gold, strode into the room. She took in Akina, her clothes, the tea, and Dog in quick flickers of her direct, piercing green eyes.

"Akina."

Akina stood and brushed her hands on her trousers, dislodging a few crumbs. "White Dragon, it's been a while. Thank you for seeing me." She bowed, a quick bend of her neck, her eyes never leaving the White Dragon's.

The older woman stepped closer and stared hard at Akina's face, then nodded. "Azure Dragon. Forgive our rudeness. I was not expecting your visit. We had some questions as to your identity."

Akina smiled. "Of course, you did! It's been, what, ten years? Twelve? I can't expect your guards to recognize me, can I?"

The White Dragon nodded. "May I join you?"

Akina sat back down. "It's your house, of course you can."

The older woman nodded and waited while a servant pulled a chair out for her. She lifted a hand and two others went scurrying for more tea.

"Welcome to White Dragon Fortress, Azure Dragon."

"Thank you for your hospitality, White Dragon." Akina sipped her tea, snapped another cookie in half, and fed the broken piece to Dog.

"How are you? How is your clan?"

Akina sighed. "I have been better, White Dragon. My clan is much reduced, as you know."

"I greatly regret the fall of the Azure Dragon Clan." An earthenware cup was set in front of her, a clay pot quickly placed next to it. A servant poured steaming liquid from one into the other.

"That's kind of you to say, though we're not completely fallen, are we? I'm still around."

The White Dragon nodded. "As you say."

"In fact, I have heirs. Future Dragons, one or both of them. Which is part of why I'm here."

The older woman blew across the surface of her tea, then sipped it. "Congratulations to you on your heirs, Azure Dragon. My own are the joys of my life. We should gather the dragon clans to recognize them. Are they traveling with you?"

Akina smiled grimly. "That's the crux of the matter, isn't it? My children have been taken from me, and I am here to get them back."

The White Dragon sipped her tea, her face stony and emotionless. "Are you accusing my clan of kidnapping your children?"

"No, no, that's not what I meant. I know who took them. I need some help getting them back, that's all."

"I see. We would be glad to offer you whatever assistance is prudent."

"Yeah, that's great! Really, I appreciate it. But I'm afraid I'm going to need some pretty imprudent assistance. The Reaver has them."

Silence reigned as the White Dragon nibbled on a cookie of her own. She swallowed, her eyes locked on Akina's.

"Akina, I do not have the resources to take on the Reaver. Even if I were willing to throw my clan away to help you."

"I know. Don't worry, I didn't come here to beg you to come with me on some kind of suicide mission to get my girls back. That would just be embarrassing for both of us, don't you think?"

"Then, and excuse my forwardness, why *did* you come here?"

Akina smiled. "I'm not here for just *your* help. I'm here to get *all* the dragon clans to help."

The White Dragon swallowed. "What are you saying?"

"I'm going to ring the Epoch Bell."

The servants and soldiers in the hallway behind the White Dragon erupted in incoherent mutterings and veiled threats. Weapons were drawn and sheathed; Akina could feel equal parts anger, fear, and confusion from the warriors.

"So it's true. You have the Millennium Qi. It was said your grandfather meant to give it to you."

Akina shrugged and sipped her drink, her right hand scratching Dog's ears. "This isn't about the Millennium Qi. As the Azure Dragon, head of one of the dragon clans, I have the right to attempt the Epoch Bell. It's always been this way."

The White Dragon's eyes narrowed. "It's always been the case that the clan heads had actual clans backing their claims. You have no such thing, little sister."

"Are you saying no? Telling me I can't try it?"

"The Epoch Bell hasn't been truly rung in a dozen generations. Your grandfather tried and failed. What makes you think you can do it? Have you been east? Is that why you disappeared for a decade?"

"Here's the thing, big sister. It doesn't matter. It doesn't matter where I've been, or what I've been doing, or what abilities I've acquired, or what my chance of success is. Every Dragon has the right to attempt the Epoch Bell once in their life, and I'm claiming my chance. You don't need to know anything else."

"You want to ring the bell, but you have nothing to offer as a leader of the Dragons. If you succeed, you'll simply be dragging all the clans into your personal vendetta."

Akina nodded. "I won't argue. All valid points. But look at the rules. It doesn't say, 'any Dragon with a powerful clan and lofty goals can try to ring the Epoch Bell and unite the dragon clans.' That's your interpretation.

The rule is just that every Dragon gets to try to ring the bell. Once. I'm here for my try. Thanks for the tea, now please take me to your storehouse, pull the dustcloth off the bell, and let me ring the damn thing so we can start planning the rescue of my girls."

"You are very confident."

"And you are procrastinating."

The White Dragon sighed. "If you ring the bell and pull us into war, you could destroy the dragon clans. I have a responsibility to prevent that."

"Do you? Funny, I don't remember that in the Dragon lore. I thought you were just here to guard the bell. So tell me, how are you going to prevent this apocalypse you foresee?"

The older woman took a long sip of tea, her fingers strong and steady on the hot cup. "I will need you to prove yourself before I let you touch the bell. I need some reassurance that you're more than just a lunatic out to destroy us."

Akina slapped her palm on the table. "Fair enough! What proof do you require? Hurry up, time is something I don't have in abundance."

"You will fight. To prove you're more than just a dawn wind."

Akina locked eyes with Dog, who panted and lunged forward, licking her chin before she could pull her head away.

"That's fine. Who do I fight? You?" *I hope she says no. I'm not sure I can beat her.*

"I have nothing to gain by fighting you. I am old and my reputation is set. You will fight my daughter. The next White Dragon."

Not sure I can beat her either.

"No."

"What do you mean, 'no'?"

"Why do people keep asking me that? Is it a hard word? I mean, no, I won't fight your daughter. I know her, or at least, I knew her. She's too skilled. To beat her, I'd have to kill her. Or at least hurt her badly. And I need her strength, for when I ring the bell and usher in the Azure Epoch and lead us all after the Reaver."

The White Dragon's eyes widened around brilliant green irises. "You are confident."

"If I didn't know I could beat your heirs in battle, I wouldn't be trying to ring the bell. It would be a waste of time, wouldn't it? Come on, you know me. My reputation. I'm not stupid. Or crazy."

"Then what do you suggest?"

"I'll fight the younger one. Your boy. If he beats me, which he won't, then that's a boost for your clan. Your at-most-third-strongest warrior beat the Azure Dragon in one-on-one combat. Big kudos all around, right? But you and I both know I can knock him bloody without crippling him. Which leaves your son with a valuable lesson, your clan with no loss of face, and me with my shot at the Epoch Bell."

"I always liked you, Akina."

"I always liked me, too. Does that mean we're good? I fight your son, try really hard to beat him without killing him, then ring the bell? Or do we have to argue more about this?"

The older woman sipped the last of her tea, putting it down with her hand over the top to prevent her servant from refilling the cup.

"Let it be so."

17

Puppy Training

Akina sat cross-legged on the floor, Dog's head in her lap, idly scratching his ears. Two attendants stood by, faces tight and tense as she faced her upcoming match with nonchalance.

"Ma'am, would you like to warm up? Stretch? Partake in preparatory exercises? We are here to bring you whatever equipment you require."

Akina continued stroking Dog. "I don't think I need to warm up for this fight, do you? It's not like it's a serious challenge."

The attendant swallowed and her compatriot, a man barely out of boyhood with a prominent Adam's apple and the scruffy neck of someone bad at shaving, cleared his throat. "It couldn't hurt, could it? And there's no reason to make him angry by fighting unprepared."

She looked up at the young man and nodded, lifting Dog and setting the animal into his arms. "You may have a point. Bring some hot towels. I'll walk about a bit."

The attendants scurried away and she began to walk a figure eight pattern across the well-packed earthen floor of the training area.

White Dragon Clan members had gathered around the edges, standing in groups of two or three, whispering and pointing at the Azure Dragon suddenly reappeared after a decade-long absence. Akina recognized a few elders she'd seen at various functions in her youth.

A stir at the far side of the practice field indicated the arrival of the White Dragon's oldest son, Kru-lin.

He was no longer a boy. A bit taller than average and with a slender build, he moved with the grace and assurance of a martial arts master. He wore white robes edged in gold that draped near the floor and sandals with straps that wound up his calves to his knees.

Kru-lin paused at the other side of the field and began a simple training form. He squatted, lowering himself first on one leg, then the other, cycling his arms through large movements designed to increase blood flow and loosen tense muscles.

Akina continued her walk, eyes on the White Dragon heir. Circle to the right, then to the left, head shifting seamlessly to keep her gaze locked on her opponent as each sure-footed step took her through the infinity symbol that defined her art.

The attendants returned with hot towels. Akina stopped in the center of the pattern, took the towels, and wiped her face and hands. Then she pulled down her cloth wraps and wound them around her hands. She pointed at the female attendant. "Watch Dog. He'll try to jump into the fight if he thinks we're playing. Don't let him."

"Yes, ma'am."

The White Dragon entered the arena from the side, showing preference to neither combatant, and stopped near the center.

"The Azure Dragon is here to prove herself worthy of an attempt to ring the Epoch Bell. She will fight my son Kru-lin and if she wins, we will uncover the bell." She turned to her left, waiting for Kru-lin to nod in agreement, then to Akina.

Akina smiled.

"Then let it begin."

Akina glided across the dirt, feet skimming the surface, balanced perfectly.

Kru-lin was grace personified. He stepped forward, his feet moving so smoothly she suspected he was levitating above the ground.

"Akina."

She grinned. "Kru-lin. Is it cliché to say you've grown? Because you have. Last time I saw you, I think you were chasing the other kids around the gardens behind the practice fields. Now here you are, attempting to fight me one-on-one."

He cocked his head to the side and studied her. "Are you trying to embarrass me so I will fight poorly? I am well beyond such petty tricks."

"I just like teasing people. It's not a tactic so much as a habit."

"I do not understand why we are doing this. I can gauge your qi, and you do not have the power to ring the bell."

"You're worried about the bell? Son, you have a fight on your hands. You should be worried about surviving that before you think about what I might do after."

They began to circle one another, each moving to their right, hands raised in fighting positions. Kru-lin held his left arm outstretched, hand open and fingers pointed at the sky, his body bladed to present Akina with the smallest cross section. Akina's posture was more square to the center, her hands in fists, left across her belly and right by her jaw.

"I prefer to understand the reason for a fight."

Her grin widened. "Does that help you win? I heard you were the greatest analyst of this generation. Yet you're not the strongest fighter in your household, are you?"

His mouth tightened at her words. "My sister is strong."

"And that's just this clan. What about the rest of the world? All that analytical ability and what does it get you?"

"I am strong enough to see that you can't beat me without expending so much energy that you'll be unable to affect the bell. Which brings me back to my first question."

She slid forward, launching a quick series of attacks. Left straight punch, right hook, duck the counter, right low kick.

Kru-lin parried, slid back, countered, then moved away from the low kick to escape unharmed.

Akina chuckled. "Infinity Bagua: Basic Sequence."

Kru-lin shook his head. "Why do you call it that?"

"Because it's so simple. Or maybe I should say . . . foundational."

"It's exactly what I'd expect you to open with."

He's not wrong. He saw every move before I threw it. His reputation is well deserved.

She grunted and closed again, launching another salvo.

Left jab, right straight. Right hook, right kick straight up into his ribs.

He parried the first jab and slid smoothly to his left, avoiding the second. Ducked the hook, then reached down to drag the kick across the front of his body, ending the sequence with a solid punch into Akina's kidney.

She spun away, cracking her neck and wincing at the pain in her back. "Intermediate Sequence."

"Again, exactly what I expected. It's a natural progression from the first. I've read your style, Dragon. You can end this now, before I embarrass you further. We can have tea and discuss your clan's future. I will help you get your girls back. Perhaps even discuss an alliance."

She shook her head. "Sounds good, but I've got this stubborn streak I can't seem to break."

She slid forward. A jab, then another with the same hand. She lifted her right knee as if to kick, planted it, and swung a tight left hook instead. Her right knee rose again, twisting into a round kick to Kru-lin's temple.

It was a more complex combination, yet Kru-lin avoided the jabs, ignored the feinted knee, leaned back just out of reach of the hook, and stepped inside the round kick, landing a hard punch to Akina's sternum and sending her stumbling back.

She coughed and rubbed her chest as they resumed circling.

"Intermediate Sequence Two."

He smiled. "Frankly, I expected more from Infinity Bagua. This is over, Dragon."

"Is that what you think?"

She hopped forward, energized by his words.

A jab, then another, with the left. Feinted right kick, then a hard left hook, and a right kick to the head.

The second jab snapped his head back and the final kick clubbed his shoulder with enough force to send him stumbling across the field.

The crowd muttered. Kru-lin shook his head, more annoyed with himself than hurt. He resumed his stance.

"Intermediate Sequence Two. Maybe we aren't done?"

"That wasn't a progression. That was the same sequence as before."

"Good eye, nephew. Weren't you expecting that? With all your fancy analysis?"

He tightened his lips and closed on her, engaging with his own series of techniques.

His strikes were direct and powerful, his form precise and linear in a way that screamed of thousands of repetitions under the most exacting of instructors.

She ducked and weaved and bobbed out of the way, then returned fire.

"Intermediate Sequence Two."

When they separated, blood poured out of his nose.

He brought back another sequence; she avoided most of it and jabbed him again. "Intermediate Sequence Two." He staggered back, confusion and disbelief warring in his eyes.

Kru-lin planted his foot and spun, his legs lashing out with the motion, first left foot, then right heel, then left foot again, his feet barely touching the ground between kicks.

Akina backpedaled and ducked, then set her feet and closed, jamming his last kick. "Intermediate Sequence Two." Her second punch landed even more solidly, staggering the man.

"I don't like repeating myself, but I will. Had enough?"

He snarled, then let out a breath and relaxed the muscles in his cheeks, blowing anger out through pursed lips. He resumed his stance. Akina shrugged.

"Intermediate Sequence Two."

Her final kick caught him flush on the temple, knocking him to the ground.

She leapt onto his prone body and raised her fists for a finishing blow.

"Enough!" The White Dragon strode onto the arena.

Akina looked at her, then at the prone man beneath her. She saw him relax.

The White Dragon took in the onlookers. "The fight is over. Prepare the storehouse. We enter in one hour. Now, clear this area."

The attendants lowered Dog to the ground and left, following the rest of the crowd as they filed out. Dog trotted over to Kru-lin and licked the man's face.

Akina faced the White Dragon. "Satisfied?"

The woman looked down at her, eyes squinting. "You're still strong, Azure Dragon. I'm not sure I understand how you beat my son with such simple techniques."

She looked at the man, who gently pushed Dog away from his face and stood. Blood stained his white robe.

Akina cracked her neck. "Other people say that when you fight, you should use the other person's weaknesses against them."

Kru-lin's cheeks reddened. "You're saying that I'm weak?"

"You didn't let me finish. I said *other* people say that. Not me. I use other people's strengths against them instead. Much more reliable. You can't always find somebody's weakness, can you? But they'll always show you their strength. Especially in a fight."

The White Dragon nodded slowly. "Your grandfather might have known what he was doing after all."

Kru-lin shook his head. "I don't understand."

Akina patted his shoulder. "You'll belong to me soon, so I'll explain. Maybe it will help you.

"Your strength is your analysis. Your ability to predict.

"You saw the techniques I was using, and you know I'm a skilled fighter. With every exchange you analyzed my movements and anticipated the way I would vary and change my attack with the next pass. Which would normally be pretty smart, right?

"But I knew you would be doing that. So I fought like a beginner. I charged in and ran the same combination over and over again. And just when you were certain I would change it up to surprise you, I instead surprised you by keeping it exactly the same."

"You're telling me that you defeated me by fighting poorly."

She shrugged. "That's one way of looking at it. Really, I beat you by fighting in a way you wouldn't expect."

He sighed and bowed his head. "Thank you for the lesson, Azure Dragon."

She patted his shoulder again. "Thank you for the match! Now let's go ring that bell."

••••••••••

Dog stood on the bare stone floor and stared at the Epoch Bell, tongue hanging out of the corner of his open mouth. He looked impressed, or perhaps stupefied. *As if there's a difference with him.*

The White Dragon waved toward the bell. "Impressive, isn't it? I never get tired of this view."

Akina nodded. The bell was a near perfect cylinder, two hundred feet tall and fifty across. It hung from chains mounted in the chamber ceiling far overhead, the lower section suspended inside a well dug into the stone floor.

The bell's surface was a material Akina had never seen anywhere else: silver-colored bone so polished it could reflect light, like the surface of a still pond.

"I've never even seen it before."

The White Dragon turned to her. "No? Well, it's not surprising. We only open the chamber for attempts to ring the bell. And those are, as you well know, quite rare. You weren't here when your grandfather tried it."

"No. I was . . . elsewhere. What do I do?"

The older woman swallowed. "You don't know?"

Akina shrugged. "Nobody ever told me. Am I supposed to hit it?"

"Yes. As hard as you can, but only once. If you hit it very hard, it will ring out a sound that will pierce your soul. But to invoke the Epoch, you have to hit it so hard that it rings three times."

Despite being belowground, the chamber was more than large enough to house the bell, hinting at the tremendous size of the catacombs beneath that housed the White Dragon Clan's treasures.

"How does it work?"

The White Dragon shook her head, white hair shifting around her shoulders with the movement. "I'm not sure. I think there is a separate mechanism inside, and when you strike the bell, the piece inside sways back and forth and hits the shell."

"What happened when my grandfather tried it?"

"He was the first person to make it ring twice in five centuries. My father made it ring once."

"And you?"

The older woman smiled. "I haven't tried. It's not my destiny to have an era of my own."

"I never thought it was mine, either. I don't believe in destiny, though." Akina took a stance, left shoulder pointing at the bell. "You going to stand back?"

The White Dragon paled. "You're doing it right now? You won't give me time to gather the other Dragons?"

"I'm in a hurry. You should stand back. Just in case."

"How will they know that you rang it? Assuming you're successful. They might think we're making up a story. Colluding to gain control of the dragon clans." Kru-lin nodded from behind his mother's shoulder.

Akina looked over the half dozen White Dragon Clan elders that had taken up positions behind their Dragon. "If it rings, everyone on the continent will know. That's what my grandfather told me. Now stand back. Like I said, I'm in a hurry."

The White Dragon bowed, just a tip of her head, and the clan members retreated to the edge of the circular room.

Akina looked at the bell, laughing when she saw her own distorted reflection in its surface. "It makes me look fat! And thick! Look how big my arms are! Lay out a rope, here I come, ready to wrestle anyone in the fortress. Ten bone shards to try; anyone who beats me takes home a hundred!"

Kru-lin snorted; his mother hushed him.

Akina shook her head, dismissing the joke, wrapped her hands, and walked a quick double loop on the flagstones.

As she walked, energy began to circulate through her core, rushing hard and heavy through an infinity pattern, building fast.

Got to make this look good. The girls are counting on me.

The White Dragon and her elders stepped back, forced away by the spillover of Akina's qi. Specks of dust blew back from the floor, pressed immediately into the far corners of the room where the walls met the floor. Even the Epoch Bell moved, shifting ever so slightly on its massive chains.

Dog stood firm and barked.

Akina added arm movements to her walk; as her left foot led, she pulled her right hand back to her hip, palm up, while her left hovered over it, palm down. As she crossed over the center point of her pattern, her hands switched to her left hip, left hand on bottom.

Left; right. Left; right.

Energy built inside her.

Give this everything I have.

She closed on the bell, right foot in front.

Crossed her left foot over and planted it.

Braced her belly and let all her power transfer through her body, torquing up from her core into her sternum, then her shoulder, elbow, and finally into her right fist.

A grunt; she struck the bell.

It absorbed her energy with no apparent effect. The bell hung in place, its stillness itself a judgment.

Akina inhaled slowly, stepping back from the bell and staring at its glossy surface.

She turned to the White Dragon, ready to leave, when the bell emitted a thunderous peal that knocked Akina to the ground, the sound vibrating in her bones.

As she looked up, she saw the clan members on the marble floor, apparently struck unconscious, the White Dragon left with glassy eyes and a face devoid of color.

Akina rubbed her numbed ears and turned to the bell.

A second peal rang out, sending Akina tumbling onto her back, legs kicked up into the air.

She had a sudden sense of what was happening to the bell: Her own energy pulsed through a sphere suspended inside the cylinder, swinging back and forth through a restraining medium. Water? She couldn't tell.

The sphere swung back to the edge, losing momentum, coming achingly close to the shell.

And it stopped.

It swung back to the center, Akina's energy dissipating. She lost every sense of what was going on inside the bell.

Dog stood at the edge of the well, nose just a few feet from its surface, and barked three times.

Akina looked back. The White Dragon was the only other person who was conscious; trails of blood leaked down from her ears and nostrils. She stared at Akina with wide, bloodshot eyes.

Akina rubbed her ear with her knuckles; they came away bloody. She swallowed, the sound echoing inside her head. She adjusted her hat, knocked askew by her fall, and began circulating qi into her eardrums.

The White Dragon rolled onto hands and knees, tried to stand. She fell, catching herself on a weak arm.

The younger woman pushed against the ground with her own hands, trying to stand. The world spun and lurched; she fell back down. Dog waddled over.

"Come here, boy." Her voice was dull and distant. *Hope this goes away soon.*

Dog licked her face. "Not now, boy. Help me up."

He grunted softly. She put a hand on his back and pushed herself to her feet. Akina closed her eyes, resisting a moment of vertigo, then opened them again.

Kru-lin was stirring as the White Dragon tried to regain her feet. Akina took one step, then another, toward the older woman, growing steadier with each attempt.

She stood over the White Dragon, looked into the older woman's eyes, and saw relief. And fear.

"Come on." Akina stuck out a hand and grabbed the older woman's wrist, hauling her upright with one tug.

The White Dragon swallowed. "So close."

Akina let her head hang, letting the brim of her hat hide the smile on her face, then straightened. "I guess it's not my destiny after all."

• • • • • • • • • • •

Six hours later, Akina sat in a hot stone bath set into the floor of an inn five miles up the Turtletail from White Dragon Fortress. It had taken her one hour to recover, two more to take full advantage of the White Dragon's hospitality and enjoy a meal, one and a half to travel to the upriver town and secure lodging and a bath for herself, one to get rid of her White Dragon escort, and half an hour to strip and soak the worst of the soreness out of her bruised body.

Dog barked from the bucket where he was soaking. Zhu and Remy entered the room, stripped, and settled into the water across from her.

"Did you do it?"

Zhu nodded and held out Akina's black silk pouch. "As ordered. Here's your pouch back."

Akina smiled, took the pouch, and set it down next to the bath. She sank into the water, letting the heat work on tight neck muscles. "Good. Thank you."

Remy sighed as the water enveloped his hairy chest and shoulders. "First time I've ever broken into a treasury to make a deposit."

Akina nodded. "I wasn't sure it would work. The White Dragon kept procrastinating. Wanted me to prove myself worthy, wanted to wait for the other Dragons to observe the attempt. I thought she'd refuse to open the treasury and undo the seals. But I have to hand it to her: She knew the rules and she followed them. Didn't like it, but she did it."

Zhu dipped her face in the water. "Tell me again what that was all about?"

Akina smiled. "I can't tell you again, since I didn't explain it to begin with."

Zhu looked at Remy, who shrugged and held his hands up defensively, water dripping off his elbows. "Don't look at me, I'm a henchman. Just following orders."

Zhu turned back to Akina. "Please?"

"You can figure it out if you try. You have all the pieces."

Zhu scratched her nose. "I really can't."

"Okay. First, the Boneshapers will realize their Ancestor Pearl is missing, right? Any day now."

"Sure."

"When they look for it, where will it be?"

"I don't know. In the treasury of the White Dragon Clan?"

Akina smiled. "Exactly! And who will they blame for taking it?"

"I guess . . . the White Dragon Clan?"

"Yes. So they'll march in and demand that the White Dragon Clan opens its treasury so the Boneshapers can get their sacred treasure back. Which the White Dragon will have to refuse because of stupid pride. And an unwillingness to admit that she let someone stick a sacred treasure into her storehouse without her knowledge."

"Oh."

"Because I just rang the Epoch Bell, even if only twice, the rest of the dragon clans will be at White Dragon Fortress when the Boneshapers arrive. They'll wonder who rang the bell and what it means. It's only the second time in a thousand years that someone has gotten two rings out of that stupid thing."

"So they'll . . . fight?"

"That's what I hope."

"What about the griffins?"

Akina cracked her neck and scratched under her fingernails, loosening some dirt. "Try to understand what the Wind Clan soldiers actually saw. They didn't know we were there, not really. They saw a Bat and a Hound damaging their dome and letting the griffins out. In other words, they saw two animal clan members humiliate them in the eyes of the Emperor."

"So they'll be mad too. And they'll want to fight."

"Now you're catching on."

Remy coughed. "None of these plans give any of these clans a reason to go after the Reaver, though. Isn't that what you want?"

"I need all these clans busy so the Tae Kun are free to help me take on the Reaver."

Zhu's nose wrinkled as she thought. "We're starting a war between three groups of clans just so the Tae Kun aren't busy watching their backs? So they're free to help us?"

"That's right."

"And this was your plan all along?"

"Basically."

"You couldn't think of anything simpler?"

"Not really, no. I tried."

Zhu nodded and lowered herself into the water, blowing at its surface so bubbles formed. "The Reaver doesn't understand what he's up against, does he?"

"No. He does not. But he will."

18

Breaking the Law

The sky was clear, leaving the bright sun reign to shine unimpeded on the colored stone mosaic floor of the open-air court where Akina and company sat and ate.

Zhu mumbled around a mouthful of fried rice. "This is so good!"

Remy held up a wooden spoon. "Try this one, it might be even better. The pork bits are soft as butter."

Akina sipped from a wooden cup, the sparkling wine tickling her lips. "Petrik and I always wanted to do this. Never had the chance."

The courtyard was shared by two establishments, restaurants famous across the northwest region of the Empire. Each utilized their own discrete section to serve as outdoor seating in good weather.

Upon arrival, Akina had dragged one of the tables to the center and loudly insisted that staff from both restaurants bring food and drink out so she and her companions could share.

She plucked a bit of pork out of one dish and held it low so Dog could nibble. "We should get some noodle dishes. Waiter!" She waved to one side, summoning a server, then turned and repeated the gesture in the opposite direction.

Two servers rushed forward, one clad in the gray and white of the east side restaurant, the other in a matching outfit in blue and yellow. Upon seeing the commotion, higher ranking hosts from both sides came forward as well, their foreheads pinched in matching expressions of consternation.

Akina patted Dog and muttered, "Remember your parts."

Remy smiled and popped a dumpling into his mouth. "We've got it, Akina." Zhu nodded, the food in her mouth muffling her words.

The east host arrived first. "Ma'am, this really isn't an appropriate place for a pet. I'm sure—"

Akina waved him away. "It's fine, no need to apologize. Dog is very understanding. He doesn't mind, do you, Dog? See, you can tell by the way he's humping your leg right now that he's not upset at the lack of suitable accommodations. Such a good boy. Aren't you a good boy, Dog?"

The man's face reddened, clearly disconcerted by the amorous attention directed toward his calf.

The other host spoke. "We really do need to put this table back where it was, ma'am. We can't have you ordering from both establishments. I'm sure you'd prefer to be over there, where the culture is more suited to your needs. We're happy to help you move to that side of the courtyard."

The first host reddened further. "Clearly your palates are more acclimated to *their* food. My staff and I would be happy to move your table over to their side so you can continue to enjoy their fine cuisine in peace."

Zhu swallowed hard and half-stood. "Are you trying to drive us away? Do you even know who she is? That's Akina Azure, the Spiral Witch! You should both be begging to bring her whatever she wants! She's an Imperial treasure, and you two are mere servants!"

Akina held her straw hat in her hand and fanned her face while shaking her head. "Now, now, Zhu, no need for all that vitriol. And maybe you shouldn't be saying my name aloud. Remember, there's a price on my head everywhere in the Empire." She smiled sweetly at the hosts, whose reddened faces rapidly drained of color.

The first host swallowed. "Price? Akina Azure?"

She held up a pair of bone shards. "Not to worry, I'm not wanted for stealing. Just some misunderstandings about a few dozen deceased soldiers."

Remy tugged on the arm of one of the servers. "I hear you have fire noodles? Could you bring us a large order of those? And another jug of the rice wine. It was excellent." The man nodded, took a quick glance at his stunned boss, and hurried back toward the kitchen of the west side business.

The other server turned to leave as well, but Remy caught him and repeated his instructions.

"Yes, sir, fire noodles."

Remy frowned. "Don't forget the wine."

"But, sir . . ."

"I like to compare! Also, I've been sober for days. Do you hear me? Days! My liver thinks I've abandoned it. Poor thing. There, there, precious, we have work for you to do today." He patted his right side as he spoke.

"Yes, sir."

The hosts backed away, each in the direction of their respective businesses. Dog barked after them. Akina bit into a dumpling.

Remy smiled. "When did we come here? Wait, did we come here? I don't remember us being this far west."

"*We* didn't. Petrik and I came here. On our honeymoon."

"Ah."

Zhu looked at Remy, then at Akina. "Who's Petrik? Wait, he's one of the Five, right?"

Remy patted her arm. "He was. And Akina's husband. He passed."

Zhu nodded. "Sorry. He was your husband?" She pointed at Remy and Akina. "So you two never . . ."

Remy and Akina snorted with laughter, the big man pounding on Zhu's back as he worked to catch his breath. "Oh, the idea of us as lovers! I haven't laughed this hard in too long!"

Zhu looked at Akina again. "What's so funny?"

Akina shook her head. "I lack certain . . . attributes that Remy looks for in a partner. We are old friends, that's all."

Remy patted his stomach and drained another cup of rice wine. "What do you think will come first, the fire noodles or the Tae Kun?"

Akina looked up at the flags flying over the corners of the square, all bearing the orange and blue of the Tae Kun. "We'll find out soon enough. Meanwhile, eat up. No idea when our next decent meal is going to be. Right, Dog?"

Dog barked and ate more pork as she scratched behind his ears.

Remy ran fingers through his beard, checking for morsels of food as he scanned the perimeter of the courtyard. "Oh damn."

Akina raised one eyebrow at him. "What?"

"They're here, and I was really looking forward to the fire noodles."

Akina nodded and looked down. "You ready, Dog?" He stood and barked, tail wagging.

Zhu stuffed another dumpling into her mouth. "I see them too."

The background chatter in the courtyard subsided, then ceased altogether, replaced by chairs scraping on stone as people hurried to stand and exit the space.

Tae Kun soldiers appeared in the courtyard's exits: first a pair to the north, then the south, then more filing out of both restaurants. They wore heavy bone armor: helmets of trimmed and polished ogre skulls, jerkins of heavy leather embedded with vertebrae and finger bones, and kneecaps and skull fragments reinforcing shoulders and elbows. The pieces were painted in orange and royal blue, the sigil of the Tae Kun displayed prominently across the soldiers' backs.

The soldiers themselves were heavily built, thick bands of muscle showing wherever the armor left skin exposed at the neck and forearms. They carried long spears and heavy axes, vicious repeating crossbows stocked with bone-tipped arrows strapped to their backs.

Zhu stood. "You sure I shouldn't get us out of here?"

Remy shook his head and drained a jug of wine. "Stick to the plan, girl. You'll be safe. Mostly."

"Not a girl."

"You can register your complaint with the Tae Kun magistrate."

"Well, maybe I will!"

Akina coughed and got to her feet to face the soldiers. "They're coming. Remember, make it look good, but not too good."

Remy stood and patted her back. "We know."

• • • • • • • • • • •

As the last few patrons left the courtyard, jugs of wine and skewers of food clutched in their hands, two of the soldiers stepped to the side to let a bigger man pass. He stood half a head taller than the others, with a gold stripe as wide as his palm painted across each shoulder.

He strode to a clear spot five yards ahead of the soldiers and faced Akina. Tilting his helmet back, he exposed a pockmarked face and smiled.

"Are you Akina Azure?"

Akina looked at him and tilted her head. "Who's asking?"

"I am Sergeant Mar Quhn of the Westlock City Watch. I am here on a mission sanctioned by the Tae Kun. Are you Akina Azure?"

Akina looked left and right, taking in Zhu's and Remy's stern expressions. "Nope."

The sergeant was about to continue, but her answer stopped him with his mouth open. He cleared his throat. "Excuse me?"

"I said no. You have the wrong person. I'm sure it's embarrassing, causing all this trouble for no reason. Sorry. Have a nice day."

"You're *not* Akina Azure? The Spiral Witch? The Azure Dragon?"

"Never heard of her."

"I . . . don't believe you."

"You know, I should be offended by that, but it's your lucky day. I'm in a generous mood. The dumplings here are really good, and I've had some wine, so I'll forgive you. Now go on about your business, Sergeant."

"I'm sure you are Akina Azure."

She leaned forward and squinted at him. "Are you?"

"Yes, I am. Quite sure. You can't fool me."

"Is that a bet?"

"You're making this difficult. I know who you are."

She sighed and pulled lengths of ivory cloth out of her sleeves. "You see, this is the kind of thing that always bothers me. You come out and you ask me whether I'm Akina Azure. So I answer, as any reasonable person might, and you say you already knew. If you already knew the answer, why did you ask the question? Why not just come out and say, 'I know you're Akina Azure; come with us'? It's disrespectful."

"I never thought of it that way. I was just giving you a chance to surrender." Ten more soldiers filed into the courtyard, forming a wall along the north side.

"Surrender? You could have asked, you know? Just say, 'please surrender.' It's not so hard, is it? But no, you have to come out here and ask a rhetorical question of me like you're some kind of bigshot."

"I wasn't trying to be disrespectful. I do need you to come with us." He swayed back and forth, from one foot to the other, his eye twitching as she spoke.

"Well, I need to stay here and finish my meal. It sounds as though our needs conflict. How are you going to resolve that?"

"I'm—well, I mean, my men and I will force you to come along. If we have to."

Zhu stepped forward. "You can't force her! She's the Spiral Witch. She's going to paint this mural red with your blood if you try to take her by force!"

Akina cleared her throat. "Zhu, when I tell people I'm not the Spiral Witch and then you tell them that I am, it's very confusing."

"He didn't believe you, though."

"I know, but you have to commit to the bit. Also, let's not get too hasty with the threats of violence. That's a very graphic image."

"Well, these guys aren't showing you the proper respect."

Ten more soldiers filed in, blocking off the south.

The sergeant lowered his helmet over his face. "I don't want any bloodshed, ma'am, but if you insist, you'll find us more than capable."

Akina turned to Remy. "You take the ten on the right, I'll take the ten on the left."

Remy pointed at the men, counting silently. "That still leaves about fifteen soldiers. For Dog?"

Dog barked, his tail wagging.

Akina shook her head. "Dog doesn't fight. Zhu, stay back."

Zhu nodded. Remy drew rope darts and began spinning them overhead. Two soldiers stepped around and in front of the sergeant, locking heavy shields together to protect him.

Akina pointed. "Last chance to walk away."

The sergeant shook his head. "It's your last chance to surrender before things get ugly."

Akina bent her legs into a quarter squat, then exploded up and forward, leaping thirty feet through the air at the sergeant and his men. She cocked back one fist while midair, punching directly into the center of the two shields as she landed.

"Infinity Bagua: Partial Function."

Her energy, combined with the kinetic energy of her fist, skipped through the shields and the men and into the body of the sergeant.

With a crack like a hot stone left in a bonfire the sergeant fell, his head bouncing roughly off the mosaic.

The soldiers looked at each other, then at Akina. One shouted, "She's using skip techniques! Reinforce shields!"

The soldiers began to weave their qi into their shields, forming barriers similar to Remy's den techniques.

"Remy!"

"I see it."

Tae Kun martial arts were developed to fight the Wedge north of the Dreadwall, where the largest tyrants and leviathans roamed. Few humans could fight in single combat against a fifty-foot-long, twenty-thousand-pound undead lizard. The Tae Kun tactic required shield bearers to use martial techniques to nullify the Wedge attacks while the strikers waited for openings to launch massive counterattacks.

The strategy worked fairly well on the Wedge; it doubled as an effective way to fight martial heroes like Akina.

Dog trotted over to the fallen sergeant as the soldiers closed on Akina, linking their shields to form a wall of magically reinforced bone.

Remy sent two rope darts flying at the soldiers opposite the sergeant's position. Akina leapt up, stomping the ground as she landed. Dog closed on the sergeant. Zhu traced circles in the air with her arms.

Lifted shields blocked the darts with matching clangs.

"Medium Wave." The soldiers near Akina shifted as the ground rippled under their feet, but they were alert and agile enough to stay upright.

Dog reached the sergeant, looked around, lifted one leg, and loosed a stream of urine on the man's torso.

Zhu grunted. "They're sealing me in. I can't form a gate."

Remy nodded. He cleared his throat and raised his voice, enunciating carefully. "I don't see how we're going to get out of this one, Akina! I think we're trapped."

Akina sighed as she spun and kicked a pair of soldiers back. "I know! After all these years, I think we're finally in a situation we can't get out of! It's so sad!" The words came slowly, as if she were reading off a script.

Zhu shook her head and muttered, "I told you guys to rehearse more."

Remy looked at her and whispered, "We're fighters, not actors."

"Watch your back."

Remy grunted as a descending spear grazed his hair, severing a tuft that drifted to the tile, and continued into the ground, splintering colored stone pieces with the impact. He spun, lashing out with a kick that sent the spear wielder stumbling back. More shield bearers closed on his position.

Dog barked and trotted over to another fallen soldier. This one was conscious; he waved the animal away with a dagger.

A group of soldiers had linked shields in a tight circle around Akina. She feinted left and struck right, her blows having little effect beyond slowing the advance of the Tae Kun.

Remy lowered his head and charged the shield bearers near him, ramming his shoulder into the shield wall and knocking four of them off their feet. He growled as more danced forward to replace and protect their comrades.

Akina took a breath. "It is truly looking hopeless now, old friend! Save yourself if you can!"

Remy looked up, lips moving before he spoke. "I won't leave you, Akina! I'll never abandon my precious friends!"

Zhu picked a jug of wine off the table and sipped from it. "Please end this quickly."

Shield walls formed around both Akina and Remy. Soldiers with spears stood outside the rings, waiting for an opening. When they saw a back turned to them, the shield bearers would part, letting the spears stab between them for a quick strike.

Remy blocked three of the strikes with a Lesser Den while Akina spun and danced to save herself.

Remy called out, "I'm running out of strength! I don't know how much longer I can last!"

Akina swore as a rock chip struck her cheek, drawing blood. "Just hold on!"

Zhu tilted the jug back, swallowing as rice wine spilled down her face. She lowered the jug, coughing at the burning in her throat. Four soldiers approached her.

"Drop it!"

She looked at the jug, shrugged, and let it fall to the ground. She held her arms up, hands open. "I'm just sitting here. See, no weapons?"

Remy flinched and spun as spear swings and thrusts came closer and closer to his body.

Akina slipped on stone loosened by the soldier's blows and fell to a knee.

Two soldiers came to Zhu and tied her hands together. "We have the girl!"

Zhu struggled, pulling at the leather tie. "I'm not a girl, I'm a woman! What is wrong with everybody?"

Remy dropped his rope darts and punched at the shields closest to him. He knocked back two soldiers, but two behind him drew closer and slipped leather straps around his ankles.

Within seconds, Akina had also been tied. Dog barked; a soldier scooped him up in his arms; the animal licked the man's face. Two soldiers fitted their shields into a litter, then rolled their unconscious sergeant onto it. Two others came, grabbing the corners, and they carried him away.

Akina looked at the ropes tying her hands together. "We should never have come to Westlock, Remy. We should have known better than to challenge the Tae Kun."

"What? Oh, right. Um . . . We should have known! I'll never forgive myself! Never, I tell you!"

A dark hood fell over Akina's head.

Only then did she let the smile she'd been fighting creep across her lips.

19

In the Doghouse

The magistrate was a small woman with dark hair and flat features that reminded Akina of the nursemaid who'd raised her.

She wore gray robes, their simple cut belying the quality of materials, broken by an orange and blue patch on the chest showing the source of her authority. A tall, square hat perched precariously on her head, forcing her into an unnaturally erect posture and slow, deliberate movements.

Akina fought to resist the powerful urge to knock the hat off.

"Are you, in fact, Akina Azure?" The woman's voice was confident and strong, deeper than her frame would suggest.

I need her to keep me here but not get so frustrated that she starts cutting pieces off Zhu. Or Remy.

"I've been over this already. I'm not her. But the fact that you've had me brought here suggests that you don't believe me." She looked around at the square room, featureless other than the simple wooden table and two singularly uncomfortable wooden chairs placed in its exact center.

The magistrate nodded, ever so slightly, and Akina braced as she expected the hat to teeter off the woman's head.

"I am aware of what you said. However, I have met Akina Azure, and you look exactly like her. If you continue to insist that you are someone else, I have to verify that claim."

"How do you plan to do that?" Akina, hands bound behind her, wrinkled her nose to relieve an itch.

"I will have a team of physicians come in and give you an exam. They will look for any signs of methods used to disguise yourself as Akina Azure."

"I see."

"It will be a most invasive and unpleasant exam. Which we can skip if you admit to who you are."

"You know, I have a theory about physicians and their exams." Her itch unrelieved, Akina twisted her neck, trying to reach far enough down to rub her nose on her collar.

The magistrate sighed. "Do tell."

"Physician visits are always unpleasant. Needles going in all sorts of places. And the inevitable probing examination of nether regions which simply can't be the source of every problem, can they? Why would anyone need to probe my ass to understand why I have a cough? Can you tell me that?"

"I cannot, not being a physician."

"That's the thing. They can't either. And they know it, too. They make their exams unpleasant, so you don't bother them with trivial complaints. You have to be really sick to put up with what the physician is going to do to you. Saves them time and energy helping people who aren't really desperate for help."

"Do you think so? Shall I call some in to discuss your theory? We can even conduct a small wager between us. On whether a rectal exam does, in fact, become part of their determination of your identity."

"Oh, please. You know it would. What would I get for winning?"

"If you're right, I'll bring someone in to scratch your nose. Or you admit to being who I think you are and I can untie you right now."

"Why would you do that? Aren't I your prisoner?"

"Yes, but the real Akina Azure would be able to snap those ropes effortlessly. If you admit to being her, I'll admit they present a meaningless inconvenience and remove them."

"Then doesn't the fact that I haven't snapped them prove I'm not Akina Azure?"

The magistrate narrowed her eyes. "It proves something. Perhaps that you are trying to waste my time. Which is not something I understand."

"Don't try too hard, you'll injure yourself. You don't have enough of the full picture to figure things out."

The magistrate clapped her hands once. The door opened and a uniformed soldier entered with two mugs of tea. He set them on the table between the women and left, shutting it behind him.

Akina tilted her chin to point at the cup. "I can't exactly reach that. Are you going to lift it to my lips so I can drink?"

"No. I will sit here, drink my own, and watch yours grow cold."

The magistrate proceeded to do just that, sipping carefully at her drink while maintaining eye contact with Akina.

This bitch is good. I've been tortured before, but never with cold tea.

She let out a sigh. "All right, you win. I'm Akina."

The magistrate nodded. "Very well."

"Now will you untie me?"

"I think I'll finish my tea first."

"Oh, come on. That's just cruel."

"I don't think you and I have the same definition of cruelty. You haven't spent much time on that side of the table, have you?"

"I'm a knight errant. I spent most of my life north of the Dreadwall, killing Wedge for their bones. I wasn't on either side of any tables."

"Of course. I'll free you now, but you have to give me something else."

"What do you want? Your men searched me. I don't have anything to give you. And, for the record, I'll want my stuff back when you release me."

"Your belongings are safe. I want to know who the others are."

Akina paused. "My dog is named Dog."

"Okay."

"He's called that because—"

The magistrate cut in. "I don't care. Who are the other two?"

"Didn't they tell you themselves?"

"I want to see if your stories match."

"The man is Remy. He's one of the Five Fangs. He's famous, you should have heard of him. The girl told me her name is Zhu Hsa of the Star Clan. I spared her life and she's under sworn parole."

The magistrate nodded, set her tea down, circled the table, and released Akina's hands.

"Don't try to escape. Not that I think you will."

"Why is that?" The Spiral Witch rubbed her chafed wrists.

"I think you want to be here. What I don't know is why."

"Your soldiers were very skilled. They overwhelmed us."

"Don't patronize me. We never would have known you were in the city if you hadn't practically shouted that information to the world. And those soldiers were skilled, but they couldn't have captured two of the Five Fangs without sustaining heavy losses. Not if you were trying to resist. Unless you two are severely diminished from what you were."

"It has been a long time." Akina picked up her tea and drank from the still-warm liquid. "When did you say we met?"

"I didn't. And we didn't actually meet."

"Ah. Nice one."

"Thank you. It's good to be appreciated. Care to tell me why you were so eager to see the inside of a watch station?"

"Not really."

"I would very much like to know."

"Maybe it's not here that I want to be."

"What does that mean?"

Akina swallowed. "You're not going to keep me here forever, are you? This is just temporary. I'm sure you've sent word to the higher ups in the Tae Kun that I've been captured. Something tells me that Arha is going to hear about it and he's going to want to speak to me."

"He might. Or he might order you executed."

"Doubt it. He'll consider it, I'm sure, but then he's going to start wondering what I'm up to. That's his strength, you see. His curiosity. He's not very bright, but he is very inquisitive."

"You haven't had contact with Arha Tae Kun in a long time."

"No, I guess not. Has he changed? Your face isn't telling me that I'm wrong."

"What is my face telling you?"

"Actually, nothing. You must be hell to play tiles with. Your features are like cold bone."

The magistrate smiled. "I'll take that as a compliment. If you wanted to meet with Arha, why not just go to his fortress and ask for him?"

Akina stretched her arms to the sides and behind her, relieving tension in her shoulders. "I don't think that would have worked. Guards at the gate, me not being on the list, you know the drill. Who would take the initiative to bother the chief over me? But cause a ruckus, get involved in a fight, having a reward on my head . . . that's a way to attract attention."

The magistrate set her empty mug on the table. "If that is, in fact, your plan, I can't fault it. I do wonder, though."

"What?"

"What do you want with Arha?"

Do I tell her?

"I need help from the Tae Kun."

"With what? Perhaps I can assist you."

"My daughters were kidnapped. I need help getting them back."

The magistrate stiffened. "Daughters? So that's why you disappeared these past fifteen years."

"I was south, raising my girls. But they've been taken, and I need to get them back."

"I see. Care to tell me who took them?"

"I'll tell Arha."

The magistrate nodded and stood. "I am satisfied for the moment. I may have more questions for you later."

"Sure. I'm not going anywhere."

"That is correct."

"Can I see Dog? And Remy and Zhu?"

"You mentioned Dog first. You care more about your pet than your friends?"

"Dog doesn't understand what's going on. He's just missing me. Remy and Zhu can take care of themselves."

"Very well. I'll put you in a cell together while we wait for word from Arha."

"Thanks."

....

Dog barked from the inside of the cell, his tail wagging as Akina, led by three soldiers, approached.

A spear-carrying soldier turned the lock with a key cut from the finger-bones of a sea ogre, then swung the heavy door open. Akina entered the cell, kneeling to pet Dog as the door thudded shut behind her.

"How are you, boy? Were you worried? No, of course you weren't." He licked her hand, then hopped up on his back feet to try to lick her face.

Remy grunted from where he sat, back against the wall of the cell. "You all right?"

She looked at him. "I'm fine. How rough did they get with you?"

He smiled as he leaned into the light, showing her bruises on his face. "You should see the other guy."

"Why? Did you hurt him?"

"No, but he was cute."

Zhu stood at the other side of the cell and used her fingers to undo knots from her tangled hair. "He's fine. He's been grumbling since they stuck us in here, worried about you."

Dog whined and Akina scratched the back of his neck. "The magistrate doesn't want us hurt, she just wants to know what's going on."

Remy nodded. "The magistrate might not hold any anger toward us, but she's not the only one in here."

"The Reaver wants us alive. The Emperor might want us dead if he knew we were starting a war, but I doubt he does. So they need me under control, and you're the leverage. I told you, I have this figured out."

A fresh voice came from the slats in the door. "Is that what you think?"

The sergeant who had first accosted them stood at the entrance, six soldiers flanking him; different from the ones who had escorted Akina. The muscles along his jaw were clenched, his eyes narrowed, nostrils flaring with every breath.

Remy stood and Zhu got to her feet. Dog barked once. Akina turned to face the door.

"What do you want?"

He leaned to the side and spat on the floor. "I should probably say something like I want to know what you're up to, or what your plans are, or why you involved us in whatever ridiculous scheme you're planning. But really, I just want a bit of good old-fashioned revenge."

Akina locked eyes with him, then looked over the other soldiers. They returned hard glares devoid of sympathy.

"Look, we didn't kill anybody." *Yet. Best not to mention that part.* "I get that you're embarrassed, and I'm sorry. I needed the attention of your clan, and this was the best way to get it."

The sergeant nodded. "You didn't just assault me. You attacked the pride of our clan. That filthy animal assaulted the pride of our clan. If you turn him over to me now, I'll walk away and leave the rest of you to whatever bullshit you're trying to do."

Akina looked at Dog, who barked happily. *Still not very bright, are you?* "You can't have Dog."

"That's what I thought you'd say. Before I'm finished, you'll be begging me to take that mutt off your hands."

He reached into a pouch hanging at his belt and pulled out a white ceramic vial about half the size of a fist.

"Remy, get ready to make a den."

"I don't have my darts, and the walls are reinforced with seals that are going to interfere with whatever I do."

"Just . . . try."

He sighed and let out a deep breath; Akina could feel him gathering qi.

Zhu edged toward the back wall of the cell. "I can't gate us out of here. The walls are imbued with spells that block me."

Akina nodded and started to pull up her own qi, swirling it in a figure eight centered on her belly. "I know. We'll be okay."

The sergeant shook his head. "You really won't be. This is filled with spittle from a green tyrant. You know what will happen after I drop this in your cell? It will evaporate, releasing the most corrosive gas known this side of the Dreadwall. It might not kill you, but I can promise you'll never be pretty again."

"The magistrate doesn't want us harmed. How are you going to explain this?"

He shrugged. "This is a jail. Criminals get in here. It's your bad luck that someone with a grudge against you managed to sneak a weapon like that past us. Still, it happens. We're soldiers, after all, not jailers."

"If you wanted to use that, what are you waiting for? I bet that stuff is expensive, isn't it? It's pretty hard to bottle. Dangerous. I've been close to green tyrants. Have you?"

Zhu cleared her throat. "Akina?"

Akina ignored her. "I don't think you want to drop that vial. If it is what you say it is. You don't want to have to explain to the magistrate what happened. You're bluffing. You think I'll wet myself and hand over Dog, begging you to let us live."

"Akina, there's something you should know."

The sergeant's face reddened, skin ruddy under his pockmarks. "You should watch your mouth, bitch."

"No bitches here. Dog's a boy, as I think you're aware. And no, I'm not handing him over to you. He's a very good boy, and you're not a very nice man."

Remy prepared to use a technique.

The sergeant growled, "I don't want to use this, but you're forcing my hand! Give me the animal!"

"You have my answer already. You're really bad at this, you know? You keep asking questions when you already have the answers. It's a failure in communications skills. You should ask around, maybe there's a teacher who could help you. It's a big city, after all."

"Akina, there's something going on outside."

The sergeant sneered. "You're trying to distract me. It's not going to work. Last chance before I toss this vial into your cell."

Akina shook her head. "It's your last chance to walk away without something very unpleasant happening to you. I suggest you take it. You do not want firsthand knowledge of how I got my nickname."

Remy laughed. "Spiral Witch. I almost forgot that story."

The sergeant's face paled as he stuck his arm through the slats in the door, lifting the vial up and preparing to slam it toward the floor.

"Remy, now!"

"Way of the Bear: Lesser Den." Remy's qi swirled out and formed a bubble conforming to the inside of the cell, pinning the sergeant's arm against the door.

The pockmarked man grimaced. "What?"

Zhu walked up to Akina and tapped her shoulder. "You have to listen. There are gates opening. Three of them. Strong ones, right outside. I can feel them."

Akina blew air through tightened lips. "That was faster than I expected."

"Is it the Reaver?"

"I can't imagine who else it could be." She walked up to the sergeant and reached for his clenched fist and the vial within. Remy's energy blocked her from it as much as it trapped the sergeant in place.

Soldiers shuffled forward, crowding at the sergeant's sides to examine his predicament. Two grabbed him by his jerkin and tried to pull him free.

"Stop! My arm is bent through there. You'll break it if you do that!" They released him.

"What should we do?"

"Get spears! Stab them!"

Two of the soldiers ran off to find more weapons.

Akina turned to Zhu. "How many people could come through those gates?"

The younger woman shrugged. "A lot. An army. Are they here for us?"

Akina smiled. "It certainly looks like it."

20

Into the Fire

Horns sounded from a distance. The soldiers traded glances. "Sergeant, that's the call for reinforcements."

The sergeant turned to face them, arm still trapped inside the cell, sweat beading on his forehead. "I know what the horns mean!"

"Sir, what should we do?"

He turned to look into the cell, then faced his men. "Go! I'll be fine."

Zhu looked at Akina. "What do I do?"

"All you can do is focus on those gates. Try to feel where they are, or what's coming through them. If you can."

Zhu nodded and walked to the back corner of the cell, closing her eyes. Remy was breathing hard, the air from his nose rustling his full mustache, cords showing in his neck as he turned his head from side to side.

He can't hold on much longer.

"Remy, drop the den on my signal."

"If you wait much longer, I'll be dropping it on my signal, which will be me passing out." Dog barked and trotted toward the door.

"If you have the strength to make dumb jokes, you're strong enough to hold out for a few more seconds."

The soldiers hurried up the hallway and away from the cell. Akina waited until they had turned a corner, leaving nothing but their sergeant and the echo of a door slamming behind them.

Another round of horns sounded, followed by distant screaming.

Akina looked into the sergeant's eyes. "You called me pretty, but you threatened Dog. Teenage me might have called us even, but unfortunately for you—" She signaled Remy with the hand behind her back.

The den dropped, freeing the sergeant while removing the barrier between Akina and his hand.

She grabbed his wrist in her right hand and whipped it up and around. Her left was cupped below his hand.

The sergeant's upper arm snapped like a dry branch. He opened his mouth to scream just as he dropped the vial.

Akina caught the vial in her open hand and twisted the sergeant's arm back in its original direction, grinding the bones against each other. He screamed, eyes bloodshot and angry.

"As I was saying, not a teenager anymore." She pulled on the arm, setting a foot against the door for leverage, and dislocated his shoulder. Then she let go, shoving slightly so he fell away from the door.

She turned to Remy. "What are you thinking?"

He leaned forward, hands on his knees. "We can't stay here. They know how dangerous you are; they'll come at us with overwhelming force. We have to meet them on our terms."

"Agreed. How?"

The sergeant climbed to his feet, holding on to the door to overcome the shaking in his legs, and muttered curses through the slats.

Remy looked at Zhu. "They might break the seals preventing a gate, then she can get us out."

"I'm not betting on Faceless making a mistake like that. Too risky."

"Then we have to get out and fight free. Take the door down first, then maybe get our weapons. I feel naked without my armor."

Akina nodded. "You were here overnight. How tough are the walls?"

The sergeant laughed between shallow breaths. "These cells are designed to hold martial artists. You can't break free."

Remy shook his head. "Akina, you're strong enough to batter them down but it will take time, make noise, and leave you drained."

"What about together?"

"Same. And it's all around. Floor, ceiling too." He straightened, breath caught, and cracked his neck.

Zhu opened her eyes. "I know where the gates are. Two to the north, one to the south. I can't tell exactly how many came through, but it's at least ten men in each."

Akina locked eyes with Remy, who glanced at the vial. She nodded. "Can you contain the vapors?"

"If we time it carefully. I don't see any other choices."

"Neither do I. Be ready."

The sergeant watched her approach the door. "What are you thinking? You can't . . ."

Akina held up the vial of corrosive fluid, waited for Remy's nod, and smashed it against the back of the locking mechanism on the door.

Wisps of green gas immediately wafted away, tracing ghostly lines through the air. Remy held his hand out in front of his heavy body, whispering, "Way of the Bear: Hold the Cub." Energy shed off his hands and onto the door, forming a sphere around the lock.

Zhu walked forward; Akina grabbed her and pulled her to the side as one of the trails of gas almost touched the younger woman. "Watch those."

Zhu's eyes widened. "Oh. What does it do?"

"That liquid will eat through the lock." She looked up at the fear blossoming on the sergeant's face. "Sergeant, I'll be sure to let the Tae Kun know who provided us with our means of escape."

He scrambled to the door, reaching through in a vain attempt to grab her with his good arm. "You can't! But I didn't!" Sizzling and popping sounds came from the lock.

"I'm pretty sure you did."

Remy grunted. "Steam is building up in there. The pressure is growing, Akina. I'm not sure I can hold it."

She eyed the lock, then shook the door. It was still stuck. "Remy, you can control the shape of the den, right?"

"Of course."

"Open the back. Vent some of the gases. It will be fine. It's eaten halfway through the lock already."

The sergeant looked to the spot where his lower belly was pressed against the lock on the outside of the door. His mouth dropped open as Remy adjusted the den.

An explosion of steam, superheated air, and corrosive gases blew out of the lock and into the sergeant's midsection, slamming him into the wall opposite the door. He slumped to the ground. The blowback tore apart what remained of the lock, leaving splinters of bone and fire-hardened wood opened in the hole where the mechanism had been set.

"Remy, keep holding it until we're ready to run past. Zhu, cover your face and hold your breath. Ready?" They arranged themselves and nodded.

Remy released the den; Akina yanked the door open; Zhu sprinted through the opening, Dog behind her, Akina taking the rear after Remy.

They ran up the hallway, heading further into the station, away from the horns and sounds of combat. Dog paused to squat and shit next to the sergeant's body.

Zhu turned one corner, then through a doorway. Trails of green gas followed them.

Remy crashed through, then Akina. Zhu grunted. "Come on, Dog! I have to close this door!"

Dog barked, sniffed the air, and ran to catch up. As soon as he cleared the doorway, Zhu slammed it shut.

"Will that hold the gas?"

Remy ran fingers through his beard. "It was a small vial; the gas will dissipate quickly. My guess, it will be safe to walk through there within an hour. Maybe less. It's not the sort of thing that would poison the entire building."

"Okay. Where to?"

Remy looked around, then pointed. "They took our belongings this way. Hopefully it isn't far."

He led the way down a corridor. The air smelled faintly of smoke and blood; they could hear shouting and the clashes of bone-on-bone impact.

Remy waved. "It's this way. I can sense my weapons."

They followed him down one abandoned corridor, through another set of doors, then around a corner. He stopped short and Zhu ran into his broad back.

Akina looked around her friend and saw an alcove. It held a small desk supporting a ledger, a bone-tipped pen, and a small jar of ink. At the back of the alcove was a pair of double doors, ebony wood reinforced with strips of bone until barely a grain could be seen.

Standing before the twin doors was the magistrate, her square hat towering over her head.

Akina stepped around her friend. "We need our things. Bones, weapons."

The magistrate looked over the three, then down at Dog. "You're all still prisoners of this precinct."

Akina shook her head. "We'll be out of this precinct within an hour. Only question is whether we go with them," she pointed over her shoulder in the general direction of the sounds of combat, "or leave on our own."

"Why should I help you escape?"

"You can help us or help the other guys. And while you might not like us very much, the other guys are killing your men right now."

"Because of you."

"What was it you were telling me? If they wanted us, they could have asked nicely. Petitioned Arha for custody. Instead, they came storming in and started slaughtering people. So, choose."

"I'm thinking."

"Thinking for much longer is choosing them over us. They have blood on their hands. I'm just trying to save my girls."

The magistrate nodded, then stepped aside. "Take your things. Go save your girls. I will feel less generous the next time I see you."

"Fair enough." Akina faced the door.

Remy looked down at the magistrate. "Key?"

She sighed and pointed. "It's already open."

"Thanks!" He smiled and followed Zhu through the door.

Zhu was staring at the shelves, stacked high with boxes. "Can we take some stuff?"

Akina sighed. "We're not here to steal. Just get your things. What are you missing?"

"My punch daggers, a little money, some armor, and my pack. Nothing valuable, really."

Remy grunted. "Here's mine. Look in these boxes, yours should be close."

Akina held up a box. "My pack's here. Get your armor on, we're fighting our way out."

The magistrate looked through the open door. "What does the Reaver want with your girls?"

"Nothing. He wants me."

Remy settled his jerkin over thick shoulders and began buckling on strands of bone-reinforced leather. Akina opened her purse and eyed the bone shards inside.

"For the Millennium Qi?"

Akina shrugged. "That's what they're saying."

"Have you considered just giving it to him?"

Akina tucked hand wraps inside her sleeves and slung her pack onto her back. "You want a guy willing to order a slaughter to be even stronger?"

"It's not as if you can stop him. Handing over the Qi is probably your only chance to save your family."

"It's not going to happen, magistrate. Thank you for your advice, we'll be going now."

"But you'll allow slaughter like this to continue?"

"Don't hold me responsible for the foolishness of power-hungry men, magistrate. Goodbye, and I hope you survive."

Dog jogged over to the magistrate and licked her leg, then looked up at her, waiting for a head scratch. She shook her head at him and he trotted after his humans as they left.

Remy looked up and down the next corridor. "Which way?"

Akina pointed. "Gates opened north and south, so we go east."

He drew two rope darts, held them loosely in his hands, and led the way.

• • • • • • • • • • •

Zhu knelt by a pair of bodies; men wearing orange and blue. "They're dead. Not even soldiers."

Akina pointed. "Wounds?"

Dog nuzzled one of the bodies, then turned his head and let out a cough. Remy looked up. "Nothing. Maybe poison?"

"Maybe. Come on."

Remy turned as he heard a growl from behind them. "Bao?"

A giant strode forward, arms spread, fingertips trailing the walls on either side as he stomped. Nearly eight feet tall, the man wore armor decorated in the purple and black of the Reaver. War clubs dangled from each hand: three-foot lengths adorned with heavy knobs of bone around the last foot.

His face did, in fact, resemble that of Little Bao, if Little Bao had tripled in size. And not been dead.

Akina stepped toward the giant. "Wait, are you Little Bao's brother? The simple one?"

Remy started swinging his darts, forming small circles in the tight hallway. "It's Stupid Duow! I remember him!"

The giant swung both clubs in a wide arc; Remy formed a quick den and blocked their path.

The giant growled and lifted the clubs, tearing long gouges into the ceiling.

Akina ducked low and slid forward, kicking at the giant's ankle. "It was Duow. But not Stupid Duow. It was something else." The clubs came down, aimed at her head. A sharp pivot and backstep got her out of harm's way.

Remy shot a dart at the giant's neck; it was blocked with a flick of a club. "No, you're right. Not Stupid. But it was something."

Two Tae Kun soldiers came around the corner from behind the giant, nearly colliding with his back. He swiveled his massive head on his thick, shapeless neck and grinned.

Darts of black light speared from the giant's eyes and pierced the soldiers' chests. Their eyes widened as their faces shrank, cheeks hollowing and skin withering in seconds.

Akina grunted. "You're supposed to tell them what you're doing. That's a Reaver's Reap. Your brother used something similar."

The giant turned to her, the shafts of black light pulsing as energy was sucked into him. He smiled, jagged teeth each as big as Akina's thumbs peering out between dark lips. The soldiers dropped to the floor.

The giant swung his clubs again, but this time Remy's den crumpled under the impact.

Remy fell to a knee. "He's stronger."

Akina grunted. "Of course he is, Remy. That's what the Reap does."

The giant stepped forward and swung at Remy. Akina stomped the floor. "Infinity Bagua: Minor Wave."

The floor rippled, interrupting the giant's balance. Remy ducked under the clubs.

"I remember, he *was* stupid, but we didn't *call* him stupid. Different things."

The giant recovered and prepared to swing again. Dog barked.

Akina jumped, her knee rising to meet the giant's chin. "Cubic Function. Zhu! Go around a corner! Don't let him use the Reap on you!"

The younger woman followed orders as the giant brought his clubs up, absorbing the strike from Akina. He pushed them forward, throwing her down the hallway.

Zhu called out, "What about you? Won't he drain you?"

Remy grunted as twin beams of darkness lashed against his chest. "We can resist it. For a time. You're not trained for it, lass."

Akina landed on her feet and charged forward just as Duow swung his clubs at Remy. They caught his shoulder, sending her friend into the wall, wooden boards splintering with the impact.

The giant leaned in as Akina struck, smile unwavering, his own energy reinforcing his face and dissipating the impact of her strike. He sent her flying with a backhanded swing of his club. Dog stood in the center of the hallway and barked.

Akina panted, watching Remy stand and shake his head to clear it.

He's too strong.

The giant's smile widened as he brought his clubs to a ready position. His body pulsed with stolen energy, a spiritual bonfire of black flame and sickness.

Remy coughed. "It was Dumb Duow. Because he couldn't speak."

Akina nodded. Dog kept to the center of the hall and barked. The giant looked down at the animal.

"Dumb Duow!"

The giant looked at her.

"Talk to your brother lately?"

He narrowed his eyes at her.

"Oh, you don't talk at all, do you? But if you did, you wouldn't have talked to Little Bao. Not lately. You want to know how I know?"

He stared.

"I know because I killed him."

Silence.

"I didn't particularly want to, but the Reaver took my girls, and Bao was in my way, and . . . you can guess the rest, can't you?"

Remy straightened and started spinning his rope darts again.

"I know the Reaver has given you power, and position, and a place in the world. I get it. I do. And maybe you even believe what he's telling you about why he needs the Millennium Qi or why it's important.

"But you and I both know that's not an excuse for taking my girls.

"Anyone who stands with him is going to face my wrath, Dumb Duow. Right now, that means you.

"Drop the clubs and back away or I'm going to leave your mother grieving two of her boys instead of one."

For a moment, he seemed to consider it. Then he raised his war clubs overhead and roared.

It was worth a try.

Akina leaned to the side and scooped up Dog. "Sic him." With an effortless underhanded toss, she threw the animal at the giant's face.

Duow grinned, lowering his clubs, and shot streams of black light from his eyes, hitting Dog full in his small, furry face.

Dog barked and struck the giant in the chest, paws flailing at Duow's skin as he slid to the ground. The beams of black light flickered and faltered, fading with every swipe of Dog's paw.

Didn't expect that, did you? There's a reason Dog is fearless.

Duow looked down in confusion.

Remy launched both darts, faster than Akina had ever seen, on parallel tracks to Duow's face, one just behind the other.

The giant raised his clubs and blocked the first dart.

Dart number two sank deep into his right eye.

He opened his mouth to roar, but Akina was flying toward him. Her knee slammed into the base of the second dagger, driving it through his eye and inside his large but underutilized brain.

Dumb Duow stood, head turning to Akina, then to Remy, then back to the Spiral Witch. He toppled over backward.

Akina panted and looked at her pet. "Sorry, Dog. Dire circumstances. You understand."

Dog hopped onto the giant's torso and barked.

21

Stop Licking That

Zhu walked over to Akina. “Where to now?” Behind her, Dog sniffed at various parts of Duow’s body. The sounds of combat were diffuse and distant; the smell of smoke grew stronger by the minute.

“The building has you sealed in, correct?”

Zhu scrunched up her nose and paused. “Yep. I can form a gate inside the building but not to the outside.”

“Can you tell where the seals are?”

“You mean where we need to walk to before I can gate us somewhere far?”

“Exactly. Is it just the building? Is it the city? Somewhere in the middle?”

“Hold on.”

Remy stroked Dog’s back, trying to calm the animal. He grunted and bent closer to the giant corpse.

Zhu held up a hand. “I’m not sensing anything other than what’s in the walls of the station. But if my brother is with the Reaver’s men, he can seal me off pretty much anytime he wants.”

Akina nodded. “Can you tell where he is? Which direction?”

“Only if he does something. And it would have to be something big.”

Remy called out. “Akina? You should see this.”

She rubbed her temples. “If it’s not a way out of here, then it can wait.”

“I’m not sure it should. Dumb Duow has left us a gift.”

"What?" She turned.

Remy knelt by the body, a red lumpy sphere held in each of his hands, each twice the size of a closed fist. Akina fell back a step. "Are those what they look like?"

Remy shrugged. "Pretty sure."

Zhu walked over to him and reached out to touch one. "What are they?"

Remy snatched the ball away from her. "Be. Very. Careful."

Akina let out a breath. "Zhu, those are fragment packs. Rare and very dangerous."

"What do they do?"

Remy held it up to examine in the light. "Have you ever been hit by a flying fingernail? Minding your own business, perhaps sipping a cup of wine, one of your mates is on the other side of the campfire, clipping their nails, and one comes flying over . . ."

"What? Gross. No. Maybe? I don't know."

"At most, it stings a bit. But what if that fingernail were thrown at you?"

Zhu crinkled her nose in disgust. "Who would throw a fingernail at another person? Where do you get these ideas?"

"Now imagine that fingernail fell with the speed of a diving griffin. Or more. Faster than the fastest wind. A hundred miles an hour. Five hundred. A thousand."

"Okay, sure, that would really sting."

"Fast enough to tear skin and split bone. Fast enough to rend the very air around it."

"Why is it that you never bother to explain anything to me? And now you're talking about this horrible weapon and, all of a sudden, you're some kind of poet?"

Remy nodded. "I admit I find it fascinating. This ball is filled with hundreds of bone shards, each about the size of a fingernail. When activated, they come flying out in all directions. Each fast enough to tear completely through a human body."

"That sounds nasty. Couldn't you put up a den or something to block it?"

"Maybe. If I was quick enough. But the projectiles come out at different angles, and there are a great many of them. Stopping them all is difficult."

"Wait. Why don't we use these all the time? That sounds amazing."

Akina walked over and took one of the fragment packs, hefting it carefully in her hand. "The materials are expensive. They take forever to make. If I tried, I could make one in a year. And they kill everything near the detonation, which, all too often, includes the person who threw them."

"That sounds less great."

"I think they were invented as a joke. Or to prove a point."

Remy stood as Dog kept his eyes locked on the second fragment pack. "Akina, they can be useful. We've used them on Wedge."

"Right. Get a black tyrant to swallow one and it's done for. One of the sure ways to get a one-shot kill on those bastards."

Zhu pointed at the pack. "Why did Duow have them?"

Remy shrugged. "We didn't call him Dumb Duow just because he couldn't speak. The question is, can we use them?"

They turned to Akina, who was turning slowly, studying the walls. "We need to keep moving. We can't escape from inside the building, so logic tells me we have to leave the building."

Zhu looked at her. "Won't Faceless and the rest of the Reaver's men be waiting outside?"

"Logic says that, too. It's a good thing we're not shy about fighting our way out of these situations."

••••••••••

The four escaping prisoners made their way to the station's east exit. The halls were lit by skylights: sections of ceiling covered by translucent waxed paper and exposed to the sun. With every dead end and wrong turn Akina grew more tempted to punch through the walls instead of going around them. *If the Tae Kun hadn't put so many reinforcing enchantments on every surface, we could have been outside ten minutes ago.*

They turned a corner and saw an entrance hall with large windows and a pair of enormous doors open to the avenue outside.

A pair of soldiers in purple and black shouted, "They're here!"

Zhu skipped up and tapped Akina's shoulder. "Gates are forming. They're moving to this side."

"As expected."

Akina took three long steps and leapt, cracking a knee into the back of one soldier. "Infinity Bagua: Cubic Function." Things popped and cracked in his neck and the soldier fell face-first to the ground.

A whistling sound to Akina's right heralded a pair of rope darts sailing across the entrance hall and into the lower back of the second of the Reaver's men. He collapsed soundlessly.

Bodies lay strewn about the entrance hall, all wearing Tae Kun orange and blue. Only half were armored, the rest obviously clerical or support staff, not soldiers.

Dog trotted from body to body, sniffing each one. Akina walked to the open doorway, Remy at her side and Zhu trailing behind.

Zhu pointed. "They're right outside."

Akina nodded. "Remy, give us some cover."

He nodded and began spinning a pair of rope darts.

"Way of the Bear: Greater Den."

Side by side they approached the open doorway. Akina stepped out into the sun.

Another half dozen soldiers lay unconscious or dead in the courtyard, blood splatters telling a tale of a savage and very short fight. Akina counted, noting that three of the bodies wore purple, not orange. *Reaver's men. The Tae Kun aren't going down without a fight.*

Standing among them were two men she knew and a handful she didn't.

Faceless began moving his hands as he saw her. Bru Wei spoke, his words carrying across the courtyard and into the building with the perfect clarity of his sound-controlling martial technique.

"If you thought the Tae Kun would keep you safe, you were sorely underestimating us."

Akina shrugged. "We didn't come to them for safety. They captured us. Seems there's a reward on our heads. Weird coincidence, right? The Reaver wanting me and the Emperor putting out a bounty on us at the same time."

"The Emperor's had a bounty on you for a dozen years. Everyone wants control of the Millennium Qi."

A slender soldier with dark hair and narrow eyes stood behind Faceless, the cut of his tunic suggesting Clan of the Star. *Must be Zhu's brother. Looks like they left the blond one behind.*

Bru Wei lifted a hand as if to direct an attack on Akina, but Faceless reached out and pulled it back. The black-leather-clad Bat adept turned, and they exchanged a flurry of soft words and hand signals.

Remy looked at the forces arrayed against them. "Why doesn't Faceless want him attacking?"

Akina pointed at the walls around them. "If they damage the building, they break the seals keeping us here. He doesn't want us to escape."

Zhu stuck her head between them. "What do we do?"

"Do you know any of them?"

"Yeah, duh. Faceless and Bru Wei. That's my brother behind them. The other four are the Reaver's men. Maybe not as tough as Duow, but each one is close to his level. Together . . . I don't know. It's not good."

Remy looked at them. "Shouldn't we be whispering?"

"It won't matter." Akina shook her head. "Bru Wei will hear everything. Those ears on his cowl can pick up any sound. They say he can hear your actual thoughts."

The Bat Clan adept laughed as she spoke but didn't respond.

Akina stepped to a spot just outside the doors and just inside the edge of Remy's shield. "I'd rather die than be taken by you, Faceless. How does that serve the Reaver's goals?"

Faceless' hand motions were a blur. Bru Wei spoke. "If you die, the Reaver has no reason to keep your daughters alive. But if you come with us, he'll have no reason to harm them."

"You're going to have to do better than that if you want to convince me to give up without a fight."

Faceless stopped and considered. The men flanking him shifted from foot to foot, their eyes gleaming with battle lust.

Faceless' hands began moving again. Bru Wei continued, "Another Surge is coming. More than that, a Great Surge. The last time we saw a Great Surge, life on this continent almost ended.

"The Emperor is too arrogant to take the necessary measures. He thinks he is invincible after coming back from the east. But he's not strong enough for this.

"We need every weapon available to fight the Wedge, Akina. We can't afford to have you taking the Millennium Qi and wandering off somewhere to live your quiet life. That path dooms us all."

Akina looked over the Reaver's men. "I was teasing when I asked you to do a better job of convincing me, but you know what? I think you're right. I give up. Take me to the Reaver, I'll surrender. Look at all these dead soldiers. For what?"

Remy cleared his throat. "Akina?"

Zhu leaned forward, putting her chin over Akina's shoulder. "Seriously?"

Bru Wei stepped forward, but Faceless grabbed his shoulder. They communicated some more and Bru Wei faced the station again. "Drop the den and come out into the courtyard."

Akina answered with a snort. "I guess you can't hear my thoughts or the sarcasm in my voice. Look, Faceless, Bru Wei, whoever's talking, have you actually thought about this ridiculous story you're telling? Doesn't it seem convenient that you have this power-crazy guy coming along, digging up forbidden techniques, absorbing the life energy of other people, and, oh yeah, by the way, it's all justified, because there's a threat coming that will wipe out humanity if he doesn't save you?

"How many people will he consume while saving us from this Great Surge he says is coming? Will there be anybody left? Will you line up village after village for his black light to pierce? Human lives snuffed out to fuel his power?

"If my grandfather had wanted someone like him to have the Millennium Qi, he could have passed it to the Reaver. But he didn't, did he? What does that tell you?"

A flurry of hand motions.

"The Great Surge is real. I can sense it." Bru Wei pointed to Faceless, indicating who authored the words. "The Emperor knows it, too. He's sent emissaries east, looking for aid. He's been to the temples to request help from other worlds. This is no conspiracy. The Reaver is our best hope."

"You're a coward, Faceless. You're willing to abandon everything that matters because you're afraid of a Surge. If humanity can only be saved by baring our necks to a man who eats souls and kidnaps children, then we don't deserve to survive."

"That isn't your choice to make."

"I think it is. It's everyone's choice. The Reaver set himself against me, so he's going to have to deal with me. And if the Wedge come, Surge or no Surge, they're going to have to face me too. And they'll wish I offered them a chance to slink back to the western hell that spawned them."

Remy swallowed. "I can't hold this much longer, Akina."

She nodded and held a fragment pack in her hand. "Look familiar?"

Faceless motioned and Zhu's brother stepped forward. He held his hands up, preparing to execute a technique.

"Zhu."

"Yes?"

Akina cleared her throat. "I'm going to toss this. Your brother is going to form a gate, probably send the pack off into the wilderness somewhere. Or underground. I want you to make your own gate, one that opens right in front of his and takes the pack somewhere in the middle of their formation. Can you do that?"

"Hell yes, I can do that."

"Remy, hand me the other pack." He placed it in her left hand. "When you see me throw, drop the den."

"Got it."

Bru Wei looked at Akina, then back at Zhu, then at the others. "Scatter! She's going to gate the pack right between you!"

Zhu's brother shook his head. "I can outmaneuver her!"

Zhu patted Akina's shoulder. "He's wrong. I'll take care of it."

Akina nodded. "I'm counting on it. Faceless!"

He stepped forward, his eyehole pointing directly at her.

"The Reaver will destroy you all. I mean, he will if nobody stops him. Luckily for you, I'm here, and I'm feeling generous. So I'll save you and the rest of his people from the consequences of your own stupid choices.

"I just wanted to tell you that now so you can die with a clear conscience."

Dog barked.

Akina hurled the first pack directly at Faceless' mask.

Remy dropped his den just as the pack was about to impact its inside edge.

Bru Wei leapt into the air.

Zhu's brother fell to one knee and opened a gate on the pack's trajectory.

Zhu grunted and held her hands up, opening her own gate in front of her brother's.

The Reaver's soldiers dove for the ground on either side, getting low and crawling for cover.

Faceless stood motionless.

Akina took two steps into the courtyard.

The pack hurtled toward Zhu's gate.

Zhu's brother dropped his gate and turned his head from side to side, looking for the exit Zhu had formed. He spun and saw it behind him.

Remy tossed a dart at Bru Wei.

Akina whipped her arm through the air, launching the second fragment pack back at the wall of the station.

Bru Wei dodged Remy's dart.

Faceless took two steps back.

The first pack went through Zhu's gate, coming out the exit traveling in the opposite direction, directly into her brother's chest.

Akina spun and leapt through the station's double doors into the entrance hall.

Faceless waved his arms in the air, pointing at the second pack as it impacted the wall of the station.

Zhu shouted wordlessly as her brother opened a gate against his skin, redirecting the first pack to some unknown exit.

Shards exploded out of the station wall, obliterating an outhouse-size chunk of the structure and shedding fragments of bone in a cloud of destruction.

Faceless knelt, drawing his cape over his body and reinforcing it with his qi. Shards bounced off it like hailstones off a tile roof.

Other fragments shredded Bru Wei's leather wings.

One of the soldiers died, chunks of stone tearing through his eyes and obliterating his head.

Akina dropped to the ground inside the station.

"Zhu, step back!"

Zhu nodded. "He got rid of the pack, but he strained himself to do it!"

"I know! Now get us out of here!"

"I can't, the . . ."

Akina waved her arm. "The second pack broke the seals. Get us out of here."

The younger woman nodded and formed shapes with her hands. "Path of the Star: Chieftain's Gate."

Her brother spun, ready to interfere, but the storm of fragments tore the skin on his face and neck, breaking his concentration.

A hole appeared in space, a bit larger than it needed to be to accommodate Remy's height, opening to a well-lit forest.

Akina shoved Remy through, then watched as Dog leapt after the man. Zhu jumped after the animal and Akina followed right on her heels.

The four stood in a clearing and looked around.

Remy cracked his neck and leaned back, breathing deeply. "That was close, wasn't it? It seemed close. Was that really the plan?"

Akina shrugged. "It was *a* plan. I'm not sure it was *the* plan."

He looked at her. "I can't believe we had two fully working fragmentation packs and couldn't hold on to them for a full hour."

"Did you have a better way to get past Faceless? I didn't."

Dog barked. Zhu's gaze swiveled between them. "Wait, how did you know we were going to find those packs on Duow? Was that just luck?"

Akina knelt and petted Dog. "I would have come up with something else. It might have been harder, but we'd have gotten away."

Zhu turned to Remy. "Is she being serious? That sounds crazy. Are we crazy? Is this whole thing planned out or are we just stumbling through each step hoping for the best?"

Remy smiled. "You're committed either way, aren't you, little one? This is always the way things are with Akina."

"That doesn't answer my question."

"You want to know if she's crazy? We'll find out after the fact. If we survive and rescue the girls, then we can all say she's a genius. If we wind up dead somewhere, then Faceless can stand over our corpses and say she was crazy. That we were all crazy."

Akina straightened. "Remy, I'm hungry. Tell me you stole some food, then help me plan my introduction to Arha Tae Kun."

22

Mark of the Bear

Dog whined and bumped Akina's leg with his nose. She squatted in the short grass and dropped her pack to the ground.

"Remy, you have any food for Dog?"

The big man patted himself down, eyes brightening as he found a sack. He opened it and pulled out dried scraps of meat.

"Here you go, boy." Dog trotted over to him and inhaled the food. "Do we need to move again?"

Akina turned to Zhu. "Can you shift us another hundred miles?"

The younger woman rubbed her temples. "I'm not a horse, you know, just dragging you guys from place to place all day. I need to rest."

"No rest. Use infinity walks to rebuild your energy. How long?"

Zhu paused. "If you give me an hour, I think I can do a hundred miles. Does that work?"

Remy pointed in the general direction of Westlock. "Will they follow us? Can your brother track the gate you formed?"

She scratched her nose. "I don't think so. He was distracted when we left. The technique he used to save himself is trickier than it seems. It would have drained him."

Akina nodded. "Good. You cycle your energy. Remy, how are your injuries? The guards worked you over a bit."

A hard slap broke the silence of the forest as he patted his belly. "I could use a nap to fully recover. But I'm more or less fine."

"Great."

"What's next? Do we need to draw anybody else into this little conflict of yours?"

Akina shrugged. "Who else is there?"

"I mean, the Pink Lotus? There are other monastic orders you could pull in. If you want to create a true catastrophe."

"Come on, Remy. There's a purpose to this. The Pink Lotus are neutral between the Reaver, the Emperor, and the Tae Kun. They wouldn't support any sides in those fights. There's no need to draw them in. I'm not trying to cause chaos for its own sake."

He tipped back a waterskin, then ran fingers through his beard to catch the water that spilled. "No, you're right. Should we head to Eastlock? Visit Arha Tae Kun and get him on our side?"

Dog trotted to the edge of the small clearing and began sniffing at the undergrowth at its edge. "We need to give it a bit of time. I need word to spread that the Reaver's men attacked that station and slaughtered a bunch of Tae Kun soldiers."

"Makes sense. I'll take that nap now. You tell me when it's time to throw ourselves into the next fire."

"Don't lose your nerve now, Remy. You're my ticket to see Arha."

"My nerve is intact, Akina. Which is more than I can say for my skin. Now let me sleep."

Akina stepped away as Remy lay on his side, back propped against a tree, and began to snore. Zhu continued working on the knots in her hair.

Akina walked over to the younger girl. "Let me help with that."

Zhu looked up. "What? Oh, no. I can just cut it off. I'll get my knives."

"Don't be silly. Sit." She held the younger woman's shoulders and pressed her gently but firmly to the ground.

Zhu sighed. "What are you going to do?"

"Just fixing your hair." She pulled a comb out of a pocket and began at the back, gently working out the knots.

Zhu winced, ready for the pain of pulled hair, but none came. "How do you do that? Without snagging?"

"It's the comb. Saurid ribs, enchanted to be slippery. I'll get you one. Makes getting the knots out easy."

Zhu shrugged. "Sounds good."

"Your mother never bought you a good comb?" Akina moved higher on Zhu's head, pulling the comb over her scalp.

"She wasn't much for that sort of thing. Never had time."

"Hmm. If we survive, we should get you a proper haircut too. Your hair looks like it was cut by a drunk Wedge."

"I thought we'd be enemies if we survive."

"If you want, we can be. But I have plenty of enemies already. I don't need more."

Zhu sighed and relaxed as the older woman continued working on her hair.

"I could have just chopped it off, you know. I don't mind."

Akina sighed. "You can always chop it off later. Let it not be said that I didn't take care of my prisoner, okay? There, all straight. You look lovely."

"Thank you."

"Don't thank me, walk your pattern."

Zhu grunted and stood. She found a clear area and began walking figure eights in the grass while Dog busily marked every fifth tree within a hundred yards.

Akina went over the fight at the prison in her mind. After several minutes, she looked down at the crescents her fingernails had dug into her palms. She sniffed and wiped dampness off her cheeks with the backs of her hands.

That was too close. Hold on, girls. Mama's coming for you. Just hold on.

Reaver, I know you can't hear me, but you'd better be keeping them safe. If any harm comes to them, there won't be a place on this world where I won't find you, and no gods strong enough to protect you from my wrath.

••••••••••

The next day, Akina asked Zhu to gate them to Eastlock, the city that housed the clan house for the Tae Kun.

She had skipped them to a different wilderness location the previous night and if they were being tracked, there was no sign of it.

The guard at the front gate of the city stopped them.

"No animals, ma'am."

Akina looked up at the heavily armored woman, thick bones embedded in the leather of her jerkin, a shield of bone and sinew at her side.

"Those people up ahead went in with animals."

"Those are livestock, ma'am. No pets allowed."

"This isn't a pet. He isn't even a dog. Have you heard of the Bosun Clan?"

The guard frowned at her, unimpressed. "They're a myth, and that's a dog. You're not trying to convince me that's a weredog, are you?"

Remy put a hand on Akina's shoulder and smiled at the guard. "Forgive my friend, she has a sense of humor as overpowering as a Wedge Surge. That is not, of course, a weredog. But he is a sacred beast, a warhound of the Azure Dragon Clan, and this is the Dragon of the Azure. She and I are here to meet with your own illustrious leader, Arha."

The guard straightened and looked up at Remy's face. "You're here to meet with our chief?"

"Indeed, we are. He and I are old friends."

"Are you now? And who might you be?"

Remy smiled. "I am so sorry. I assumed all would recognize me. I am Remy of the Bear Clan, founding member of the Five Fangs. As I mentioned, Arha and I are old friends."

The woman narrowed her eyes slightly. "If you're not really Remy, you'd better say so now. Arha won't go easy on you if you're an impostor."

"I am Remy, and Remy is me. True words."

The guard nodded. "Then, sir, you may pass. All of you, even the dog. For at least the past ten years, the first thing every guard in Eastlock learns is that if Remy the Bear comes to the gate, he is to be allowed inside immediately."

Remy smiled. "I'm glad to have been remembered!"

The guard leaned in. "Before you go, sir, would you tell me how you made such an impression on our chief?"

Remy's smile broadened. "I'm afraid that's not my secret to share. It's a thing between men, I hope you understand."

She shrugged, plates of bone shifting and clacking with the motion. "I had to ask. Carry on." She looked over his shoulder. "Next!"

Remy waved Zhu and Dog through the gate.

Akina looked up at her friend. "You were serious."

"I'm always serious. Wait, about what?"

"About Arha owing you a favor. I half thought it was a tall tale, that you'd back out and we'd have to find another way to talk to him."

"I was as serious as gallstones. When do I ever lie to you, Akina?"

"I don't know. You're always exaggerating things."

"No, I'm not. Name one thing!"

"Well, I thought this was one thing, but obviously I was mistaken. Now I'm going to have to reevaluate our entire relationship. What else have you been telling the truth about?"

"What? Everything! That's what I'm trying to tell you! I'm a very honest person!"

"See? That's a lot of things I have to think about, and it's all your fault! Always making such big claims, and the way you tell them. You're also drunk half the time. You never *sound* like an honest person. Why would anyone think it's true? It's very misleading, Remy."

"I suppose I need to beg your forgiveness for enjoying a drink now and again! Or for saying precisely what I mean to say when I speak!"

"Maybe you should do exactly that!"

Zhu cleared her throat. "Guys, I'm getting a little dry here. Could we stop for some tea? Or something?"

Remy grunted. "We can just go to the citadel. We may not see Arha right away, but they'll serve us tea while we wait."

Akina snorted. "Tea? The way they regard you, they'll do more than serve us tea. I bet you'll get your feet washed. Maybe a massage. A full meal. A bucket of wine." She stomped the ground, startling Dog, then stopped to rub her temples.

Zhu sighed. "I just want tea."

••••••••••

The Tae Kun citadel was a martial arts school run wild: barracks for two hundred students, training halls with weapon storage and indoor exercise areas, a kitchen big enough to feed those two hundred students in groups of fifty that rotated in and out throughout the day, and a ceremonial hall with room for exhibitions, greeting visiting dignitaries, and private living quarters for the clan leaders. A griffin landing patch was empty, the attached aviary unused.

The citadel had taken over a quarter of Eastlock, dominating the town's economy with its demand for food, equipment, and repairs. In turn, bones flowed out of the citadel, making the local craftsmen wealthy.

Above all, the favor of the Emperor was on display. Tapestries hung on wooden walls, stitched with threads dyed in restricted colors. Busts and paintings and ornamental bushes dotted the grounds, made with techniques known only within the walls of the Imperial Palace.

Dog lay on an embroidered cushion, his head cradled by a second, softer cloth, and yawned. Zhu sipped her tea as Remy popped a syrupy pastry into his mouth.

Akina drank her own tea and looked over her friends. "I'm sorry for underestimating you."

Remy grunted. "You should be. What's wrong with you today?"

She sipped again. "I don't like depending on other people."

"We sailed up the river without lifting a finger. You were fine with that. I've seen you bathe in water heated by servants."

"Those things are different."

"Are they?"

Dog yawned again, let out a loud fart, then settled his head back onto the pillow. Zhu held up a piece of paper that was rough and cheap with writing printed over both sides. "While you two were arguing, I bought this. The town is pretty upset about the Reaver's soldiers attacking Westlock."

Akina nodded. "I overheard soldiers on the road talking about the same thing. It's good. They need to have a reason to attack the Reaver that's more than whatever favor Arha owes Remy."

Remy drained half a goblet of wine and belched loudly. "Does it say anything about conflict between the other clans?"

Zhu scanned the paper. "Yeah. It's looking like war, but mostly this is speculation about who exactly is going to side with whom."

The door opened and a servant in lush robes bowed to them. "The chief is here."

Remy brushed crumbs off his chest and stood. Akina and Zhu followed suit.

The servant stepped back to make room for a thickly built man dressed in an orange and blue casual robe.

"The Bear! Good to see you, my friend. It's been ages!"

Remy smiled and stepped forward, greeting the shorter man with a hug. "Arha! Over a decade. You look good!"

Arha disengaged and flashed a broad grin at the women. "And you look fat. Now, who are your friends? I heard dear old Remy was accompanied by a pair of beautiful women and I thought to myself, of course he is, that sly old beast." His eyes twinkled as he took in Zhu but rested for longer on Akina.

Her curtsy belied the smirk on her lips. "Chief Arha. We've met before, though I don't expect you to remember me." *Careful, Akina. Keep your tongue in check. You need him on your side.*

Arha frowned and turned to Remy. "Is she who I think she is?" His eyes were dark.

Remy smiled, a hint of anxiety flashing across his face. "She is exactly who you think she is. And you will hear her out, Arha, because you owe me."

Arha's hands clenched into fists, muscles bunching across his shoulders and neck. "You're not in a position to make demands, Remy. I'm clan chief now. It's one thing to come here unannounced and expect food and hospitality and quite another—"

Remy shook his head and interrupted. "I'm not the one making demands here, Arha. It's your own honor that requires you listen to her. Give Akina leave to speak and your debt to me will be considered paid."

Arha's frown intensified. "You're sure? I always thought you'd ask for a position here. Retire as an instructor to the Tae Kun or something. Grow fat and pinch the bottoms of the servant girls." Akina let out an explosive cough, covering her mouth with one hand while waving apologetically with the other. Zhu stepped to the older woman and patted her back.

Dog raised his head, barked softly, then laid it back down.

Remy nodded. "Please. It's important. More important than my life. Or hers, for that matter."

Arha sighed. "Then sit. I'll hear what you have to say." He clapped and the door opened, two servants entering with fresh tea and snacks.

Zhu waved at the clan chief. "I'm Zhu of the Star Clan. I'm their prisoner. Pleased to meet you."

Arha nodded. "Welcome to clan Tae Kun. Please enjoy our hospitality while you are here." He popped a small cake into his mouth, then picked up a cup of tea, composing himself as he drank.

Dog stood and walked over to Arha, nuzzling the man's leg. He reached down and scratched behind the animal's ears.

"Dragon of the Azure, our differences lie in the distant past. I am ready to hear you out."

She nodded and let out a breath. "I don't like coming to you to ask for help, but I need help."

She paused and waited. He stared at her face for a hard moment, then nodded. "Go on."

"I have two daughters. The Reaver has taken them prisoner. I'd like them back."

Arha flinched when she named the Reaver. "You want me to negotiate for their release? Act as an intermediary? What does he want? The fortune you accumulated as part of the Five Fangs?"

"Not exactly. If he wanted bones, I'd give him bones. I have no need for them. He wants the Millennium Qi. And that I cannot let him have."

Arha swallowed hard, put down his teacup, and stroked his jaw. "The Reaver is very strong. If he gains the Millennium Qi . . ."

Remy leaned forward. "He would rule the martial world. Or beyond. We think he has designs on the Empire. He wants to be the one to stop the next Surge. Given your connection to the Emperor . . ."

Arha grunted. "We'd be forced to defend the Empire. Even if he loses that conflict, we'd be caught in the middle. And because of where we are, my clan would bear the brunt of the casualties."

Remy nodded. "After which the other clans competing for the Emperor's favor would be in an advantageous position. Giving up the Millennium Qi would be bad for Akina, but it would also damage the Tae Kun."

Arha nodded. "What do you suggest? Offer him alternative payment? You said he had no interest in bones."

Akina let out another long breath. *So much rides on this conversation. I wish I was better at talking.* "I do not want to negotiate for my daughters' freedom, I want to kill the Reaver and tear his men apart, limb by limb, until they beg me to take my girls back."

"As I would expect from the Spiral Witch."

"But I'm not strong enough to do that on my own. Even the three of us can't handle the Reaver and his army. But with the help of the Tae Kun we have a chance."

"I want to help. My clan is clamoring for revenge against the Reaver. But while it pains me to admit this, the Reaver's men are strong. I can't simply send every soldier out into the Wilds to take them on. We have cities to guard, Wedge to watch for."

"I don't need your whole army, just a portion of them. One thousand men. Remy and I can handle the rest."

Arha sputtered. "The most I could possibly free up is five hundred soldiers."

"I accept."

Arha looked at Zhu, who smiled and crunched into a pastry.

"My options are still limited. We have other clans nipping at our heels, all fighting for the Emperor's favor. If we march on the Wilds, they will take advantage."

Akina held out a hand; Zhu passed over the printed newssheet. Akina passed it to Arha. "Your enemies are otherwise occupied."

He took the paper and scanned it, then turned to Remy and snorted. "Did you do this, you rascal? Start a war so I'd be free to help your woman? Not that I'd expect any less from you."

Remy smiled as Akina coughed again. "Akina did the planning. She is very motivated. Given the situation."

Arha nodded. "I never thought you were the planning type, Dragon."

She shrugged. "I never was. However, circumstance and age have had their way with me."

"Still, that is a tremendous risk for my men. Many will die. Most of them aren't used to the Wilds. And the Reaver is strong. His men use the forbidden techniques to great effect. If it were just me, I'd help. I owe Remy at least that. But to risk the lives of so many of my followers? That's a much bigger thing to ask."

Akina waited for him to continue. Instead, he picked up his tea.

Remy looked between Arha and Akina, as if wondering what he could offer to enhance their bargaining power.

Remy, you sweet man, you don't have anything else to give. But that's okay.

She caught Remy's eyes, gave a slight shake of her head, and turned to Arha.

"I know what I'm asking for. And I'm willing to compensate you for that risk and those losses."

"I'm listening."

"Help me free my girls, and when we're done, you can have me."

Arha swallowed. Zhu's eyes widened and Remy's mouth fell open.

Remy stood. "Akina, there must be—"

"If there was another way, I would have found it. It's for the girls. Arha, what do you say?"

He swallowed again, then sipped his tea. "What do you mean? To punish? I'm not so angry at you for what happened fifteen years ago that I need to see you beaten for it."

"Not to punish. I meant to have. However you want."

"You'd be my concubine? Bear me children?"

She shrugged. "If that's the limit of your imagination, so be it."

He looked at Remy quickly, then back. "Are you offering your life? You'd give me the Millennium Qi?"

She spread her arms wide. "All of myself. No restrictions. My word, on my honor as a knight errant."

Arha stood, matching Remy, his hand clenching and unclenching with excitement. "The Millennium Qi! I'd rival the Emperor with that. I could take it east, come back. Wait, your grandfather already did that. I could use it myself. With the clan at my back . . . we'd be unrivaled in the martial world."

Akina swallowed. "Don't forget, we'd also be removing the Reaver from the equation. Your biggest rival, gone. And you'd have everything I could give you on top of it."

Arha looked at Remy. "You'd let her do this? You understand what it means?"

Remy closed his mouth and sat on the cushioned chair. "It's not up to me, is it? Akina is the one making these choices. They're her girls."

Akina sat next to him. "I'll need you to look after them, Remy. Keep them safe."

He slumped in his chair. "I'm probably not the best choice—"

"You're the best choice. The only choice. Keep them safe. Teach them. For old times' sake. Okay?"

Remy nodded as Arha's eyes gleamed. "I can't say no to you, Akina. I'll do whatever you need."

She looked up at Arha. "Do we have a deal? Your army marches with me to the Reaver. We free my girls. They walk away with Remy and Dog, and you can have me."

"How can I trust you to hold to the bargain, Akina?"

She sighed. "I'll swear to it. On qi and clan, if you help me get my girls to safety, I'll turn myself over to you."

His eyes widened and he looked up at the ceiling, his lips twitching as he talked to himself.

Checking for loopholes. Finding none. He looked down, catching her full in his gaze, and smiled widely enough to show off sparkling eyeteeth.

"My dear Akina, seeing you again has brought back such unpleasant memories, yet somehow it has turned out to be such a lovely surprise. Yes, we have a deal. Swear your oath and I will begin preparations immediately."

Remy clasped her hand in his own and gently shook his head. "I . . ." His voice trailed off.

Akina smiled. "Mourn later, old friend. We have a war to finish, and I need you clear-headed for it."

"I'm here, Akina. I'm here."

23

Enter the Princess

Remy squatted on his heels, arms spread wide as if reaching for the far corners of the practice yard. He wore nothing but breeches, his armor having been taken by Tae Kun servants for cleaning and repair. His red hair was matted with sweat, his beard a mess.

With a grunt he swung his hands into a tremendous clap, then rubbed them against one another as if grinding spices in his palms, slowly drawing them toward his chest. Muscles bunched and writhed under his skin.

Akina paused and leaned forward, breathing deeply through her nose. *He's lost weight. Hopefully he'll have a chance to gain it back after we've rescued the girls.*

Zhu walked her pattern, the flow of qi around her core much closer to the desired shape than it had been a week earlier. *She's talented. They were wasting her potential.*

A servant hurried over with a pitcher of water and a handful of dried cocovado slices. Akina paused, then took the water. "Thank you."

"Yes, ma'am." The servant retreated.

Remy stretched his arms out and brought them together again with a clap that echoed off the clay walls of the surrounding structures.

Zhu stopped and turned to Akina. "In this part, in the middle, what am I supposed to be doing with my hands?"

Akina smiled and demonstrated the motions, moving just in front of Zhu so the younger woman could mimic her more precisely.

A different clap, softer and more subdued, sounded from one of the yard entrances. Arha entered, body encased in armor of black bone plates held together with knots of shiny tendon. His head was bare.

The knights errant paused and turned to face him.

Two attendants trailed behind Arha, encased in similar armor of paler bone, quills and parchment in their hands as they scribbled messages their leader was dictating.

". . . rations for a fortnight, and one and a half water rations for the same time. Got that?"

The attendant wrote furiously, waited for a nod from Arha, then ran off.

The clan leader turned to Akina and Remy. "We'll be ready to move at dawn."

Remy combed his damp beard with warm fingers. "What are we doing about transportation? It's a long walk to the Reaver's fortress."

Arha shook his head. "We have Star Clan adepts contracted to get us there."

Akina narrowed her eyes. "Will they fight?"

"They've been paid to get us there and back and to set up a seal around the fortress so the Reaver can't escape. They won't step into the fight, even if we're losing the battle."

Remy counted on his fingers. "That will cost a fortune. You can spare that sum of bones?"

Arha's lips curled back in a grim smile. "I didn't have to."

A different voice called out from behind him. "My father has agreed to fund this expedition."

Zhu whispered from her spot behind Akina, "Another one? How many people am I supposed to remember?"

Arha stepped to the side and held his arm out to welcome the newcomer forward. She was close to his height, slender, and dressed in pale robes. Her hair was white, not the color of age but of fibers bleached by the sun.

She had skin tanned nearly as dark as Akina's and her eyes were a violet so intense they seemed to glow.

She stepped forward and Akina caught her mistake. *Her eyes don't 'seem' to glow, they're actually glowing. I could read a map in the dead of night by the light she's giving off.*

Arha's voice was soft and careful. "My darling, these are two of the Five Fangs. Akina the Spiral Witch, the Azure Dragon, and Remy the Bear." He turned to the knights. "This is my wife, Her Highness, Princess Ramat."

The princess stepped forward and pinned Akina with her violet stare. "I know you by reputation, Spiral Witch. My father has spoken of you."

Akina shuffled her feet. *Should I bow?*

She didn't bow.

"Princess, it's a pleasure to meet you. I didn't realize you were in the city."

"Oh, I wasn't. I was visiting the palace. Then we got word about a commotion and my father became curious."

"Did he?"

The princess closed on Akina, looking downwards to meet the older woman's eyes. "He was surprised you didn't come to him for help. After all, the Reaver attacked and killed his men and was involved in releasing his griffins from their aviary."

Akina shrugged. "We're not exactly on speaking terms, are we? He put a price on my head. I didn't think I could just dance into the palace and ask for a favor from my old friend from the east. Besides, if he wants to attack the Reaver, he's perfectly capable of doing it without me."

"Yes, quite." The white-haired woman turned to Remy. "Now you, I don't know. Yet you seem quite familiar."

Remy chuckled and ran fingers through his hair, eyes darting left and right, searching for a robe or something else to cover his near nakedness. "Familiar? Me? Oh, it's the beard, I'm sure. With all this hair all bearded men look alike."

"No, I've seen men with beards before. There's something else, from years ago."

Arha stepped forward and placed his hand under her elbow. “My precious flower, the most essential treasure of my soul, your mind is too pure to be sullied with memories of this barbarian. I am sure that if you have ever crossed paths, you are better off having forgotten him. Come, let us get you tea and some rest.”

She smiled at her husband. “You can have tea brought here. I would like to speak with the knights who are dragging my husband off to war.”

Zhu stepped next to Akina. “Nobody’s dragging anybody anywhere, you know. He took the deal, and—” Akina covered her mouth with a sweaty hand.

“Hush, Zhu. This is the Emperor’s daughter. No reason to antagonize more powerful people, is there?”

Her response was muffled. “But she—”

“I said hush. That’s an order.” Zhu nodded and Akina let go of her mouth. Dog jogged to the princess.

“Is this your animal?”

Akina sighed. “Oh for—” The princess knelt on the packed dirt floor and scratched Dog as he licked her other hand.

“He’s very cute! What breed is he? He reminds me of something. A dragon clan hound.”

Akina pushed Zhu back a few steps. “He’s a mutt. Just a dog we found. Nothing special.”

Dog barked approval.

The princess stood and wiped her hands on the sides of her robe. “Anyway, my father is very interested in this expedition. He is funding the Star Clan assistance and, pursuant to his wishes, I will be accompanying you.”

Arha’s face tightened further. “My sweetness, love of my life, my eternal soulmate, surely you have better things to do than join us on this grubby adventure?”

She pursed her lips. “You are sweet, dear husband, but you are overreaching. I do not need your protection. I am the daughter of the Emperor." The glow from her eyes intensified, casting a purple tint over his forehead.

He licked his lips. "Of course, dear. That's not what I meant, not at all. No one here doubts your ferocity in combat. I simply think you would—"

"I will let you know when I want you to think, husband. Now, tell me when we are leaving so I can be ready." Arha gritted his teeth and looked to Akina, as if for help.

Akina looked at her. "Just you? Are you bringing any soldiers? I know who your father is, but the Reaver is only part of the danger. We'll be in the Wilds."

"My father has sent two dozen of his bodyguard to escort me. That is in addition to the twenty score Tae Kun soldiers we are bringing. With you fighting alongside I am sure I will be perfectly safe."

Remy cleared his throat. "Princess, I am certain you can hold your own in combat. I worry, though, about the men."

"The men?"

"Yes, the men. And women. The soldiers. I fear they will take unnecessary risks in an attempt to catch your attention and your favor. That they will fight foolishly. Which could put us all at risk in a battle of this size."

The princess looked up at him. "You really do seem familiar. Regardless, you make a good point. I will stay in my palanquin as much as possible so my presence does not incur any undesirable fervor in the soldiers. You will keep me appraised of progress in the battle personally. Is that understood, Remy the Bear?"

He smiled and nodded. "Yes, Your Highness. It will be my honor."

"Of course, it will. Come, husband, let us retire for the night. Preparations are being made."

Arha smiled. "You go on without me, my darling, most blessed nectar. I will join you shortly. We need to do a little more strategizing before dawn."

"Very well." The princess cast a long stare Akina's way, then left the training yard.

Arha turned to the knights and spread his hands.

Akina grumbled. "What are we supposed to do with her?"

"She's bringing her bodyguard, you heard. And if she has to fight, she's as fierce as anybody in the clan. You saw her eyes. She has the Emperor's power."

"Just so long as you're not expecting us to drop everything and protect her."

Arha shook his head. "You save your daughters. I'll worry about my wife. All I want is for you to fulfill the conditions of your oath."

Akina nodded. "Fair enough, then. Let's plan."

••••••••••

Dog yawned wide while Akina ran her fingers from just behind his eyes down his back and over his haunches. She smiled as he lowered his belly and lifted his butt up into the air, stretching.

"Good boy, good boy. Did you want some food? We have leftovers from lunch. Let me get you some food." He stood and watched while she assembled a snack for him.

She stepped back and let him eat. Remy and Zhu had gone to the bathhouse, leaving Akina alone in the small suite they were sharing.

She picked up a hollow bamboo filled with sticky rice and scooped some into her mouth as the door slid open.

Akina grunted. "Princess. What a surprise." Her tone was flat, belying her words.

The princess smiled as she slid the door shut behind her. "Akina. I wanted a few words with you in private."

Dog chewed noisily, ignoring the women.

"Isn't your husband expecting you? I thought you told him you were retiring."

The princess shrugged. "He can wait. He understands I have responsibilities that go beyond his needs."

Akina looked around the room. "My etiquette is a bit rusty. I'm in your compound, but these are my rooms. Who's the guest here? Should I be offering you tea, or should you be offering me?"

The princess waved a well-tanned hand. "I'm not particular about those sorts of things. Did you need tea? I can have some sent in."

"No. I'm good. What did you want to talk about?"

"You've put me in a very awkward position."

"Have I? I don't remember that. Were we grappling? Why don't I remember? Did I get a concussion? Dog, you should have told me."

Dog looked up and barked as she said his name.

The princess sighed. "I was speaking metaphorically. As you are well aware. Your banter is quite off-putting."

Akina shrugged. "I didn't realize it was my job to put you on. That didn't sound right. Turn you on? No, that made it worse."

"Are you trying to make me angry? Are we adversaries?"

Akina readied a retort; reconsidered. "Sorry, it's my default mode of communication. As far as I know, we have no reason to be adversaries."

The princess nodded. "Good. Now, about that awkward position."

"If this has something to do with Arha, I swear you're thinking of someone else. I haven't seen him in over a decade."

A tan hand rose. "Perhaps you could allow me to continue? This is not about my husband. I trust him, and his devotion, implicitly."

"That's a relief."

"Besides which, I'm sure you're not his type. He prefers his women to be slenderer."

"That was really unnecessary, you know."

"I don't have to fit the princess stereotype and have you flogged for mocking me, but I can't just let you get away with it completely unpunished, can I? It's a matter of reputation."

Dog finished his meal and waddled over to Akina. She bent and scratched his neck. "That's fair. What's the awkward position, then?"

The princess looked around the room, taking in the luxurious, though sparse, furnishings. "My father admires you. He has spoken of you numerous times over the years. When he heard that you had returned to his domain, he declared that he would like you for a concubine."

"Wow. Okay. I can see how that's awkward for you. Nobody likes to be around someone their dad wants to bang unless it's, like, their mom. I think. Maybe even then, you don't want to think about it."

Ramat shook her head. "I'm used to that part. He's the emperor, after all. I grew up in a palace filled with his wives and concubines and a menagerie of half-siblings."

"What's the awkward part, then?"

"My father wants me to bring you back to him. But you are sworn to my husband."

Akina nodded. "Ah. That is a bit of a situation. It's terrible for you, really. You want to be loyal to your father and take me to him to be a sex slave, but in fact your husband is going to kill me first, so you won't be able to do that. I'm deeply sympathetic."

"Nobody was going to kidnap or enslave you. My father wanted me to extend an offer, that is all. You could be his first concubine, with all accompanying privileges. He didn't ask me to force you. He doesn't do that."

Akina gave Dog a last rub and stood. "I know, I'm playing with you. Your father actually has a decent reputation on that front."

"It is earned. He does not abuse women."

"He does have two dozen wives and how many concubines, though, doesn't he?"

The princess shrugged. "All with him by choice, and all treated well."

"Fair enough. We can leave any discussions about the ethics of this polygamy to the philosophers. As you noted, I'm not in any position to accept a position as your father's concubine, so that question is answered."

"But would you consider it? If you were not beholden to my husband?"

Akina paused. "To be honest, I might, if it were just me."

"Pardon?"

"Your father's good looking enough. I've met him. He actually does seem kind. And being an Imperial concubine? Life of luxury, living in the palace. I could do worse. I have done worse."

"So?"

"It wouldn't be just me, would it? I'd have to bring the girls."

"That would be expected."

"I can't give away their freedom like that. It's not mine to give, it's theirs."

"I see."

"So there's no conflict. Even if my deal with your husband were somehow nullified, I wouldn't go slinking back with you to the Emperor."

"Unless you needed his help to free your girls."

Akina shrugged. "You can spend as much time as you want dancing through hypotheticals, but it won't get you anywhere."

"No, I realize that. There is something else."

"Someone else wants me dead or as a seventy-ninth mistress? I've been back for less than two months and I'm this popular?"

"Not that. My father's advisors have doubts that you are still the warrior you once were. They suspect that your mission to stop the Reaver will fail, and that your failure will bring down the Tae Kun."

"So what? There are always more clans to take its place."

"Still, to have the Emperor's favorite clan brought down like this? He would lose face. He wants you tested before this campaign is allowed to continue."

Akina straightened. "Tested? We're supposed to fight?"

The princess held her hands up, open. "That is what he wanted, yes."

Akina cracked her neck, then paced the width of the room three times while the princess stood in place. "You don't want to fight me. That's what you're saying. Your father does, but you don't."

"It does seem like a waste of effort. What would it prove? If you beat me, that doesn't mean you can necessarily defeat the Reaver. And if I win, that simply shows that you're not equipped to handle my particular skills. Which are not the Reaver's."

"I see."

"But I need something. Some kind of . . . assurance."

How am I supposed to stay sarcastic when she's being reasonable?

"Okay. What did you have in mind?"

"Can you give me any evidence that you're the kind of warrior you used to be?"

Akina stopped pacing. "I killed many of the Reaver's men already. I fought Faceless and Bru Wei to a standstill. But it's not my hand-to-hand combat skills that should reassure you."

"No? Then what? I need to have enough confidence in you to face my father's questions without flinching."

"I don't know if you'll understand. Do you have children?"

The princess' nostrils flared. "What does that mean?"

"Look, I'm out of touch. I don't know if you and Arha had any kids. Are you a mother?"

"I am unable to bear children. A side effect of the power from the east that burns through me."

"Okay. I'll have to explain this another way."

"Wait. We have children. Adopted children. Three boys. Their parents died of a fever and I took them in as infants. Raised them myself."

Akina let out a deep breath. "Good, so you understand."

"I do? You won't argue, say I'm not a real mother because the children didn't come from my womb?"

Akina rubbed her temples. "Look, tell me. Are you a mother to those boys or not?"

"I say I am."

"That's good enough for me. You don't have to worry about me failing because I will not let that happen. I'm not the warrior I was when I was part of the Five Fangs. I'm ten times as dangerous.

"I might not be as fast or as strong, but I'm willing to do anything to save my children. I started a war between the elemental clans and the dragon clans just to distract them from the Tae Kun. I tricked Bru Wei into ruining your father's aviary. I let the Tae Kun capture me so the Reaver's men would slaughter your soldiers at Westlock. I stole and fought and manipulated half the continent to get what I want.

"You don't have to worry about your husband's safety. Unless he decides to get in my way."

"You're the cause of all this strife?"

"Of course. Hadn't you figured that out already?"

"Why are you admitting this to me?"

"You were wondering whether I was dangerous enough to carry out my plans. I'm telling you that I'm far more dangerous than that."

"How do you know I won't give you away? Tell my husband that the rift with the Reaver is your fault?"

"Because you're a mother too, and you understand that I'm only doing this for my girls."

The princess stared with wide, glowing eyes as if seeing Akina for the first time. "I'm not sure that makes sense."

"How about this, then: The Reaver is dangerous to your father. He would be even more dangerous if he got his hands on the Millennium Qi. Backing my plan is the best way to make sure the threat of the Reaver has ended and the Millennium Qi is kept safe. Your husband wins and your father wins. All you have to do is not interfere."

The princess drummed nervous fingers against her side. "May I bring my boys? I think they'd like to pet Dog."

Akina relaxed her back and neck. "Better hurry. We're going to war in the morning."

24

The Real Wilds One

The following afternoon, Arha took off a bone-reinforced gauntlet and wiped the back of his hand across his face, then frowned at the smear of blood and other fluids that stained it. "I don't remember the Wilds being this crowded with Wedge. Am I just getting old, or was it less dangerous back then?"

The sounds of combat echoed across the plain: Tae Kun soldiers fighting knots of Wedge all around them.

Akina faced him and nodded, her expression blank. "I'm not sure, but I think you should duck."

"What? Duck? Why?"

She let out a breath and lifted her chin slightly. "Are you sure you should be asking me questions? You ought to try listening for a change. I'm telling you to duck."

He looked over his shoulder, eyes widening as he folded at the waist. A pair of rope darts screamed over his back, burying deep into the eye sockets of a fifteen-foot-long, white-skinned reptilian Wedge.

Arha straightened and spun, hammer in hands, relaxing when he saw the monster slump to the ground. A saurid, it walked on two legs, like the larger tyrants, its massive head counterbalanced by a long, muscular tail.

"You almost killed me!"

Dog waddled over to the Wedge and relieved himself into its open mouth, urine mixing with the toxic saliva dripping off the creature's jagged teeth. Zhu followed the animal, her punch dagger out as she looked for a good place to start cutting into the body.

Akina shook her head. "That white almost killed you. Remy just saved your life." Remy walked up to the corpse, planted his foot on its snout, and pulled his darts out of the skull by their ropes. He gave them a quick spin, spraying gore and brain around the field. Zhu cut into the creature's torso and started working a rib free with her daggers.

They stood on broken, rocky terrain. Off to the north, they could see the Spine of the World: uncrossable, white-tipped mountains that stretched east and west in an almost straight line. The land between the Spine and the Dreadwall to the south was bleak; shrubs and occasional hardy trees sprouted in thickets between boulders and stretches of cracked stone.

A flat patch a hundred yards across held a set of supply wagons drawn by battle oxen dressed in bone armor, the army's support personnel, and four Imperial griffins standing guard and occasionally snapping at the head of a stray wedge with their sharp beaks.

Remy palmed his rope darts and pointed one west. "There's a big one coming. I'm not sure these soldiers can handle it."

Akina tightened her rich blue jacket around her shoulders, chilled by the icy wind that came from the north. Groups of Tae Kun had formed shield walls in various places, blocking the paths to the wagons, the axe and spear wielders striking from carefully placed gaps in the wall.

The shield and spear tactics had worked well against the swarm of smaller Wedge that had been attacking ever since the army emerged from their gate into the Wilds.

She looked in the direction Remy had pointed. A head bobbed over a ridge, dropping back down. A tyrant, at least thirty feet high.

Arha looked at her. "Those things used to be rare. Did we make a mistake gating so far from the Reaver's fortress? Should I have asked the Star Clan adepts to take us in closer?"

She shook her head. "You have some good qualities, Arha. You're good to your wife. You're reliable. You have just enough charisma to keep your clan soldiers loyal to you without looking like a threat to anyone above you in the power structure."

"Why is it that when you compliment me, it feels like an insult?"

"I have that effect on everybody. But I was building up to something. You have flaws. You second-guess yourself. You made a call. Wondering if it was the right call, right now, is pointless."

"So you *do* think it was a mistake."

Remy laughed. "That's not what she said, Arha. If we had gated in closer to the Reaver, his men would have sensed it and ambushed us as we exited the gate. You did the right thing. None of us really expected this many Wedge out in the Wilds."

Zhu looked up. "I did. It's been like this for years now."

They turned to her. Akina cleared her throat. "Excuse me?"

"Well, Remy said none of us really expected all these Wedge, and I just said that I did, because, you know, I was living in the Reaver's fortress up until a few weeks ago. It's been like this for a long time."

Akina nodded. "You didn't think that maybe mentioning this to one of us might be important?"

Zhu shrugged and fell back on her rear as a rib came free in her hand. She flipped it back and forth, sighting along its length, looking for flaws. "You didn't ask. Also, I thought you knew. I heard the Wilds used to be safer or something, but I never saw it myself."

Remy looked at Akina, his forehead thickly creased. "Could this be the start of a Great Surge? For real?"

His friend shrugged her muscular shoulders. "Well, let's see. Why don't you compare what's happening here to some of the detailed records of the last Great Surge that we've all studied at length? Then we can make an educated guess as to whether this matches."

He sighed. "I've never read any of those records."

"Of course you haven't, because they don't exist. Humanity barely survived the last Great Surge. It took everything they had to stay alive. Nobody was bothering to write anything down or do any scholarship."

"You're saying we have no idea what presaged the Great Surge."

Akina nodded. "We know it happened. Wedge larger and in greater numbers than had ever been seen before came. They crossed the Dreadwall and rampaged across the southern lands. We know how it ended, more or less. And we've seen the monsters that came along at the end. Did it start like this? I have no idea."

Zhu pulled out another rib and shoved it through her sash, then moved over to the teeth. "There are fewer of the Wedge closer to the mountains, but that's not where the fortress is."

Remy tilted his head. "Are you sure? There are usually more of them as you go further north."

"Not anymore. They all come this way, near the fortress. It's why the Reaver's men are so rich. They get a concentrated river of Wedge to pick bones from. They call it fishing."

Akina and Remy shared another glance. She pointed at the ridge to the west. "Yes, I'm thinking the same thing. But right now, we have to kill that tyrant before he eats our army."

"How do you suggest we do that?"

She grinned. "Bearapult? As soon as it climbs over that crest."

Zhu crinkled her nose. "What's a bearapult?"

Remy sighed. "It's further proof of Petrik's questionable sense of humor."

Akina smiled. "You love it and you know you love it. Now set up."

Remy hung his head, beard scraping the bone-in-leather armor covering his broad chest, then nodded. He walked fifty feet west, gaze fixed on the ridge. "Here?"

Akina backed up. "Too far. You're out of practice."

He nodded and walked forward. "Good?"

"Perfect!" Remy turned his back to the ridge, cracked his neck, and laced his fingers together, palms up. Akina stood about fifty feet away.

Dog barked and Zhu stared. "Are you doing what I think you're doing?"

Akina smiled as she wrapped her hands in lengths of white cloth. "Probably. Not a mind reader."

Remy looked up at her. "Tell me when."

"You'll know when I start running at you, Remy. Just like always."

"We haven't done this in fifteen years. Maybe we should have practiced?"

Dog barked. Zhu pointed at the ridge. "I think I see it."

A head rose up over the hill, swaying left to right with ponderous rhythm. Its skin was as white as bleached human bone, cross-hatched with pink scars and oozing abrasions. Vertically-slit green eyes set into blood-red sclera scanned the ground without emotion.

Zhu hopped up and down. "Those teeth are as long as my arms! We're going to be rich!"

Remy snorted. "Only if we survive."

Akina looked at him. "I think it could swallow Remy in one bite. Should we test it, Remy?"

"I'd rather not, thanks."

"Fine, we'll go with plan A."

She jumped forward, spinning and facing to her left when her foot punched the ground. She rose higher, spinning faster, and hit the ground again.

Her next leap had both feet land squarely on Remy's interlaced hands. She squatted down into his hands, a fierce grin curling her lips.

Remy grunted and stood, extending at the hips and knees, hurling Akina up and over, the way men from his native village would hurl heavy stones over horizontal poles during sporting events.

She extended at the same time, leaping out of his hands, combining all the momentum of her run with the strength in her own hips and legs, both of them pouring qi into the motions.

She exploded out of his hands with a snap of air, suddenly thirty feet higher than the tyrant's head. Her energy spun furiously, a figure-eight torrent so dense she was sure it was visible to the naked eye.

The tyrant looked up and roared.

Remy, overextended, fell to his back but rolled, stood, and faced the tyrant. He threw two darts at the creature while Akina reached the apex of her leap, hands pulled back behind her shoulders, and began to descend.

Remy's darts tore lines across the monster's throat. It flinched and lowered its chin, pinning him with a venomous gaze.

Akina dropped.

"Infinity Bagua: Decreasing Function."

Her right fist rose up over her shoulder, over her head, and down, knuckles pointing at the ground as the weight of her entire body torqued through her elbow.

She shouted wordlessly, a scream that rose from the pit of her belly, loud enough to startle Wedge and Tae Kun soldiers alike as they fought.

Her knuckles struck the tyrant directly between its eyes.

Akina had spent two years taking down thousand-year-old trees, over a hundred feet high with trunks fifteen or twenty feet across. Teams of lumberjacks would weaken the bases until they were ready to fall, then give one final push. The crack as eight to ten feet of wood gave way to the weight that stretched up into the sky would echo across the entire valley.

The tyrant's skull was louder.

The creature stilled, then dropped, pitching forward and hitting the ground with a thud that shook the plain.

Akina landed next to it, panting with the exertion. Remy ran up, darts spinning overhead, ready to finish the tyrant if it showed any signs of life.

It didn't.

Dog followed on Remy's heels, barking at the fallen tyrant. A small cheer rose from the Tae Kun who were in position to see the size of the monster that had almost descended on their positions.

Akina leaned over, hands on thighs, and took deep breaths. She smiled at Remy. "Like old times, eh?"

He shrugged. "Most of it seems familiar, but not you being this tired afterwards." Zhu ran up and climbed onto the tyrant's head, looking at its eyes and teeth as if deciding which to carve out first.

Akina straightened. "Cut me some slack, I'm not young anymore. Do the others need help?"

Remy turned and surveyed the knots of soldiers finishing off the smaller Wedge around the area. "It does not appear so."

Dog barked several times, loudly.

Zhu stood straight, hand on her forehead to shield her eyes from the sun. "Guys?"

Remy looked at her. "What is it?"

"I think this guy brought friends."

••••••••••

Akina stood on legs less steady than she liked. "I probably shouldn't have blown so much energy on that first one."

Remy clapped her on the back. "You were just giving Arha a speech about second-guessing himself and now you're doing it? You couldn't have known. Three tyrants this size moving together was unheard of when we roamed the Wilds."

"That's not going to be much comfort to the soldiers who find themselves turned into tyrant scat. Any ideas?"

Remy frowned. "Tae Kun tactics are good for fighting large creatures like this. They'll win, but they'll also take heavy losses and we're counting on these soldiers to take out the Reaver."

Arha walked up to them, long axe handle slung over his shoulder, eyeing the tyrant corpse. "What's going on?"

Remy pointed. "Two more Wedge are coming, around the size of that one. We're not sure we have enough in reserve to take them on."

The Tae Kun chief dropped his axe. "We can handle them."

Remy shook his head. "I appreciate your confidence and your pride, old friend, but I'm afraid it's misplaced."

Princess Ramat walked toward them. If she wore any armor, it was subtle and hidden under white robes. Two heavily armored soldiers flanked her, both wielding swords of bone and wearing the Emperor's colors.

She narrowed her glowing violet eyes. "We'll take care of the two tyrants. You can move toward the fortress."

Arha shook his head. "My love, I couldn't bear to see you harmed. Those creatures are dangerous."

She levelled her gaze on him. "Sweet husband, so am I."

"But this isn't your battle."

"My father has not given me leave to fight the Reaver directly. But the Wedge are enemies to us all. This is the only way I can help. Besides which, I could use the exercise. It has been too long." She snapped her fingers and her two bodyguards drew their swords: three-foot lengths of sharpened bone.

Akina turned to face the central open area where the officers had gathered. Four griffins were held in place there by leather halters. "Will they be using the griffins?"

"We won't need them. And I'm not eager to explain to my father why some of his precious mounts have been injured, especially after what happened at the aviary."

Akina smiled nervously. "Right, that. Sure."

Two heads rose over the ridge, each matching the size and coloration of the first tyrant. Their eyes passed over their dead cousin without flinching. The creature on the left let out a roar.

Arha turned and shouted to his men. "Cover your eyes! Turn away from the princess!" He took a heavy cloth from his belt, of a type used to bandage a bad cut or stabilize a broken bone, and quickly wrapped it around his eyes.

Remy turned to Akina. "Have you ever seen the Emperor's bloodline in action?"

She shrugged as she tied a cloth around her eyes. "Has anybody? Isn't that the point?"

"I suppose." He began to bandage his eyes.

Zhu called out. "What are you doing?"

Akina, sightless, pointed in her general direction. "Cover your eyes."

"Is it forbidden to see the Emperor's power?"

"Just do it, Zhu. It's an order. We'll explain."

"Can I peek?"

"You really shouldn't."

"Fine."

Akina felt Remy's body heat as he stood close to her and spoke in a lowered voice. "Will she listen?"

"It's up to her. She should, though, it's an order."

"What about Dog?"

"He'll be fine. Probably. Maybe. You know, I should really do something about Dog." She raised her voice. "Here, Dog. Come here, boy."

A moment later, the animal was nuzzling her leg. She knelt and covered his face. He licked her palm.

The princess called for her guards. "Raise me."

"Yes, ma'am."

The tyrants roared. Akina could feel vibrations through the ground, stone and earth shaking with each enormous lizard step.

Dog barked, squirming to get free, but Akina held him tight. "You'd probably be fine anyway, but the girls would never forgive me if I let you get hurt. So quiet down and let me protect you for once."

He barked again but settled.

The princess called out again, louder. "Way of the Emperor: Solar Flare!"

Akina could sense an eruption of spiritual energy from the princess' direction that would have impressed even her grandfather. Her exposed skin burned as it might after lying in the sun for too long; her back warmed as if she had come too close to a bonfire. Dog barked.

Both tyrants began to roar in a different, higher pitch. They stomped the ground in a sudden staccato frenzy.

"Finish them!"

Akina let go of Dog and shouted, "You can look now! Help finish them!" She quickly uncovered her eyes and turned toward the tyrants.

The creatures rolled, stood, and stumbled, roaring and snapping at . . . nothing. The princess' bodyguards closed with drawn swords, slicing neat chunks of meat out of both creatures with methodical precision. The tyrants snapped back, biting and clawing at air, but missed widely with each attack.

Akina led her band closer.

Zhu exhaled. "Their eyes. Why are we even bothering to finish them?"

"They're still dangerous."

The red eyes of each tyrant were reduced to smoking craters, blackened flesh deep inside their skulls exposed to view.

The princess knelt, a smile on her dark cheeks, the glow from her eyes dimmed to near absence.

She looked at Akina, then pointed at the tyrants. "My value is not only in being the Emperor's favorite daughter."

Akina waved at Dog, who trotted to the princess. She petted him, relaxing with the movements. "Nobody doubted you, princess. Will you be all right?"

The princess smiled. "I might have been overeager. I'll be fine unless, in the way of comedic plays, there are three more tyrants behind those two."

Remy laughed. "If there are three more tyrants, and four more beyond them, we'll never have a chance to see how we match up against the Reaver."

Zhu looked at them. "I don't think that's funny. Is that supposed to be funny? And should the next wave be three or four? Then eight? Aren't they doubling?"

Akina laughed. “Zhu, under other circumstances, with that mathematical acuity, you’d be at the top of my list of potential disciples of Infinity Bagua. But I think we’re safe for now. Let the princess rest.”

Ramat put a hand down and pushed herself to her feet. “We shouldn’t stay here. My guards can carry me. Let us take this fight to the Reaver. I have questions for him.”

25

Siege on Reaver's Keep

Dog pawed at the gravel surface of the Shattered Plain, moving pieces of broken rock so he could bury his feces below the mostly flat surface.

Akina stood next to him and eyed the wall of soldiers that had formed between them and the Reaver's citadel, about a quarter mile from the hundred-and-fifty-foot-long skull that contained the keep's entrance.

Remy let out a breath. "I forgot how big that three-horn is. Five hundred feet long when it was alive?"

"Closer to six. And two hundred feet high. Makes you wonder how they ever managed to kill it."

Zhu pointed at the fortress. "Makes me wonder why it's facing west. Did it turn around and try to run before they finished it off?"

Akina turned to her student. "That's an interesting question. Not that we'll ever know the answer."

Arha disengaged from the Star Clan adepts he had been speaking with and approached the knights, his wife at his side. "They've sealed the area. Nobody within half a mile of that fortress can form a gate large enough to transport a person. The Reaver can't get out, and he can't get your girls out."

Akina nodded and watched as a dozen soldiers in the Reaver's colors made a break across the plain for the fortress. Tae Kun soldiers blocked them off, the shield bearers holding them back while the axe-wielders decapitated them. The leader of the Reaver's men drained his surviving companions of their life force and used the energy to electrocute the Tae Kun, killing two, before losing his head in retaliation.

Akina looked at Arha and the princess. "How many soldiers have you lost?"

His eyes tightened with regret as he shook his head. "Two dozen. We anticipated that. Not that it makes things any easier."

I almost told him I was sorry. I'm getting soft.

"What's next?"

"I'd like to break through the sides, but I'm being told that we can't. It's been reinforced by bone and spells for centuries. Which means we're going to have to go straight in through the mouth."

The skull, by itself larger than some towns Akina had lived in, was blunt-nosed, with three horns and a broad frill of bone framing its rear. The flesh had long since rotted off the body, but the spaces between bones had been filled in with wood, leather, and the carcasses of other creatures, leaving the open mouth the only obvious entrance.

The skeleton's sides had been similarly reinforced. Akina could sense the spells of sealing and protection from where she stood.

Living Wedge were chained to the sides: tyrants and saurids, smaller three-horns and ogres, leaking blood and missing limbs, chains of bone embedded in their flesh and anchoring them to the base of the fortress.

"Incoming!" The shout came from the soldiers. A flight of black-tipped arrows came from the top of the fortress, falling toward the Tae Kun formation.

Arha stepped between Ramat and the arrows but held out a hand. "We'll be fine."

The arrows struck an invisible barrier above the shield wall and clattered harmlessly to the grave.

Bear grunted approval. "How long can they hold that?"

Arha grinned. "They rotate maintaining the barrier. We can keep it up for weeks, I think. If we start to take losses, that changes things."

She looked at the mouth of the skull. Armored soldiers waited just inside the jaws, their expressions betraying no hint of fear or anxiety.

A fresh volley of missiles emerged from the fortress. Larger arrows, small boulders, and bundles of pitch set on fire were launched at them.

The griffins locked their gazes on the missiles, but none made it through the field above the shield wall.

Akina rubbed her temples. "They can't get out but we're going to have a bloody hard time getting in. This is a siege."

Arha nodded. "Were you expecting something else? This fortress has stood inviolate for hundreds of years. It only changes hands when the owner dies of old age. Or assassination. Come to think of it, never old age. But not open attacks, either."

"I know. I thought . . . never mind."

Zhu pointed at a makeshift platform in front of the skull's ocular cavity, in the shade of the upper-left horn.

"He's coming to talk to you."

"How do you know?"

Zhu shrugged. "There's motion up there, and that's what he does. He won't let you hang out here. He's going to want to taunt you some."

A voice boomed across the plain, far beyond what any human vocal cords could have produced. "Welcome, visitors from the Tae Kun. To what do I owe the pleasure of your visit?"

Dog stopped scratching at the gravel, faced the fortress, and barked. Remy spun toward it, then back to Akina, his eyes darkening as he listened.

Arha looked at Akina, eyebrows raised. She gritted her teeth. "Bru Wei is amplifying the Reaver's voice. He's an adept of the Bat Clan."

"Can he hear us if we answer?"

Zhu looked up, using her hand to shield her eyes from the sun. "Yes, but you'll have to be somewhere Bru Wei can notice you."

Arha waved an arm. "Bring the banner."

A heavily armored soldier, features lost between a double-shell helmet, jogged over. He planted the butt end of a ten-foot lance in the ground at Arha's feet, the clan's orange and blue banner fluttering near the sharp end.

The clan chief looked up at the tri-horn's eye socket and waved. "Hey, there." He turned to Zhu. "Can he hear me?"

The voice rang across the plain. "I hear you, Arha Tae Kun. Are you here to surrender the Spiral Witch to me? Perhaps along with a certain Imperial princess I understand is in the camp?"

Arha grinned. "You couldn't handle either of them, so I'll save you the face you'd lose from trying."

Something moved on the platform, then a chuckle echoed out from the fortress. "Your concern is touching, if misplaced. Surely even you are capable of seeing reason? The Millennium Qi does nobody any good while hidden away. We must harness it, use it to fight the Great Surge that's coming."

Arha shrugged. "My father-in-law will stop the next Surge, and the one after, just as surely as he went east and returned. Such is his sacred duty. Your words are hollow, Reaver. You seek power for yourself, not protection. Return the children. Forsake your forbidden techniques. There is still a chance for you. This does not have to end in your death."

"Do I hear fear, Arha Tae Kun? Do you seek to avoid confrontation?"

Remy faced Akina, his cheeks reddening fast. "I know that voice, don't I, Akina?"

She shook her head hard. "We can't do this now."

"Then when?"

"Later, I promise."

Arha straightened. "You say that you seek to preserve humanity's strength to fight the next Surge, yet you risk the lives of all these soldiers in your quest for personal gain. Your actions belie your words, Reaver. End this. I won't ask again."

The only response was more laughter.

Akina pushed Remy to the side to make room next to Arha, gripped the banner, and lifted her chin. “Reaver. Show me my girls. Now.”

“Fierce as ever, Akina. I’m glad. I thought you’d lost your spirit. Why should I do that?”

She swallowed. “If you don’t, I’ll assume they’re dead. I’ll invoke my death curse and burn my lifeforce to come after you. I’ll tear that fortress down with my bare hands.”

Remy stared into her stony expression.

A pause.

“That will result in your death and the destruction of the Millennium Qi.”

“If my girls are dead, I have nothing to live for anyway. Show them to me, healthy and whole, or this ends at nightfall.”

“Are you so sure you can breach this fortress? Even under a death curse?”

“I’m sure I’ll try. And I’m sure it will kill me. Even if I fail, you won’t get what you want. That’s a good enough outcome by my assessment.”

A rustle.

“I am starting to think you’re serious.”

Akina began to cycle her qi.

Gravel stirred and shook near her feet. The banner fluttering above her stilled, then stiffened into an arc pointing away from her. Soldiers standing nearby stepped away, leaving only Arha, Remy, Dog, Ramat, and Zhu near the banner.

Dog, facing the fortress, barked.

The Reaver’s voice rang out across the plain. “Wait, wait, Akina. They’re safe. I can only imagine what you think of me, but I’m no monster. Give me a few minutes to fetch them.”

She grunted as smaller pieces of gravel lifted into the air, swirling slowly around the group, tracing lazy circles in the air.

Remy cleared his throat. “Give him his time, Akina. He wouldn’t hurt them. No matter what he’s become. And how foolish would you feel for invoking the death curse only to find them alive and safe?”

Her cheeks tightened as the rocks spun faster.

Dog barked and ran to Akina. He put his paws on her thighs and licked her pants.

Zhu pointed and Remy nodded, scooping up the animal. He held Dog to Akina's face.

Dog licked her face, rough tongue scraping over her cheeks.

The stones settled to the ground.

Arha looked at Akina with wide eyes. She lowered her head and panted. Remy patted her back, Dog held to her face in his other hand.

Remy put his lips close to her ear and spoke. "Relax, Akina. Not yet. We'll get them back. You'll see."

She nodded, her shoulders shaking with the effort of self-control.

Dog barked; Remy put him down. "Akina, the Reaver . . ." His voice cracked.

She shook her head. "We'll talk later, Remy. I promised."

He turned to face the fortress, then back to her. "Later. We'd better."

"I said it."

Zhu looked at each of them. "What's going on? I missed something. What did I miss?"

Remy shook his head. "Later. She promised."

Zhu sighed. "I never understand anything. It's very frustrating. Oh, look, something's moving up there again."

They faced the fortress. The princess pointed. "Would you like a better view?"

Akina nodded and spoke, her mouth dry. "Please."

"Way of the Emperor: Magnify."

The air in front of the princess bent and warped, the image of the skull leaping at them so violently that Akina and Remy took involuntary steps backward, as if avoiding a collision.

The edge of the platform looked close enough to touch.

Ramat exhaled slowly, her hands extended, shaping the technique. "This isn't a gate. You can't step through it onto the skull. It's just an image. But it's true to what's up there."

Bru Wei stood at the front of the platform, eyes on the Tae Kun formation, the whirls and gnarls of the leather ears built up out of his cowl by Bat Clan artisans plain to see in the magnified picture. Soldiers milled about, several leaving the platform to create more room. The Reaver stood at the rear of the platform: average size, a purple mask covering his face, black bone armor over his torso and head. He moved and waved his arms as if speaking to the others, but no sounds were conveyed by the princess' technique.

Two soldiers stepped to the back of the platform, then down some stairs. Finally, figures climbed the stairs.

Akina swallowed.

Pooja came first, her eyes tight and fierce, gaze never leaving the soldiers around her. She was darker than most, though not as dark as Akina, with long black hair tied back in a simple ponytail.

Sneha followed. Two female soldiers flanked her: beefy women who kept firm grips on her shoulders as she walked. She reached the top step and stumbled, knocking one of the women hard enough to send her down the stairs before catching her balance.

The girl mouthed something that looked an awful lot like an insincere apology, her cheeks twitching in a familiar grin.

Two other soldiers took the big woman's place, corralling Sneha onto the platform with gentle hands.

Not manhandling the girls. That's good.

The Reaver waved at Bru Wei and said something. The Bat Clan adept nodded and waved the girls forward.

Pooja looked at him, then rushed to the edge of the platform, her eyes on the Tae Kun banner. She opened her mouth and Akina heard her daughter's voice for the first time in months.

"Mama!"

Dog barked.

Sneha's grin disappeared as she joined her sister. "Is she down there? Who are they?"

Pooja shook her head. "Shh. Listen."

Akina cleared her throat. Remy patted her shoulder.

"Girls, I'm here. Did they hurt you?"

Sneha gave a little hop. "You should be proud of me, Mama. I killed six of them, and Pooja got five."

Pooja twitched, hitting her sister with an elbow. "We might have escaped if you hadn't kept killing the guards, you know. You kept them on high alert."

Sneha shrugged. "What was I supposed to do, just follow orders like a *good girl*?"

Akina smiled and wiped her cheeks with the back of her hand. "I'm proud of both of you."

Sneha pointed at the plains below. "We got to travel through a really big gate, Mama. And see the Wilds. But we missed you."

Pooja nodded. "We walked our pattern every day, Mama. At least a hundred times. At least."

The Reaver walked up behind them. "You see, Akina? Safe and sound. As I promised. Now turn yourself over to me and I'll see that they stay that way."

Sneha shook her head. "You have to kill this one, Mama. He does bad things. Not to us, but still. His qi is ugly. Don't you worry about us, we'll be fine. Gather your friends and kill all of these bastards."

The Reaver sighed. "Do you see what I've been putting up with? Honestly, it will be a relief to let them go."

Akina loosened her hands, which had tightened into fists. "Girls, you stay good. And watch out for each other. Mama will take care of everything. I'll kill all of these—Sneha, don't use bad words."

"Sorry, Mama."

Pooja snickered. "She's totally not sorry. You should hear what she calls them when they're not—"

"Enough!" The Reaver gestured and the female guards ushered the girls back toward the stairs.

Pooja twisted her head and called out, "Sneha's right, Mama. You have to kill him."

Dog walked away from the magnified image and toward the supply wagons.

Akina smiled as their heads dropped below the border of the magnified image. "I will, girls. Don't worry. You can relax now."

The Reaver faced her. "Parents always lie to their children, don't they? Tell them they're special. Tell them everything will be fine. Tell them the Wedge aren't coming to steal them from their beds. It breaks my heart to see."

"You haven't hurt them, so I'll give you one last chance. Let them go, or I swear on qi and clan I'll break your heart in truth. With my fists, directly through your sternum."

Remy wheeled on her. "Akina! You can't . . . Don't—"

The Reaver laughed. "Of course she can, Remy. That's been her intention all along. Sweet, loyal Remy. She didn't tell you, did she?"

Remy's cheeks paled. "She didn't."

Akina looked into his eyes and shook her head. "I didn't know."

The Reaver shouted. "Tell the truth! You weren't sure he'd follow if he knew. Wouldn't go against me. So you didn't say."

"No, that's not right. I wasn't sure, Remy. I'm sorry."

Remy swallowed. "You suspected, though. I can see it on your face."

Dog barked.

She sighed. "We can talk about this later, Remy. Surely you can see—"

Remy shook his head, beard flapping with the motion. "Don't you dare. You should have told me, Akina."

She slapped his chest hard enough to knock him back a step. "I said later, Remy! They took my girls. I told you I'd do whatever it takes to get them back. Safe."

He stared at her, pain and anger warring in his eyes.

Zhu tapped Akina on the shoulder. "Something's bothering Dog."

"What? Dog? What's bothering him?" She spun in the direction Zhu pointed.

Dog stood twenty feet away, tail stiff and upright, and barked in the direction of the supply wagons. Akina walked closer; Ramat and Arha followed.

Zhu snapped her fingers and pointed again. "There, the gravel near my clanspeople. Do you see it?"

Akina muttered. The gravel was rustling. "Shit. He was distracting us. Come on."

She launched herself through the air, spinning faster with each leaping step, not looking to see if the others followed her.

Unluckily for whoever that is, I'm in the mood for a fight.

Arha shouted. "To the rear! Attack from the rear!"

Remy yelled after them, "They're coming from the mouth of the fortress! Arha, it's too many to ignore! Keep the wall in place!"

Arha cursed and fell back.

A patch of gravel fifteen feet across stirred, rotating like the surface of a whirlpool, the center sinking rapidly and revealing a pit.

Soldiers emerged in the Reaver's livery: purple and black cloth over cages of bone.

"Infinity Bagua: Major Wave."

Akina took one final leap and landed with legs outstretched. A wave tore through the gravel, concentric circles radiating outward from her landing point, knocking half the soldiers off their feet and sending plumes of loose stone over everyone nearby.

One squat man was first to his feet. He gripped another man by the shoulder, black light pouring over his fingers and into the other man's flesh. The squat soldier tilted his head back, taking an exaggerated breath, then threw his head forward, mouth so wide his uvula was prominently displayed.

Akina paled as she recognized the technique.

Remy's voice was in her ear: "Way of the Bear: Greater Den."

Flame poured out of the squat soldier's mouth, erupting in a column headed directly for Akina's position.

It struck Remy's shield, spreading and clawing at the technique, looking for a way to her, a hole to squeeze through or an edge to ooze around.

The drained man collapsed inward on himself, skin shriveling into his bones. He wasn't armed. In fact, his hands were chained together, his armor perfunctory at best.

Remy grunted next to her, the effort of maintaining his technique quickly using up his reserves.

Akina snarled. "They're draining prisoners. Or slaves."

The big man huffed. "He's lost his way, Akina. We have to help him. Mau—"

She interrupted. "He's beyond help, Remy. Look at what his men are doing."

"I know. But . . ."

"Duck."

Remy ducked as Akina leapt over his head, driving her knee into the face of a soldier coming up behind him. The big man spun and tossed a rope dart into the soldier's throat, finishing him.

Akina shouted, "Zhu, we can handle them. Check on the other front! The shield wall!"

"Got it!" Zhu turned and ran toward the fortress.

Remy retrieved his dart and set it and its companion spinning overhead. A cluster of soldiers had regained their footing and were moving toward the Star Clan formation.

"Remy, we can't let them reach. Those adepts can't defend themselves and maintain the seal around the area at the same time."

"Give me a moment." He rooted himself in the gravel, the rope darts spinning faster and faster, then shouted, "Winter Den."

A fresh shield of shimmering energy spread out from his darts, arcing out to the sides, then forward, closing into a circle in front of the running soldiers. It was much larger than any previous iteration.

The soldiers turned to face Akina. One of them laughed. "So much for the great Bear of the Five Fangs. You missed! That shield can't protect you! You're trapped in here!"

Remy chuckled. "I didn't miss. We're not the ones who are trapped."

Akina bared her teeth and set her feet. "Simultaneous Equations."

26

Castling the Storm

Ramat's eyes flared with violet light, casting a purple haze over the dark corners of the command tent. "Dear husband, I'm sure it's very gratifying to order our soldiers into futile frontal attacks on that fortress and see them shed blood on your orders, but it is not going to result in victory for our clan."

Arha stood across a folding wooden table from her, rubbing his eyes. Blood and gore stained his outer robes; they had sufficient drinking water but not enough to bathe. "I am aware, oh flower of my dreams, that our strategy is not working. Do you have any suggestions? I am composed of nothing but eagerness to absorb your wisdom."

Akina smiled. She sat on a rug a few feet away, scratching at a patch of blood that had dried on her jacket.

Ramat nodded. "I have studied strategy, honorable husband. In the capital we have libraries full of books on the waging of war. If you had overwhelming numbers, perhaps we could force our way through the front, but we simply do not."

Arha nodded. "What else can we do? Retreat?"

Akina's nostrils flared. "You promised to help me."

"I did, but I cannot do what I cannot do. I won't waste the resources of my clan on a helpless cause, no matter what I promised."

Remy cracked his neck. "Can we wait them out? We're outside, they're inside. They'll run out of food and water eventually."

Zhu paused her pacing to shake her head. "They have a cocovado grove inside the fortress. There's also an underground stream. Starving them out will take forever."

Arha waved his hand. "It doesn't matter. The Star Clan adepts can't maintain their lock forever, remember? I said weeks, at most. And that's assuming no more adepts are lost in surprise attacks." Sorties from the fortress had tried for the adepts three times already; during the second attempt, they'd managed to kill one of them. "Once the seal fails, the Reaver's men will be able to gate in and out at will. No more siege."

Remy ran fingers through his red beard. "Can we smoke them out? Light a fire?"

The princess snorted. "On an open plain? And with what? Are you aware of a nearby forest full of kindling I have missed?"

The big man shrugged. "I'm just thinking out loud."

Arha looked at his wife. "Darling, you know I hold you in the highest esteem for your intellect as well as for your beauty. Do you have any suggestions for me? Any thoughts, no matter how nascent?"

Akina struggled not to laugh out loud. "Yes, please. Any suggestions? We're all experienced fighting Wedge but not humans in a fortress."

Ramat pinched her chin between thumb and forefinger. "In the stories, the attackers find some weakness in the fortress. They sneak in through the water supply or uncover a secret exit." Dog nuzzled her leg; she stooped to scratch his back.

Zhu stood and nodded. "I remember stories like that! We need someone on the inside to open a back door! Someone willing to betray the Reaver!"

Akina stood, noticing the younger woman's excitement. "That's a good idea! Can you think of anybody? A friend of yours? Somebody dissatisfied with their place in the Reaver's power structure? Someone we could bribe?"

Zhu sagged back onto her heels. “I can’t think of anybody. Sorry. Most of the Reaver’s men are fanatical in how they support him. Just eager to make their way up the ranks and learn the Reaver’s Reap. The ones who don’t like how things work either leave or get killed pretty quickly.”

Remy looked at her. “Is there any way to gate inside?”

Zhu shrugged. “I can’t gate a person anywhere inside this seal. So, no.”

Remy and Akina locked eyes. Akina turned to Zhu. “What if the seal wasn’t there?”

Zhu looked back. “What do you mean?”

“What if *we* broke the seal? Could you gate us in?”

Zhu paused. “Kind of. Maybe.”

Remy sighed. “A little clarity, please.”

Zhu blew hard through loose lips. “The skeleton is sealed. You can’t form a gate through it. When we gated away from the fortress, we’d leave the fortress, form the gate to wherever, then walk through.”

Remy looked down at her. “That does not sound like a ‘kind of,’ let alone a ‘maybe.’ Perhaps you left out some details?”

She shrugged. “Well, there’s a way in. The spells follow the body of the three-horn. It was pretty heavily armored. Except for the mouth, obviously. That was open. Otherwise it couldn’t eat. So the Reaver had to make sure to set up a special set of seals around the mouth area to prevent people from just gating inside through it.”

“And those seals are . . . what? Are they vulnerable somehow?”

Zhu squirmed, rubbing her ear on her shoulder. “Well, no. The mouth is sealed shut. But I realized that if the mouth was a potential entrance, since food had to pass through it, there had to be a matching exit. On the other side.”

Akina snorted and brushed a lock of hair off her forehead. “The three-horn’s anus.”

“We checked, just out of curiosity, and the opening is, well, relatively small, but it’s not enchanted. You’d have to be really precise to bend space through it.”

Remy laughed. "Can you do it, girl?"

"Not a girl. And yes, probably, if not for the seal my clanspeople are keeping."

"We can work around that."

••••••••••

Akina walked an infinity pattern in the open area west of the Tae Kun camp. She kept her eyes on the edge of the approaching nightshade as it cast darkness over the Shattered Plain, a line of shadow stretching north to the Spine of the World and disappearing into the southern haze. Dog snored nearby, lying in a small indentation he'd dug in the gravel. The growls and whines of injured Wedge, chained to the fortress, wafted over the plain between them.

The line of night struck the tail of the Reaver's fortress as Remy walked close to her and cleared his throat. She sighed and stopped in the center of her pattern.

"What is it, Remy?"

"It's later, Akina. That's what it is."

I had a feeling he was going to say that.

"You didn't come to me that first day."

"We've been busy fighting his men. And I needed to cool off a bit. I didn't want to talk while hot-headed."

"Very mature of you."

"I'm an old man. I've learned to still my temper, and I can wait for the right time to talk about something troublesome. But I won't go without answers forever, and now seems like the right time."

Her sweat dried quickly in the cool breeze.

"What do you want, Remy? An apology?"

"How could you?" His voice was tight.

"How *couldn't* I? They're my girls. They're my world. More than that. I told you up front that I would do anything for them. I meant it."

"You should have told me who the Reaver is. Especially with what he meant to me. To us. Instead, you lied, Akina. You didn't even have to."

"I couldn't take the chance that knowing would keep you from coming with me. And I never lied. Did I tell you everything? No, I suppose not. But I never lied."

They turned as crunching gravel signaled someone's approach.

Zhu walked up to Dog and rubbed his back. "You called me? I thought I heard my name."

Akina shook her head. "Nobody called you, Zhu."

"Really? I could have sworn you called me. It's the Shattered Plain, you know. Playing tricks with sound."

Remy looked down at her. "What do you want?"

"I told you. I thought you called me."

"Really."

"Also, I wanted to know what was going on. With you and Remy and the Reaver."

Akina exhaled. "Go back to camp, Zhu."

Remy turned to her. "Why? Why shouldn't she hear? She's come this far with us. Risked her life for us. I say she stays."

Akina stared at him for a dozen heartbeats, then at Zhu. "Fine. She stays."

Zhu sat on the ground and nodded. "So, what's going on? Why was Remy so freaked out by the Reaver? Is his voice weird? I don't think his voice is weird, but I've heard it before."

Remy grunted. "Nothing so simple. You know of the Five Fangs?"

Zhu shrugged. "Of course. You guys."

"Yes, but not just us. There were five of us."

"I know that. You were the *Five* Fangs. I'm not a moron."

"There was Petrik, who died. And Rei, who we think is off to the west."

"Right. What's his name told you about Rei. The map guy."

"Which leaves one more."

"I know. I told you, I'm not a moron. I can count to five. I bet I could even count to ten. Twenty, if I take my shoes off."

"Girl, do you want answers, or do you want to demonstrate how obnoxious you can be?"

"Can't I have both? I mean, sorry! Sorry. I'll be good."

"Mau-rhi, Rei's sibling. I've told you about him."

Zhu nodded. "So, what? Your old friend is the Reaver? Is that the big deal?"

Remy's cheeks darkened. "Yes."

"I don't get it. What's the problem?"

"He's our friend."

Akina grunted. "Was our friend."

"Fine, *was* our friend. We saved one another's lives, too many times to count. He fought Arha to save Akina from, well, whatever Arha had planned."

"Arha? You mean to tell me that the Tae Kun you fought in a bar the first time you met was Arha?"

Akina laughed. "You thought he disliked me for no reason?"

"I didn't—are you messing with me? If you fought with him, why does he like Remy so much? He treats you like his best friend."

Remy smiled. "Years after that incident, I found myself in a position to render Arha assistance. Which was of great value to him."

"What could you have possibly done for the leader of the Tae Kun to balance out beating him up in a bar?"

Akina chuckled. "Yes, tell her, Remy. Whatever did you do? Did you guard him on some epic quest? Defeat some Wedge threatening his holdings? Save him from the Reaver's assassins?"

Remy looked at her as he slowly shook his head. "Don't do this, Akina."

Zhu sat up straighter. "Do what? Is it a bad thing? I want to hear! Somebody tell me something, please."

Remy groaned. "I helped him with a situation, is all. Nothing dramatic."

Zhu shook her head. "I bet it was dramatic. So dramatic. If it wasn't, there's no way he'd have treated you like his best friend. If you don't want to explain, I can always go and ask him myself. I'm sure he'll be happy to tell me. I'm very persuasive."

Akina snorted. "That's one way to describe you."

Remy sighed. "Don't do that. I'll tell you. I helped him with a lady problem."

"What kind of lady problem? Was someone pregnant? I mean, on accident? That seems to happen to guys like Arha a lot. I'm not sure exactly how."

Remy's cheeks colored again. "No. Well, not at first. Arha was in love. With a woman. Who had no interest in him. I helped him rectify the situation."

Zhu snorted. "You? How? Did you kidnap her?"

"What? No! How do you think romance works, young lady? I can tell you, kidnapping is rarely part of it."

Akina walked to Dog's other side and joined Zhu in scratching him. "I don't think 'rarely' is the word you want to use there, Remy."

"Regardless, the answer is no, there was no kidnapping. I simply advised him in the appropriate way to romance a woman of quality."

Akina smiled. "You did more than advise him. You hid in the bushes and whispered instructions to him during their chats, didn't you?"

Zhu looked up at Remy. "You? You're trying to tell me that you're an expert in seducing women?"

Remy coughed, pounding his chest to clear his lungs. "Not an expert, exactly." His breathing returned to normal. "I'm just a good listener. I understand what women are looking for. And I so informed Arha. It was easier than you'd think."

Akina pointed at him. "Then there's the tongue thing. Don't forget that, Remy."

Zhu looked at her. "What? What?"

Remy shook his head. "I passed along a tidbit I had heard. From a lady friend. About something that greatly pleases a woman. Simply a rumor, nothing more. A suggestion."

Zhu looked at her hands, tapped her fingers together, then blushed. "Oh! I know what you mean. I think. I mean, I've heard. Not *know*. You told him to do *that*? And it worked? By the Emperor, what would happen if the princess heard about this?" She stood and spun, eyes narrowing as she stared into the darkness all around, looking for eavesdroppers.

Night crossed over them.

Remy sat heavily on the gravel. "I'm sure this would come as no surprise to the princess, Zhu. I'm not sure she'd appreciate finding out that you know about it. Though if you really want to bring up the subject, I suppose I can't stop you . . ."

"Wait, is this woman you helped him with—is it the princess? Is that what we're talking about? You helped him find a wife?"

Akina chuckled. "Not just *a* wife. *The* wife. Perhaps the most beautiful woman on the continent. Certainly one of the most influential. And one far above even Arha's station."

"And you coached him into landing her for himself. Nice work. Not what I would have expected from you."

"Zhu, you wound my pride. When have I given you cause to doubt my insight into the female condition?"

"Well, you're kind of a big, fat oaf. How was I supposed to know?"

Akina leaned over and jabbed her elbow into Zhu's shoulder. "Don't judge a person by their appearance, Zhu. Let this be a lesson for you."

"Okay, I'll believe I was wrong about the Bear over here. But I still don't understand one thing."

Akina picked up a small stone and threw it into the distance. "Just one?"

"Ha ha. Seriously. Why does it matter that he was your friend once? Back to the Reaver. If he was still that guy, your friend who saved your lives, he wouldn't have just kidnapped your daughters, would he? So he's clearly become something else. Why is killing him so devastating to you then?" She looked at Akina when she started but shifted to Remy by the end.

He ran his fingers through his beard. "You're young, Zhu. You don't have our experience. Yes, people change, but not so much. Not without a reason. Yes, he took Akina's daughters. But he didn't hurt them. He just wanted her attention. I don't think he meant them, or her, any harm."

Dog shifted in his sleep as Akina stopped petting him and stood. "That's why I didn't tell you, Remy. You can't let yourself believe he's become a monster. Because you're too nice. Too kind. Too generous. You don't think he's become insane because you don't want to think it. You care about him too much, even after all this time. But we've already seen enough here to know you're wrong."

"We just have to talk to him, Akina. He's afraid of the Wedge. You know that. The next Great Surge. Tell him you'll help. Tell him you'll fight alongside him. Tell him we both will. We can stay here. Your girls will be fine. Or send them somewhere safer. They can stay with Rei. We don't have to spill one another's blood."

"Remy, I love you like a brother, but you've gone soft in the head if you think that's going to work. He's been using the forbidden techniques. The Reap. There's a reason they're forbidden; it's poisoned his mind. His very soul. There's no going back, no saving him. He's a threat to us all as long as he draws breath. A threat to us and to my girls."

"Don't say that, Akina. I . . . just don't."

Zhu cleared her throat. "You are worrying an awful lot about whether you should kill the Reaver when you have no idea how to kill him. Have you seen him fight? Wasn't he nearly as tough as you two, way back when? And now he has the Reap adding to it."

Remy pointed to Akina. "She has the Millennium Qi now. And Mau-rhi was never as tough as her."

The younger woman stood up from Dog's side. "I don't know about that, but I've seen her fight, and I've seen the Reaver fight. I'm telling you, this is a discussion you don't need to have. You want me to gate you in through that three-horn's butthole so you can steal your daughters back? Great. I'll do it. But if you think you can fight the Reaver, just the three of us? When he'll probably have Bru Wei and Faceless by his side? No chance."

Akina's lips tightened. "Four."

"Four? Four what?"

"You miscounted. There are four of us who will go in to fight the Reaver."

Zhu pointed at them. "One, two, three . . . who am I missing? Is Arha coming? The princess?"

Akina shook her head. "Not them. Dog."

"What's he going to do, hump the Reaver to death?"

"He'll be our courage. I keep explaining, Dog isn't afraid of anything."

Zhu looked at Remy. "I appreciate confidence as much as the next person, but I think she's going to get us all killed."

Remy shrugged. "It does seem likely. Better make your peace with your gods tonight, little one. I don't think you'll get many more chances."

27

Counter-Siege

Arha sat at a table in his command tent and sliced a section off a cold meat roll. It was the same food his soldiers were breaking fast with around the camp, though they weren't sitting at polished tables and using fine bone utensils.

"Explain it to me once more, but slowly, and use simple words, as if I were a child. Because I am certain that I am missing some key component of your request, and only through plain language and patronizing clarity will I be sure that I am correct." He put the greasy chunk of bread in his mouth and began the onerous process of chewing it.

Akina's stomach grumbled; she hadn't eaten yet. Zhu's stomach answered hers. Dog barked and sat near Arha's feet, eyes big as he stared at the food. Akina turned a beseeching glance on Remy, who nodded and spoke.

"Arha, old friend, it's not as crazy as it sounds. We want you to muster your troops and attack the fortress from the front. Then, once the defenses are fully engaged, we want the Star Clan to drop the seal."

Arha swallowed. "Drop the seal. Which is the only thing stopping the Reaver from taking the children and running away." He sliced off another chunk of his roll and passed it under the table to Dog. Zhu twitched as if she were about to steal the food, but she held her ground.

"Well, yes. But only briefly. Zhu can form a gate to get us inside the fortress, but only if the seal is down. So during the fighting, drop the seal and we'll get inside. Then we'll rescue the girls and you can disengage your troops." Dog dropped the bread to the floor and bit pieces out of it.

Akina nodded. "He won't run, Arha. He doesn't really want to. He wants me. If I go inside the fortress, he'll leave the battle to face me. We'll fight and I'll end this little war with my own hands."

Remy shook his head. "It's not about what we do or don't do to the Reaver, Akina. This is about rescuing your daughters."

Arha snorted. "You two need to coordinate your plans better. Are you stealing the girls out from behind the Reaver's back or going in there to end the threat he presents?"

Remy said, "Steal the girls."

Akina said, "Kill the Reaver."

They glared at each other. Zhu snorted a laugh, quickly covering her face with her hand to stifle the sound.

Arha shook his head. "This sounds like the worst sort of rubbish made up by storytellers and minstrels. How are we supposed to coordinate these things so precisely? If they drop the seal before you're ready, the Reaver will have time to send his own troops through gates and disrupt our attack. Meanwhile, we can't gate inside because the fortress is still protected by its old enchantments. And what are you going to do if you succeed? You'll have to find the girls somewhere inside that enormous fortress. If you're right and he turns back to face you, then what? You'll have no backup, no support. You'll be facing the Reaver and Faceless and who knows how many other of his lieutenants while locked inside with him. You're asking me to throw my men's lives away for nothing."

Akina stepped closer to him and put her palms on the table, leaning toward the clan chief. "Zhu will sense when the seal is dropped. We'll be ready to go that second. If that's not enough for you, we can time it by nightfall. Say, when the nightshadow strikes the tip of the fortress' tail. Or something. And I can finish the Reaver. Don't forget who I am."

"If you were so confident you could take out the Reaver, why did you bother dragging my clan all this way?"

Akina leaned back. "I couldn't face him and his entire army. As long as your men are at the mouth of the fortress, they'll be occupied. Remy and I can take the Reaver and Faceless. And Bru Wei if we have to."

Arha bit off another chunk of roll. "Remy? Is she right? Can you beat them? Are you going to help her bring me his head?"

Remy paled. "His head? But I'm not sure—"

Arha slammed the hilt of his knife into the table. "I didn't bring my men this far, sacrifice so much blood, just for those two girls! I came here to get rid of that menace! If you're second-guessing that goal, I'm going to have to second-guess my involvement in this carriage wreck of an excursion!"

Remy sputtered. "No, that's not what I meant. We're going to stop him. We have to. But that doesn't mean we have to kill him. There are other ways. Always, there are other ways."

Akina rubbed the bridge of her nose. "Remy, please. We've talked about this."

He turned to her. "You've talked. I've talked. That's not the same as *we've* talked. You're not listening to what I'm saying. I'm not sworn to your service, I'm your friend. I'm not just going to follow your orders without question."

A soldier pulled aside the flap covering the entrance and stepped into the tent. "Imperial messenger here for you, sir."

Arha nodded. "Send them in." The soldier nodded and turned away, letting the flap close. Dog barked, then waited for Arha to give him more food.

A woman entered, dressed in purple and gold, her long dark hair in disarray. She wore thick leather leggings and carried a scroll case.

"Chief Arha?"

Arha stood and reached out a hand. "That's me. You have something for me?"

She nodded and popped open the scroll case, pulled out a roll of parchment, and handed it over. "Yes, sir. It's an informal communication only, sir. His Majesty wanted me to relay that very explicitly. And to relay the contents verbally as well, in case there are any concerns."

"Of course. Please, go ahead. You can talk in front of them."

"Yes, sir. The war in the martial world has progressed significantly. Early battles were inconclusive, and both sides have pulled in allies and so on. At this point, every major clan across the north and south has committed significant forces to the war. Early casualty reports indicate over a hundred dead."

Arha exhaled. "Go on."

"His Majesty hopes you will be able to return soon and with sufficient force to assist in ending the conflict."

Arha unrolled the parchment and read it. "That's not an order."

"No, sir. It is his hope. His Majesty was very clear on that point."

"Is he asking me to abandon this siege?"

"His Majesty also expressed his sincere hope that he can soon wake up without the need to concern himself with the Reaver or his abhorrent practices. Sir."

Arha sighed. "I understand."

"One last thing, sir. This isn't on the scroll, but His Majesty wanted me to wish you the best of luck."

Arha snorted. "Really?"

"Yes, sir. And, between you and I, His Majesty has a most unique sense of humor, but I believe he meant that with complete sincerity."

"Did he now? That's interesting. Please, avail yourself of whatever hospitality we have to offer, and convey my thanks to His Majesty."

"Of course, sir. My griffin and I will be on our way. My thanks."

She turned and left the tent.

Akina looked at Arha. "I don't speak Emperor. What does all that mean?"

Arha snorted. "It means he wants me to hurry the hell up. But since he won't help me take out the Reaver, and can't suggest any methods of doing so, he won't order me to do anything specific. Just express generalized hopes that things happen the way he wants."

"So, what are you going to do?"

Arha shook his head. "This war presents opportunities. Both to gain power and to gain my father in law's favor. Good opportunities for my clan. But I can't take advantage of them if three quarters of my soldiers are killed in the mouth of that fortress. So for now, we're going to do nothing but wait here until the Reaver loses patience and does something stupid."

A voice rang out across their camp. "Arha Tae Kun! Come and speak with me! I grow impatient!"

Remy and Akina exchanged confused glances. Arha stood and wiped his mouth on a cloth napkin before tossing the last piece of his breakfast to Dog. "Let's see what that lunatic wants now." He left the tent.

They formed a circle around the Tae Kun banner still planted in the gravel where the clan herald had placed it three days earlier. The princess was already there, accompanied by two of her bodyguards.

"I'm here, Reaver. Are you ready to surrender?"

The eye of the fortress was far enough away that they could barely make out the Reaver, the masked figure moving about on the platform. Bru Wei stood in front of him, manipulating their voices so the groups could hear one another as clearly as if they stood on opposite sides of a dinner table. Akina found her hands tightened into fists and slowly worked her fingers loose while he spoke.

"Your presence is annoying me. There is work to be done, and this siege is interfering with it. To the detriment of us all."

Arha nodded. "Surrender and I'll end the siege. We can get to work doing whatever it is that you think needs doing. Without the poison of your forbidden techniques."

"Those techniques are our best chance of defeating the next Surge, Arha. You've faced Wedge attacks these past few days, have you not? What will you do when faced with a Great Surge? With tyrants ten times the size of the ones you faced last week?"

Arha and his wife traded glances. Arha faced forward. "Say what you have to say, Reaver."

"My fight is with the Wedge, not with your people or even the Emperor. Leave now. We'll call this battle a stalemate. Nobody needs to lose face. Leave with your forces intact."

"Or else . . . what, exactly? You'll continue to cower inside your fortress, hiding from combat with those whose strength you denigrate?"

Akina nodded. *You're smarter than I remembered, Arha. Making him angry. Maybe it will work and he'll do something stupid.*

"If you don't leave of your own accord, I'll have you destroyed."

"Destroyed? How? The odor of your corpse fortress? Boredom? Do you think we'll yawn ourselves to death?"

A pause.

"You mock me. I understand. You have no other weapons at hand. Unfortunately, the same cannot be said for me. Leave, or you will be destroyed. Sunset tomorrow. Remember, this is not the outcome I desired. My quarrel is not with you."

Arha opened his mouth; closed it. Turned to his wife. "What do I say?"

She shrugged, her violet eyes dim but steely. "Say nothing. There is nothing to say, after all."

He nodded, hung his head for a long breath, then looked around at his friends. "Can anyone block that eavesdropping? Or can Bru Wei hear whatever he wants, whenever he wants?"

Remy drew his rope darts and started spinning them. "I can block him. I've been working on a way to make my shields stop sound. Way of the Bear: Quiet Den." A film of energy rose around the group.

Arha looked around. "Is he bluffing? What's going on here?"

The princess shook her head, casting shifting shadows as the lights of her eyes changed direction. "If he had a secret way to destroy you, why wouldn't he? Why warn you off? What does he have to gain?"

Remy grunted. "You don't know him. You're thinking of him as a mad, power-hungry warlord establishing a base out here in the Wilds."

She lit him purple with her gaze. "Are you trying to say he's not exactly that? Are my eyes lying to me?"

"Perhaps he is those things. But his words, his philosophy, are not just a way to control his followers. He believes what he says. He thinks his way is the best way, or the only way, to save humans from the Wedge. It's not just something he says to attain loyalty from his men."

"So?"

"He genuinely doesn't want to kill us. If he destroys us, he'll weaken the forces of humanity. You have over four hundred highly trained warriors, each the culmination of over ten years of disciplined practice. And there's Akina. Whatever secret weapon he might have, it could hurt her. And he doesn't want that; he wants the Millennium Qi. I don't think he's bluffing."

She nodded. "What is this secret weapon, then? Since you're so sure he's not lying."

Remy shrugged his heavy shoulders. "I have no idea. But that doesn't mean there isn't one."

Silence fell. Akina studied her companions.

"What are you going to do? Are you withdrawing?"

Arha sighed. "The Emperor wants us to kill the Reaver, so retreat isn't an option. We don't have the numbers to attack the fortress. So we continue as we were and hope his secret weapon involves charging out the front gate and attacking."

Ramat nodded. "He's a madman. That's why the Reap is a forbidden technique; it damages the soul. He'll come out of his fortress and we'll destroy him out on the plain."

Remy shrugged, out of arguments. Dog let out a snore from his spot ten feet away.

Akina exhaled and pulled a strand of hair back from her forehead, tucking it under her straw hat. "We think we have a way into the fortress. We told Arha earlier."

The princess nodded. "If you have a way in, why aren't you using it?"

Arha interrupted. "She needs us to start a full-frontal assault. And drop the Star Clan seal. And she's not sure it will work. I said no."

The princess sighed. "That is a tremendous risk. I think you're making the right call."

Akina cracked her knuckles. "We can end this. Prevent any surprises from biting us in the backside. It just takes a little commitment. You're not willing?"

Stony faces gave their answer.

Akina sighed. "I understand. We'll wait. Come on, Zhu. I noticed something in your form. I want to fix it before it becomes habit. Remy, keep an eye on Dog. If you don't mind." Her tone was cold.

Remy swallowed and nodded as Akina led Zhu to the open plain west of the camp.

Zhu tugged at Akina's sleeve. "Are you mad at Remy?"

"What makes you say that?"

"I don't know. Your super angry voice, maybe. And the way you stare at him like you wish he'd be struck by lightning and fall over dead."

"Is that how I stare at him?"

"Only now. Not usually."

Akina walked a hundred yards before answering. "He doesn't see what needs to be done. He's letting his feelings get the better of him. The Reaver can't be saved; he's gone too far."

Zhu nodded. "Sure, absolutely. I see that. But what if you're the one letting your feelings get the better of you?"

"I'm not the emotional one."

"Still, they're your daughters. But if you say so, sure. I mean, it's not up to me."

"No, it is not."

They walked another two hundred yards.

Zhu cleared her throat. "I had another question."

"I hope it's about the flaw in your cycling technique."

"No, I figured you were going to tell me that without a question. Something else."

"Fine. Go ahead."

"I get that you want to save your daughters, really, I do. It's sweet. It's sure as hell more than my mom would do for me." She paused to breathe.

"That's not a question."

"I know. I'm getting to it. Sorry. The thing is, a lot of people are dying because of your plans. Like, a *lot* a lot. Do I have this wrong, or didn't you start like a huge war to get the Tae Kun to help you?"

"Keep that to yourself. But yes."

"That's a lot of other people who will lose their daughters so that you can save yours. I don't know, is that okay? That doesn't seem okay. Maybe."

"Are you going to try to stop me?"

"Me? Oh, no. That's not—that's not what I'm saying. Trying to say. I'm sworn to you, that hasn't changed. For, I don't know, a bunch more days. I lost track."

"You should pay more attention. That's the sort of thing you need to remember." *I lost track too. I'm getting old.*

"So how do you justify it? Causing all that death and suffering just for your girls? Breaking other mothers' hearts to save your own? And what if the Reaver is right? What if working with him is the only way to stop the Great Surge? He and Faceless believe it's coming. I feel like you haven't considered that."

Do I argue with her? Tell her that it's the clans' own fault? If they had just talked to each other, they could have avoided all this? Tell her that they're always looking for an excuse to fight? That if not for me, they would have found something else to war over?

Or do I admit the truth—that none of that matters? That I would have sacrificed all those children for mine regardless?

Akina stopped, gravel skittering away from her planted foot. She faced Zhu, who flinched back when she saw Akina's face.

"Girl, did you think I was the hero of this story? Or the villain?"

Zhu swallowed. "I don't know. Compared to the Reaver? He's awful. And you're a mom just trying to save your kids. I guess I figured you were the hero."

Akina nodded. "Perhaps you figured wrong. Now come, I'll show you where your weight shifts too early when you walk the pattern."

28

Through the Triceratbottoms

A day and a half passed. The fortress was quiet, other than the endless cries of crippled Wedge; no sorties occurred.

A rainstorm came and went.

Akina cycled qi, walked her pattern, and felt anxiety build inexorably in the base of her gut. Zhu practiced nearby, eyeing the older woman's movements, looking for the secrets to her techniques.

Dog slept and occasionally barked, facing west toward mile after mile of nothing.

Remy stayed clear of his friends, resting and training on the other side of the camp.

The nightshade was fast approaching from the east when a Tae Kun soldier ran up to Akina's practice area. The soldier skidded to a stop, gravel spraying, and threw a quick salute.

"Azure Dragon, Chief Tae Kun requests your presence."

Akina stopped in the center of her pattern and focused on the soldier. "Why? So he can tell me we're going to wait out here doing nothing for another week? A month?"

"I do not believe so, ma'am. Please, come with me."

Akina shrugged. "Zhu, come. As my disciple, when my time is wasted, yours should be as well."

Zhu shrugged and followed her teacher into the camp, Dog trotting behind. The soldier held open the entrance to the command tent. Remy was already inside.

Arha pinned her with his eyes. "We have news."

Akina shrugged. "Does this have something to do with the flurry of griffins that have been coming and going recently?"

His face was grim. "We've been using the griffins for long distance scouting. There's a pack of Wedge approaching. From the west, as you'd imagine. But these are different than normal."

Akina looked at Remy, who wouldn't meet her eyes. "What do you mean? How?"

Princess Ramat rubbed her hands together. "It's a big pack. The tyrants leading it are larger than the ones we fought. At least a dozen tyrants, each twice the size of the three we defeated earlier. Several score lesser tyrants and flocks of saurids. Two three-horns."

Akina let out a soft whistle. "I hate to ask, but are you sure? Did a griffin rider see a normal pack and panic?"

Arha barked a humorless laugh. "That was my first thought. We sent a second scouting team to confirm. We're sure."

"Could it be an illusion? A technique? A pack that size isn't quite a Surge but it's . . . historic."

Arha looked to his wife. "You see? Same thing I said."

She patted his arm. "Your wit is as keen as ever, my husband." She turned to Akina. "We sent adepts skilled in piercing illusions. Either the Wedge are real or they're the product of an illusion magic more advanced than anyone has ever seen."

Akina looked at Remy, who continued to avoid her gaze. "When do they arrive?"

Arha looked at a canvas map stretched across the table before him. "Nightfall tomorrow. Perhaps a bit later."

Akina nodded. "So, what's the plan? Or did you call me here to ask me for ideas?"

The princess shook her head. "We're leaving. We might lose face, but we can't stop a pack that size with the forces we have here. Not on an open plain. It's untenable."

Arha nodded. "I'm sorry, Akina. I tried. But this has turned into a suicide mission, and I'm not risking my clan for it."

Akina rubbed her temples. "You're just going to run?"

"I don't see what choice we have."

"Attack tonight. Using the plan we came up with. Take out the Reaver. Be gone before the pack sets a claw on the Shattered Plain."

"Nothing has changed in the fortress, Akina. We can't do it."

I need to force his hand.

"You have to do it. You don't have a choice."

Arha's voice darkened. "What do you mean? You're not threatening me, are you?"

"The Reaver is in collusion with the Wedge. He told you he had a weapon that would destroy you, and a day later a pack the likes of which we haven't seen in a thousand years comes marching down to nip at your backside. Are you trying to tell me you think these things are unconnected? He called for them, and they answered. There is no greater sin than working with the Wedge. You have to kill him. Or help me kill him."

Remy wheeled on her. "You don't know that. You can't be sure."

"Don't I? More importantly, what will everyone else believe when they hear the story? The Emperor? They'll see that the Tae Kun observed direct evidence of collaboration with the Wedge and, instead of handling it, turned tail and ran. You could have left yesterday or the day before and suffered no more than a simple loss of face. Now? It's a lot more serious."

Arha looked at his wife, whose lips tightened into colorless lines. "She might be right."

Ramat shook her head slowly. "I don't know. Even if she is, what can we do? I certainly can't stop those Wedge. I could possibly take my bodyguard out and slow them down, but we'd die in the process, and it wouldn't gain you much advantage."

She's no coward, I'll give her that.

Akina stepped closer to the pair. "You don't have to fight the Wedge. A day? That's plenty of time to take out the Reaver. After nightfall, loan me a couple of griffins to fly my team out to the east of the fortress. Attack the mouth at dawn. We'll go through Zhu's secret entrance and kill the Reaver. Get the Star Clan adepts ready, and by midafternoon you can start gating back to Eastlock."

Arha and Ramat traded a long stare. He shrugged. "It's either do what she says or kill them now so they don't spread these stories."

Remy cleared his throat. "You'll not find that so simple, Arha. Don't forget who we are. And don't forget the Millennium Qi."

Ramat shook her head. "No, we're not killing anybody. At least, nobody here. We promised to help this woman save her daughters; that's what we're going to do."

Arha nodded. "I'll begin the preparations."

••••••••••

Of the four, only Dog was left with steady legs after riding the griffins to a spot east of the fortress under cover of darkness.

The griffins were terrifying; twenty feet long with an eighty-foot wingspan, they could each eat an entire ox in a meal. Dog had made quick friends with both of them, licking their talons and trying to wrestle with the animals before they returned to the camp.

The knights huddled together for warmth, bracing against the cold northern breeze. They spent the bulk of the night in awkward silence.

Akina woke with the edge of the nightshade barely visible to the east. She ate cold food, drank water, and woke the others.

"Get ready. Dawn's approaching."

Zhu and Remy woke and prepared. Dog ate from Akina's pack and went back to sleep.

Akina held Zhu by her shoulders. "Are you ready?"

Zhu nodded. "I guess. After all, what's the worst that can happen to me? I die?"

Remy chuckled darkly. "Some would consider having one's soul consumed by the Reaver a worse fate than death."

She shrugged. "Dead is dead. If I wanted to stay safe, I would have stayed home. I'm ready."

Akina nodded and exhaled slowly, emptying her lungs, her head hanging loosely on her shoulders. Then she straightened. "Thank you. Thank you both. I wouldn't be here without you."

Zhu smiled. "You didn't give me any choice! But I guess you really meant Remy. He had a choice."

The big man slumped where he sat. "I never really do. She knows me too well."

Akina smiled. "It's not my fault you're easy to manipulate. But come on, it's not like you're doing something that's against your nature. You're saving Petrik's children."

He grunted. "Not everything you're asking of me is in accordance with my nature."

She nodded. "Fair enough."

Remy scratched his beard and cracked his neck, then set his shoulders. "When will the seal drop?"

Zhu shrugged. "When the nightshade comes and its shadow strikes the tip of the tail. Which means the attack should have already started, to cover for us."

Remy stood and faced the fortress. He couldn't make it out from that distance. "Men and women are dying as we speak."

Akina shrugged. "Don't go soft on me now, Remy. I didn't start this."

"No. I just wish I understood why *he* did. What happened to him. What broke him. This isn't how he used to be. This isn't the man I . . . knew."

"This is not the time for philosophy, Remy. Get yourself ready for a fight."

"I'm as ready as I'll ever be."

They waited as the dawn line slid across the plain of shattered stone.

••••••••••

Zhu raised her hand to attract attention. "It's almost time."

Remy stepped closer to her. "Is the seal in place?"

"Yeah. But I won't feel anything until they drop it, and that will happen suddenly, without warning. We have to stay ready."

Dog barked. The four huddled close, staring west, waiting for a sign from Zhu.

A bead of sweat was trickling down Akina's neck when Zhu waved. "It's down."

Akina held her shoulder. "Let's go."

Zhu brushed her hair back, rolled her shoulders, and exhaled. She rooted her feet, twisting them into the gravel for better purchase, and traced circles in the air with her palms: one on top, one below, moving clockwise, then counterclockwise.

Dog barked.

The space inside the circle blurred and wavered, then snapped into a new orientation. Through the hole Akina saw shadow, the broad green leaves of growing cocovado trees, and walls of bone and leather. A moist, warm blast of air rushed out of the gate.

Zhu sighed. "We're in. It's tight, but we're in. They'll sense it soon, so go quick."

Remy patted her shoulder. "Good job, Zhu."

Akina faced the young woman. "You don't have to come with us. Stay here. You can gate yourself to camp, wait out the battle."

Zhu looked up at the sky, then shook her head. "Nah. I want to see this through. Let's go."

Remy led the way through the gate.

Akina's nose crinkled at the acrid combination of trees, compost, and human sweat. Zhu grunted as she followed Dog through the gate and let the spatial rift snap shut.

They stood surrounded by trees. The ground was packed dirt, well fertilized and spongy beneath their feet.

Akina rubbed her hand under her nose. "I forgot what this place smelled like."

Remy ran his eyes over the perimeter. "Lots of people and not much water. I wish the unpleasant odor were the most significant of our challenges here."

A voice rang through the trees. "You're so predictable, sister. I knew you'd bring them here."

Zhu stiffened and looked at Akina. "He knows about the, er, back entrance."

Akina nodded. "Obviously."

He appeared between two trees: slender, with dark hair and eyes, pale skin, wearing the white-trimmed gray of the Star Clan. His face was lined with healing wounds.

"My name is Lang, of the Star Clan, and I am going to take the Spiral Witch to the Reaver in chains. My sister will stay to answer for her betrayal. Bear, you can take the dog and leave now or die by my hands. Your choice."

Akina shook her head. "Get out of my way, Lang of the Star Clan. You're no match for us."

"Perhaps not. But I can hold you here while the Reaver and his lieutenants come this way. And I'm sure they'll take a detour to pick up our lovely little hostages. What were you thinking, really?"

Zhu stepped forward. "I won't let you, Lang. Let us pass or you'll have to fight me, dagger to dagger."

He smiled. "Sister, you were never a match for me. Did you forget? Let me serve you a little reminder."

Punch daggers covered both of his hands, same as Zhu's. He stood forty feet away, well out of range for a normal attack, but still thrust one dagger into the air.

A small gate opened in front of his fist and the dagger emerged inches from Zhu's throat.

Dog barked; Remy and Akina backpedaled, startled by the speed of his attack.

Zhu slid to the side, her feet moving in a pattern familiar to Akina as she spun up her own qi and stabbed through a gate of her own.

Her blade nicked Lang's shoulder.

He looked at her with wide eyes. "How did you do that while moving that way?"

She smiled and brought her blade close to her mouth, tongue extended as if to lick it; at the last moment, she wrinkled her nose and shuddered. "That's so gross. Why would someone do that? They do that in the stories. It's so dumb."

Lang's eyes narrowed. "You're mocking *me*?"

"I've been a prisoner of the Spiral Witch for a month, Lang. Did she *have* to train me? No, she could have just ordered me to crawl down an outhouse pit when she didn't need me. Instead, she taught me. For a month. Which is more real training than I got from you or mom over years. Want to see what else I learned?"

She spun, leaping to the side, then back in the original direction, turning her back to her brother and stabbing through another gate.

He tried to defend, but the gate opened behind him, and the tip of her dagger sliced into the back of his neck. He growled and punched with both hands, creating two separate gates in the air.

One of his daggers sliced across his sister's leg.

Zhu smiled, wincing at the pain in her thigh. "You haven't lost a step either, have you?"

"Of course not, sister. I'm the talented one."

"Talent won't be enough. Akina, take Dog and Remy and follow that trail at the outside of the grove. The cells where your daughters are kept are against the ribs on the right side, down at the base. Pass the composting stations and head down."

Lang growled. "They're not going anywhere." He stabbed through space, the dagger coming close to Akina; Zhu waved and opened her own gate; his blade thunked into the trunk of a tree on the other side of the grove.

Akina looked at her disciple. "Are you sure?"

"Of course. This is what I've been training for."

"Can you beat him?"

Zhu shrugged. "Probably not, but I'm sure going to enjoy trying."

Akina nodded and walked along the trail at the right side of the grove, the tail of the three-horn behind her.

Remy spoke from behind his friend. "He'll kill her, you know."

Akina stopped in place, hung her head, and pressed both palms into her forehead, nails digging lightly into her hairline. She let out a shaky breath.

"You're probably right."

"We could work together, overwhelm him."

"It will take too long. He can gate himself around, and he can strike at us from anywhere. Even if we finish him, it would give the Reaver time to get to the twins."

"Akina, if we lose that girl—"

She froze at his words, then looked up, her eyes hard. "Not a girl, Remy. She keeps telling you. A woman. She made a grownup choice. Offered her service to help me. Help us. Knowing it might cost her life. We're going to honor that."

He sighed. "If Lang kills her—"

"Then he can gate himself east to the Heavenly Plains or west to Wedgesource and he still won't be safe from my vengeance. But for now, we trust that *woman* to take care of herself, the same as we would with any other comrade."

She continued. Fifty feet of silence passed as they pushed through the trees lining the edge of the fortress.

Remy coughed. "I think Dog will miss her."

"Dog isn't making the decisions."

29

Facing Faceless

The knights errant stepped out of the grove and into the cavernous interior of the fortress. Akina wrapped her hands, punching each fist into the opposite palm to test her work.

The cocovado grove covered the top of a stone, dirt, and bone mound a hundred feet high, yet the tops of the trees were still well below the framework of vertebrae and ribs that loomed overhead. In front of the knights the mound sloped steeply to the base of the fortress, a dozen staircases set along the decline to help the climb.

The thoracic cavity of the fortress was closely packed with buildings: barracks, foundries, mess halls, food storage, training spaces, and a library. Some buildings were dozens of stories tall, their roofs touching the spine overhead, supported by anchors set into the fortress ribs. Winding stairs, swaying rope bridges, and bone ladders connected the buildings to one another and to the sides of the fortress with a complexity that was hard to follow.

Dog lifted one leg and peed on a tree at the very edge of the grove.

Akina nodded. “Yes, Dog. It’s all yours now. Good boy.” He barked.

Remy pointed a rope dagger at a solid structure at the base of the mound. “Is that it?”

"I'm surprised you don't know where the prison is in this place. Don't tell me you never got into a bar brawl in the days before the Reaver took over."

"I did, but I was so drunk I can't remember where they locked me up."

Akina picked a set of stairs and began descending. "Well, that's where Zhu told us to go. Must be it."

Remy ran after her, floating down the stairs with a dexterity he hadn't shown a month earlier.

Akina peered at him through the brim of her straw hat. "Have you lost weight?"

"Maybe some. Don't worry, I can still fight."

"One way or another, we're almost done. You can get back to eating and drinking too much and fill back out."

"Assuming I survive. If I don't, I'll haunt you for a dozen lifetimes over the indignity of leaving a skinny corpse. Oh, the shame if my clan saw me like this."

"Relax, Remy. I said you're thinner than before. By normal standards, you're still portly."

The space was all but deserted, servants scurrying from place to place in the distance. Remy grunted. "Everybody's in the mouth. Fighting the Tae Kun."

"Look, that's the prison. Two guards."

Akina's heart fluttered as she picked up her pace. Dog trotted along.

The cell was a simple, rectangular structure with wooden walls heavily reinforced by slats of bone. Its single entrance was guarded by two soldiers, both gazing intently toward the mouth of the fortress and the mortal combat going on there.

Akina grunted. "Oy. You two."

One soldier turned; she leapt, dirt and stone kicking up with the force of her launch, knee intercepting his face at the apex of her flight path with a crunch and a spurt of blood.

She twisted in the air, landing with her hands between herself and the second guard.

He was down with a rope dart firmly embedded in his left eye.

"Nice shot."

"I was aiming for the other eye."

She faced the door. "Key?"

Remy shook his head and stepped up to the entrance. He lashed out with one heavy foot, shattering the reinforced double doors. "There's my key."

Akina exhaled and prepared to enter the prison when a voice washed over them from behind.

"That is far enough, Spiral Witch. Your invasion ends here."

She turned and looked up. "Bru Wei. And Faceless."

They stood on the flat roof of a stone-walled, windowless two-story warehouse. Fat sacks of grain were stacked five high against its walls. Faceless remained covered, no exposed skin visible even behind the two holes in his otherwise featureless ivory mask. Bru Wei stood at his side, a full head taller, dressed in black leather from cowl to wings to split-toed boots.

Faceless nodded to her, his hands dancing in the air in front of him as Bru Wei interpreted. "Your reputation does not do justice to your intellect. You embarrassed us at the Aviary. I didn't realize you were capable of cunning."

"Shucks, Faceless, I'm blushing. Are you blushing, too? I can't tell, because, you know. No face. Oh, sorry. Is that a sore subject?" She began cycling qi, building a double loop of energy that met at her core. Remy cracked his neck and whipped his rope darts into a slow spin.

Bru Wei watched Faceless' hands, then nodded and turned to the knights. "Last chance. Surrender and we'll let the Bear live."

Remy growled. "You won't find me so easy to kill. Besides, if she cared that much about my life, she would have left me on the South River."

Bru Wei nodded and spread his arms. Long flaps of thin leather fell, stretched from wrist to ankle. He crouched, then leapt into the air, extending his body so the flaps formed wings like a bird's.

He swooped down on the pair, his mouth open to emit a scream of energy-imbued noise.

Remy stepped forward. "Way of the Bear: Quiet Den."

Bru Wei's eyes widened behind his cowl as his attack dissipated against Remy's shield. The knight immediately dropped his den and sent both rope darts up into the air on tight arcs aimed to intercept the flying man's path.

Faceless stepped off the roof and rode a slide of pure qi to the ground, drawing his long bone sword from its sheath as he fell.

Akina growled and ran to intercept him. From twenty feet away she leapt into the air.

Dog ran forward to a spot in front of Remy and barked, looking up at Bru Wei. The Bat Clan adept changed direction, folding in half and sending himself back toward the storehouse with a powerful sweep of his wings.

"Infinity Bagua: Major Wave." Akina landed, sending a pulse of energy through the ground in a broad arc.

Faceless hopped over the wave of dirt and stone, no expression on his bone mask as he closed on Akina, sword edge menacing in the bright light that filtered through the skeletal roof of the fortress.

One of Remy's rope darts cut a line across Bru Wei's leg while the other sailed past harmlessly. He reeled it in with its silk tether and ran after the flying man.

Faceless twitched and his sword slashed across the space between him and Akina. She stopped suddenly, leaning back to avoid decapitation. Her foot rose with the same motion, toes piercing the space where his head had been, but he hopped backward to safety. They stood facing one another, and he gave her a brief nod.

Respect? Acknowledgment? Just a crick in his neck?

She angled her body, left shoulder toward Faceless, left hand by her belly, right fist by her cheek.

She leaned forward, lashing out with her left fist.

Faceless shook his head.

He's telling me I'm too far.

She was suddenly on top of him; she had pulled her right foot up past her left while punching, and her hand had blocked his line of sight. She was a full step closer than he realized.

A right punch landed solidly on his ribs. He flicked his sword at her, forcing her to pivot and step away.

If the blow had hurt, he gave no indication.

Bru Wei had flapped his great leather wings twice more, echoing a wave of sound off the ground to add lift, and regained footing on the roof of the storehouse. Remy stood near its base, faced with no easy way to climb and rejoin the fight.

Bru Wei prepared another scream. Remy spun his rope darts and formed a Silent Den. Dog ran up to the base of the storehouse and barked, then ran in a small circle and took off toward the side of the storehouse.

Faceless' free hand contorted in the air.

Bru Wei called down, "You might fight me to a draw, but while your companion's technique is impressive, it's draining him quickly. He will soon tire and fall. Within minutes we'll both be attacking you."

Akina shrugged. "I guess I'm going to have to make those minutes very unpleasant. Infinity Bagua: Subtraction." She feinted a punch at his ribs, causing him to raise his sword in defense. *I guess that first punch hurt him after all.*

She dipped her hips and spun, lashing out with a leg to sweep his feet out from under him. Faceless hit the ground rolling, twisting and coming to his feet, but not before Akina landed another pair of palm strikes on his ribs.

Bru Wei's scream ended; Remy dropped his den. The big man ran to the edge of the storehouse, calling after Dog.

Faceless thrust his blade straight at Akina's face. She ducked and slapped it up with a palm strike. He mimicked her earlier move, lifting his foot to kick her, aided by the momentum of his arm swinging with the force of her strike.

His kick caught her in the belly, knocking her back.

She let out a slow breath, patting herself to check for damage. *Hurt but not injured.*

Remy growled. "There's a staircase on the outside, Akina! Dog's climbing it."

"Don't worry about Dog! Fight your fight!"

Remy paused and looked up at Bru Wei crouched on the edge of the roof. He was preparing for another swooping attack. With careful deliberation he sheathed his rope darts.

"I said fight your fight. Do not give up!"

"That's not what I'm doing. Take care of Faceless."

She ducked under another swing of Faceless' vicious sword. Her hand dropped as if to catch a fall, and she struck the earth with enough force to cause another wave of stone, knocking Faceless off his feet.

Bru Wei stood and prepared to drop off the roof once again.

Remy leaned forward and picked up a sack of grain. Markings on the canvas said they were each one hundred pounds. He smiled as he hefted it in both hands, turning his back to the storehouse.

Bru Wei jumped off the roof, thirty feet off the ground, a scream on his lips.

Remy lowered the sack in outstretched arms, bending at the hips, then swung it up, his entire body extending in a violent convulsion of muscular energy.

"Bearapult."

The Bat's attack lanced through Remy's body, the sound so heavy that the air was distorted by its passage, like the shimmering over a candle flame.

The sack of grain struck the Bat in the midsection, folding him in half and driving all the remaining air out of his lungs.

They both fell. Remy from a considerably lower height.

Dog looked over the edge of the roof and barked.

Akina turned to Faceless as he scrambled to his feet. “Fractions.” She kicked him, her instep slicing into the tendons just under his kneecap.

Bru Wei thudded into the ground. Remy groaned; Akina turned to him.

Faceless stood on one good leg and thrust his sword into her left side.

She grunted as pain flashed through her body. Her left hand pinched shut over the blade, trapping it inside her, and she pivoted on her right foot, spinning ferociously.

The blade came free of Faceless’ grip, leaving his empty hand outstretched and grasping. She continued her spin, left foot rising in a sweeping arc that intercepted his chin with a thud like an axe taking down an oak tree.

“Remy!”

He groaned and stirred as she pulled the sword out of her body, energy pulsing into the wound to seal the blood vessels that Faceless had severed.

First things first. She looked at Faceless. He lay stretched out on the gravel like a corpse, but his chest rose and fell.

She looked at the sword, considered ending him with it, then tossed it to the side and looked to her friend.

A fresh voice came from the storehouse roof.

“Not bad, Akina. Not what I expected of you, but not bad.”

•••••••••••

She panted as she looked up at the roof. “Mau-rhi.”

“I prefer to be called the Reaver these days. An affectation, but still. And since you are here, in my home, I expect you to extend me that courtesy.”

She grunted, hand pressed to her side. *I can heal this, but it’s going to take most of what I have left.*

“What do you want, Reaver?”

He leaned over the edge of the roof, dressed in purple and black robes, a bone mask with holes for both eyes covering the rest of his face.

"That's a ridiculous question, Akina. I want you. I want the Millennium Qi. I want to end the threat of the Wedge."

"Seems to me you *are* the threat of the Wedge. You seem to be controlling them, after all."

"Pfsh. I can't control them. I can draw them here, that's all. And I can drain them of their energy. It's . . . different from human energy, you understand? More potent. More fiery. It's quite delicious."

She realized a chained saurid was scratching at the roof next to him.

"That's a forbidden technique, Reaver. Twice over. You're damned."

Remy rolled onto his side, then almost onto his belly, but fell back with a pant. Dog barked from the roof.

"I'm sure the Emperor would prefer I not use these techniques. I'm sure he wants us all beholden to him for our safety. That's what they do, isn't it? Keep us under their control. But when I show everyone that we don't need him, we'll be free. We won't need him or his family anymore."

"Is that what you're after? Undercutting the Emperor? So, what, you can be in charge instead? Is that it? You want to sit on the throne?"

"You think so small. I want to change everything, Akina. End the Wedge. Change the world."

She exhaled slowly and lifted her hand. The flow of blood was slowing.

"Why are you talking to me? Why don't you come down here and fight me?"

"I would, but something's not right. I expected more of you. With the Millennium Qi, I was sure you'd make short work of Faceless. I thought, maybe you're soft, living in the south for these last fifteen years. I gave you plenty of time to get in shape, harden those edges back to the Akina I knew. But for some reason you haven't."

"Great. You're disappointed? I'm so sorry, but obviously I'm not what you need to accomplish your crazy plan. I'll just take my girls and go now. Good luck! I hope I don't see you again for another decade and a half, at least!"

He straightened and stretched both arms over his head. "No, that's not going to happen. I need to see what you really have. I don't think you're angry enough yet, Akina. I thought for sure, this would be enough, but for some reason . . . it isn't. Maybe you've gotten too old."

"Yup. Too old. I'll just go and you won't have to waste more energy puzzling this out."

"That won't do. I told you, I need the Millennium Qi. I just have to motivate you to show it to me. What should I do? I suppose I could kill Remy."

The big man rolled over again, this time making it to his belly. He pressed his arms into the ground and began to lift himself up.

"He's suffered enough, Reaver."

"It must have broken his heart to realize you were going to kill me, Akina. Did he scream? Did he cry?"

"Shut up, Reaver."

"Oh, good, there's some anger. But not enough. I would like to drop down there and finish him, or at least part of me would. But I don't think I'm there yet. There's still some humanity left in me. Too much to hurt poor Remy."

"Come down and fight me, Reaver. I'm tired of all this."

"That's just it. I don't want to fight *tired* you. I want the angry you. I want you to show me the Millennium Qi."

He crouched as Dog licked the side of his leg.

Akina called up, "Get away from him, Dog. He's bad. Like Wedge shit. You shouldn't lick him."

"Will this do the trick, then, Akina? I can't hurt poor Remy. Not after all we've been to one another. But this creature. It's so sweet."

"Leave him alone, Reaver. Or so help me—"

Dog yelped as the Reaver picked him up and stood. "Or what? You'll show me your power? Done!"

He drew a dagger, red bone sharpened to an edge that could split stone or cut the sun. He lifted the blade high in the air.

Dog looked up at the Reaver, tongue lolling out of his mouth.

The Reaver drove the blade down, directly into a spot between Dog's sad eyes.

30

A Very Good Dog

The blade fell.

Akina leapt forward, twisting as she landed, planting her right foot hard into the ground, propelling herself and rotating more. *Too far.*

The tip of the blade struck the sensitive skin between Dog's eyes.

Remy pushed himself to his knees, eyes widening in shock as he caught sight of the rooftop scene.

She landed on her left side, her back to the storehouse, and pushed off again with more lift, aiming for the edge of the roof. Qi spun from her core, into her limbs, turning her leg into a spring and blasting the ground away from her.

The Reaver's eyes widened behind his mask as his blade stopped, the point denting the surface of Dog's skin without penetrating it.

Everybody kept saying I had the Millennium Qi. I only claimed to know where it was, that it was safe. I never said it was in me.

Akina rose into the air, spinning as she flew, and aimed at the Reaver.

He tensed, pushing down on the knife with all his strength, his own energy pouring suddenly into the weapon.

Dog's body shivered as he sneezed, spraying droplets over the Reaver's bone mask.

"How? What is this . . . this power?"

People should listen to what I say and stop making assumptions.

Akina, velocity shed by her flight, landed on the edge of the roof. She stepped up to the Reaver.

He turned his mask to her. "The Millennium Qi? It's in—"

She slammed her palm into his chest. "Infinity Bagua: Partial Function."

His eyes widened further. He touched his chest, dropping Dog, feeling his sternum for damage. "What? What did you do?"

Remy was on his feet, heading for the stairs.

She reached down and scooped up Dog, who promptly licked her cheek. "I never quite mastered Partial Function when we fought together, did I? It's a way to project the force of a blow through an intervening barrier. It skips over something and lands on the other side. I caught the hang of it about ten years ago. Caring for toddlers gave me a surprising amount of time to practice."

He let out a burbling cough, reaching up to slide his mask off his face.

His skin had become sallow, a yellowish tint she didn't remember standing out against bloodshot eyes. His cheeks were sunken; formerly thick hair grew only in patches.

He leaned forward and coughed again, releasing a torrent of blood and bile onto the roof. "Is this . . ."

"You're dead. It's just taking your body a minute to recognize it. You shouldn't have gone after my daughters, Mau-rhi. Or my dog."

"The Wedge . . ." He fell to his backside, arms behind him to catch his weight. Akina stroked Dog and held him in her arms.

"If there's a Surge coming, I'll end it, Mau-rhi. After all, my girls are here. And I'm not about to let anybody harm them. Human or . . . otherwise."

Remy reached the roof, his skin pale as death. He ran to the Reaver's side, sliding to his knees by the man's head.

"Mau-rhi. Mau-rhi. Oh, you fool. You shouldn't have done this." He reached down and cradled the Reaver's head in his hands, leaning forward to press his forehead gently against the other man's.

Akina dripped blood onto the floor and watched her best friend hold the love of his life as the latter coughed his last onto the granary roof.

•••••••••••

Remy's choking sobs echoed off the distant walls of the deserted fortress. Akina's gut twisted at the sight of one old friend dying while another grieved his loss.

Remy deserved better. I should have done better for him.

Akina freed her right hand and wiped the dampness off her cheeks. "I'm sorry, Remy. I had to."

Remy's tears stained his old lover's face. A fresh cough from the Reaver brought a bubble of blood and he raised a weak hand to stroke Remy's beard.

Remy nodded. "I know. I just . . ."

"I know. You always loved him."

Remy's shoulders shook and he rocked back and forth on his heels, head still touching the Reaver's. "Always. I'll always love you, Mau-rhi. I should have stayed. Fought harder. Protected you. From yourself."

The Reaver's lips moved, then stilled.

Akina looked. "Did you hear what he said?"

Remy shook his head. "I shouldn't have let this happen, Akina. I should never have let him drive me away. I knew he was hurting, but I never thought he could have become . . . this."

"It's not your fault, Remy. You couldn't fix what he became. Maybe it's my fault. Or mine and Petrik's. I don't know."

A crash sounded behind them as something broke inside the prison. Footsteps sounded, and a pair of familiar voices rang out from the base.

"Mama!"

Pooja and Sneha ran up the stairs. Akina held Dog tight and walked to meet them, leaving Remy cradling the Reaver's corpse.

She settled Dog on the ground and spread her arms wide, scooping her girls into a hug.

"Oh, girls. Oh, I've missed you so much."

Pooja sniffled. "Are you okay, Mama?"

"Just a stab wound. Nothing your mama can't handle. Are you okay? Not hurt?"

Sneha shook her head, tears dripping down her cheeks. "They weren't so bad, Mama. Not to us."

"My brave, brave girls. I'm so proud of you both."

Sneha disengaged first. "Is that Uncle Remy? Why is he crying?"

"Yes, that's your uncle. He was friends with the Reaver before he became a bad man. We both were. He's sad that we had to kill him."

She sniffed. "They must have been very good friends. He's really sad."

Akina laughed beneath her tears. "Maybe they were a bit more than friends." She let go. "Can you girls do something for me?"

Pooja nodded. "Of course."

"You remember Zhu? The Star Clan girl a few years older than you? I want you to climb up into the cocovado grove. I know, it smells bad, but do it anyway. Go see if she's still alive. If she is, see if she needs help. If she does, help her."

Sneha nodded. "Do you want us to bring her here, Mama?"

Akina shrugged. "Only if she wants to come. Don't force her, all right? And you can tell her that she's free of her obligation to me."

The girls nodded, turned, and leapt off the edge of the roof.

Akina knelt next to Remy and draped her arm over his shoulders. "I am so sorry, old friend." Dog snuggled next to her.

"I know." Remy's voice was weak; his shoulders shook.

"But you're not done."

He sank a bit, leaning further onto the Reaver, then sat up. "What is it?"

She sighed. "I need you to take care of the girls for me."

"What does that mean? Where will you be?"

"You're forgetting. I promised Arha he could have me when this was done. It's done."

"Arha? What? Oh . . . Oh. You were serious? You're not going to run?"

She shook her head. "I can't run. You know that. There wouldn't be anywhere far enough. And I swore on qi and clan. How far would I get with the Tae Kun chasing me and my powers broken?"

"You can find a way. Emperor knows you've shown what you can manage when you put your mind to it. I'll help. I'm strong enough for us both. You can't just give your life away."

"Maybe Arha will have mercy." Remy snorted. "Either way, I have no choice. I can't force my girls into that life."

"I bet they'll happily live life on the run if they can keep you with them."

"Maybe they'd say so now, but in the long term it will limit them too much. What happens when they want to re-establish the Azure Dragon Clan? The martial world won't accept their claim, not if their mother ran from an oath like that. This is the best way."

He lowered the Reaver's body to the ground and gently released it, then leaned his head back and looked up through the skeleton roof and into the sky.

"I don't know if I can do this, Akina. I feel drained. Hollow."

"You're the strongest man I know. You can do it."

He shuddered and let his head hang.

She reached her other arm around his chest, rested her head on his beefy shoulder, and held him.

••••••••••••

Pooja and Sneha carried a bloody and semi-conscious Zhu up the stairs to join their mother. The Star Clan adept was bandaged in strips cut from her own clothes; none of the wounds appeared life-threatening.

Sneha pointed at Bru Wei and Faceless sprawled out on the ground below. "Mama, should we finish off those two men? Faceless is starting to move."

Akina shook her head. "There's been enough of that for today. With the Reaver dead they have no reason to be my enemy anymore."

Pooja looked at her. “Mama, what’s wrong? Are you upset about your old friend?” Akina felt tears stream down her cheeks.

“Yes, but that’s not it.” She knelt on the ground, all strength gone from her legs. “I have something else I have to do. I’m not sure I’m going to survive.”

Sneha snickered. “Nothing can kill you, Mama.”

“That’s what we thought about Papa, too. Remember?” *Too harsh. But they need to understand.*

The girls quieted.

“Listen. I have to do this. It might turn out fine, but it might not.”

Pooja nodded. “Can we help you? We’ve been training.”

“Yes, you can help me. You can go with your Uncle Remy. He’s going to take very good care of you both. But he’s going to need some help, so I need you to be good.”

“What does Uncle Remy know about girls, though? He’s very big and hairy.”

“Nothing, but he’s a good listener and a good man. Will you help him?”

They traded glances and nodded.

Akina sighed. “Good. Now, let’s go show the Reaver’s body to his troops, end this war before more soldiers die needlessly.”

Remy stood. “I’ll carry him.” He scooped the Reaver up in both arms, like a groom carrying his bride over the threshold, and walked stiffly toward the staircase. Dog barked.

Zhu regained full consciousness as Remy passed her. “What’s going on?”

Sneha patted her shoulder. “We’re going to stop the fighting. Do you want to come with us? Mama said you don’t have to.”

“Mama . . . oh, right. Right. Did I survive?”

“Yup. I’m not sure about the other guy, though. You cut him up pretty bad.”

“Did I? Huh. Yeah, I’ll come with you.”

“Cool. Sit up. We’ll help you walk.”

Pooja set a shoulder under Zhu’s other arm and they helped her stand.

Their awkward procession made its way to the mouth of the fortress and out.

••••••••••

Five people and one dog carried a corpse through the front entrance of a triceratops corpse.

The fighting, ferocious at first, began to die down almost immediately as soldiers of the Reaver and of the Tae Kun recognized what Remy held.

Akina led the way past a few dozen fights, then took a deep breath and yelled, reinforcing her voice with a shock of qi.

"This war ends now!"

Her words were loud enough to physically knock back the nearest groups of soldiers. Those farther away jumped and hopped, turning to face her in groups.

Remy stepped to her side, pressing the body of the Reaver overhead. Tears continued to stream down his cheeks.

The closest soldiers in purple and black looked to their leader's corpse, then to Akina's fierce eyes, and fell to their knees.

Their most recent opponents, all in blue and orange with heavy shields, shouted triumphantly.

One of the Tae Kun looked into Akina's face, then to the kneeling enemy, and knelt beside them.

The shouts faded.

More and more of the Tae Kun settled, heads lowered, kneeling before Akina.

She and Remy made their way through the battlefield, sparing nothing more than hard glances for the soldiers who knelt. Dog led the way, tongue hanging out of his mouth, letting out an occasional yip.

When Akina reached the command tent of the Tae Kun, the field was quiet and not a single soldier was left standing.

• • • • • • • • • • •

Two days later.

Remy let out a loud snore, his breath catching in his chest, coughed, and woke with a start. Akina sat on her bed across the room from him, watching.

"Akina?"

"Hey. How do you feel?"

He lay back and groaned. "Where are the girls?"

"Out playing with Dog. They're fine."

"Where are *we*?"

She laughed. "You passed out. We're in Eastlock. In Arha's compound."

"Ah. That."

"What else do you want to know?"

He sighed. "Why did you do it, Akina? The Millennium Qi? Why didn't you take it for yourself?"

"Because I wanted it."

"Of course. No, wait, not of course. What does that mean?"

"Remy, did you see what I've done to this world in the past two months? Just me, without the Millennium Qi?"

"I suppose I have an idea."

"Now imagine me with it. As soon as my grandfather came to me, I wanted it. I wanted to rule the world, Remy. So badly. And I could have. It was so . . . so much. So I knew I couldn't have it. The temptation would have been too great."

"You didn't want to be Emperor, Akina? That would have been fun. Servants. Big palace to decorate. You would have enjoyed it."

"I don't think I would have, Remy. I think I would have raised armies. Gone west and east. North, over the Spine. Created a real empire. When my grandfather came, for a night and a day, that's all I could think about. Then Petrik came in and held me and . . . none of us would have been happy. Not me. Certainly not Petrik. And not the girls."

"Ah. Well, good choice then. Dog seems perfectly content with it. He's not running about trying to conquer the world."

"Exactly."

"So I understand that. Sort of. What's next? What are we doing now?"

She let out a long breath. "I'm out of time, Remy. I have to go see him."

"Him? Arha?"

She nodded.

Remy sighed. "Now? Like, right now?"

"Yes. He asked for me yesterday. I can't stall anymore."

"Oh." Remy eased himself upright. "I'm not sure what to say."

"You're famous for knowing the right thing to say. That's how you won Arha's favor to begin with."

"It's not working. Must be that blow from Bru Wei."

She smiled. "I had a good run, Remy. It's fine for it to end here. As long as the girls are safe."

"They will be, Akina. I swear it. If it costs me my life."

"What was that thing you used to say, Remy? You're willing to sacrifice your life for your cause, but you'd much rather make the other guy sacrifice his life for *his* cause."

"That's very smart. I should write that down. I said that?"

"You did. You were pretty drunk, so it's no wonder you've forgotten."

They sat in silence for ten dozen heartbeats.

Akina sighed. "Tell me something nice, Remy. Just once."

"Nice?"

"Yeah. I don't know. Tell me you forgive me."

"I'm not sure about that, Akina. I mean, I will. Forgive you. Eventually. Maybe. One day."

"Tell me anyway. Can't you lie?"

"Not to you. I never could. You're too perceptive for your own good. Or for my good. Whatever."

"You have nothing nice you can say to me that's *not* a lie?"

He smiled. "Well, there is one thing."

"Yes?"

"Since giving birth to the girls, your breasts look great. You're really filling out that jacket nicely."

She laughed. "Since when do you care about a woman's breasts, Remy?"

"I mean, I might not want to do anything to them myself, but I can still admire them aesthetically, can't I? The way one might admire a fine painting. Of hills. Or even some mountains. Or a pair of jugs of rice wine."

She stood, a smile straining her cheeks. "That will do. Thank you, Remy. For all of it." She hugged him, hard and fast, and left the room.

No reason to put this off any longer. Except all the reasons. But none of them will make it easier.

She nodded to the Tae Kun soldier standing outside the door and followed him to Arha's office.

The chief and his wife were in his sitting room, two monks in heavy robes behind his seat. A wide grin had cemented itself on Arha's face.

Akina let the guard close the door behind her. She approached Arha's heavy bone and wood chair. *Almost throne-like.*

"Chief. Princess."

They nodded to her.

Arha leaned forward, elbows on his thighs. "Akina, I never liked you. For . . . reasons. But you have made me a very happy man today. I am feeling very generous, so I'd like to give you something."

She nodded. "How about letting me go?"

He laughed. "Not that. I still need the Millennium Qi. Something else. A position for your girls? I can adopt them into the clan. No, forget that. I'll adopt them myself. They'll be equal heirs to the Tae Kun."

Akina watched the princess. If the woman had any reservations about her husband's offer, she didn't show it.

"That's very generous, but I don't want to make that kind of commitment for them. Please just let them leave with Remy. They'll find their own way."

"Of course they will. They're your daughters, after all. So, to business. I assume you need to begin some sort of ritual, purifying your qi for the move. How soon will it be done? When can we transfer the Millennium Qi from you to me?"

Akina shook her head. "We can't."

He looked at her, then turned to look at the monks behind him. "What do you mean we can't? I realize the procedure is a risk, but that was part of our agreement."

"I mean, we can't, because I don't have it."

"What? What?" He looked at his wife, who shrugged in ignorance. "Where is it, then?"

"It's in Dog."

Arha stood, his mouth working around words that wouldn't come. "You put the greatest weapon of the martial world inside a filthy animal?"

"Actually, he's not filthy. Have you really looked at his spirit, Arha? It's the cleanest, purest thing I've ever seen."

Arha spun, pointing at the monks, who shrugged. He shouted. "Check her!"

They nodded and approached Akina, hands held up in supplication.

She nodded. "Go ahead."

They flanked her and ran their hands over her skin, inhaling and exhaling in synchronized rhythms.

After a few moments, the female monk turned to Arha. "She speaks the truth, Chief. There is no weapon inside her."

Arha turned on Akina. "You swore!"

She shook her head. "I swore you could have me, however you wanted. I never said I had the Millennium Qi."

He turned to the monks. "Go! Get some soldiers and bring me that dog!"

Akina stepped back, putting herself between the monks and the door. "I never agreed to let you have Dog. If you go after him, our agreement is void. I'll fight to protect him. And Arha, you don't want me for an enemy."

He sputtered and looked at his wife.

Is the princess smiling? Must be my imagination.

"Your life is still mine, Witch! I'll have you on the rack. We'll flay your skin from your body for a hundred days. You'll beg me to kill you."

She nodded. "That I'll accept." She held her hands out. "You'll have to bind me well. I expect I'll thrash about a bit when you get to the ticklish parts."

"Are you serious?"

She shrugged. "An oath is an oath. I didn't expect to leave this room alive. I promised you my life: I meant it. But you can't have Dog or Remy or the girls. Or the Millennium Qi."

He sputtered again and looked at his wife.

The princess smiled. "Dear husband, you were in such a good mood, moments ago. Remind me why that was."

His mouth snapped shut. "We did end the Reaver's threat. And we recovered enough bones to make the Tae Kun the richest martial clan in the Empire. Our status has never been higher. New recruits are already flocking to our banner in record numbers."

She nodded agreement. "See? It's been a wonderful week. Don't spoil it."

"What do you mean?"

"I mean, this woman upset an entire continent because her girls were threatened. She is currently your ally. And while her oath may be fulfilled on a technicality, she knows she still owes you a debt. Right, Akina?"

Akina shrugged. "I can accept that. Within reason."

"As I said. Show your magnanimity. Celebrate the Spiral Witch, with whose help you have attained such heights. Let all know that she is an ally of the Tae Kun."

He wheeled on Akina, mouth working again, then back to his wife. Then he slumped to his chair.

"You win. Both of you. Go, Akina. We're not enemies, but I'd prefer not to see your face around this city for a few months at least."

Akina's heart leapt. She looked at the princess, who nodded, then back to Arha. "Thank you, Arha. I'll repay your kindness one day."

He waved her away. "No need. My dear wife is right, you have done much for me. Just go. Raise those girls of yours. Keep Remy out of trouble."

"I'll try, Arha. Seriously, thank you."

She left the Tae Kun sitting room sniffling back tears.

•••••••••••

Two days later, Akina, Zhu, Remy, Sneha, and Pooja sat around a table inside an inn on the other side of the city, drinking tea and wine and eating steamed pork buns. A server brought two jugs of rice wine to replace the ones they had already emptied.

Zhu looked around. "What's the plan? Are we just going to drink our way across the continent?"

Remy looked at her with bleary eyes. "What's wrong with that plan?"

Akina drained her cup, exhaling as the alcohol burned away tension that had been held in her chest for months. "We should see Rei. Tell her about her brother."

Remy sighed. "I really don't want to. But yes, we should."

Sneha held out her cup. "Disciple Zhu, more tea."

Akina glared at her daughter. "Sneha."

"What? Don't we outrank her?"

"Technically, yes. But be nice anyway."

Sneha frowned and sighed. "Fine. I can pour my own tea."

Zhu shook her head. "Wait. Watch this." She picked up the teapot, turned away from the table, and tipped it over the floor.

The stream of liquid disappeared midair. Sneha looked down and smiled as she saw it splash into her cup. "Neat!"

Pooja held up her cup. "Do me next!" Dog barked from his spot next to her feet. Akina leaned over and fed him a piece of pork.

Zhu smiled and poured more. "Is that it? We all go visit Rei?"

Sneha snorted. "Of course that's not *all* we have to do."

Zhu turned to the girl. "What does that mean?"

Pooja nodded with her sister. "We do that first, but that's not *it*. Did you forget? We have a Great Surge to stop."

THE END

Will the adventures of Akina, Remy, Zhu, Pooja, Sneha, and Dog continue?
What am I, a fortune teller? Maybe!

What's Next

The adventures of Akina and company have come to an end, at least for now.

If you enjoyed this book, please review it on Amazon and/or Goodreads and tell your friends about it! They'll enjoy it, and you'll seem cool and smart to have done so.

You might also enjoy the Hybrid Helix, starting with Wistful Ascending. It's by the same guy.

Please also go to jcmberne.com and sign up for the Book Berne-ing newsletter for updates about upcoming project, possibly including another story about Akina and the people who learn to greatly regret pissing her off. Follow JCM on twitter (@JoeBerne1), check out his Facebook page or YouTube channel (@jcmberne), or find him on the back channels of Discord. Who knows, he might even start a Patreon or show up on Bluesky.